Blood
Mud

*Also by K. C. Constantine
in Large Print:*

Family Values

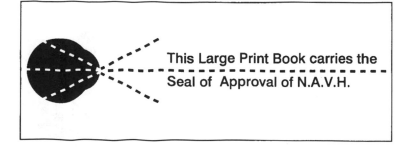

This Large Print Book carries the
Seal of Approval of N.A.V.H.

Blood Mud

K. C. CONSTANTINE

Thorndike Press • Thorndike, Maine

LP
FIC
CONSTANTINE
K

Published in 1999 by arrangement with Warner Books, Inc.

Thorndike Large Print ® Mystery Series.

The tree indicium is a trademark of Thorndike Press.

The text of this Large Print edition is unabridged.
Other aspects of the book may vary from the original edition.

Set in 16 pt. Plantin.

Printed in the United States on permanent paper.

Library of Congress Cataloging-in-Publication Data

Constantine, K. C.
    Blood mud / K.C. Constantine.
       p.   cm.
    ISBN 0-7862-2031-7 (lg. print : hc : alk. paper)
    1. Balzic, Mario (Fictitious character) Fiction. 2. Police
— Pennsylvania Fiction. 3. Large type books. I. Title.
    [PS3553.O524B57   1999b]
    813'.54—dc21   99-30875

Blood
Mud

Gina Hite's slow burn was gaining speed. What she'd thought she was getting was a new Mustang. Red. A convertible. With black leather seats, automatic transmission, CD and cassette players, quad speakers, air-conditioning — that's what Herb Tanyar had said he was going to buy her, but that was not what he was parking at the curb, no thank you very much.

"What is this?" she said, flipping her palm at the car as Herb came bounding around the front end, beaming triumphantly. Gina flounced from one hip to the other, her mouth open in a pout of disappointment growing wider by the second.

" 'What is this?' Is that what you said?" Herb's beam grew dimmer. "You kiddin' me? This, hey, Gina, this is a classic. This is a '73 Mustang, that's what this is. You're not gonna believe what I got it for. Listen to this, you ready?"

"This is a used car," Gina interrupted him, her lips curling away from the word *used* as though it were moldy cheese.

Herb guffawed nervously. "Used? Hey, Gina, this is not what we call *used*, sweetheart. This is, uh, this is *restored*. This is a classic car."

"You can call it what you want, Herbie, it's still a used car," Gina said over her shoulder as she marched up the walk toward the front door of her apartment building.

Herb shook his head hard to try to shake out the goo that had just filled his ears. He bolted after her, caught up to her as she was reaching for the door handle, and tried to turn her around by her arm without giving her whiplash. "Wait a minute, wait wait, what're you doin'? When you walk away, you sayin' you're not takin' this car? You sayin' you don't accept this? When you're sayin' 'used' and you're walkin' away, you sayin' you don't want this car, is that what you're sayin'?"

An elderly couple was trying to come outside, and Gina used their presence to intimidate Herb into freeing her arm. Once the couple had passed, she backed up two steps, folded her arms across her ample chest, and said, "Well you got that part right at least. That's exactly what I'm sayin', Herbie."

"Hey. I've told you before, you know? Nobody calls me Herbie. Herbert, Herb, Mister Tanyar, Mister Councilman, okay?

No Herbie. And before you get back on your high horse, Gina, I want you to do something you do not normally do, but right this minute you better do it, which is stop jumpin' to conclusions for once and start thinkin' about what life has just handed you —"

"Life?" Gina said, snorting. "Life just handed me something? What, that lemon back there? I thought that was you handed me that — or tried to. And what am I supposed to do with that, Mister Councilman — make lemonade or something? Where do I get a pitcher big enough to fit that lemon into?"

"That lemon as you call it," Herb said, making a fist and then pushing the knuckle of his index finger against his teeth before putting both fists on his hips. "That lemon cost me fifteen thousand dollars. You hear what I just said, Gina? Fifteen thousand — and a lotta grief, which I'm not gonna explain. But on the way over here, when I stopped to get gas? A guy offered me thirty — you hear what I just said — thirty?"

"Shoulda took it. 'Cause then you could buy me the Mustang you said you were gonna buy me and you'd still have plenty left over to send your kids to that school you think's so great."

9

"My kids aren't part of this, Gina. They're not up for discussion here, they're none of your concern —"

"Oh. Okay. So I'll just stick with the car we looked at — the one you swore up and down you were gonna buy me — if you can remember —"

"Gina, Gina, whoa, you're not listenin' to me. And you're not thinkin'."

"No, Herb. You're the one's not listenin'. I'm your new girl. I want a new car, which is what you promised me. A new Mustang. You wanna give that old car to somebody? Give it to your old lady. I'm not your old lady. I'm your new girl, which I have been for almost a year now, which you keep tellin' me is what I am, and which you also keep tellin' me, if I'll just be a little more patient, you know, be a little more patient, Gina, and someday real soon now you'll be my new old lady, and to prove this to me you said you were gonna buy me a Mustang. A *new* Mustang, Herb. That's what *you* said — but I'm startin' to get the picture why your old lady does such a number on you —"

"I know what I said, Gina, but I'm tellin' you, sometimes better things come along, and when they do you need to be smart enough to recognize them, you need to be

10

quick enough and smart enough to recognize something better than what you were plannin' for, understand? And don't be worryin' what kinda number my old lady does on me, that's not up for discussion here either —"

"Okay, so forget her. Back to the car. A secondhand car might've been part of *your* plans," Gina said, shaking her head emphatically, "but a secondhand car was never part of any plans I thought *we* made —"

"Will you listen to yourself?" Herb said, struggling to keep his composure. "I'm tryin' to tell you that what I'm givin' you isn't just a car but an investment. Will you stop thinkin' like some ditzoid and put two and two together here?"

"Oh I'm some ditzoid now, huh? Last night I believe I was the blood of youth flowin' in the arteries of your heart. Last week I was spring in the middle of your winter, I was the cause of your hope, your courage, your energy, your stamina — what I really was was the cause of your hard-ons, Herb, that's what you were really sayin'! I gave you back your hard-ons, okay? And for givin' you back *your hope* and *your courage* and *your energy* and *your stamina,* for this I get a secondhand car? I don't think so."

11

Herb cleared his throat and tried harder to collect himself. He redoubled his efforts to soften his face, to smile, to look like the mediator he prided himself on being. "Gina, listen carefully. I am not giving you a secondhand car. This is a classic car, this is not a used car. This car has been restored by one of the best mechanics and bodymen I've ever known. And he sold it to me for a fantastic price. Half what it's worth. Which means you can drive this car for as long as you like, take it to my mechanic, who will maintain it for you, and all you have to do is make sure you get it cleaned, waxed, keep it in a garage when you're not drivin' it, and you've got an investment here, which —"

"I don't want an investment, Herb, alright? I want the car you said you were gonna buy me —"

"Which, as I was sayin', as long as you take care of the car the way I just said, this car is gonna be worth twice what a new Mustang's gonna be worth in two years, three for sure. Seriously, Gina, I know you don't think about investments but I want you to think about this one."

"Yeah?" Gina said. "Is that what you want? Well next time you want these lips around your you know what, Herbie? You think about what you see walkin' away from you right now. 'Cause what I want is what you said you were gonna buy me, which is what you promised you were gonna buy me, which is a new Mustang convertible — the red one we looked at? At Highway Ford? Case you forgot, that was six months ago, and that was how long ago you told me I could start lookin' forward to it — which I remember if you don't! This of course was before you started talkin' about where you were gonna get the money to pay for your kids' school, which now is supposed to be none of my concern. Okay. Fine. None of it's any of my concern now, Herbie. Bye!"

She got through the door of her building before he could catch hold of her arm again. He watched her walking through the lobby, every move of her legs and hips and buttocks sending tremors of fire, doubt, desire, and anger through his mind and body.

You stupid cunt, Herb said to himself. How can anything that looks like that be that stupid? Moves like that, do what that does, how can she be all that and be that fucking dumb? Huh? Whoa — who's the dummy here? I'm the one just put myself in the middle of a goddamn felony for this

13

and she walks away from it like it's a goddamn malignant tumor?! Jesus Christ, I
don't believe this. . . .

"So, uh, Ronnie, what? You don't watch the
Weather Channel?"

"No I don't watch the Weather Channel.
How come every time you start talkin' you
stop shovelin'?"

"If you'da watched the Weather Channel, Ronnie, you'da known we was gonna
be freezin' our ass off out here."

"I told you fifty times my old lady ain't
goin' for no cable —"

"Told me twice. And both times I told
you Joey B.'ll hook it up for you for half a
yard, what's the problem? Big-timer like
you, you can't spare half a yard?"

"My problem is every time you start
talkin' you stop workin'."

"Well if you'da been watchin' the
Weather Channel, which if you'd get up
offa some cheese our old lady could have
it, you know? And you'da known it was
gonna freeze tonight —"

"Hey I ain't payin' you to talk. I'm
payin' you to shovel, okay?"

14

"Speakin' of which —"

"Don't even say it, okay? Don't . . . fucking . . . say it, okay? I told you when you was gonna get paid, and that's when the fuck you're gonna get paid, and you ain't gonna get paid a fuckin' second before you're done, okay? So shut up and fucking shovel, okay?"

"All I'm sayin' is you woulda known it was gonna freeze you woulda maybe brought a pick, okay? That's all I was gonna say. You know, shit freezes too, man. Water freezes, mud freezes, I mean all that shit freezes, you gotta know horseshit's gonna freeze too, you know, temperature goes down low enough —"

"No shit — is that what I would know? And I would know this if I had cable, huh? Can't figure out why I didn't think of that myself, you know? But I'm gonna tell you somethin', and this is the last fuckin' time I'm gonna tell ya, Lennie, you hear me? You don't shut up and do what I hired you for? You know? Shovel? If you don't shut the fuck up and shovel, I swear to you on our sister's crooked tits, I'm gonna bust your fuckin' face with this shovel so money'll be the last thing you need to fuckin' be worryin' about, understand?"

"All I'm sayin' —"

"Hey, Lennie, honest to God, don't make me hit you!"

"Aw come on, Ronnie, Jesus Christ —"

"No! Don't say nothin'! Not another fuckin' word! But if you ain't gonna shovel, least go down the end of the barn and make sure that asshole's still watchin' TV, alright? Think you can do that? And while you're down there, okay? Just think about this. If we didn't have the same mother I wouldn't even piss on your leg, understand? I want you to think about that while you're doin' this one little fuckin' thing I'm askin' you to do now, okay?"

"Aw man, I'm ruinin' my shoes, my pants, my only good pair of gloves, I'm gettin' horseshit all over me, and you ain't even told me what you want this shit for."

Ronnie straightened up slowly, his face full of menace, which Lennie could see clearly even in the half-moon. He'd seen that look before, and he knew how close he was.

Ronnie raised his shovel over his right shoulder like it was a spear and placed his feet in such a way that it looked like he was getting ready to drive the blade into Lennie's face, pinched now not only with cold but with old and deep fear.

Lennie immediately dropped into a

crouch and gingerly put his shovel down with his left hand while holding up his right. "I'm goin', Ronnie, I'm goin', I'm goin'." He backed away, losing his balance several times over the frozen horse dung and disappearing around the corner of the barn.

"Stupid fuck," Ronnie grumbled to himself, turning once again to hacking and scraping and shoveling horse dung into a plastic garbage bag. After ten minutes he'd succeeded in filling only one. He had three more to go. Must've been nuts to hire this asshole. Biggest waste of sperm in the history of the world. But that's what you get when you marry a Polak. Wouldn't listen to me, noooo. She'da listened to me, she'da married a dago. Did she listen? Noooo, not her. No, she could pick a husband out all on her own, didn't need no help from me. Married that fuckin' Polak, and what do they produce? Leonard Derzepelski, that's what they produce. Biggest fuckin' waste of sperms and eggs in the history of human breedin'. And genius me, I gotta listen to her. Hire him, she says, he's a good worker, he can help you. Takes orders good, she says, he can't help it he can't hold no job, it ain't his fault. No, fuck no, nothin's never his fault. Stupidest motherfucker in

17

Rocksburg . . . in the whole fuckin' state . . . in America . . . in the whole fuckin' world — no, he ain't the stupidest — me, *I'm* the stupidest! I hired the mother-fucker!

Soon as we get here, what's he start bitchin' about, huh? He goes, " 'What'd you have to bring such a big goddamn flashlight for? I'm gettin' a cramp in my jaw bitin' this fucker.' " Tell him don't stop shovelin', what's he do? Goes, " 'Couldn't you bring one of them small ones? Like a pen?' "

Tell him don't stop, what's he say? " 'Whattaya mean, stop? I'm fuckin' sweatin' here already, I ain't stoppin', who's stoppin'?' "

Tell him put the fuckin' light back in his mouth, can't see what the fuck I'm doin', what's he say? " 'It's makin' my jaws hurt, I ain't gonna stick this thing in my mouth no more, I'm just gonna hold it.' "

Tell him you just hold it, asshole, I'm gonna wind up doin' all the work, and that ain't what I'm payin' you for.

And what's he say? Starts in about the fuckin' money. " 'Yeah right, ain't seen none of that money yet, ooooh that biiiig money.' "

Tell him shut the fuck up and put the

thing back in his mouth and keep shovelin', and what the fuck's he do, huh?

Drops the motherfucker, that's what he does. He ain't shittin' me, that motherfucker, he dropped it on purpose, I know him.

I says, "You dropped it? What? Like accidentally, huh? You dropped it on purpose, you lazy fuck."

He goes, " 'It slipped!' "

My ass, slipped. Tell him pick it up, what's he say? " 'And do what, huh? Wipe it off I guess and put it back in my mouth, huh? Hey, Ronnie, you stick it in your mouth, I ain't fuckin' touchin' it.' "

Tell him he's wearin' fuckin' gloves, what's he say?

" 'I ain't got gloves in my mouth and they're my good ones anyway, I ain't gonna ruin 'em worse than they are.' "

What'd he wear good gloves for? He gets fuckin' dumber every day, man, swear to God, what's he say?

Goes, " 'Yeah? Least when I come outta my house all dressed in black nobody calls me no fuckin' Italian ninja.' "

Tell him that guy's an asshole, nobody listens to him, tell him c'mon, man, get shovelin' here! Quit talkin'! What's he say?

" 'Man, ain't we got enough yet?' "

Tell him we would if you'd do somethin' besides stand around whinin', what's he say? " 'The fuck people get outta ridin' horses anyway?' "

The fuck you care — shovel, huh? Okay? What's he say? " 'I was just thinkin', that's all.' "

Tell him no, what you do ain't thinkin'. What you do is stop workin' and start talkin'. Think you keep that up long enough I'm gonna get pissed off enough and do all the fuckin' work myself, that's what you're doin'. Which is naturally just what the fuck happened. . . .

Once again, as he'd done half a dozen times already, Ronnie used the shovel like a wedge, driving it into the pile of frozen horse dung until he broke enough loose that he could shovel it into the bag, holding the bag with one hand and the shovel with the other. It was slow going, and even though the temperature was in the high twenties, he was sweating so much he had to take his knit cap off.

Then he heard somebody coming and he couldn't be sure it was Lennie, so he hurried to the stone wall of the barn and pressed his back against it, raising the shovel like an ax, ready to brain whoever it was, but it was just Lennie coming back.

"Fuck'd you go, man, Cleveland?"

They slipped and slid their way back around the side of the dunghill they'd been shoveling from.

"Well? Still there?"

"Yeah, he's asleep or drunk or somethin', ain't movin'. This shit's startin' to stink, you know that? Must be meltin'. Makin' my nose burn, my nose is burnin'."

"That's what shit does, genius. It stinks. That's what it's supposed to do, you know? Like what you were supposed to do was fuckin' shovel once in a while, you know?"

"What you gonna do with this shit anyway — you ever gonna tell me?"

"How many times I tell ya it's none of your business, huh? C'mon, tie a knot in this one and get me another one and hold it open. Ain't gonna shovel, least hold the fuckin' bags — c'mon, man, we gotta get movin', we been out here way too long. And just so you know, I wish to fuck I'da never listened to my mother, you hear me? And I'm thinkin' seriously 'bout cuttin' your pay."

"She's my mother too."

" 'She's my mother too,' " Ronnie mimicked him.

"Aw come on, man, what the fuck, my gloves're ruined, I'm freezin', don't be

21

jaggin' me off like 'at, you promised."

"All I promised you, jagoff, was I'd pay you if you worked. I didn't say nothin' about payin' you for watchin'."

"Man, Ronnie, you're a real prick sometimes, you know that?"

Ronnie stopped shoveling again, straightened up, and glared at his half-brother again, walking toward him until their faces were inches apart. "Lennie? You ever even think somethin' like 'at again, and I think you're thinkin' it? I'm gonna bury your fuckin' ass right here, you fuckin' hear me, you stupid fuckin' half-Polak motherfucker you, you hear me?"

"Hey, c'mon, Ronnie, hey, man, you know, I was just . . . I was just clownin' around, man, that's all, I didn't mean nothin' —"

"Yeah? Well I did, motherfucker. Every motherfucking word."

Arturo Chianese was scowling, his thick lower lip protruding even farther than it usually did when he wasn't angry. He didn't like Charley Babyak the first time he'd seen him, forty years ago, when Babyak was barely two years old. Chianese liked him even less now, and he was still pissed that he'd let his sister talk him into hiring her son just because he felt sorry for her because the cancer in her breast had spread to her lymph glands.

But Chianese hadn't trusted his sister any more than he trusted anybody else, so he had his attorney, Louis Ghia, call all the cancer specialists in the Conemaugh County Medical Association to make sure his sister wasn't handing him a crock just to try to get her son something cushy for his old age. Once Ghia confirmed for Chianese that his sister was indeed getting chemotherapy from an oncologist named Beilmann, Chianese reluctantly hired Babyak to run his numbers for him in Hunkytown, the six or so square blocks of row houses behind where Knox Iron and Steel had had their rolling mill before they moved their entire steelmaking operation to Brazil.

Now that his sister was dead, Chianese's contempt for Babyak had risen again in his throat like too many canned anchovies eaten too close to bedtime. When Babyak showed up every night with the Hunkytown take, Chianese went out of his way to find something messy for Babyak to do in the deli, like cleaning the grease pit under the grill or the deep fryers or the sausage machine. All such jobs were bad enough by themselves, but were made worse because they were done in the presence of the cousins Serra, Jimmy and Angie, who took turns letting Babyak know they thought he was the sorriest white man they'd ever seen.

Tonight, Chianese wanted Babyak to do all three jobs, and also to sweep the snow off the sidewalk and spread some de-icer around.

Physical strength had never been one of Babyak's qualities. He'd never thought he had what he called a strong constitution; he'd always thought of himself as being on the weak side, especially in the lungs and stomach. Didn't take much of a strong odor or an unpleasant sight to turn his stomach. But cleaning the grill's grease pit and the fryer baskets didn't have the combination of labor and lousy stimuli that the sausage machine did; the sausage machine always took him over the top, especially because lately he'd been fuming that twelve hours a day manning the phones in the cellar of his mother's house ought to've been enough to satisfy anybody. That it didn't satisfy Chianese made the deli jobs smell, look, and feel all the worse.

Ten minutes after starting on the sausage machine, Babyak went lurching into the alley behind the deli, where he lost the chicken soup and peanut butter sandwich he'd had for lunch. It took four Tums to settle his stomach down enough to finish the job, but when his uncle told him to get a broom and shovel and clean the sidewalk, Babyak did something he'd never done since he'd started working for Chianese, more than two years ago. He complained.

"I'm not feelin' real good, Uncle Arthur. And I'm real tired. Maybe Jimmy could do it, or Angie, whattaya think? I'd appreciate you got one of them to do it, you know?"

"Tired?" Chianese said sarcastically, his heavy eyelids going up. Chianese was hunched over at the neck and had a bulbous belly. Babyak called him "Fat Buddha" behind his back, because he resembled pictures of statues of the Buddha Babyak had seen when he worked in the library at Southern Regional Correctional Facility when he was doing his last stretch for burglary.

"Yeah I'm tired," Babyak said. "Throwin' up does a number on me, Uncle, you know? I got a bad stomach, I can't help it, and that sausage maker, that gets to me, that's all. I don't know why you make me do that. I thought takin' bets for you, you know, I sorta thought that was enough for a day's work."

"Is that what you thought?" Chianese shuffled into the back room, crooked his finger at somebody, and came shuffling back out to the front door.

He was followed by Angie Serra, a one-time defensive tackle at the University of Pittsburgh who'd lost his football scholarship because one of the three whores he was pimping out of his apartment four blocks from the Cathedral of Learning had given gonorrhea to a city councilman's administrative assistant. There followed an immediate but unpublicized raid on Serra's apartment, where Pittsburgh vice detectives found one of the whores sick with a raging need for a fix and eager to cooperate. Angie, having nowhere else to turn, sought the counsel of his cousin Jimmy, who had been in Arturo Chianese's employ for some years.

Jimmy appealed to Chianese, touting Angie as being not only one of the largest human beings in southwestern Pennsylvania but also one of the quickest and meanest, qualities Chianese admired. Jimmy

26

also added, "He's also worked the last two summers in Jersey, at the shore there, as a short-order cook. And he's already a pimp. Kid with this much talent, I think he'd fit right in, Mister Chianese."

Chianese, always on the lookout for talent, agreed, and sent Attorney Ghia to counsel Angelo Serra at his arraignment before a city magistrate in East Liberty — and to take along a paper lunch bag half full of twenty-dollar bills, just in case. Ghia conferred with City Magistrate Elroy Futch, who happened to mention that his Oldsmobile was black and was parked behind his office. Ghia excused himself, found the Olds, and shoved the lunch bag under the front seat. He then returned to the tiny courtroom and advised Angelo to plead no contest to three counts of promoting prostitution.

Magistrate Futch started sneezing and declared a brief recess, saying he had to get some allergy medicine out of his car. When he returned he was much less allergic and also much more observant because he quickly noted that two numbers in Angelo Serra's address had been transposed on the search warrant.

Rebuking the vice officers who'd served the warrant, Magistrate Futch then lectured Angelo sternly on the evil that women with loose morals do on society, reminding him how lucky he was to be the benefactor of police incompetence, otherwise he would be looking at three counts of a third-degree felony. And coincidentally, with the profound dejection of a man weary of dealing with such morally weighty matters, Futch said he had no choice but to dismiss all charges because of the mix-up on the address.

Thus, Angelo Serra's total punishment, after seven and a half minutes of the best justice in East Liberty at the time, was a blistering warning delivered by an indignant magistrate never again to consort with the three women who had been sharing his apartment at the time police arrested him. In return for which Angelo began his new career as a maker of sandwiches and salads and all-around good fella in the employ of Arturo Chianese.

"Angie," Chianese said, pointing to Babyak, "throw this cocksucker outside with that broom and that shovel and make sure he stays out there till my sidewalk's clean. And then make sure he spreads the de-icer around. And he gives you any shit? Sit on his stomach."

"Yessir, Mister Chianese."

"Aw c'mon, Uncle," Babyak said. "Jesus, I don't deserve this."

"You don't deserve nothin'. You wasn't my sister's kid, if you fell down with a heart attack I wouldn't call nine-one-one. Now go shovel the sidewalk or Angie's gonna give you a real bellyache, which you'll have to call nine-one-one yourself, only you'll have to crawl somewhere else to do it 'cause you ain't gonna use none of my phones."

"Don't waste your energy on me, Angelo," Babyak said, collecting the broom, snow shovel, and bag of de-icer and heading out the front door, where he worked as quickly as he could manage, given his advanced state of fatigue. When he'd almost finished spreading the de-icer and while he was lost in one revenge fantasy against his uncle after another, he looked up and saw Angelo poking his enormous head out the front door and calling his name.

"Now what?" Babyak said.

"Mister Chianese says when you're finished he wantsa talk to you, you got that?"

Babyak nodded glumly, tossed another handful of de-icer down, and went back inside, dragging broom, shovel, and de-icer into the back room. Chianese was sitting at his desk in the wobbly swivel rocker he was always bragging he'd stolen from his junior high principal's office the day after he quit school at the end of the eighth grade. Chianese's lower lip seemed to Babyak to be sticking out even farther than usual.

Chianese waved for the cousins Serra to go out front. Like honor Dobermans at an obedience school, the cousins practically trotted to the front room of the deli.

Babyak felt a major quiver in his stomach. What was coming wasn't going to be said to impress the faithful. Something was up, and Babyak knew he was up for it, he just didn't know what it was just yet. He instinctively shot a glance toward the door to the alley to see whether it had been rebolted since he'd had to go through it to throw up. It had been rebolted, which meant there was no way he could get out before the Dobermans got to him.

Babyak wracked his mind about what he could've done to piss Chianese off even more than usual. There were so many things Chianese didn't like about him, it was hard to single out any one thing. Whatever it was, Babyak knew, it was no small thing or he would've been hearing it from one of the Dobermans.

"Ain't you got somethin' to tell me?" Chianese said, shifting around in his chair, the wood creaking and groaning. The only other sound Babyak could hear was the steady hum of the refrigeration units.

"What's the matter, Uncle? I do somethin'? Like what?"

"If I have to ask you again, I'm gonna call the Serras back in here. Is 'at what you want?"

"No no, definitely not, no, but I don't know what you're talkin' about, Uncle, honest. Do my job every day, come here with the take every night, turn over every nickel, never hold out a penny on ya, then whatever you want done around here, I do it, so I mean, what's up? I don't get it. I'm not doin' nothin'."

"Not what I hear."

"What? Whatta you hear? I don't know what you're talkin' about," Babyak said, but suddenly it hit him. He knew what this was about. Somebody had seen him with the bikers, the Pagan wannabes, that had to be it. Couldn't be anything else. Everything else he did, he did alone, so this had to be about the crank.

"Swear on my sister's grave you're not doin' nothin'."

"What? Oh, you talkin' about the crank?"

"Ohhhhh, the crannnnk," Chianese said.

31

"Now your brain is workin', yeah. Okay. So tell me about this crank you think you can sell under my nose without tellin' me, why don't you do that, huh?"

"Hey, Uncle, my stomach, you know? My arthuritis? I ain't got any insurance. That medicine I gotta take? That's expensive. Month's wortha stomach pills cost me a hundred and nine bucks. All that calcium and shark cartilage'n stuff I take for my arthuritis, that stuff adds up too. I'm just movin' a little crank to cover my medicine, that's all, I ain't doin' nothin' else. And I ain't doin' enough to hurt you —"

"I decide who hurts me, not you. You think you could do this, you didn't have to ask me first? How about everybody starts thinkin' they can go into business around here without askin' me first — or tellin' me afterwards neither? 'Cause I'm still waitin' to hear you tell me how you think you could get with those biker assholes, huh? And I'm not gonna find out? You wanna explain that, you schemey little prick?"

Babyak shrugged and looked away and said, "Look, Uncle, I'm not doin' enough business to hurt you or anybody else. All I am, really, honest, I'm just a middleman, that's all. I put people in touch with other people, that's the whole thing right there, nothin' else. And for that, they throw a couple yards my way, that's it. And what — this makes you mad? C'mon. Whatta you want — ten percent? If that's what you want, I'll give it to you —"

"*You're* gonna give *me* ten percent?" Chianese laughed and snorted, echoed by the creaking wood under him. "I'll tell ya what you can give me, you cheesy little Slovak prick. You can give me a change in your fuckin' attitude, that's first —"

"Half-Slovak, Uncle," Babyak interrupted him. "My mother was same as you."

"Don't tell me what my sister was, and don't fuckin' interrupt me again. I know what she was. You gonna explain yourself here? Or am I gonna call Angie, what's it gonna be? You think your stomach hurts now? How 'bout Angie sits on it for ten minutes?"

"Aw whatta you want from me, Uncle? I ain't even allowed to make extra to cover my medicine? Doctor bills? Jesus Christ, six months ago I was in the emergency room at Conemaugh Hospital! Man, four fuckin' hours I was in there, the bill come to six twenty-nine and change. I still owe 'em three. What you pay me, Uncle, hey, that covers the back taxes on my mother's house, and my food, and my car payments, and that's it. 'Cause I guess what you forgot is your sister couldn't afford to pay her school taxes, you know? For the last ten years, you didn't know she couldn't make her real estate taxes? You didn't know that? You tellin' me she never asked you for it, huh? Don't tell me that, 'cause I know she did. And she told me what you told her too —"

Chianese pointed his thick, stubby index finger at Babyak. "Hey. You better watch your mouth."

"You told her to get it from me, that's what she told me. Meanwhile I was in the fuckin' joint seven of those years, which what? You forgot? Huh? Or maybe you just didn't hear about it? Shit."

"I ain't gonna tell you again. Watch how you talk."

"Or what? You're gonna call Angie? Huh? Fuck him, go ahead, call him, I don't give a shit no more. My stomach hurts all the time, my fuckin' hands hurt, my knees hurt, my elbows hurt, fuckit. I'm sicka tryin' to catch up on those fuckin' taxes — on what you're payin' me? Gonna take me three more years at least — and I ain't cleanin' your fuckin' sausage machine no more. Turns my fuckin' stomach every

34

time. So go 'head, call him, you gonna be-grudge me two yards a month. I don't give a shit, call him, fuckit, get it over with. 'Cause believe me, where I am ain't para-dise, I don't give a shit how much you think I'm makin' on the mouse."

"Well ain't you the mouthy little prick all of a sudden."

"Ain't nothin' sudden about it, Uncle, it just sounds that way. 'Cause if there's one thing I learned inside, it's everybody got a limit and then after that, fuckit, you can just take so much, and I don't care any-more, that's all. So if you're gonna do it, do it."

"Lookin' at you makes me sick," Chia-nese said. "Get outta here. Just remember, I got limits too. You can have it for your medicine, but don't let me hear about you doin' somethin' else, you hear me?"

"Nothin' wrong with my ears, Uncle. Probably the only thing I got works like they're supposed to."

"Is that a fact? I was you, I wouldn't let 'em get any bigger."

"Never turned anybody yet, Uncle. Not gonna start with you."

"Yeah? That's good. 'Cause you ever do? Think kolbassi. I'll have an Easter special on your ass. Two ninety-nine a pound."

A bolt of electrical pain shot through Babyak's stomach. He doubled over, retched, and ran away from his uncle and out the front door. On his way across the street to the bank parking lot where he parked his Ford Escort, he had to stop to throw up again, and when he finally got the door open and his key in the ignition, sweat was running down his bony chest, despite the fact the neon sign above the bank lot said it was 19 degrees.

Ronnie Cozzolino slouched with one cheek on the stool at the bar in the Ground Round, both his heels keeping time to music only he heard, the song of impatience that had been playing in his inner ear as long as he could remember. He ran his fingers through the condensation on his beer mug, pretending to be interested in it while waiting for Jackie Slaney to get right with the register. What he really wanted to do was take the beer mug and jam it into the teeth of the assistant manager, the geeky little corpozoid who was always taking his shot while Jackie was cashing out. Every night that he watched her, Ronnie heard the same music, the same words.

Look at him. Thinks he's so cool 'cause he drives that fuckin' Camaro. Owes some bank five years' worth of his life for the privilege of thinking he's Mister Coolmaro. And someday, whoopee-fuckin'-do, if he works real hard and sucks enough ass, he's gonna move all the way up to manager. Asshole. I oughta take that fuckin' Camaro to Cleveland, cover the motherfucker with Steeler stickers, leave it on the street, see how long it takes to get turned to junk.

Cozzolino's eyes were stapled to the assistant manager, hanging by Jackie's back, sticking his chin into her hair while he pretended to point something out, then making a big deal of brushing her hair away from his face and laughing, trying to be so cool. Go 'head, motherfucker, let me see you bump your dick up against her leg, go 'head, I'll fill that fuckin' Camaro fulla road-killed skunks.

Finally, Jackie slipped away, smiling, always smiling, always working for tips even when she wasn't, big smile here, light touch on the forearm there, telling people that whatever they ordered or thought or said was always right, good choice, the right thing to do, the way to go. Ronnie admired her for it as much as he was disgusted by it; he knew that's how she made the kind of tips she made, but he couldn't stand seeing her do it.

"Hi," she said, slipping onto the stool next to him.

"Why won't you tell me where that creep lives so I can fuck him up good?"

Jackie smiled brightly and said, "Hi, Jackie. How was your night? How'd you do on tips? Hungry? Get a chance to eat? Wanna eat something? Oh fine, Ronnie, I'm just fine. Had a great night. No I'm not hungry, I had plenty of chances to eat. I only worked sixty-three dinners by myself tonight 'cause that girl who started last night? She quit already — wow, Ronnie, you smell like, yuk, horses."

"Why you gotta bust my balls, Jackie, huh? Just tell me where that creep lives, I'll fuck him up so good, he'll never bother you again, why won't you tell me that?"

"You answered your own question, Ronnie," Jackie said, opening a pack of cigars shaped like cigarettes and reaching behind her for a pack of matches and an ashtray. "Hey, Freddie, give me a Diet Coke when you get a chance, huh, please? How come you smell like that?"

"Whatta you mean I answered my own question?"

"If I tell you where he lives, you'll do it, and where's that gonna leave me, huh? He's only seen us together about a gazillion times now, that's all. That'd be just great, right? You eff him up, he calls the cops, tells them who you been sittin' with, who do you think the cops're gonna wanna talk to first? Duhhhh."

"Why won't you listen to me? I keep tellin' ya, when it comes to the cops, you don't know nothin', you never know nothin'. That's kindergarten."

"Kindergarten, huh? Maybe yours, Ronnie, not mine. I don't know what I see in you. I must be nuts, you know that?" Jackie said, exhaling toward the ceiling. "You gonna tell me why you smell?"

"You don't know what you see in me? I'll tell you what you see. What you're too scared to say, that's what you see. Speed, baby. Danger. Ex-fucking-citement. I don't come in here, all you got is your old lady and that apartment and those books you think're gonna get you off the floor here and into some kinda pinstripe office or some shit. Speakin' of which, I hope you remember somethin'. Like what night to-morrow is. And never mind why I smell. I don't smell —"

"Oh Ronnie, Jesus —"

"Ho, whoa! 'Oh Ronnie Jesus'? Don't oh Ronnie Jesus me! I been workin' on this too long now, I don't wanna hear no 'oh Ronnie Jesus' shit —"

"Ronnie, honest to God, you wanna do what you wanna do? Fine. I don't care. But I don't like you making me a part of this, I don't understand why I'm in this, just 'cause you wanna do something —"

"Whatta you mean *makin'* you a part of this — what is this shit? I ain't *makin'* you do nothin'. Nobody held a gun to nobody's head here, this was fun! Oh yeah! Fun fun fun, yeah, your eyes turned orange neon, babyface, from the git. All I hada do was start talkin' about it and you were right here." He held up his left palm and jammed his right index finger into it three times. "So I don't know where you're gettin' that makin'-you shit all of a sudden 'cause nobody was doin' any makin' anybody here. But we're here now, babyface, and there ain't gonna be no U-turns. I told you what you have to do, which is small enough you don't have to sweat it, I'm the one gonna be doin' the work, all you gotta do is what you gotta do. Which is a simple thing and nobody's gonna know nothin'."

Jackie clenched her fists and brought

them down on her thighs. "Ronnie, listen to me. He's not stupid, Ronnie. You think he's stupid, you think everybody's stupid, but everybody isn't stupid. Not as stupid as you think they are. And soon as the cops ask him where he was, soon as they ask what he was doin', soon as they ask why he wasn't doin' what he was supposed to be doin'? C'mon, Ronnie, you can say he's stupid all you want, but I'm tellin' you he's gonna tell 'em. Then what? It's right back to me again, and that's conspiracy, Ronnie —"

"Keep it down, will ya? Freddie's comin' with your Coke. You keep sayin' he's okay, I don't trust the motherfucker —"

"Oh, he's okay, Ronnie. You're the one's not okay. This thing started out as a big joke, and if you tell me it didn't you're lyin' — thanks, Freddie, oh God I'm so thirsty —"

"You better be right about him 'cause he's practically gettin' a cramp in his neck tryin' to hear what we're sayin' here —"

"Freddie's not the problem, Ronnie. You are. 'Cause you just refuse to understand what I've been tryin' to tell you for the last week. At first it was funny, and the more you talked about it, the more I played along with it, the funnier it got, 'cause he's so pathetic, but it's not funny anymore

41

'cause now I know you're serious —"

"*Now* I'm serious?! *Now?!* Hey, Jackie, I was never not serious! And you better get serious too, 'cause this thing's happenin', you hear me? Tomorrow it's happening. Big joke? This thing was never a joke. I know what you're doin', Jackie, I ain't stupid either, you know?"

"Oh I'm doin' something? What? What am I doin'?"

"You're tryin' to cop out it was all a joke, that's what you're doin'. That's bullshit, Jackie. That's what people say when they get called on somethin' — oh I was only jokin', that's all, what'sa-matter with you, you can't take a joke — all that stupid shit. But this ain't no joke, Jackie, it was never no joke, I don't care what you say now, and it better not be no joke tomorrow night, you hear me? Better not hang me up, Jackie, I'm tellin' ya."

"Don't look at me like that, Ronnie. And don't talk to me like that either. You scare me when you talk like that."

Ronnie leaned back and smiled, very satisfied with himself. "There. That's what you like about me. You're scared to admit it, but that's the whole deal, right there, that's it. I scare you. But you suck it up. Good little girl loves to be around the bad boys. But when a real bad boy shows up, and she gets a little taste? Oh man, then she can't stand it. It's an old story, Jackie, I've seen the movie a hundert times, and so've you, don't tell me you haven't —"

"This isn't a movie, Ronnie, Jesus Christ —"

"You got that right, babyface. It ain't. So tomorrow night, when he comes in here to get a refill on his Thermos? You do what you said you were gonna do, you hear? You keep his ass in here till I told you when. It's gonna take me till then to do what I'm gonna do. Don't hang me up, Jackie. I'm tellin' ya. Don't. 'Cause you hang me up — you listenin' to me? You hang me up tomorrow night, I don't care what we had goin' here, it'll be over. You understand over, Jackie, huh? I mean as in over over? You and your old lady both."

"You're scaring me, Ronnie. I mean it. You really scare me when you talk like that. You should see your face."

"You should see yours. You got thrill jones spread all over it. You got the hunger, babyface —"

"Oh God — *thrill jones?!* Do you even know what you're seein'? Do you even know what you're sayin'?"

"Yeah, right, thrill jones, I know what

43

I'm seein'. 'Cause pizza and Diet Coke ain't never gonna do it for you, don't shit me, you got a bad thrill jones, you know you do. And that's what scares you. But tomorrow night, you do what you gotta do. Or I'll do what I gotta do."

Balzic was sipping coffee and reading the *Pittsburgh Post-Gazette* at the far end of the bar in Muscotti's when Valcanas walked in. Balzic looked away from the paper long enough to see who'd come in, then returned to it with a snort. "Hey, Panagios, you should know this. The people that print this paper, don't they own a piece of the Pirates?"

"Nonvoting share," Valcanas said, easing onto the stool next to Balzic. "One-sixth as much cash investment as the principal owner is what I seem to recall. But don't trust my recall."

"Yeah, well that's what I recall too," Balzic said. "I'm tellin' ya, all you read in this fuckin' paper? Sports pages, editorial page, they're fuckin' relentless, the Pirates absolutely gotta have their own ballpark, Pittsburgh absolutely needs another sta-

dium, Cleveland got a new stadium, Balti-
more got a new stadium, Pittsburgh absolutely got to have a new stadium, otherwise
Pittsburgh's gonna dry up and blow away.
Whatta they call this stuff now? Infor-
mercials? Advertorials? Used to be they'd
call it what it was, you know? Propaganda?
Makes you sick the bullshit we're swim-
min' in."

"Don't make me sick," Vinnie the bartender said.

"Nothin' makes you sick," Valcanas said.

"Ho, wrong there! Youns guys, yo, every
day I go home with a headache."

"That ain't what I'm talkin' about,"
Balzic said. "It's this shit, Pittsburgh needs
another stadium. Like I need another
asshole — who they think's gonna pay for
it? Clinton signs that welfare reform for
the poor — disgustin' what they did there,
all of 'em, oughta be ashamed of themselves. You'd think after that they'd have
the decency to go to work on these free-
loaders own sports franchises, huh? How
long we s'pposed to carry those guys?"

"You just talkin', or you talkin' to me
now, what?" Vinnie said.

"I'm talkin'. You wanna listen, listen.
You don't wanna listen, don't listen."

Vinnie grunted. "You're gettin' bad as

Iron City Steve, you know that? Better watch it, Mario, I'm tellin' ya. You keep makin' speeches, one day I'll be sendin' you to the bank to pay Dom's electric bill."

"The day I start runnin' for you, that's the day I go find my blackjack and beat myself to death."

"Watch what you say now. Remember Steve? Huh? The way he used to come in here? Carnations in his lapel, diamond stickpin in his tie — remember? Look at him down there. Ain't open a half hour, already he's in a coma."

Balzic ignored Vinnie, turned the page, glanced at Valcanas, and said, "Man, you're in here this early, you must be tryin' to keep somebody outta family court."

"Tryin' and failin'," Vinnie said, shaking his head and smirking. "Have hope, will travel. You oughta get some cards printed up like 'at, Greek, no shit. Get yourself a van, put some loudspeakers on the roof, your marriage can be saved, four monthly payments just twenty-nine ninety-nine —"

"If only you'd shut your loudspeakers off. How about working for a change, why don't you?" Valcanas said, nodding toward Balzic's coffee and motioning for Vinnie to bring him one. "And put a little

Sambuca in it."

"A little Sambuca," Vinnie said, rolling his eyes. "What the fuck's a little — you want two drops, you want a teaspoon, what?"

"Astonish me. An honest ounce."

Vinnie raised his palms and rolled his eyes. "My old man told me, learn a fuckin' trade. Said it once, said it eight fuckin' thousand times. Did I listen? Nooo, not me, fuck no. Me? I shoot for a career in retail alcohol."

Iron City Steve raised his head off his forearms, flung out his bony hands, and bellowed at the ceiling, "I know I'm goin' to hell, but am I expected to walk? Let's have some transportation!" He sawed the back of his hands across his mouth, folded his arms on the bar, farted, and eased his forehead back down onto his arms.

Vinnie brought a mug of coffee, the Sambuca, and a shot glass. He set them in front of Valcanas and grinned at Balzic. "Hear that, Mario? Huh? Keep sittin' here talkin' back to the paper, that's you, two years tops."

"Uh, do you mind?" Valcanas said, pointing at the empty glass between Vinnie and the coffee.

"Do I mind what? Huh? What, you have

47

a stroke, you paralyzed or somethin', you can't move your hands? Get some money up — and before you give me any shit, Dom told me, okay? No more tabs. State cops shut us down next time, it's gonna be thirty days, and it's gonna be my ass 'cause it's my writin' on the fuckin' paper, okay? So come up with somethin' here."

"If I pay you, will you promise to leave? I have business to conduct here and I'd like to do it privately, if you don't mind." Valcanas reached into his inside coat pocket and brought out his wallet. He licked his thumb and index finger, drew out a five, and laid it on the bar.

Vinnie smiled, nodded, poured, picked up the five, and said, "You want privacy, why the fuck you come here, huh? Explain that to me, okay? Only not now, I don't wanna hear it now." He brought the change, slid it onto the worn wood, and headed for the far end of the bar, singing, "Some enchanted evening. . . ."

Balzic folded up his newspaper and squinted at Valcanas. "You want privacy with me? I should leave right now."

"Relax. Nothing to be alarmed about."

"Oh shit," Balzic said, snorting and laughing, "for sure I should leave. Should be runnin'. And believe me, if I could run, I would —"

"It's nothing, believe me, you can take care of it in two days, three tops."

"Hey. Every time somebody says somethin' is nothin'? And they're lookin' at me? I start to get heartburn, you know that?"

"How long have we been friends?"

"Huh? Oh man, you gotta ask, it's been about a minute too long —"

"No, I'm serious. How long?"

Balzic scowled over his glasses at Valcanas. "Now I'm really startin' to get heartburn. First, it's nothin', then it's how long we been friends —"

"I'm not calling in chips   I was just thinking about it on my way down here."

"Okay, '46, that's how long. Since '46."

"Well see I know it was later than that —"

"Nah, uh-uh, '46. I got outta the Marines December '46. I was home for Christmas '46. You got outta the Coast Guard —"

"On the way down here, I'm thinking, ask Mario, see what his memory is, you know, just to see if your memory corresponds to mine, that's all, and already you're wrong. 'Cause after I thought about it, I remembered I have my VA card in my wallet, I'm still carryin' it, don't ask me why. Says in black and white I was discharged February twenty-fifth, 1947 —"

"Oh, so that's where we are, huh? Where you're askin' me — and you got the evidence right in your wallet? What's next, you gonna start bettin' me? Christ."

Valcanas poured the Sambuca into his coffee, stirred it, and took a sip. "Amazing, our memory, you know? You spend a life building a career on your memory? Pass all these tests, jump through all these hoops, and then what? One day you wake up and suddenly it seems very important to remember when certain things happened. And you can't."

"Yeah, well, we live long enough, we're all gonna be in diapers again. Know how good your memory was when you were in diapers the first time? Anyway, what's this about, this other thing?"

"You know Albert Bertelli, right?"

"The insurance guy? Yeah. We're not social, and he's not my insurance guy, but we speak, yeah."

"Well normally I'd get Joe Buckner to do this, but he's up to his eyes. I've got this really complicated case, four insurers for four vehicles, two of them commercial, seven occupants, totally contradictory depositions —"

"Aw, hey, c'mon, Greek, too cold, I don't wanna be rentin' flamethrowers so I can measure skid marks, Jesus Christ, it was seven degrees when I woke up this morning —"

"Mario, what I was just talking about has nothing to do with Bertelli. I was telling you why I can't have Buckner do it."

"Oh. So what's with him — and remember, I don't have a license, okay? You do remember that, right?"

"Yes I remember that. You know it, I know it — has anybody asked to see your bona fides so far?"

"You kiddin' me? Everybody. Christ, half the people in the courthouse. To them, I'm just another nosey geezer."

"Mario, you don't feel like working, fine, but don't tell me you don't know how to talk the talk." He took another sip of coffee. "Pays fifty an hour."

"How much?"

"Oh, *now* I have your attention. Okay, listen. All you have to do is talk to the same people you always talked to — or whoever fills their seats now. Still have the letter I gave you?"

"What letter?"

"The letter I gave you establishing your relationship to my practice —"

"Oh, that one. Yeah, I still have it. Some-where."

"Never mind, I'll have another one typed up —"

"Why? I just said I still have it, you don't need to have another one typed up. I know what to say anyway, I don't need a letter says I'm waitin' on Harrisburg to process some bullshit application —"

"Mario, why do we have to go through this? Why don't you just get a license and be done with it?"

" 'Cause I don't wanna pay the goddamn fees they charge, that's why — why do you keep askin' me? Same reason I'm tired of payin' taxes so those bastards can give it to their rich friends that own sports fran-chises — you hear what our genius gover-nor wants to do now? Huh? With the state stores? Wantsa sell 'em, use the money to build sports stadiums — you feature that bullshit?"

"Mario, they're never gonna let him get away with that, so quit worryin' about it —"

"Who's not gonna let him get away with it?"

"All the legislators from all the hick towns between Pittsburgh and Philadel-phia, that's who. You think *they're* gonna let him sell the state stores? And give it all to a handful of guys in the two big cities? Never happen. Not as long as we have the problems we have payin' for the schools, never mind the sewerage that's goin' to hell, they'll never stand for that —"

"He's a Republican, he's got Republican majorities in both houses there —"

"They may say they're Republican, Mario, I'm not arguing that, but they're not the same kind of Republicans, never have been, not gonna turn into 'em now. I don't care how many there are in the majority, they're not gonna tolerate sellin' off a system worth all that money just to give it to a handful of people in the cities while their own people are bitchin' about payin' for schools with real estate taxes. Trust me. I don't claim to know much about Pennsylvania politics, but I do know that much."

"Yeah, that's what you know, right. What I see comin' is another shuck and jive headin' for us like Volkswagen. Bring in those fuckin' Germans, lend 'em millions to train the grunts, give 'em all kindsa tax dodges, build 'em the roads, build 'em the rail spur, and when the tax dodges run out, all that's left is us suckers payin' off the bond issues. Which they did again with the fuckin' Japs and Sony. Same fuckin' building for crissake. What the fuck did we fight Big Two for, can you tell me that?"

"Mario, listen, some other time I'd love to debate who lost Big Two, okay? But not now, okay? Bertelli?"

"Yeah yeah, okay, go ahead — and you're on the square about fifty an hour? Why so much? That's double what you paid me last time —"

"On the square, plus expenses, and don't worry about it. It won't take you three days even if you transcribe the interviews yourself —"

"Aw be serious, I do that, it'll take me a month."

"Well I don't have that kind of money, so just give me the tapes, my secretary'll transcribe them. Cheaper to pay her overtime — anyway, where was I? Oh. Listen, here's the deal. This gunshop that was burgled in the mall — you hear about that?"

"Yeah, I read about it," Balzic said, rolling his eyes. "What? Bertelli stuck for that?"

"Why're you rollin' your eyes? You know something?"

"No, I don't know anything. Just what I read, that's all."

"And?"

Balzic shrugged. "Hey, all I said when I read it, I said either the reporter got the numbers fucked up or this guy's workin' a swindle, that's all, it was obvious."

"Obvious why?"

" 'Cause there's no way he had that kinda inventory, not the numbers I read. Coulda been typos, you know, with the *Gazette* you never know, but the numbers I read were strictly for the tourists."

"Which *Gazette*?"

"The local. Not this one," Balzic said, tapping the *Pittsburgh Post-Gazette*. "I don't recall the numbers exactly, but they were way outta line."

"Well, he's got a claim for forty-some handguns and thirty thousand rounds of ammo, office furniture, carpets, showcases —"

"Well that sounds sorta like what I read, so I guess it wasn't typos. Guy owns the shop? His name's not familiar to me, who is he?"

Valcanas finished his coffee and said, "Listen, talk to Bertelli. I need to get movin' on this other thing. And just so I'm sure now, you're gonna do it, right? You're gonna talk to him? Today? If he calls me, I can say that and mean it?"

"Sure. Why not? Put me on the clock right now. 'Specially since Vinnie thinks

55

I'm in trainin' to become the future Iron City Steve. Man, that's scary. Guess I'm gonna have to stop makin' speeches."

"Fine," Valcanas said, finishing his coffee and standing. "Here's Bertelli's card."

"Who wrote it up? The state? Who else, stupid question."

Valcanas stood, buttoned his wool overcoat, and said, "What he said to me was, they gave it a nod in passing. Ask them yourself, see what they say." Valcanas shrugged a small wave good-bye and was gone, out the door into biting wind whipping in around him.

Balzic had started to follow him out, but stopped short at the rush of cold. He happened to have stopped behind Iron City Steve, who picked that moment to rise up, spin slowly on his stool, and stare gloomily at Balzic. "Tell me the truth," Steve said. "This war on drugs? Is there gonna be a G.I. Bill or what? And if so, you think there might be a little somethin' extra for us POWs?" He spun slowly back to the bar, folded his arms, and lowered his head to them with a noisy sigh.

Man, Balzic thought, the G.I. Bill. Jesus, I had about five years' worth and didn't take one damn course. All that college I could've had, and never even thought about it, never hesitated. Not once. Just bought the house with the VA mortgage. Be a cop, be a cop, that's all my little brain could understand. Got outta one uniform, got into another one. And here I go again, gotta go home, put on a shirt and tie. . . .

Balzic pulled into the macadam parking lot in front of Bertelli-Jacks Independent Insurance Agency at the top of a hill on Rider Road in Westfield Township. The building was a nondescript three-story rectangle of red brick and inset windows. It housed, in addition to Bertelli-Jacks IIA, offices for a podiatrist, a chiropractor, an optometrist, a family and marriage counselor, a CPA, and four attorneys. The usual mix, Balzic thought, in pretty much the usual kind of building. The words *professional building* seemed to come attached to them. The *Smith Building* or the *Jones Building* wasn't enough. It had to be the Smith Professional Building, or in this case the Morton Professional Center.

They'd been sprouting around Rocksburg for decades. Inside Rocksburg, they tended to fill the once grand residences around Conemaugh General Hospital where the mine owners had lived at the beginning of the century; but in the surrounding townships, they seemed to turn up anywhere bulldozers could get access to carve a level space out of a hillside. It seemed to Balzic that there was an equal ratio: the more manufacturing facilities closed in and around Rocksburg, the more of these buildings there seemed to be. Full of professionals, Balzic groused, whose principal reason for doing business in a building not their homes was that they needed someplace to go to get away from their spouses and kids. Which they would deny. What they'd want to talk about was all the tax pros and cons of doing business in the home versus owning or renting office space.

What the hell, Balzic thought. He envied them anyway. Only place he had to go to get away from the home was Muscotti's, and sometimes listening to Vinnie was as trying as. . . .

As trying as what, he asked himself as he got out of his Chevy and locked it. C'mon, what were you thinkin'? Listenin' to Vinnie's startin' to get as tryin' as . . . never mind. Jesus, maybe the Greek's right, maybe I do need to get a license. Maybe rent a storefront. As many of those as there are on Main Street, probably could get one for fifty bucks a week. Phone, lights, heat, water, coffeepot, one of those little refrigerators, a hot plate, file cabinet, a desk, two chairs, a lamp, a broom, a mop, a cup, a dish, a spoon, some paper towels, toilet paper — oh man, just stop it. Just go inside and talk to this Bertelli, quit fantasizin', you're not gonna pay those fucks in Harrisburg what they want for a license and incorporation fees, who you kiddin'?

Fuck them, don't get a license, don't incorporate, just get the office, pretend you got the license, who asks for it anyway? Oh right, yeah, "Uh, pardon me, Detective, are you bonded? I don't know much about the law, but if you're working for me and something goes wrong, I mean accidents happen, well, uh, are you bonded? Do you have insurance? That can't be part of the fee if something goes wrong — I mean, people sue — are you covered?" Yeah, right, absolutely, I'm covered. In clothes that're gettin' older by the minute. Like me. . . .

"I'm here to see Mr. Bertelli," Balzic said to the fortyish woman on the other side of the counter. She had the kind of hair his wife told him was supposed to look like it just happened that way, that nobody had really spent any time or effort making it look like that, but it reminded him of the nests of small animals anyway.

She brought a tiny square pad and a ballpoint pen to the counter and said, "And your name, sir?"

"Balzic. Mario. I'm here for Attorney Panagios Valcanas." *Here?* I'm *here* for attorney Valcanas? I'm not *working* for him, I'm just *here* for him. What kind of bullshit is this?

"Oh he just called, I just now hung up. Let me tell Al you're here. Mister Valcanas just called not two minutes ago. I'll be right back." She hurried out from behind the counter and rushed down a short corridor where her head and shoulders disappeared as she held on to the door frame with both hands and announced Balzic's arrival. She reappeared, gave him a couple of quick waves and a bright smile, and said, "C'mon, Mister Balzic, he can't wait to see you, believe me."

Bertelli had put on a few inches around the middle and his hair was now the color of sooty snow, but otherwise he looked like Balzic remembered, even though it had been probably five years since they'd last met. Bertelli was broad-shouldered, thick through the neck and chest, with great tufts of black hair on the backs of his hands and fingers. When Balzic came through the door, Bertelli was buttoning his shirt collar and tightening his tie as he came around his desk.

"Mario, good to see you. It's been a long time. Mo said he thought he could talk you into this, even though you probably wouldn't want to do it." He shook hands with Balzic, his grip as soft as Balzic's. "Sit down, sit down — can I get you a coffee? Huh? Tea? Coke? That's it, that's my beverage list. Any of those suit you?"

"Nah, nothin', I'm fine. Already had too much coffee." Balzic took a seat in the chair Bertelli dragged up beside his desk. "So, uh, Mo said you have a problem with this gunshop?"

"A problem, yes," Bertelli said, sitting and drawing his chair toward Balzic and leaning toward him. His voice dropped so low that Balzic had to lean forward as well.

"Listen, uh, sorry to ask, but you're gonna have to speak up a little, Mister Bertelli, I must be gettin' ready for a hearing aid —"

"Al. Please. I'm sorry. Anytime I get nervous about something like this, I guess I, uh, you know, start whispering, start acting like I'm in some dumb movie or something."

"Somebody, uh, around here you don't trust?"

"Huh? Oh God no. Absolutely not, no, these girls, they're all solid. God, they've been with me for years. Doreen's the youngest but she's been here fifteen years at least. Hell, they run the place, I could leave for a month, they wouldn't know I was gone. But one of them's off for a week, I go crazy. Sometimes I wonder what I actually do around here."

"Well, you know, gets ya outta the house," Balzic said.

"Yeah, but I mean aside from that — anyway, just tell me if I start sounding like a bad movie or something."

"Oh I will, don't worry. So this gunshop, uh, why's your nose open?"

"Why's my nose open, yeah. Well, see, the volume, I mean, it's just crazy. I mean, my antenna went right up. Forty handguns? I mean forty different ones, yeah. Maybe? But all of them 9mm semi-auto pistols — except for, uh, lemme see here, one .357 Magnum. Yeah, a Ruger Model 707 .357 Magnum with a short barrel, and, uh, a .44 Magnum. Also a Ruger.

Long-barrel. Both of those stainless-steel. But all the others? Nine-millimeter Berettas. Model 92F. Thirty-eight of them alone, and thirty thousand rounds of 9mm ammunition, that's just crazy."

"Why?"

"Why?"

"Yeah, why? Why do you think — I mean, do you have a specific reason for thinkin' it's crazy? Is it not possible? Or what?"

"Here's the thing, Mario. Soon as I heard it, I mean the first thing I asked him —"

"Who's him by the way?"

"Oh. Bemiss. Soloman Jacob Bemiss, but he's not a Jew. Don't ask me what he is, I don't know, I just always associated those first two names with Jews, but, uh, with this guy I'm wrong. First time I met him, he made a point of telling me he's not a Jew. Told me he didn't spell his name the same way. It's S-o-l-o-m-a-n, Solo-man."

"So, okay, so he's not a Jew, so what? More important, is he a cherry, or does he have history?"

"I don't know."

Balzic felt his mouth turning down at the corners. "You guys don't keep this on your computers?"

"I do, of course. And the companies

used to — God knows they're supposed to."

"But what — you tellin' me they don't anymore?"

Bertelli fidgeted and laughed nervously. "Well, to be honest — I mean I hate to say this, but what it's like, I mean this is just my opinion, but it's gettin' a lot like airport security is what it's gettin' to be, you know?"

"No, I don't know. Haven't been on a plane, God, must be twenty years."

"Well believe me, every time I get on one I wish I wasn't, but I don't have a choice. Thing is, airport security, hey, I mean, it's a joke. They bring these people in, they pay them minimum wage, they train them for about a day, and the turnover is, uh, God, I shudder to think — I don't want to know what it is. And you know why? You guess?"

Balzic shrugged. "You mean the turn-over? Probably 'cause they get caught not doin' what they're supposed to be doin'."

"Exactly. But what's scary is they know who's testin' them! They know, for cryin' out loud! They see the tester comin' and they still let the damn stuff go through. God it's really scary to think about it. Only way I can get on a damn plane, I swear, it's

Scotch and Valium, I admit it, I just get swacked, try to sleep through it."

"So, uh, you sayin' the insurance companies are doin' the same kinda hirin'? Same kinda trainin'?"

Bertelli shrugged and sighed. "What do you think? Cut back, cut back, that's all we hear, hell, that's all I read. Listen, I don't care what anybody says, you keep cutting back on personnel, cutting wages, forcing the people you keep to take up the slack — something has to give. I don't give a damn how much money they're making for their stockholders, there are screwups. More and more of them. And not only are they more frequent, some of them are lulus. You complain, they say they don't need all these people, they've got these great computers. It's crap. Come on, I mean, hey, even I know a computer's nothing but an electronic file cabinet. You got people who don't know what they're doing taking care of your filing, what you got is file cabinets full of useless information, what's the difference whether it's on paper or on those, uh, what the hell they call 'em, silicon chips?"

"So what you're sayin' is there's no record on your guy here?"

"Yes. That's what I'm saying — God,

American General Casualty, believe me, I've called that office sometimes and I've gotten people I could not understand ten words they said — I'm not exaggeratin'. I say where're you from, you know, I mean, I'm not being a smart-ass — what the hell, all my people were immigrants — but honest to God I can't understand them. They say Iraq, Pakistan. I mean, Jesus, who puts people like that on the phones? What the hell are they thinking? Hire people who can't speak the language? That's your first contact with the company? I mean after those goddarn menus? You sit, and you wait, and you push another button, and the first live person you get you can't understand him? Or her? Jesus. I'm sorry, this has really got me upset, making me think, you know, maybe it's time to, uh, just pack it in, get out while the gettin's good — ah, listen to me."

Balzic chewed his lower lip for a moment. "Listen, how much we talkin' here? Can't be that much — I know nobody wants to pay a phony claim, I don't care how much it is, but, uh, I mean, we're not talkin' a couple hundred grand here, right?"

"Well, the Berettas, they go for, uh, generally now, they usually retail for six twenty-six and change apiece —"

"Wait, wait — that's not what he paid?"

"Oh no, but pretty close. His markup's not a whole lot."

"I know it isn't, but what'd he pay?"

Bertelli shrugged. "His markup's about two percent, more or less."

"So instead of six twenty-six, it's what?"

"I think he said six thirteen and change."

"So he's sayin' what, thirty-eight times six thirteen and change, what's that?"

"His claim is, uh, lemme check here," Bertelli said, shuffling paper. "Here it is. Twenty-three thousand three hundred and twelve dollars and twenty-four cents — that's for the Berettas. He's not sure what he paid for the other guns, he's still checkin'."

"He's still checkin'?"

"That's what he says."

"Okay, so he's checkin'. So what's his markup on the ammo?"

"Twenty percent. Approximately."

"And what's he claimin' there? Thirty thousand rounds at what?"

"He says it retails for thirteen ninety-nine a box, fifty rounds to a box, that's six hundred boxes, he says it was eight thousand three hundred and ninety-four, so eighty percent of that, that's another six thousand seven hundred and fifteen and twenty cents."

"And he's got paper to back this up?"

"Well, see, that's the problem. He says they, uh, dumped his paperwork and they defecated on it, smeared it all around, plus they brought in horse manure and spread that all around too. All over everything, ruined all his furnishings, shoved it into all the locks, everything has to be replaced."

"I see," Balzic said. "It was not the work of, uh, what do they call 'em? Anal retentives?"

"Mario, I'm just repeating what the man said."

"I understand that, I didn't mean to get wise there, but, uh — never mind. Who wrote this up for the state, you have a name?"

Bertelli shoved some papers aside on his desk, found a notebook and read it. "Uh, Trooper Claude Milliron. Troop A Barracks."

"Uh-huh. And he's got photos of all this, uh, destruction by defecation, right? You get copies?"

"Not yet."

"When'd this happen?"

"Week ago Sunday."

"Uh-huh. What's this guy's deductible, by the way?"

"A thousand."

"So, uh, what's his claim on the office damage? He have replacement costs or what?"

"Oh replacement, yeah, of course, what do you think?"

"So what's he sayin' there, total?"

Bertelli picked up a sheaf of forms and peeled them back until he found the one he was looking for. "He's saying a desk, chair, two lamps, a computer, a phone, answering machine, fax machine, copier, scatter rug, small electric heater, two four-drawer file cabinets, two two-drawer file cabinets, coffeepot, two coffee mugs, assorted stationery supplies including but not limited to pens, pencils, staplers, thumbtacks, corkboard, Post-its —"

"They spread the crap over everything?"

"That's what he says."

"Sounds to me like he wants to redecorate. What's the total — his claim, I mean — wait a minute, you said computer?"

"Yeah, that's what he said."

"So, uh, what? He's sayin' he doesn't have the invoices in the computer, he just had 'em on paper? Or is he claimin' they wrecked the computer too? And the, uh, whatta they call them, those things — the, uh, the disks?"

"Everything either smashed or smeared with excrement."

"How convenient for him." Balzic squeezed his eyes shut, took off his glasses and rubbed his right eye with his knuckle. "I'm thinkin', you know, ammo's heavier'n hell. Fifty rounds per box, how many boxes in a case — Christ, I can't remember anything anymore. I do know it's heavier than hell."

"What are you saying?"

"Well, I'm sayin' somebody broke a major sweat humpin' it outta there — at least one somebody. And it had to take a while, I mean, spread all that crap around, hump the ammo outta there — they didn't do that in five minutes, where was security? Who's security out there? Vanguard has that contract, don't they?"

"Not anymore. Some new outfit, uh, Bulldog Security. They've got an office out on Route 79, about eight, eight and a half miles this side of little Washington."

"Never heard of 'em. How long they been in the mall?"

"Not long, two years. Not even that long."

"What happened to Vanguard?"

"Bankruptcy is what I heard. Tried to re-organize, but that didn't work apparently. Supposedly liquidating — course this is just hearsay now. All I know is they're no longer in business, but that part's not hearsay, but what stage of bankruptcy they're in I shouldn't't've said 'cause I don't know."

"So this trooper, uh, this Milliron? He had proof of forced entry? Or is he holdin' his nose — never mind, I'll ask him. What did you say the total was on the office and furnishings — did you tell me already and I forgot? Please don't say you told me —"

"I didn't."

"Oh good. My memory's for shit anymore. Don't worry, I use a tape recorder, I just forgot to get it, you know. Mo said you were kinda anxious to get goin'. Anyway, so the total on the office is what now?"

"Approximately fifty-two hundred."

"Okay, so the guns're what again? Twenty-three what?"

"Twenty-three three twelve twenty-four. And the ammo's six thousand seven fifteen twenty."

"And the office is fifty-two hundred, so, uh, that's what?"

"It comes to thirty-five two twenty-seven."

"And you've covered him for how long?"

71

"Eleven months."

"How long's he been in the mall?"

"Same. Eleven months."

"What's his premium? And how's he pay, monthly, quarterly, what?"

"He pays quarterly. It's a thousand a month."

"So, uh, he timely? Covered for the year?"

"Yeah."

"So you got him for twelve and he wants you for thirty-six, approximately, is that it?"

"That's it. But not me. American General Casualty."

"Uh-huh. What'd he do before guns? Anything? Where's he from? You know?"

"I'm not sure. Something sticks in my mind about a pickle line at, uh, U.S. Steel, acid, he worked with acid, but I don't know why I'm thinking that. Maybe he delivered acid, Mario, I'm not sure."

"What, he get laid off, get hurt, what — you know?"

"He got hurt on the job somehow, I think that's how he got the money to open this shop. But I don't even know why I'm saying that, it just popped into my mind when you asked, but I'm not positive about that. Should be easy enough to check though, right?"

"Well, let's hope. Okay, Albert," Balzic said, standing, stretching his chin upward. "God, I got this goofy pain in my neck, don't wanna call it pain, it's not even that, it's just, you know, it only used to bother me when I was walkin', especially goin' up steps. Now it's startin' to bother me all the time. Ah well, you know what they say, huh? Gettin' old ain't for sissies."

"Aw tell me about it," Bertelli said, laughing. "Every day I wake up, my shoulders hurt so bad I gotta warm up, you know, swing my arms around, circles or whatever, you know, just to get loose enough to brush my teeth. Honest to God, it got so bad last summer, I had to learn how to shave and brush my teeth left-handed. I finally had to get an electric razor, I was cutting myself so much, it was ridiculous. My wife said what's wrong with you, you been shaving twice a day since you were in high school, you don't know how to shave anymore? I tell her my shoulders hurt, she tells me I'm a crybaby, you can't win. I'm tellin' you, you can't win with women. Maybe it's just my wife. I say something hurts, she says you never had a baby, don't tell me about pain, have a baby, then you can talk. What the hell you

73

gonna do, huh? Listen, uh, you'll let me know, right? How things're going?"

"Well, I can call you every day if that's what you want —"

"No no, that's not necessary. Just whenever — well, uh, when are you gonna report to Mo?"

"We didn't even talk about that. He just told me he thought I could cover everything in two days, three tops, so I didn't say to him, uh, you know, when I'd be checkin' in. He just told me to give my tapes to his secretary —"

"Personal assistant."

"Huh? Oh, yeah, right, I keep forgettin'. Don't call 'em secretaries, Jesus. *Secretary* — is like, man, I don't know what, hunky, dago, nigger. What the hell's so bad about *secretary*? When'd that turn rancid?"

"You really want to know, ask Doreen, she'll tell you. I made the mistake of introducing her to some guy about five years ago. Man oh man, soon as he left, she comes flyin' in, shuts the door behind her, wow, she gave me five minutes of why she wasn't an-y-bod-y's secretary, and don't you forget it, Mis-ter Bertelli. Oh yeah."

"I'll bet she did. Yeah, personal assistants, right — you better not forget either. Yeah. Okay, so anyway, I was gonna drop

74

off the tapes in his office every night, Mo's, or, you know, next morning, but that's as far as I got, thinkin' about it. But I'll call every day if you want. Or if you prefer I'll call ya at home every night — oh, which reminds me. Give me every phone number and address you've got — for everybody, save me a lotta time — better yet, you got cards for 'em? Got a copyin' machine? I'll just lay 'em in there, put 'em all on one sheet, you can keep the cards, how's that?"

"Fine. We can do that right now."

The copying of business cards completed, Balzic shook hands with Bertelli, wished all the personal assistants a good day, and was on his way to his car when he got that sensation again. It wasn't pain exactly, sort of like heartburn but not like heartburn. It started on both sides of his esophagus and rose upward into his neck and then into his jaw, especially on the left side. By the time he got to the Chevy, it was up into his left cheek, somewhere above his upper molars. Probably just some goofy muscle spasm. Pinched nerve. Probably ought to go see a chiropractor, get the neck cracked, the whole back, what the hell. Go home, put a cold gel pack on it for fifteen minutes, take a couple aspirins, forget about it, get the tape recorder, check the batteries, go to work. But don't say anything to Ruth, Christ. Says all you do is complain anymore. Bitch, bitch, bitch. Everybody has things wrong with them, what do you think gettin' old is? Huh? Gettin' old means gettin' things wrong with you, joints, God, Mario, listenin' to you, you'd think you're the first person in the world ever had cartilage break down in his joints. What, you never heard of osteoarthritis? What do you think your mother was complaining about all the time? Didn't you listen?

Shit, just shut up about it, dummy, don't be layin' it off on her, nobody wants to listen to this kinda bullshit all the time. Think up somethin' else to say.

God that feels goofy, what the fuck is that? Can't be heartburn, I didn't eat anything. Is that the fuckin' coffee? Has to be the fuckin' coffee. But what the fuck else am I gonna drink in Dom's? I hate tea. Start askin' Vinnie for tea, he'll be bustin' my balls till next Christmas. Aw fuckit. . . .

When it finally spread to every corner of his mind that Gina Hite was blowing off his generosity with a contemptuous snort, Herb Tanyar could neither move nor breathe for almost ten seconds. He kept trying and failing to understand that she'd actually, physically turned her back on a restored '73 'Tang because all she could see was a used car! This had not been part of his plans. He'd anticipated a wildly different end to this evening, and now he was being forced to improvise, something he was, by his own admission, not particularly good at when women were involved because the one thing he knew he couldn't do was take the car home, much as he wanted to. And God, how he wanted to. This '73 'Tang was exquisite, a jewel, the most beautiful car he'd ever had the good luck to drive. But if he couldn't think of something else and fast, all the mediating skills he thought he possessed with men would not save him from his wife's blistering inquisition.

One of the reasons he'd bought this car for Gina instead of the one he'd promised to buy was the possibility that at some future date he would finesse her out of it, though he'd never gotten very far into the details of that plan. Now that it was painfully clear she didn't want it, he didn't have to plan how to finesse her out of it. That was the only good news here. Everything else was bad. If he didn't come up with the Mustang she wanted, he could say bye-bye to everything about Gina that had made him do the things he'd done to get this 'Tang. But if Missus Herb saw him anywhere near this car, as much as he'd bored her over the years with all his talk about different models of 'Tangs, she'd be on him like white on a blizzard. And as pissed off as she was from his last two flings, one with another 'Tang and the other with another exotic dancer, her next step would be to hire that son of a bitch from Bulldog Security again.

After all the times Tanyar had covered that lazy prick's ass when he was a detective in the Knox PD and Tanyar was chairman of the safety committee. Covered his ass a half dozen times, but did that make him hesitate when Missus Herb came callin'? Fuuuuuck no. Didn't stop him from hounding Herb for two weeks either, which wasn't the worst part. The real kick in Herb's stones came when the bill was delivered to Herb's Freight Liquidation, his furniture store, the windup being that Herb paid for his own surveillance, all because Missus Herb's nitwit sister had moved into Gina's old apartment building!

Tanyar still couldn't believe it — how could that fuckin' broad say no to this car?! How could anybody be that stupid?! Nobody's that stupid! You have to get elected to the state House to get that stupid!

When he couldn't come up with any coherent move because every thought was fogged and fuzzed by images of either Gina with her tongue dancing on his nipples or of Missus Herb dancing on his mind with her three-inch stiletto heels, Herb did what he always did when he needed a break from thinking. He drove. Took the 'Tang out onto Route 22 and drove like a maniac for an hour, pretending he was Burt Reynolds in one of those Smokey and the Bandit movies, though he was smart enough to know he didn't have the reflexes to put the pedal to the floor — not in this car.

What was under the hood in this one was about a hundred horses too many for him and he congratulated himself for having sense enough to recognize as much. Metzger, that son of a bitch, what a genius!

Some guys could do bodies, some guys could do engines, Metzger could do both. And what he'd done with this engine, God, giving this car to that stupid broad — what a waste! Too bad Metzger was such a compulsive jerk, I could do things with that guy. Couldn't stop stealing, couldn't stop gambling. Herb grinned nervously — alone in this wild womb of a barely guided 'Tang — he wasn't sure whether he was describing Metzger or himself.

Aw fuckit, he thought. Enough with the self-analysis, this engine doesn't belong in this car! This engine belongs in my 'Tang, that's where this engine belongs . . . ah shit! Not my 'Tang anymore. Noooo. Missus Herb's now, ain't it — speaking of conniving broads. Took that instead of a divorce, miserable bitch, queen of the ball-busters. . . .

After an hour on the road, thirty minutes east and thirty back, with ten minutes out for a large coffee at a 7-Eleven, Tanyar had pretty much decided that until he could talk sense into Gina the only chance he had to keep this car was to take it back to Jack Metzger, who'd sold it to him, who'd also restored it, after — and this was the largest *after* Herb had ever been involved in — after he'd arranged to have it stolen out of Winkie Pietropoli's Salvage Yard on Neville Island. Tanyar had spotted it there when he was looking for a good used gearbox for his own '75 Mustang, which Missus Herb was now driving to every indoor mall in western Pennsylvania because that was the price she'd extracted for not walking out on him in the middle of the last election.

And now — shit! Herb pounded the steering wheel. Metzger's in Vegas! Bastard took the fifteen and went to Vegas! Where the fuck am I gonna put this car? Aw man. Why'd you give me balls, God, huh? Wanna answer that? Ever since they started sproutin' hair — you know that, God? — the minute they sprouted hair, my troubles started, you understand? Life'd be so much goddamn simpler if I didn't have these things, I'm tellin' you. Do you care? Ha! Why should you care — and don't give me the shit that you do 'cause you don't — aw Christ, listen to me, drivin' ninety miles an hour tellin' God he doesn't care that he gave me balls. . . .

Gina, vagina, Gina, vagina, vagina, Gina, you got me crazy, girl, completely nuts, nobody with his balls under control would do what I've just done, Jesus Christ Almighty, conspiracy to commit felony theft

81

auto, I am out of my fucking mind. . . .

Herb finally made his way back to Knox and drove aimlessly through the streets and alleys until he was hungry, and being hungry naturally made him think of one of his favorite foods, the hot sausage and sweet pepper sandwiches Artie Chianese made in his deli. Herb drove south on Main Street three blocks past City Hall, and through the alley behind Chianese's Deli where Herb knew Chianese had a garage and kept his refrigerator trucks. Used to have three or four of them, but somebody said he'd gotten rid of a couple. Maybe Chianese had room in his garage for the 'Tang. What the hell, couldn't hurt to ask, everything I've done for him, that's the least that fat bastard could do. Get a sausage and bowl of pasta salad while I'm there — if he's still open.

Herb pulled out of the alley and around the front into the bank parking lot across the street from Chianese's Deli just as Charley Babyak was driving his Escort out, and both of them had to jam on their brakes to avoid banging into the other.

"Whoa! Asshole! Watch where the fuck you're goin'," Herb shouted with the windows up.

Charley saw Herb's mouth moving and

didn't have any trouble reading his lips, so he rolled down his window as he backed up and then inched forward alongside the Mustang. "Before you start cussin' me out, Mister Councilman, maybe you oughta settle up for last weekend, huh? Case you forgot, you lost all four, which I know is why you ain't been around, but if you ain't gonna pay me the least you can do is don't be callin' me names, okay?"

"This is a brand-new car!" Herb protested, as though that explained everything.

"Yeah? Well, your losses are growin' older by the minute. And that don't look like no new car to me — course not bein' a car freak like you I wouldn't know."

"Obviously," Herb said, unable to keep from sneering at Babyak's decrepit Escort but quickly shifting attitudes. "Listen, Charley, you know I'm good for it. Never stiffed you yet."

"Knowin' you're good for it don't pay my bills."

"Yeah, alright, okay, I hear you. Listen, uh, the Buddha in there?"

"In where?"

"The deli. Isn't that where you were comin' from?"

Babyak was still woozy from the verbal

beating he'd just taken from his uncle, so it was with a teaspoon of satisfaction that he dumped part of it on this politician's head. "He was there when I left. How about I tell him you're four behind plus the vig?"

"C'mon, Charley, I'm good for it, you know that, no reason for you to be sayin' things like that, c'mon."

"My uncle thought my mother, which was his own sister, was lyin' to him when she told him she had cancer. You think he thinks you're good for it, Mister Councilman, don't call me asshole anymore."

"I thought you were gonna bang into my car, Charley, that's all! That was just a normal reaction, that's all. I just picked this car up, this thing was just restored, man. Don't take it personally, Charley, I didn't know it was you. And let's not make a big deal here, okay? I apologize, I shouldn't have called you names. I was as much at fault as you were, okay?"

"Yeah, sure, takes two to crash. But you still owe for four and I'm tellin' ya right now I ain't bookin' nothin' else till you get square."

"I understand that, Charley. I know where you're comin' from. Tell ya what — tomorrow, okay? I'll catch you tomorrow, how's that?"

Babyak snorted, wound up his window, and drove away. Tanyar parked the Mustang and locked it. He hurried across the street, head down into a wind that had suddenly freshened, looking up just in time to see the cousins Serra disappearing around the corner of the deli.

Tanyar reached the front door just as the light in the back room went out, and he pounded on the frame with the flat of his gloved hand. In a moment, the light came back on and Arturo Chianese's hulking silhouette came shuffling out of the back room, saying, "Closed, go to Mickey D's!"

"It's me, Arthur. Herb Tanyar. Let me in, man, I'm starvin'."

Chianese, still fuming about his nephew, shuffled toward the door, wondering what this asshole wanted. Nobody talked to him like that scrawny shit Babyak just did, sister's kid or no sister's kid. He reached the door finally and said, "Go to Mickey D's, I'm closed."

"Aw c'mon, Arthur, you put everything away already?"

"Oh, it's you, huh? You're kiddin', right?"

"C'mon, Arthur, I haven't had anything to eat since breakfast."

"What, you don't know what closed

means? Means turned off, shut down, put away, that's what closed means. This is new to you?" Chianese knew Tanyar wasn't there just for the food. He wanted something else. Because he always wanted something else. That was why he was so easy.

"C'mon, Arthur, you gotta have some potato salad left, some chipped ham, somethin', Christ."

"You're gonna make it yourself, I ain't makin' it for ya — and you're gonna clean up too."

"Sure, that's fine, I'll clean up."

"You know where everything is," Chianese said, letting Tanyar in and shuffling into the back room, followed eagerly by Tanyar, who liked the idea of making the food himself. He could pile the chipped ham on the good bread Chianese kept for himself. Somehow, Chianese was still able to get the chipped ham that Isaly's became famous for selling before they went out of business. And Tanyer had been hearing about the new goon Chianese had hired, how great his salads were, potato, macaroni, tortellini, seafood; name the salad, this gorilla had the touch, that was the big lunch news around City Hall lately.

Had to be something left that was good, Herb thought as he opened the door to one of the stainless-steel reefers. "Oh man," he said, his eyes widening, "all this stuff from today?"

"Don't insult me," Chianese said, trying to ease into his chair but falling the last few inches into it. "Course it's from today. Maybe you think I serve garbage, but I know you know I don't eat garbage. Or maybe you think I do."

"Course you don't eat it, Arthur, but the wrong people come in, well, you know," Herb said, laughing, thinking he'd made a joke.

There was no response behind him, so Herb backed out of the reefer with his arms full of two bowls, one of tortellini salad, the other of potato salad, and turned around to see that Chianese was not laughing.

"What're you doin' here, Councilman?"

"Makin' myself somethin' to eat, Arthur. You said I could."

"Why you always insultin' me? Every conversation I have with you, you wind up insultin' me, you know that? Why's 'at, you think, huh?"

Herb didn't know what to say. He stammered a couple of times, then finally said, "Hey, it's just me, Arthur, that's all, just the way I am. You deal with people all day, sometimes you lose your, uh, you know, you forget who you're talkin' to, that's all. I know I rub you the wrong way sometimes, but honest to God, Arthur, uh, it's nothin' personal, you know, it's not, uh, it's just the way I am I guess. Sorry, uh, if I offended you just now."

"No you ain't. That's another insult. It's late. I'm tired, I still gotta go to my club, and if you're here for some other reason, quit jaggin' me off and say it."

"Uh, okay. Okay. Sorry I caught you at a bad time —"

"Stop with the fuckin' sorries, okay? Just wastes more time."

Herb stopped dishing tortellini salad into a bowl, cleared his throat, and said, "Uh, listen, Arthur, I got sort of a, you know, a problem I was hopin' maybe you could help me with."

Chianese said nothing, just leaned back farther in his swivel chair and stared, his eyelids drooping so low Herb couldn't see his pupils. Not a good sign, Herb thought.

Fuckit, Herb thought further, just start talking and talk fast. "Uh, see, I got this car, Arthur. I was gonna give it to somebody, you know, as a gift? Only this somebody apparently couldn't get over certain mental roadblocks. So, uh, what I need,

88

uh, I need to store this car somewhere until I can make this person understand that roadblocks aren't progress, if you know what I mean. So, uh, you know where I could keep this car — for a couple days maybe? That's all it would be, no more than that."

Chianese surmised several things immediately. One, the car was hot. Two, the person who didn't want the car was Tanyar's girlfriend, Gina something or other, some whore that worked the booths in one of Leo Buckles's joints. Three, Missus Herb was still bustin' Herbie's balls big-time or he'd be takin' the car home. Four, another favor asked for by another pol was opportunity knockin', and Chianese always answered that knock. The only thing that made him hesitate was he was still stewing over Charley Babyak, which interfered with present thoughts.

After he finally forced Babyak from his mind, Chianese said, "Yeah, no problem. I got room in my garage. We're only gonna be usin' one of the trucks in the mornin'. You come back tomorrow afternoon, we'll figure somethin' else out. Kinda car is it?"

"Seventy-three Mustang."

"Oh yeah?" Chianese's first surmise about the car being hot was right. Twice over. Winkie Pietropoli had called Chianese nearly six months ago about something else and wound up complaining about losing a '73 Mustang he'd picked up in Ohio on commission from a made guy in Philadelphia who had a customer in Mexico. This is even better, Chianese thought. This is real good. For several reasons.

"What it cost ya?"

"Fifteen," Herb said.

"Fifteen for a '73? No shit," Chianese said. "Musta thought it was worth it. Kinda shape's it in?"

"Oh, it's gorgeous, man, wait till you see it. Better than when it left the factory. Engine is for sure."

"No kiddin'. Who did the work? Anybody I know?"

"Nah, I don't think so," Tanyar lied. He knew Chianese knew Jack Metzger. Anybody who'd ever had anything remotely to do with chop shops knew Metzger. "Some guy from the other side of Pittsburgh. Just kind of a hobby with him. He's not lookin' to get rich."

"Not lookin' to get rich, huh?" Chianese sputtered a laugh and sent bubbles of saliva flying. "What, he's the Mother Teresa of old cars? Just finds 'em on the street, takes 'em home, huh?"

"Nah, it's just, you know, the guy has a good job, makes a lotta money, I think he's a pilot, uh, for FedEx maybe or UPS. He doesn't do it for money."

"I heard about guys like 'at. Never actually met one though. Maybe sometime you could bring him around, introduce me. I make sausage sorta like a hobby. Maybe we could have a meetin' of the minds, somethin' like 'at, whattaya think?"

Herb couldn't think of an answer fast enough. He was starting to get uncomfortable, though he couldn't say why exactly. Just had a feeling that Chianese had figured some things out, just by the way he was sort of half-smiling. Tanyar started gulping down the tortellini salad, trying to get out of there before Chianese changed his mind about letting him store the Mustang.

"Whattaya eatin' so fast for, Councilman? Slow down, enjoy it, see if you can pick out all the flavors, that's what I do. Gonna give yourself heartburn. That's the trouble with everybody nowadays, in too fuckin' big a hurry. I didn't say nothin' to upset ya, did I?"

"Huh? No no, not at all," Herb said, stuffing the last forkful of tortellinis in his mouth and wiping his lips with a hanky.

"When you're done cleanin' up, make sure you put everything back in the reefer," Chianese said, standing with a grunt, then shuffling toward the door to the alley. "Just pull the front door shut behind ya. Bring the car in the alley. I gotta check on two guys back 'ere."

"Yeah, all right, Arthur, I'll make sure the door's closed. And thanks. I mean it. Really appreciate the food — and the fact you're gonna let me keep the car here, everything, I mean it, thanks."

"Don't mention it, Councilman. Don't give it another thought."

"Oh, Arthur? One other thing, okay? I'm a little bit rattled, uh, almost forgot."

Chianese stopped opening the back door, turning halfway to look over his shoulder, thinking now what, asshole?

"Hate to ask, but, uh, you think one of your guys could give me a ride home? I mean I park the car here, I'm on foot, and it's, uh, you know, three miles to my place. It's cold out there tonight, you know?"

"It's January, Councilman. And we're here. Gets cold here every January. This is new to you?"

Instead of going home, as he'd told Chianese he'd wanted to do, Tanyar asked the Serras to drop him off at City Hall when he spotted Police Chief Earl Butterbaugh's unmarked Ford Galaxie in his usual parking slot. It was twenty-five to eleven, and Tanyar wanted to know what the chief's car was doing there at that time. As chairman of council's safety committee, Tanyar was Butterbaugh's immediate supervisor, so wanting to know what the chief was up to at any given moment was legitimate, but Tanyar also relished every opportunity to stick it to Butterbaugh, ever since he'd learned that Butterbaugh had written a glowing letter of recommendation for that prick David Beckmaier when he applied for his PI license.

Tanyar believed in his bones that Butterbaugh's letter had clinched the license for Beckmaier, without which Beckmaier would not have been able to hound him for two weeks — and then send him the bill! That Missus Herb could have hired any number of private eyes to bloodhound him was irrelevant. It was Beckmaier she'd hired, and it was Butterbaugh who'd written the glowing letter of recommendation in support of Beckmaier's application.

That Tanyar knew he was making a fool of himself all over town by lusting after Gina Hite didn't enter into his thinking about his wife or Butterbaugh or Beckmaier, which more or less went like this: since Missus Herb was more interested in how she looked than how she cooked or made love or kept house, it was only natural Tanyar would seek other outlets for his urges, which he was the first to admit were barely under control even under the best of circumstances at home.

Thus it was that Tanyar found himself one night in one of Leo Buckles's porn shops ("live girls, all nude all the time"), gawking openmouthed at Gina Hite as she caused her tanned, taut body to writhe rhythmically in gyrations as old as the revolutions of the earth while pretending to make love to herself. In some unspeakably powerful way, she reminded Tanyar of the ideal woman whose face and figure he'd been carrying in his mind since puberty; God only knew where he'd got that female image, he didn't. He just knew he had it, and when he saw Gina, the image of her on the other side of the window melded with the one he'd been fantasizing about, and he was lost. Lost for Gina, but lost also for a reason he didn't discover until a couple of days later when he went to see Leo Buckles to ask how he might meet Gina.

From the first moment he'd seen Gina, who was just putting in another night's work, Tanyar lost every remnant of self-restraint he'd ever claimed to Missus Herb that he had. Gina wasn't like the last nude dancer he'd had a fling with. Or the one before that. Neither of them had looked anything at all like the fantasy he'd been carrying around. Any thought of delaying his gratification with Gina had vanished almost as fast as she had when he'd run out of cash that first night — and Leo Buckles's clerks didn't take plastic.

Tanyar, flushed with lust and self-importance, discovered to his shock something many other people in Knox and the surrounding communities had learned too late after they'd watched one of Leo Buckles's window dancers mime unbridled lust: that in the so-called VIP booth a well-hidden videocam was pointed at the customer's chair, and the moment the customer paid his money to see one of the dancers work, the first move in the dancer's job was to start the videocam. Leo Buckles thus had videotape of every customer who'd been in his VIP booths in every one of his shops during the last six years and seven months. "Every man has an idol," Leo said when revealing his little secret, "and mine is John Edgar Hoover. Now *that* was a man who knew how to get ahold of power. And keep it."

Tanyar could not have agreed more — especially after Leo played the tape of Tanyar making love to himself while Gina pretended to make love to herself. But Leo was gracious. All he wanted was a hundred bucks for Gina's phone number. Also, there were sixty or so parking citations in Knox, and one outstanding warrant for DUI which Tanyar, as chairman of the Knox City Council Safety Committee, might be able to resolve. That was Leo's word: resolve. . . .

Tanyar complimented the Serras on the tortellini salad and thanked them three times for the ride before hurrying into the police station's duty room, thinking about the other bone he had to pick with the chief. He found Butterbaugh nodding off at the radio console. Tanyar banged on the counter, startling Butterbaugh, who came to with a jolt and then broke into a smarmy grin as he always did upon seeing his boss.

"Mister Councilman! Out kinda late, aren't you? Something up?"

"Just passin', Earl, saw your car, thought I'd ask you the same question."

"Nothin' goin' on at all, Herb, not so far. Couple guys got the flu, Polichek's still off with his collarbone, I'm workin' a double, that's all. No big deal. Soon as John gets here, I'm gone, and, anyway, mostly what I've done is snooze my way through it, you want the truth, but, uh, long as you're here, Herb, there is something I'd like to raise with you, if you have a minute."

Herb shrugged, trying to make it seem he didn't have anything else in mind. "Only place I have to go is home, and I'm not the least bit anxious to find out how much she spent today."

"She's punishing you, Herb. I'm probably out of line for saying this, but when a wife leaves the bills out for the husband to see, I mean, she's just makin' him pay twice, that's what she's doin'."

Herb nodded, gave a little whistle, and thought, no thanks to you for greasing that bastard Beckmaier's PI application. "Yeah, some people would say that," Herb said.

"You said it, Herb. In the Legion? Last Saturday night? Said it two or three times — well, you said it more than once anyway."

"Oh yeah, I remember, sure. Hey, what the hell, you drink a little, you feel sorry for yourself a lot, it's an old story. So what do you wanna talk about — oh not about the guns again I hope —"

"As a matter of fact, Herb, I have been talkin' to some people, and I'm hearing better prices — now just a minute, hear me out now, don't just shut me down, I think I'm onto something here —"

"Earl, how many times have I said we can't do this now? So I don't know why you're havin' such a hard time under-standin' it, but the last time you raised this with me, you were quotin' prices, as I recall, almost six hundred apiece — not countin' magazines, ammo, holsters, train-ing — not only for each member of the de-partment but also for Revitski and Leffert, both of whom I'm assuming are still doin' the gunsmithin' — am I correct? They still doin' that?"

"Yes they are, you're right, but that's what I'm trying to tell you, I think we can do way better than six hundred, I've been talking to people, I think we can do it for five hundred apiece —"

"Thought you said that price was solid? Set by the manufacturer, Beretta, that's what you told me. Now you're telling me five hundred? How's that possible? You told me absolutely, no way we could do better than that, never mind that I told you it was off the table —"

"I know what I said, but I'm telling you I think it can be done for five hundred apiece, and I don't think we should pass it up —"

"Earl?"

" this is too good to let slip away —"

"Earl? Earl, whoa, listen to me. Even at a hundred apiece less, you're still talking approximately, what? Nine? Huh? Nine thousand? Not counting magazines, ammo, holsters, training —"

"Nine thousand is way better than ten eight —"

"Earl, we don't have ten eight. We also don't have nine. I told you what we had and that's five, period. First you were talkin' ten eight, now you got it down to nine, and now you think you've made some kind of progress, but the fact remains nine is still four more than we've got. This is simple arithmetic, Earl, it ain't complicated."

"Well, Herb, would you at least consider

it, huh? Will you give it some more thought?"

"Earl, what's wrong with you here? This isn't about me. I'm not stayin' up nights schemin' how I can thwart your plans to rearm your department. I happen to disagree with you about the amount of drug activity around here, but I've always been willing to concede I don't have all the answers about this. If the rest of the safety committee agrees with you, and if council agrees with the committee, I'm not gonna throw up a roadblock just for the sake of throwin' up roadblocks — why would I do that?"

"Well, Herb, since you asked, and, uh, since there's just the two of us here, I'll tell ya what I think. I think you're still real, real pissed off at me 'cause you think I had something to do with, uh, Dave Beckmaier taking the job from your wife to dog you —"

"Oh I don't think that at all, Earl," Tanyar lied.

"Yeah, well, I know you may say you don't, but I think you think because I helped him get his license, you're still sorta holdin' that against me, even though you don't wanna admit it."

"C'mon, Earl," Herb said, putting on his best look of incredulity. "That's under the

100

bridge. You know I don't hold grudges like that. How the hell could you've known when you helped Beckmaier get his license that someday down the road he was gonna wind up takin' a job from my wife to dog me? Nobody could've known that, c'mon."

Butterbaugh canted his head and nodded several times, smiling and working his lips. "I hear ya, Herb."

"What, you don't believe me?"

"Look, Herb, I've put myself in your place, and I mean, what the hell, a guy who used to work for me? Turns into my shadow? Then he has the unmitigated balls to send me the bill? I don't know, Herb, I just don't believe you when you say, you know, you're not holdin' a grudge."

"You're saying you would be holdin' a grudge?"

"Hell yeah. I think anybody would. It's a little far-fetched to work back to me, you know, from him, but still, hell, I'd be real pissed — I mean I remember the times you covered his ass — I may be the only person who was in a position to know just how many times you went to bat for him, so, yeah, I can understand how easy it'd be to, uh, you know, still be pissed at me, but I wish you'd give it up, really, I do."

"For the sake of rearmin' your department, right? Huh?"

"Well now hell, Herb, c'mon, I mean what I'm talkin' about is between us, you know —"

"And doesn't have a thing to do with you and Beckmaier and me, right?"

"Right, yeah —"

"Just two public officials here, right? Havin' an informal meeting, a little preliminary discussion about how you can get your department rearmed to combat the, uh, the growing drug menace —"

"Aw see there how you are? Now why do you have to go and talk like that? Growing drug menace, Jesus Christ —"

"Your words, Earl, not mine," Tanyar said, warming up to the other reason he wanted to see Butterbaugh tonight. "Page one, *Knox Weekly Review*, delivered tomorrow. Anything in there gonna be of interest?"

Butterbaugh looked genuinely surprised, embarrassed even. "How'd you find out about that?"

"What, you think it'd make a difference if I read it tomorrow instead of havin' it read to me yesterday? You really have to ask?"

"I didn't think, well . . . was it the kid? Or Stoudamier?"

"Who do you think, Earl? Christ, don't give me that look! You been playin' the news game as long as I have — what, all of a sudden you don't know how it works? You on some kinda medication, Earl, maybe you oughta tell me about? Maybe you shouldn't be carryin' a weapon or somethin'?"

"That's not funny, Herb —"

"Well what the fuck, Earl? You think you're gonna go public with your bitch about how your guys're undergunned? Puny little six-shooters, huh, .38s? And all these big bad druggies're carryin' Uzis and MAC-10s and fifteen-shot nines? And it's about time your department went out there with the wherewithal to fight back? Jesus, where'd you find all that bullshit? Or are you actually gonna try and tell me you believe that stuff?"

"As a matter of fact I do."

"Aw for Christ's sake, give it a break," Herb said, throwing up his hands. "How many arrests have you made — your department I mean, total, this year, Earl, for drugs? Huh? Six? Seven? How many?"

"Eight."

"Eight, there ya go, eight! And how many of your officers were killed by gunfire, Earl, huh? While making those arrests?"

"You're not gonna succeed in makin' a

joke of this, Herb, it won't work with me —"

"Just tell me how many of your men were killed? Or wounded? Or shot at? Was there one goddamn shot fired during any one of these eight drug arrests, that's what I'm askin' you, Earl, can you tell me shots were fired? I mean, as the person who eventually has to review, by law, every officer-involved shooting in this town, I mean, is there something I missed? Was I sick, or on vacation or somethin'? 'Cause I don't recall one instance since I've been on the safety committee, not in damn near twelve years, I don't recall reading an unusual incident report where those two things happened simultaneously, a drug arrest and the discharge of a firearm — by anybody! Now am I wrong about that, Earl?"

"No, no, no, you're not wrong," Butterbaugh said, stretching his neck and then settling his chin low and avoiding Tanyar's eyes.

"Well, just between us, Earl, okay? You want to discuss police policy, you do it with me first, alright? You don't do it with some goddamn twenty-somethin' kid who doesn't understand how the news game is played, alright? And then insult my intelligence by actin' like you didn't know what

104

you were doin'. I mean if you're gettin' ready to run for office, Earl, you gotta quit. You gotta retire, you can't be chief and run for council, and I know you know that as well as I do."

"Aw c'mon, Herb, you know I'm not runnin' for anything —"

"Then I don't wanna read another goddamn story about how you believe drugs're headin' our way like some goddamn tidal wave and you're the only one with eyes good enough to see it. And the only one with balls big enough to stand up to it, if only you had the right kinda firepower. Say that to a kid reporter, Earl, makes us both look like jagoffs, you know? And I got enough people thinkin' I'm a jagoff right now, I don't need anybody else, okay? In that parade? Can I have your word on this, Earl? The next time you get the urge to discuss police policy, you're gonna call me first? Okay?"

"Sure, hell yes, you got it," Butterbaugh said, nodding and extending his hand, thinking hard if there might be somebody he didn't already know who thought Tanyar was a jagoff. If Butterbaugh was ever going to get his department up to the level of the druggies' firepower, he could always use more help.

After the midweek third watch, comprised entirely of Watch Commander John Leffert and Patrolman Walter Buggs, showed up at five to eleven, and after Butterbaugh supervised the changing of the watch, he reluctantly agreed to drive Tanyar home. For months now, he'd been looking for any opportunity to get Tanyar alone so he could plead his case about rearming his department, but since Tanyar had just trashed the idea because of the interview Butterbaugh gave to the kid from the *Weekly Review*, Butterbaugh didn't want to be alone with Tanyar even for the short time it would take to drive him home. But he couldn't very well refuse, since it was freezing out and snowing.

On the way they exchanged inane pleasantries about the weather and how they could both use a good night's sleep and how everything tended to look better in the morning, but while Butterbaugh was painfully stuck for something else to say, Tanyar was enjoying the inanity because he knew how frustrated the chief was having to talk about everything except what they'd just talked about: buying those 15-shot Be-rettas for the department. Good, Tanyar thought. If he squirms hard enough, maybe the stupid bastard'll think a little harder the next time that prick Beckmaier wants a favor.

When Tanyar said good night outside his house, the chief drove on as though going home himself but waited until he was cer-tain Tanyar had gone inside and then turned around and drove back into town, heading straight for the Knox Athletic Club, the private club owned by Artie Chianese. Butterbaugh was fuming because once again that shit-ass politician Tanyar had failed to grasp the seriousness of the drug wars and the necessity of upgrading his de-partment's firepower.

Butterbaugh knew almost as much about Knox AC as Artie Chianese himself. He'd made it his business to know because his predecessor had schooled him on the im-portance of maintaining good relations with the Sicilians who were made members of La Cosa Nostra. In Knox that meant the Chianese family, starting with Artie's pa-ternal grandfather, Carlo, who in 1909 opened a club called the Palermo Football Club because he knew that men needed a place to drink, play cards, and talk their own language without the interference of the authorities or, God save them all, the interruptions of women. Artie's father, Angelo, continued the club, running it with even less tolerance for outsiders than his father, but changing its name to the Palermo Athletic Club. When Angelo died and Arturo took over, there were so few full-blooded Sicilians left in Knox it was hard for Artie to justify keeping the club open for more than two nights a week.

So, proclaiming that he was a man of the people and to show how much he believed in democracy, Artie changed the name of the club while opening the membership first to all Italian men, and soon after to all men, no matter their ancestry, excepting of course Jews and blacks, who, to Artie's way of thinking, could be called men only because they weren't as hairy as apes. The few Jews in Knox wouldn't have been interested anyway, belonging as they did to synagogues and clubs nearer to Pittsburgh. As for the blacks, Artie scouted around until he found two who were almost as hungry for money as he was, and installed them as front men in their own club, with Artie providing the building, furnishings, and stock. He called it Freeman's Club and Barbecue.

As long as Knox Iron and Steel continued to make steel up to the late 1970s, the two private clubs alone made Artie Chianese a wealthy man, particularly Freeman's because outside of their churches the blacks had no other public place to socialize. But when Knox Iron and Steel moved to Brazil in 1979, both clubs suffered like all the residents of Knox; and Chianese, like so many others, was forced to change jobs, even though his jobs until then had been strictly for appearances. It got so bad in his clubs by the early 1980s that Artie Chianese actually had to go to work every day in his own deli, which he'd been forced to open in 1953 because he couldn't find a woman to cook for him. All three of his wives had deserted him in quick succession because not only was he a bully he was also a slob. Despite his money he not only couldn't find any woman desperate enough to marry him, he couldn't find one desperate enough to cook or clean house for money. Thus he opened the deli after he hired half a dozen or so true WOPs, Sicilians With Out Papers, to prepare food exactly the way he wanted it prepared.

He had to open the deli for another reason: he wouldn't eat the food served in the four other restaurants within walking distance of his house in town. Chianese was too fat to get behind the steering wheel and reach the pedals in every automobile he'd tried to drive, so he walked very slowly wherever he had to go around town until he got the idea to have somebody push him around in a wheelchair, which he'd had custom-made to accept his width. Then all he had to do was find somebody with a small brain, large muscles, and no interest in anything other than eating, drinking, screwing, and evacuating his wastes. Thus had he hired Jimmy Serra.

Earl Butterbaugh had learned most of this from his predecessor and the rest from his own observations. Still, in a perversely snobbish way, he was proud to call himself a member of Knox AC, not only because it allowed him to rub shoulders with a made member of La Cosa Nostra, but also with everybody else in Knox who wanted to make the same claim, with everybody, in other words, who thought they were anybody.

Chianese didn't give a damn who they thought they were, just so they paid their dues on time and brought cash to the bar and to the card and dice tables. Besides, once he'd adulterated the club by letting the first hunky in, all they were to him were so many walking wallets.

After Butterbaugh had parked in the alley behind the club, he sidled through the blowing snow, was admitted by Angie Serra, and found Chianese, slurping a Sambuca and espresso and sprawled in a huge vinyl recliner in the corner between the bar and the door to the dice room.

Butterbaugh waited until he saw that Chianese wasn't talking to anyone in particular, then casually approached him and said, "Hey, Arthur, hi ya doin'?"

Chianese nodded ponderously, glancing up under his fat eyelids at the chief.

"Got a couple minutes, Arthur? I'd like to talk to you."

"About what?"

"Well, it's sorta private, Arthur, if you don't mind."

"What, you want me to stand up? And go back to my office?"

"Well, Arthur," Butterbaugh said, clearing his throat and shrugging apologetically, "it's kinda important."

"Who to? You? Ha ha ha," Chianese laughed an absurdly phony three-note laugh. Then, with the help of Jimmy Serra, he heaved himself out of the recliner and into his wheelchair, which Jimmy pushed across the sixteen-by-sixteen-foot dance floor. Once in his office, he was again helped out of the wheelchair into another recliner on Jimmy's bulging forearms. "Bring me my coffee," Artie said, "and then don't let nobody back here." He looked up at Chief Butterbaugh, who had taken off his service parka and was holding it in front of him, looking for someplace to put it.

Chianese waited, mouth open, breathing heavily. "So?"

"Maybe I should wait until you get your coffee —"

"Don't wait," Artie said, his head dropping nearer to the expanse of his chest, as though he could only hold it upright for so long before the effort became too much.

Looking at Chianese's droopy head, Butterbaugh was reminded of his new grandson who was barely old enough to hold his head up, and if Chianese lost any more of his hair, Butterbaugh thought, very soon he was going to look like the world's largest infant.

"Okay," Butterbaugh said, but knowing he was soon going to be interrupted by the goon carrying the espresso, he tried to make small talk by asking about Chianese's family.

"Funny you should ask," Artie said, his

eyelids narrowing more until they were just puffy slits. "I was just thinkin' about how it was when I took over this place from my father. Fifty-nine I think it was. There was only, like, twenty-one pure-blood Sicilianos left around here. I couldn't make no money on this place. Couldn't keep it open more'n two nights a week. I thought fuck that, I ain't makin' no money with this blood shit, so I opened it up to all the dagos, you know? Any one of 'em wanted in, fuckit, let 'em, long as they could make the dues and they brought cash, the fuck did I care whether they were blood or not. My father was dead, my mother was dead, these fuckin' Sicilianos, stupid fucks, they were marryin' Irish, Polaks, Germans, never mind them snobby fucks from the Piedmont —"

"Here's your coffee, Mister C," Jimmy Serra said, coming in and gently placing a tiny gold-rimmed cup and saucer in the middle of Chianese's upturned palm, which had been resting on the uppermost curve of his belly.

"I didn't give a fuck no more," Chianese continued. "Got so bad when the fuckin' mill closed, I started lettin' hunkies in, that's how bad it got. The hunkies, they were like the niggers in that respect, they didn't have no other place to go. So I made a club for the niggers 'cause I didn't want 'em in here, but I wasn't gonna waste no money on them fuckin' hunkies. Buildin' them a special place when this place was fuckin' dyin'? I mean, would you?"

"Huh? Oh no, no," Butterbaugh said, working hard to feign interest. He'd heard this story before. Many times. It was a story Chianese never tired of telling.

"You ain't drinkin' nothin'," Chianese said, suddenly looking at Butterbaugh's hands holding nothing but his parka. "Hey, Jimmy? Ho, Jimmy? Bring the chief a drink — beer, ain't it?"

"Yeah, that's fine. Rollin' Rock, that's good."

Jimmy Serra had just opened the door a crack when called, listened for the order, then disappeared. He was back in half a minute with a Rolling Rock and a frosty mug which he held through the door without setting foot inside the room.

Butterbaugh still didn't know where to put his parka. He took bottle and glass in one hand and then looked around for a place to put everything, including himself.

Chianese nodded to a folding chair leaning against the wall. It was the only other chair in the office. Butterbaugh had to set parka, bottle, and glass on the floor while he opened the chair and sat on it, draping the parka over the back of the chair, then filling his glass and taking a couple of long swallows while Chianese went back to his story, droning on about the history of his club's admissions policy.

"So who do you think was the first hunky applied for admission? Huh? Walter Babyak, that's who, that Slovak cock-sucker. Fuckin' crane operator in the mill, that's all he was. Then at night he had this band, one of those button box bands, you know, accordeens? Polka band, you know? Played weddings and shit. Thought he was the leader. He was the singer, you know, a regular fuckin' Frankie Yankovic, or vac or whatever. So my stupid sister, Nicolette — you ever meet her?"

"Never did," Butterbaugh said, wondering whether he was ever going to get a chance to talk or whether he was going to have to listen to this stupid club history — again — for the rest of the time he was here.

"She wasn't bad lookin', my sister. I mean you couldn't tell she was stupid just from lookin' at her, but she didn't have the brains God give a cackaroach. So one

115

night she goes to a Polak wedding, Slovak, Polak, whatever, they're all the same those fuckin' hunky weddings, so anyway, this Babyak's there with his band, and they got these black shiny pants, you know, and these white shiny shirts, and a kinda red, sashy thing around their bellies, you know, and he's singin' up there and wiggling his skinny hips around, and my fuckin' goofy sister, she falls for this asshole. Just 'cause he can sing and he got these skinny hips, and he can dance the fuckin' polka, I guess. Yeah. I still can't believe this shit, 'cept I know it's true.

"Next thing I know he wantsa join this club. Ouuu, my sister says, you gotta let him, wait'll you hear him sing, I'm gonna teach him Italian, she says, teach him all the Italian wedding songs, we're gonna sing at all the Italian weddings too, you should let him sing in here, every Friday night, you could get a big crowd in here . . . yeah. Next fuckin' thing I know, she got a belly out to there and mister brother-in-law Babyak, he's singin' and playin' his fuckin' polkas in here every Friday and Saturday night, and I'm payin' this cackaroach about twice what the fuck he's bringin' in, so they can get an apartment with a bedroom for the kid when it comes, yeah. Next thing I know, out pops little Charley Babyak, and twice a week I gotta listen to his old man massacre good Italian songs in that fuckin' Slovak accent.

"They're all dead now anyway. 'Cept Charley. He's the only pain in the ass left. You know what that little cackaroach is doin', huh? You should be real interested in this, Chief, you know? Huh?"

"What's that?" Butterbaugh said, clearing his throat and biting the inside of his lower lip in his struggle to appear to be interested. He tried to think of how many times he'd had to listen to this story, and how many times he'd come to the conclusion that Chianese told it just to irritate people, just to show how much contempt he had for everybody, especially the police. Which naturally made it worse for Butterbaugh because once again he was here to ask a favor, which meant that he'd have to listen to this story every time Chianese wanted to irritate him.

"Fucker's sellin' dope now. Ain't satisfied workin' a phone for me, noooo, no, the little cackaroach gotta go into business for himself. Dealin' with them jagoff biker assholes, them Pagan wannabes, you know?"

Suddenly Butterbaugh didn't have to

117

work to be attentive; he just had to work to catch up. He'd heard the word "dope" but he wasn't sure in what context. And he didn't know how to ask because he didn't want Chianese to know he hadn't been listening.

"Selling dope, Arthur? You sure?"

"That's what I said, ain't it? Pukey little fuck. Shoulda drowned him when he was born. Shoulda tied his scrawny ass in a sack and dropped him in the fuckin' river. Soon as I seen him, I knew he wasn't no fuckin' good. All that slivowitz, slibowitz, whatever that piss is his old man drank, that's what fucked his sperm all up. Told my sister that's what you get for marryin' that fuckin' drunk hunky. She didn't wanna hear nothin', all she cared about, ouu he's so handsome, he sings so gooooood. I don't know who's stupider, niggers or women."

"Uh, where's he selling this dope?"

"What, you're the cops — you don't know?"

"Well see, that's what I wanted to talk to you about, Arthur —"

"What, who's sellin' dope? You wanna talk to me about that, you gotta be kiddin', you needa hire some smarter fuckin' detectives."

"No no, that's not it, Arthur, I mean, I'll be happy to take any information you wanna give me, but the problem I wanted to discuss with you is Herb Tanyar —"

"Who? Fuck you wanna talk about him for, he's another jagoff."

"Yes, see, exactly my point. The man doesn't understand the seriousness of the problem we've got around here, he won't listen."

"Yeah? So?"

"Well, see, the fact is, which you know, I mean the man's chairman of the safety committee. Which of course I don't have to remind you, Arthur, you know that as well as I do. But everything I do, every requisition I submit for equipment, for training, seminars, everything I need to run an efficient department, it has to go through him."

"Yeah? So?"

"Well listen, Arthur, I mean, for cryin' out loud, we're still carrying .38s, you know? Six-shooters. These druggies, my God, they're carrying 9-millimeters. Thirteen-shot mags, fifteen-shots, seventeen-shot mags, machine pistols, MAC-10s, MAC-11s, Uzis, some of these things have thirty-shot magazines, Arthur, hell, my men, they're outgunned, that's all there is to it. We're in a war with people who've got more fire-power in one hand than any three of my men, see what I'm saying?"

"Yeah, so what's your point?"

"My point? Jesus, Arthur, my point is I've been trying to make Tanyar under-stand he's got to make a pitch to the rest of the safety committee, so they can make a recommendation to the rest of council, you know how it works, Arthur, I don't want to insult your intelligence here, but you know, uh, the fact is, uh, Herb respects you, he respects your, uh, your judgment, your ex-perience, your know-how, the way you run things, Arthur, you know what I'm saying."

"And you want what now, exactly?"

"I want you to talk to him."

"Talk?! Shit, he's a jagoff, you can't talk to jagoffs," Chianese said, taking the last swallow of his espresso and Sambuca and shouting for Jimmy Serra to bring him an-other. " 'Nother beer for the chief too."

"Oh thank you, Arthur."

"Whatta thankin' me for, I ain't givin' 'em to ya, I'm just orderin' 'em."

"Oh."

"So you want me to talk to Tanyar and say what now?"

"Well, uh, tell him what you know about this guy you said is sellin' dope — where's he selling it by the way?"

"Told ya, them biker jagoffs. Somethin' wrong with your ears?"

"No no, I heard who, I was just asking where, that's all I meant."

"Fuck you got detectives for?"

"Well is it a big operation? What kinda volume we talkin' here?"

"What operation? I told ya, it's my fuckin' jagoff nephew. Ain't no fuckin' operation. Put him in charge of a two-car funeral, he'd send one of 'em to the wrong cemetery."

"But you did say Pagans, right? They're known to be big on crank, amphetamine —"

"I didn't say Pagans, I said Pagan wannabes. Guys that think 'cause they got a secondhand Harley and a couple tattoos that makes 'em tough. Don't make 'em nothin' but tattooed jagoffs with used bikes."

"Still, it's a continuing criminal enterprise, that's what I'm saying."

"Whatever."

"So will you do it?"

"Will I do what?"

Butterbaugh almost threw up his hands. How could this fat slob be a made member of La Cosa Nostra? God, they must be desperate. Maybe the feds were right, maybe they had broken the mob since they'd put John Gotti away. "Will you talk to Herb Tanyar, that's what I'm asking you."

"And say what again?"

Butterbaugh cleared his throat and bit his lower lip to keep from telling Chianese to clean the Parmesan out of his ears. "Listen, Arthur, you want me to help you, you've got to help me. What I want you to tell Tanyar is —"

"Wait a minute. Who said I wanted you to help me?"

"Well, I mean, your nephew. Why'd you tell me about him sellin' dope if you didn't want me to bust him?"

"Bust him? You? Fuck for — already busted him. Told him he does anything else without askin' me first I'll turn his ass into kolbassi. Put him through my grinder, sell him to the rest of the hunkies. Put enough garlic in him, they won't know the difference."

"Thought you were telling me this so I could bust him," Butterbaugh said glumly. He thought he'd lucked onto exactly the kind of bust he needed to snap Tanyar out of his drug doldrums.

"Bust him? Hey, go ahead, you wanna

bust him, I don't care. Charge him with punkin' kids for all I give a shit. You wanna clear some old B and Es, fuck, charge him with whatever makes you happy."

"Then you'll talk to Tanyar?"

"You got a serious one-track fuckin' mind, you know that, Earl?"

Jimmy Serra knocked and poked his head to see if it was all right to deliver the coffee and beer. Chianese nodded and extended his hand all of an inch above his belly, turning it palm-up to accept the saucer and cup as Serra placed them there carefully. He then scooped up Butterbaugh's empty and replaced it with a full one and hustled out.

"Anyway, Earl, talkin' to Tanyar is like talkin' to that fuckin' wall behind you," Chianese went on between sips of his espresso. "Man got pussy on the brain. Split his head open, a thousand hairy pussies'd fall out. Man thinks with his nuts. Brain's practically brand-new. Only thing it ever been used for is to hold up his hair."

"I thought his wife had pretty much clamped down on him."

"Ha ha ha," Chianese laughed his forced three-note laugh again. "All his old lady clamped down on was his precious Mustang and his plastic. She don't give a shit who he screws — long as it ain't her."

"So who's he screwin'?"

"I'm guessin' nobody right now, 'cause the one he was screwin', she just crossed her legs 'cause she wouldn't take the car he bought her. Both of 'em's stupid fucks anyway, one's stupider than the other."

"Yeah?" Butterbaugh said, trying hard to not appear too anxious to get the gossipy goods on Tanyar. More than one way to rearm a police department. If spectacular drug busts weren't possible, then maybe a little old-fashioned, uh, moral suasion. That was good, he thought. Moral suasion. What did that mean exactly? He wasn't sure. He thought it was the words people used when they wanted to blackmail somebody into doing something without any actual money changing hands while at the same time believing they were on the moral high ground. "So, uh, who was this wouldn't take his car? Anybody I might know?"

"Not 'less you're hangin' out in one of Buckles's joints."

"You mean she's a whore?"

"I don't know if a broad who gets guys to whack off is actually a whore, not that I

124

give a shit. Ha ha ha. Subject come up one night, she said long as nobody's touchin' me I ain't sellin' nothin' but my actin'. Ha ha ha. Least that's what I think she said. Said long as there's glass between them and me, I ain't no different than a picture in *Playboy*. Which I thought was pretty sharp for a hunky whore, 'cause she's a whore whether she thinks she is or not. Leo Buckles never put a broad behind glass in his joint without tryin' 'em out yet. Course what the fuck I know, she could be the first."

"Uh, what's her name again?" Butterbaugh was still pitching.

"Calls herself Gina Hite. Name's Regina Hitalsky. Say this for her, she's built better'n any hunky I ever seen. Better than most of the broads you see in movies. But way too fuckin' arrogant. Her attitude's gonna get her in trouble sooner'n she thinks. Already got Herbie boy pissed off 'cause she wouldn't take his present."

"Present?"

"Yeah. The car," Chianese said, calculating how much he wanted to say and to what effect. "Found this rebuilt Mustang, guess he trieda give it to her, apparently she told him stick it up his ass. He was all worked up over it."

"Uh, when was this?"

"Tonight. Little while ago."

"Oh so that's why he was on foot."

"Yeah. His old lady got his old Mustang, and I got the new one parked in with my trucks. So Herbie owes me another one."

"Well see there, Arthur? That's the perfect opening you need —"

"Since when do I need an opening with him?"

"Well, I mean, I was just saying, you know, if you were looking for a way to get to him about what I want you to talk to him about —"

"Which is what again?"

"Berettas, Arthur. I need firepower. I need eighteen Berettas, and all that shit-ass Tanyar wants to talk about is it's not in the budget, we got so much budgeted for this and so much for that, but nobody talks budgets when you're in a war, Arthur, you know that. You talk budgets when you have time to talk about budgets, you didn't hear anybody talkin' budgets when ol' Schwarzkopf was poundin' ol' Hussein's ass into the desert over there, did ya? Hell no!"

"Gonna start a war with somebody, Earl?"

"What do you mean *start one*, Arthur? I'm *in* one, c'mon! This is what I've been

126

tryin' to tell that goddamn Tanyar for two years now, you think that shit-ass'll listen? All he wants to do is screw, how the hell do you run a police department that way — you can't! You understand me, Arthur, you know what I'm talkin' about, what you said about your nephew here, you know we can't just stand around, let assholes like that take over the streets? But Tanyar doesn't understand, stupid shit."

"How many beers you had?" Chianese said, starting to get annoyed with Butterbaugh's harangue.

"What? How many beers? This is my second one, Arthur — what, you think I'm drunk? Oh, excuse me, Arthur, sorry to've taken up so much of your time with my petty little concerns here —"

"Aw fuck you, Earl, siddown. You're startin' to sound like Jerry Vale. Every fuckin' song, don't matter what he sings they all sound like he's fuckin' whinin'. Every time you come in here anymore, that's all I hear, guns, guns, fuckin' Berettas, Christ Almighty, give it a break, will ya? I mean when was the last time your guys shot it out with anybody, huh? The next time'll be the first —"

"Preparation, Arthur! Preparation, that's the name of the game, that's what it's all about. What do you think brought the Russkies to their knees, huh? Reagan's defense spending, that's what! Showed those goddamn commies no way they could outspend us on defense, hell no! We had a national defense under that man, Arthur, God bless his presidential balls, we had a Defense Department that wasn't about to be nickeled and dimed to death by a buncha skirt-chasin' bean counters like Herb Tanyar! They were men of vision, Arthur, men with balls big as thermonuclear devices, you understand what I'm sayin'. Because that's what it took to get those commie thugs back under their rocks."

Chianese's chins sank lower on his heaving chest. "That's a peachy fuckin' speech, Earl, but what I ast you was, when was the last time your guys shot it out with anybody, it wasn't no trick question."

"And what I'm saying, Arthur, is preparation, that's the key. You get prepared, Arthur, you can't just keep up, can't just stay even, that's not good enough, you gotta get ahead of 'em, Arthur, you got to get ahead and you got to let 'em know you're ahead. What they know right now in this town, Arthur, what they know right here right now is *they're* ahead, Arthur, not me, not my department, them! They know they're ahead of us, every single step of the way. Right now your nephew is dealin' dope because he knows he's got us out-gunned —"

"My nephew? Ha ha ha," Chianese hooted, his huge body rolling with each burst of sound. "My nephew don't know which end of a gun to hold. He saw a gun once, he had to change his pants."

"Don't be shortsighted, Arthur, he's getting his dope from somebody somewhere, and I guarantee you *they* know which end of a MAC-10 to hold, I promise you that."

"Oh yeah? You think, huh? Maybe so," Chianese said, smiling crookedly, thinking that maybe this man who is so eaten up with guns, who can talk of nothing else, maybe he can be useful again for some other reason. And if he wanted to bust Charley Babyak? What the fuck, let him. Means I won't have to get my fingernails dirty with that scrawny prick.

Balzic was shivering when he got inside his house. He hollered, "It's me. I'm just gettin' my tape recorder, then I'm goin' again.

Hello? You here? Ruth? It's me, okay?" He wiped his shoes on the scatter rug inside the front door and shivered again. Why am I so cold, Jesus, what the hell am I shiverin' for?

He could hear himself breathing as he went into the bedroom and went to his closet to get his briefcase and tape recorder. Then he went to his side of the bed, got down on his knees, and felt around for the plug wire to the recharger. He pulled the recharger out, took two batteries out of it and exchanged them with two from his recorder. His breathing was getting louder, and so was the buzzing in his ears. For years now, he'd been living with the sounds of a summer night in his ears. When it got unbearable, he'd learned to mask it with music from his Sony Walkman, and when, for one reason or another, he didn't want to listen to music, he'd mask it with tapes of the surf or the rain forest or a boat sailing, all presents from Ruth to help him get to sleep on those nights when the tinnitus was worse than usual. Mostly, he'd trained himself to ignore it, but lately, along with this damned goofy sensation in his chest and neck, it seemed — though he couldn't be sure because he wasn't cataloging anything — that the tinnitus was getting worse, not like the one had anything to do with the other. But who knew that? Maybe they were related, maybe they weren't. Whatever. Christ it's cold in here — what the hell's the thermostat set at? She turn the thermostat down again?

He lurched to his feet, turned, and was startled by Ruth's presence as much as she was startled by his. Her arms were full of towels, underwear, and socks from the dryer, a white load. She dumped them on the bed and started folding them.

"I didn't hear you come in," she said. "When did you come in?"

"I was yellin', yo, Ruth, hello — you didn't hear me? Well hell, obviously not —"

"I was changin' loads, I didn't hear you —"

"Why's it so cold in here — you turn the thermostat down again?"

"No I didn't turn the — why would I do that? It was seven degrees this morning —"

"Used to turn it down all the time when you were havin' hot flashes —"

"Mario, I haven't had a hot flash in five years — God, I did not turn the thermostat down —"

"Yeah, but you used to. Used to turn it down all the time, Christ, I remember one time you turned it down to sixty —"

"I did not. Turned it down to sixty, what're you talkin' about — why should you be cold anyway, God, look at the clothes you've got on — and you're still cold?"

"Yeah, right — and thermals too, tops and bottoms, and I'm still cold —"

"I've been telling you, you need to see somebody, Mario — oh, please don't throw up your hands and turn away from me — Mario, listen to me, I told you you need to see somebody about that buzzing in your neck and —"

"What buzzing, whatta you talkin' about, I don't have any buzzing in my neck —"

"Mario, you know exactly what I'm talkin' about. Buzzing is your word —"

"I never used that word — buzzing. When, when'd I ever use that word? I never said anything about any buzzing —"

"Are you gonna tell me now that you're not gettin' any sensations in your neck? Huh? In your chest? Like heartburn? Only it's not? You used the word buzzing, one day when you were tryin' to explain it, that's what you said, buzzing —"

"Much as you didn't wanna hear it, I'm surprised you remember any words I used —"

"Mario, don't do this," Ruth said, bending forward from the hips and jabbing the air twice with her hands splayed. "Don't do this, please. Just call Doctor James and ask him about it, it's time for your physical anyway. Way past time. You should've had it done last month, what's wrong with you, why're you puttin' this off, I don't understand, just tell me that much, that's all —"

"I got a job, okay? For Mo. I gotta get to work, I just came home to get my tape recorder, that's all, I don't wanna talk about this now —"

"Mario, how many times have you said it now, there's something wrong here, huh? Look at you, no man wearin' all the clothes you've got on inside this house — where the thermostat's set at seventy where you set it and where you check it every day, sometimes twice — and don't you dare say I changed it, 'cause you know damn well I didn't, don't you dare say I did — I mean nobody should be cold. Look at you, you're shivering! You need to have this checked, you're overdue for your physical, what's the big deal here? It's just a physical, you get one every year, you've been gettin' one every year for the last — I don't know how many years now. I'm gonna call and make you an appointment — and don't argue with me, I'm sick of this. This is nonsense, this — whatever this is —"

"I'm goin' to Troop A," Balzic said, trying to slide toward the front door. "And after that I'm goin' to the mall, and if I still got time after that, I'm goin' to some security outfit, Bulldog somethin', it's out on 79, but I might not get to them today, but I'll call ya, okay? I gotta get goin'."

She dropped the towel she was folding on the bed and hurried after him. "I'm gonna make the appointment, Mario, do you hear me? Will you please stop all this selective deafness? And that's another thing you need to get checked, you're turnin' the TV up so loud, I almost didn't hear the phone last night when Emily called, she said it rang eight times before I answered —"

"Aw you were up off the couch on the second ring — eight rings, what is this, eight rings, what the hell's she smokin'? Listen, I gotta get movin', you wanna make an appointment for me with James, go ahead, fine with me —"

"Well thank you Jesus," Ruth said, raising her hands toward the ceiling, then letting them drop against her thighs. "His chiefness agrees to be examined, hallelujah."

"Aw yeah, that's sweet, 'his chiefness' now. Listen, I'm goin', I'll see ya later. If I get stuck someplace, any one of those places, I'll call. Otherwise, you know, I'll be home, like, say, probably six, six somethin'. You want me to get anything?"

"I don't know. What's on your menu tonight?"

"Whattaya mean what's on my menu — I cooked last night."

"No you didn't. Yesterday you made bread, but last night I cooked, you didn't cook. Today's Wednesday. It's your sched ule, you made it, but I'm stickin' with it. Mondays and Wednesdays it's you —"

"Okay, I know now, okay, I forgot it's Wednesday."

"And forgot to take somethin' outta the freezer too. I don't want pasta again."

"Hey. The rule was, if you're cookin' it's what you wanna cook, you don't get to pick 'less it's your birthday —"

"Yeah, right, but every time you forget to take somethin' outta the freezer the night before it's your turn, what you do, you throw some veggies in a pan, boil some pasta, hoop-de-do, it's pasta prima-vera."

"Hoop-de-do? *Hoop-de-do* now? And what's wrong with that anyway? It's healthy, it's good for you. So?"

"So I'm tired of carrots, broccoli, cauli-flower, same three all the time. They're not even fresh anymore. Used to go get 'em at least, pick 'em, clean 'em, used to cut little designs in the carrots. Now you just open a bag of frozen ones —"

"The frozen ones are better in the winter —"

"The frozen ones are never better —"

"I gotta get goin', okay? If it's my turn, it's my turn, I'll think of somethin'. And it won't be frozen."

"Honest to God you're goin' to see James and don't you dare tell me you're not goin' after I make the appointment, I'm not gonna let you do that —"

"Did I say anything about not goin', huh? I didn't say anything about not goin'. You make the appointment I'll go. I gotta go now, I'll see ya tonight."

"So go, you're goin'."

"Okay, I'm goin'. This is me, goin'. Here I go. Bye."

"So bye," she said, trying to be as flip as he was, but the way she looked at him unnerved him.

He ducked out of the house, down the steps, and into the Chevy, making sure not to look back. He knew what it was, and he wished that it wasn't, but he couldn't deny that he'd seen it. Worse, he'd recognized it. She was afraid. And she was not often afraid — or she was very good at hiding it, he'd never been able to figure that out about her. She'd look solid, she'd be steady, not even the hint of a quaver in her voice, but then after some time would go by, she'd admit it. She'd let it slip one night when they were getting into bed, after they'd been talking about somebody else's trouble, and she'd ask him to hold her. That's when it would come out. That's when she'd talk about when she was scared, and why.

But he'd seen it now for sure. All that guff about making an appointment with James, all that attitude, that tone — those were nothing but fronts. She was scared. And nothing scared him as much as seeing her afraid because in his gut he suspected that what he was seeing was not her fear but a reflection of his own.

Go to work, he thought, starting the Chevy, and be thankful you have something else to think about. So he put his mind to it, put his mind on all the questions he had for Trooper Claude Milliron at the Troop A Barracks.

But these other thoughts kept intruding, kept interrupting. He fought them while he was driving to the barracks, was still fighting them while going up the steps into the barracks, and couldn't understand why he couldn't even avoid them or evade them, but they were there as he felt the burning or the buzzing or whatever the hell it was, and heard his breathing getting louder, felt his pulses starting to hammer, heard the insects swarming. . . .

It was all probably nothing but winter anyway. Winter never had been their favorite season, especially after the girls had grown and gone, but since he'd retired winter had become the white demon, a living, breathing presence that could and would eat them alive if they didn't force themselves to escape by going out into it. Only he'd never wanted to do that; he'd always thought it was safer to play the hibernation game. It was always Ruth who'd had to coax and cajole him out of the house. Because, she kept saying, if you let it keep you inside when neither of you has a job to go to, this white demon starts to eat you alive from the inside out, it gets into your blood and one day you're snapping and snarling at each other like rabid rodents, small and mean and wildly furious and looking for the handiest target. . . .

So, in self-defense, he'd taken to hanging out in the mornings at Muscotti's and in the afternoons at the library. But best of all was to be working because if he hadn't learned anything else from the great god of retirement it was that you can only read for so long, you can only watch TV for so long, you can only sit for so long, you can only lie down for so long, it didn't matter how comfortable you thought you were, you couldn't remain in any one position for very long. The weight of your body pressing on your bones would eventually cause you pain. Every time you stretched, got up, started to walk, your body would cry from lack of movement. Sometimes it would scream. . . .

Life is movement, he'd learned again and again, no matter how many times his weakening brain would forget it: life is movement because when you stop moving, somebody is waiting, not with a scythe, but with a shovel. You can play the harmonica only so long, you can bake only so many loaves of bread, you can cook only so much food at one time, you can take only one breath at a time, you can have only this one moment at a time. . . .

But retirement in winter in Rocksburg is a white demon with a white shovel, and, fool, he's not asking to shovel your drive, he's not here to make pocket money, this white bastard is here for your lives, yours and Ruth's, he wants you both, he's here, wearing that wide, white smirk, waiting for you to tear each other's throats out with your sloth and dullness and lack of imagination about how to escape him, he's waiting with his shovel so he can bury you both in the snow. . . .

"Mister Balzic? Can you hear me? Come on, Mister Balzic, wake up, time to wake up, come on, Mister Balzic, come on."

"What? Who are you? Where the hell . . . where am I?" His voice sounded like he was talking underwater.

"You're in Conemaugh General Hospital, Mister Balzic," came a fuzzy voice out of something white and billowy. "The cardiac intermediate care unit. Do you know where that is, Conemaugh General?"

"Huh? Course . . . how'd I get here? What am I doin' here?"

"I'm not sure," the fuzzy voice said. Balzic squinted and tried to focus. It was white and puffy. Where its head should've been it was white and puffy and that really scared him. It was the white demon . . . it had a shovel in its hand, a wide, shiny shovel . . . it's not a man, it's not male, no, this white thing that wants to eat your blood is female. . . .

"Where's my glasses? Can't see without my glasses — you got my glasses? Huh? What happened with my glasses?"

"They're probably with your clothes, Mister Balzic. Don't worry. I'm sure they're here somewhere. Your wife probably has them."

"My wife? Where's my wife? I wanna see her. She knows who you are, she knows what you're doin'. You could fool me maybe, you can't fool her — goddammit what am I doin' here?"

"Take it easy, Mister Balzic, just relax, you've had a coronary event, that's what you're doing here. A cardiologist will be in shortly to explain everything to you, just take it easy, but whatever you do, don't move your right leg, okay? You hear me? You understand? Just keep your right leg very still just the way it is, okay?"

"A what? Event? What the hell's that? My mouth's all fulla cotton, why's it feel like that?"

"You're just reacting to the drugs. They gave you something to slow you down, something else to dry you out while they were doing the cath. That's normal to feel like your mouth's full of cotton, that's perfectly normal —"

"I'm not perfect . . . I'm not normal . . . normal my ass . . . I don't feel normal . . . never normal . . ."

"Mario? Mario, God, I finally found you — are you alright?"

His left hand was lifted and somebody was eating it. Whoever had lifted it, had put it to her mouth and was eating it. He could feel lips.

"Mario, it's me, can you hear me? It's me — can he hear me? Is that the drugs, the way he looks?"

"Oh I'm sure he's had some morphine, I can't say for sure what else he was given in the cath lab, but judging from his reactions, he's had at least some of that to slow him down. Do you have his glasses, he was asking for his glasses — did anybody tell you where his clothes are?"

"No I don't have his glasses, I just got here —"

"It's the white demon . . . it's a she, always thought it was a he . . . but it ain't . . . eatin' my blood from the inside, I'm tellin' ya, Ruth, run . . . run, you gotta run . . . it'll get ya, it's right there, look out, right beside ya, look out . . . it's eatin' my hand, I can feel it . . . run, Ruth, run . . ."

"White demon?" said the fuzzy, puffy cloud.

"That's a joke," the second fuzzy person said. "That's what we call winter."

"Oh God don't you hate it? Come to work in the dark, go home in the dark —"

"Uh, excuse me, I don't mean to be rude, but would you mind telling me what's goin' on with my husband?"

"It's all right, I understand, somebody'll be in soon, tell you everything you wanna know. I don't know which cardiologist did him, all four of them were up there a little while ago. I did see Doctor Fine, I'm sure he's still here, but I can tell you this much, it isn't bad, believe me, or he wouldn't be here, he'd be in the ICU, he wouldn't bc here —"

"Which one *did* him? Did what?! What did they do — how'd he get here, I don't know anything, I was at the Y, I got home, I turned on the machine, some state police dispatcher is telling me my husband's been taken up here —"

"Hi, how's he doin'? Wake up yet? You his wife?" A third fuzzy voice entered Balzic's wooly consciousness.

"Yes, who are you?"

"I'm Fine —"

"Not how are you — who are you, who, who?"

"I'm Doctor Fine. I'm a cardiologist. You can call me —"

"You're a doctor?"

"Marv —"

"My God we've got children older than you."

"So do my parents. Two of 'em. I don't mean I have two parents — I mean I do, but I meant they have two children older than me. It doesn't bother them, but, uh, you know, they're used to the idea. So how's he doin'? Mister Balzic? Yo, Mister Balzic, time to wake up, we need to have a little talk, wanna show you some pictures, c'mon, Mister Balzic, I didn't give you that much happiness, c'mon, c'mon —"

Soft gobs of goo were dropping rhythmically on Balzic's right hand. He turned away from Ruth and tried to hide his face and said, "They're tryin' to break in through my hand, Ruth . . . they wanna get in that way . . . there's two of 'em now, run, Ruth, run . . ."

"You're his wife?"

"Yes I am. What's wrong, what happened? You really a cardiologist?"

"Well, if I'm not, my mother's gonna be really disappointed, not to mention my father, 'cause I had him convinced those checks were for tuition and books, so, uh, yes, ma'am, to answer your question, I am. Board-certified and all. Listen, I don't know why he's, uh — he have any strange reactions to drugs that you can think of? Shouldn't be this woozy, I didn't give him enough to make him this woozy this long, so, uh, if you can recall any adverse reactions —"

"Well he can't take antihistamines, if that's what you mean. He takes a half of one of those? You know? Over-the-counter? Half of one of those he's gotta lie down. Takes a whole one, he's out. For hours."

"Oh, so he's one of those then."

"One of those what?"

"Very sensitive to uh, never mind. Uh, listen, I'm gonna tell you, okay? Because I have to check on other people, so, uh, are you all right to remember what I'm gonna say? I don't mean to patronize you —"

"So you're not worried about him, is that what you're telling me?"

"Worried? Not about him, nah. He's got a couple blocked arteries that's all, nothing that can't be fixed, and his heart's strong, there's been very minimal damage from this one that I can see —"

"This one what, I'm not following you —"

"They're followin' you, Ruth, they're right behind you . . ."

"Well, here, look at these pictures. See this? I know it's not very clear, but if you look under the tip of my pen right here? You see where it looks sorta like a bird's beak? See where it's all pinched there? That's as close to a hundred percent blockage as you're gonna get, and I think — I don't know this with absolute certainty — but what I think is, that's what did the number on him today, that's what caused him to pass out —"

"He passed out?"

"That's what I was told. I didn't talk to whoever brought him in, but that's what the ER people told me. He was out, pulse, pressure, breathing, they were all up. But then they got him stabilized, and they shipped him up to us, and we did a diagnostic cath on him, and, uh, these pictures are now part of your family album. Now, this other one? See here, this one in front here? You see that?"

"Yes, I think. That broken line there?"

"Yeah, that one. That's old. My guess is that's been like that for a long time, I can't say how long. He ever have a heart attack?"

"Not that I know of. Did he have one now?"

"Wellllll, yeah, you could call it that if you wanted to —"

"Do you always talk like this?"

"Huh? Like how? I don't know what you mean."

"You talk — I'm sorry I have to say this, but you talk like some drippy kid —"

"Oh, oh, yeah, I see what you mean. Well, look, Missus Balzic, if I talk to you in all the jargon, I'm only gonna have to break it down anyway. Which winds up taking twice as long, so I just, you know, start out breakin' it down. If that bothers you, yes, I could tell you that he had a myocardial infarction, minimal damage, maybe five percent, I'm estimating now, I do not intend for you to understand that, with the information that I have at this moment, that I can quantify the extent of damage to muscle tissue, so I'm estimating five percent damage to the tissue of the left ventricle — is that what you wanna hear?"

"No."

"Okay. Good. So here's the thing. This one in front? As I said, I think that's been closed for a long time. And the reason I say that is because you see all these squiggly

147

little lines coming out from, uh, on either side here — you see those?"

"Yes."

"Well, that's what we call collateral circulation. In other words, that's the body making its own blood vessels if one of 'em's blocked. And that's the reason I can say this blockage is old because there are so many of these little ones comin' out of the sides, you see what I'm saying? Your husband exercise a lot?"

"You mean lift weights and stuff like that? God no, he doesn't exercise, he just walks, that's all. We walk three or four times a week — except when it's cold we walk in the mall. When it's nice we just walk around town. But he walks all over the place, always has since he had a walking beat, but he never calls it exercise — unless we're walking in the mall. He hates that, he just does it for me. 'Cause I can't take the cold very well anymore."

"He been complaining about anything lately? Shortness of breath, chest pain, heartburn, anything like that?"

"Yes, he has. He said it was like heartburn only it wasn't. He tried to explain it to me a couple of times, I told him to stop complaining, everybody has aches and pains. When you get to be our age, just be

148

thankful you don't have some of these things other people have —"

"So what did he say? If you can remember."

"Well, one day, he said it was like heartburn only it wasn't inside his esophagus, it was like on the outside of it. And it went up into his neck, and one day it was up in his cheek. His left cheek."

"Up into his cheek, huh?"

"Yes, but he never said it was pain."

"Well, see, people describe it all kinds of ways, but that's classic angina. Then they come in here, we take the pictures, it's obvious what they were feelin'. How long's he been talking about this?"

"I don't know, six weeks maybe? At least, yes. I kept telling him to stop complaining and get his physical, it was way past time. Just today, before he left the house I told him I was gonna make an appointment, I didn't care what he said, I was tired of listening to him complain — oh Jesus. All the times I told him to stop complaining, it was all in his mind, oh God. Told him he didn't have enough to do. You sit around, God, you don't do anything, you can practically hear your joints locking up . . ."

"He have his cholesterol checked recently? Was he on medication? Who's your doctor by the way — you have a family doctor?"

"Yes. Doctor James. He had very high cholesterol once, it was way up there, I don't remember exactly the numbers."

"Once? What, was it a fluky test or what?"

"No no, I mean it was high for a while . . ."

"You're hesitating, why're you hesitating?"

"I don't know if he'd want me to tell you this."

"Uh-ha. Uhhhh, let me guess. He started having, uh, problems with his, uh, equipment, right? His male plumbing?"

"I think, you know, you should be talking to him about this."

"Well, I really don't have time to wait for his head to clear. Listen, uh, Missus Balzic, does this sound right? He was having problems, he started taking some form of testosterone? Right? And it sent his cholesterol through the roof, right?"

"You could guess that?"

"Well you didn't say how old he is, but from the looks of him, he's about the same age as my father, so it isn't exactly the mystery of the universe. My father has the same problem — had. The thing is, some men just can't take artificial testosterone, I don't care what form it comes in, but Metandren, does that sound right?"

"Yes, but I'm not sure, it was a while ago —"

"That was probably it. Came in a pill, right?"

"Yes, he took pills —"

"Yeah, same thing with my father. See, that was terrible for cholesterol, those pills. They were the worst. Almost doubled my father's cholesterol, yeah, went from like two twenty to like three sixty in, God I don't know, two months. This was what, about ten, twelve years ago?"

"Yes, around there."

"Oh yeah, I remember my father was really upset. I mean, for a while there he thought he was Ponce de León, then he has to quit, start takin' niacin heavy-duty —"

"Yes, Mario too."

"Yeah. My father wanted to sue the drug company, his doctor, he wanted to sue the world — but hey, that was the treatment of choice then. For some guys it was great, but for others, whoa, terrible. I mean, I'm guessin' about your husband, but, boy, it really, really upset my father, physically, emotionally. Anyway, back to your husband here. Here's what I think — I'll be back tonight to explain this to him when he comes back from happy valley, but, uh, this one? This old one, the artery in front here I showed you? I think we open that one, it's probably gonna close again real soon, like, uh, maybe three months. But this other one now? I think we open that, I think it'll stay open. But you see where it is? Right on that bend there?"

"Yes."

"Well, I'm thinking the way to do that is a procedure we call the Roto-Rooter."

"The what? Like a plumber?"

"Yeah. I mean that's what we call it, but that's not exactly what we do. I mean, sort of, same principle. What we do is, we feed a high-speed drill into the artery same way we fed the camera and the dye in so we could take these pictures. We go through the leg there, where that bag of sand is laying — there on his groin?"

"I didn't know that's what that was."

"That's what it is. That's to make sure the artery doesn't open. This drill has a carbide tip on it, 'cause that plaque's real hard, and we just drill it out, you know, while we're looking at it on a TV monitor."

"Is it dangerous? What're the risks?"

"The risks? Well, I'm not allowed to

lie to you, so yeah, there are risks. Heart attack, stroke, death, they've all happened —"

"Oh my God —"

"No no, no, wait, listen. I mean, if you're gonna have a heart attack or a stroke or your heart's gonna stop, couldn't happen in a better place. I mean, not that any of those is a day at the beach, I don't want to sound like a jerk here, but if you're gonna have any one of those things happen? There's no better place to have it happen, you know? You're on the table, I'm standing right there, heart surgeons are in the building, cardiac response team's right around the corner, hey, one of these happens at home, you gotta get here. It happens here, I mean, nobody has to get the surgeon off the golf course, follow me? I don't schedule these unless he's in the building, is what I'm saying."

"Oh God — wait, you're not asking me to authorize this, my God I'm not gonna make that kind of decision for him — without talking to him!"

"No no, no, I'm not asking you to authorize anything. I'm just trying to explain it, that's all. And I'll explain it to him — or you can. I'll be back later, I'm bein' paged, I have to go. The important thing for him

153

to know, and for you too, both of you. This can be fixed. I can fix this. That's what he needs to hear, believe me. We can fix this. This is no big deal. Gotta go. Bye."

When Balzic's head started to clear, the first thing he wanted was water, the second was his glasses, and the third was an explanation of what that damned thing was on his groin.

"Your glasses are there beside the phone," a nurse said. "I'll bring you fresh water in a minute, your wife must've drunk it. And that thing on your groin's a sandbag."

"Where're my glasses?" Balzic started to twist around to get them.

"Ah ah ah, don't move your leg!"

"How'm I gonna get my glasses — how'm I gonna get anything off there — it's behind me, I gotta move my leg."

"I'll get them for you if you can't reach them, but you have to keep that leg still, Mister Balzic, you understand? That artery opens up, you'll have that bag on you twice as long, believe me."

"Aw gimme a break, just tell me what's goin' on, okay? What's this thing for? Man, it's heavy —"

"It weighs twenty pounds and it's to make sure your artery stays closed."

"Stays closed? How'd it get open?"

"You had a diagnostic cath. That's how they go in."

"A what?"

"A diagnostic cardiac catheterization. He opened your artery. Probably Doctor Fine. But you only have to keep it on for about another hour — here's your glasses. Would you like me to clean them? They're all smeared up —"

"Cardiac what? Yeah yeah, clean 'em, please. Catheter what?"

"Catheterization. He made a small incision in that artery, he fed a lead in, and he injected dye into all the arteries in your heart while other people were taking a video of your X rays." She cleaned his glasses and handed them over.

Well at least the world looked a little less smeary. Otherwise, Balzic didn't know what to say. He had no memory of anything like this nurse was describing. "What was I, unconscious or somethin'?"

"Well if you can't remember it, apparently you were. You were given morphine, so, I don't know, maybe you were having too much anxiety, maybe you wouldn't keep still, I don't know how you were reactin' to being there. Doctor Fine'll be in, probably — well, he should've been down by now. He'll tell you everything you wanna know."

"You said my wife was here? She drank my water?"

"Yes."

"Where's she now? She out in the hall or what?"

A state police trooper took a couple of steps into the room and knocked on the door while leaning forward from the hips and looking quizzically at Balzic. "Ah good, you're awake. How ya feelin'?" He was young, in his late twenties, large, ruddy-faced, with reddish-blond hair cut short.

"Fine, I guess — hell no I'm not fine. I don't know what I'm doin' here. Who're you?"

"Milliron. Trooper, Claude. You came up the barracks to see me? Don't remember, do you?"

"Last thing I remember is goin' up some steps. Next thing I know, my head's fulla fuzz, my mouth's fulla cotton, I don't have a clue."

"Well, I got word somebody wanted to talk to me about the B and E in the gunshop? In the mall? Ring any bells?"

"Oh yeah . . . well. Sort of."

"So, uh, I came out, you were standin' there, I asked you if you were the man interested in the gunshop, you said you were, you started to introduce yourself, we shook hands, and then you just sorta went all pasty white, just started saggin'. I still had hold of your hand, but you started goin' down, I grabbed your coat, kept your head from hittin' the floor. Tried to get a pulse in your neck, couldn't feel a thing, then it started up, man, it'd beat five in a row real fast, then it'd skip one, then five or six more, then skip another one. It kept on like that while I was askin' the dispatcher whether it'd be quicker to call an ambulance or to get you here myself, and he said, you know, go ahead and take him. Once the ER people had you, you know, I just went on about my business. Had some time, thought I'd see how you were doin'."

"Real confused, right now. Fuzz's startin' to clear a little bit, but I don't know what's goin' on — I sagged and started droppin'?"

"Just like all the air went out of you," Milliron said, pointing toward the floor. "Whooosh."

"They're sayin' I had some sort of, uh, cardiac event, whatever that is. I never came to in the car? On the way up here?"

"Well your eyes were open, every time I looked back at you in the mirror, but you weren't sayin' anything, and it didn't look like you were focusin' on anything. Tried talkin' to you, but you didn't respond. After they got you on a gurney, I went through your wallet, that's when I found your FOP card. Called the barracks, dispatcher said he'd call your wife, then's when I called, uh, Detective Carlucci? Worked a case with him not too long ago."

"Uh-huh."

"He said you used to be his chief. He was real upset. Kinda thought he might be up here. Anyway, that's where it stood — till now. So how ya feelin' now?"

"Well aside from feelin' real confused, I'm not in any kind of pain. This bag's uncomfortable as hell, but what's hurtin' is my back, it's startin' to cramp up, but other'n that, you know, I feel okay."

"Well, you look a lot better than the last time I saw you. Uh, don't know if you're up to this, but what'd you wanna see me about?"

"Huh? Oh. Damn. Have to think — oh. I

158

know. I'm workin' a claim for the insurance agent that, uh, you know, insured that gunshop."

"Uh-huh. Well, you wanna talk about it? If you're up to it."

"What, you mean now?"

"Yeah, if it's okay, I mean, I have time now, what do you need?"

A nurse came in, excused herself to get around Milliron, and took Balzic's blood pressure, pulse, and temperature. As soon as she removed the thermometer Balzic asked, "You happen to know where my wife is? Or if you don't know that, you know where my clothes are?"

"Probably in one of those closets right there," she said, nodding over her shoulder toward closets on the opposite wall. "Your wife went to get something to eat. Said she hadn't eaten anything all day and all you wanted to do was sleep, so she's probably in the cafeteria."

"Ah. Okay, thanks. Uh, Trooper, you mind takin' a look, see if my clothes are in there? If they are, see if there's a tape recorder in my parka, top left pocket."

Milliron opened both closets, found clothes in the second, most of them folded into two white plastic bags with blue lettering that said PATIENT'S BELONGINGS.

Milliron pulled a sage-green parka out of one. "This yours?"

"See if there's a tape recorder in it — lucky if it's still there."

"Still here," Milliron said, handing it over. "You're sure you're okay with this now, huh?"

"Might as well, I mean, what the hell, wife's not here, doctor's not here, nurses won't tell you anything, hell, askin' them, it's like everything about me's classified or somethin', gotta file a goddamn freedom of information petition. So, uh, what the hell, pull up a chair, let's do it."

Balzic tested his recorder, then laid it on the bed between them, and said, "Interview with Trooper Milliron, Conemaugh Hospital, uh, got a watch? What time is it — Christ, what day is it?"

"Yessir. The twentieth. Five P.M., Wednesday."

"Uh, okay Wednesday, February twenty — least I remember what month it is, uh, no one else present. Subject, insurance investigation for Bertelli-Jacks IIA, etc., fill in the blanks, concerning B and E of gunshop in Rocksburg Mall — what's the name of that place anyway?"

"Freedom Firearms Inc."

"Uh-huh. Principal owner Soloman

Abraham Bemiss —"

"Jacob."

"Huh?"

"Middle name's Jacob. Soloman Jacob Bemiss, not Abraham."

"Oh. Okay. He's the principal owner?"

"He's the only name on the papers of incorporation."

"Well for sure he's the only name on the policy — no, I'm presumin' that because now that I think about it, I didn't even ask. I just took that for granted. Anyway. Run it down for me, if you would please."

"Well, I'll have to do it without notes, because I didn't know this was gonna happen, so bear with me. My notebook's in my briefcase. Still wanna continue? I can go get it —"

"Nah nah, that's okay. You forget somethin' we'll be talkin' again. Just go on your recall."

"Okay. Got the call approximately zero nine thirty-five hours Monday, February eleven. I responded on my way to another interview. Freedom Firearms is on the first floor, northern side of the western section of the mall, which is, I'm sure you know, laid out in the form of a cross. I believe the number of the gunshop is two oh one. Subject Bemiss was waiting for me, along with the manager of the mall, uh, last name Holmesburg, and his personal assistant, last name Evans, and, uh, an employee of Bulldog Security, William Rayford. They were awaiting the arrival of not only myself but, uh, oh what the hell's his name, Beckmore, David Beckmeyer, uh, I still have not talked to him. Anyway, he's the managing partner in Bulldog Security. Real tough man to find."

"How'd you come up on the place? Front door, through the mall? Or'd you go around the back?"

"Around the back. That's where they told me to meet 'em."

"So is it actually a back door — they have entrance doors back there, don't they? Yeah, sure they do. I know that."

"Right, right, but not that shop. That shop is actually — well all the shops on that side of the crossbar, that wing, all of them have back doors. The entrance to that wing is at the end of the wing — I mean you can also obviously get to those shops from the main corridors of the mall, on the inside, but they were waitin' for me at the back door, outside."

"What kind of door was it?"

"Metal. Nothing special. Same kind as all the other shops."

"What kinda locks?"

"Just the one dead bolt."

"No chains, no bolts? Just one dead bolt? You're shittin' me — excuse me, uh, Mo's personal assistant. Gotta watch my mouth, I don't know who's gonna be typin' this stuff. You're kiddin' me, just one dead bolt?"

"I know, I know," Milliron said, chuckling, shaking his head. "But that was it."

"And how many security people?"

"Two inside, one on each floor while the mall's open, one after it closes. Another one in a Jeep station wagon twenty-four seven."

"How long's it take to make their circuits?"

"They said their clocks are set for a thirty-minute foot circuit, but they don't start keyin' the clocks till all the foot traffic's out."

"When's that on Sunday?"

"Seventeen hundred. Twenty-one hundred the rest of the week, except for the Christmas holidays, and, uh, whenever they're holdin' their sales, the big stores, you know."

"So now the foot guys, they each have a thirty-minute circuit? No, wait, that's not what you said. They don't punch clocks till everybody's out, right?"

"Right. And then the shift changes, new guy comes on, and he's solo, makin' a circuit every thirty minutes, both floors."

"Where are the clocks?"

"The ends of each wing."

"Alarms?"

"All hooked into Bulldog Security."

"Every store? Both doors?"

"Every one. Front and back. Windows too, where applicable."

"And no alarm."

"They say not."

"They show it to you?"

"Yep. Not a mark on it."

"How about the back door?"

"Oh lotsa jimmy marks."

"But no noise in the home office, right?"

"Not a decibel."

Balzic started laughing. "You got a full plate, is that it? Or what, you stretched thin, or you just gonna sit around and wait for somebody like me to do your work for ya?"

Milliron was soon laughing harder than Balzic. "Well, as a matter of fact, we are stretched pretty thin right now, and, uh, yes, I do have a pretty full plate, and, uh, oh hell, why not? You wanna clear this case for me, I can watch, no skin off my ego."

They were laughing, nodding, looking away, clearing their throats, then glancing at each other and then rumbling into more laughter.

After a while, Balzic, trying hard to suppress more laughter, broke wind, which caused them both to burst out laughing all over again.

"C'mon now, Trooper, get serious here. This is a crime we're talkin' now. This is a felony — oh God . . . this felony here, this is obviously the work of, uh, criminal masterminds at work here. B and E, theft of property, receiving stolen property." Balzic couldn't go on, he was laughing too hard once again.

Milliron wiped his eyes finally and said, "You gotta love 'em, I mean, anybody can make you laugh like this, oh boy. That thing still turned on? Is that voice activated? Listen, you gotta remember to erase all this laughin', or we're gonna sound, uh, very unprofessional." He pulled some tissues out of the box on the table beside Balzic's bed, wiped his eyes, and blew his nose.

"Okay," Balzic said, clearing his throat hard. "Serious now. This guy in the Jeep, uh . . . oh God I'm gonna start laughin' again. No. No. Enough's enough." He cleared his throat again. "Alright, here we go. The security in the Jeep? The one that was waitin' at the back door? He's not who was on the previous night, obviously — correct?"

"No, uh-uh. This guy, I mean, he actually looked embarrassed."

"Shit, somebody ought to — scratch that. Okay, so when's their shift change, the Jeep guys?"

"They're twelve on, twelve off. For three days, then they're off four, workin' for somebody else if they're workin', but they only get thirty-six hours a week from Bulldog."

"So that guy came on when?"

"Previous midnight. Till noon, then his replacement came on."

"And he didn't see a thing."

"Well, you can't, I mean, he couldn't see the jimmy marks from where he was ridin' in the Jeep. I couldn't see 'em when I parked. You have to get, you know, within six, eight feet before you see 'em," Milliron said.

"So what's out there, uh, I mean I know there's a Denny's in the front lot, I mean close to the highway —"

"Yeah, a Denny's, and a Ground Round, and a Long John Silver's."

"They close when — that Denny's is open all night, isn't it?"

"Yeah. Sure is. Long John's, I think they close around ten, I'm not sure. The Ground Round, their bar's open till midnight, one through the week, two on Fridays and Saturdays, I'm not sure about Sundays."

"You didn't check any of them, see when Jeep-man was takin' his breaks? Or what he was takin'?"

"Like I said, we're stretched pretty thin, and I've —"

"I know, I know, you got a pretty full plate, come on now, Trooper, serious up, don't get me started again."

"I'm tryin', I am. Alright. Here we go. Serious now. No sir, to answer your question, I did not confirm the whereabouts of the driver of the mobile unit from Bulldog Security between the hours of seventeen hundred Sunday and midnight. Look, all jokin' around aside, I do have a couple more important things hangin' right now. I got a little girl missin' since Saturday out in Westfield Township, and I got a real bad spouse abuse. I don't think the woman's gonna live. That's been hangin' since the same time this burglary went down. So I really have not worked this case at all, just the initial response."

"I'm not your boss, Trooper, you don't have to defend your time to me. I had the same plate you had, I'd have 'em in the same order. So, uh, let's get back to the place. The claim's for all new furnishings, carpet, et cetera, so what'd it look like?"

"A mess. Lots and lots of excrement, human and animal, mostly horse."

"Everywhere?"

"Everywhere. Every lock, every drawer in the file cabinets, the computer, every opening you could think of. Smelled just like a horse barn. Somebody took a lot of time doin' it, considering how much time they had to take carryin' all that ammo out."

"Thirty thousand rounds I was told."

"That's what the man said," Milliron said, shaking his head and smiling. "Six hundred boxes, fifty rounds each, forty boxes to the case. One guy, that's fifteen trips to his vehicle — unless he had a dolly." Milliron succeeded in suppressing his urge to laugh. "Yes sir. Efficiency, strength, dedication. Carry all that crap in, carry all that ammo out — that was a dedicated man — or men. Somebody that dedicated oughta be workin' for us."

"You photographed all this?"

"I did. Thirty-six exposures. Be happy to share those with you, if you want, but I'm sure my boss'll want you to pay for the copies."

"Uh-huh. Uh, where was the, uh, the human crap?"

"In the swivel chair behind the desk. Right on the cushion."

"So, okay, that's personal, or it's supposed to make us think it is. Uh, aside from the Berettas, these other guns? The Rugers?"

"Yeah. The two Mags, .357 and .44, both stainless."

"Where'd those come from? Were they in showcases?"

"I'm not sure. One side of the room was showcases of pistols, revolvers, air guns, cleaning kits, reloading kits, et cetera, and the other side was, uh, knives, axes, hatchets, tomahawks, saws, shovels, canteens, camping gear, compasses, things like that. All the glass was broken, horse crap scattered over most of it, but, according to the owner, none of that's missing — from the showcases I mean. Just these Rugers — I mean in addition to all those Berettas — the two Rugers, the .357 had a short barrel, two and three-quarter inches I believe, and the .44 had an eight-inch barrel."

"Coupla trophies you think?"

"Yeah, probably."

"So how many showcases?"

"Uh, I believe six, three on each side of the store."

"Glass broken in every one?"

"Every one. Top and front."

Balzic shook his head and started to laugh again but suppressed in time.

"Yeah, I know," Milliron said. "Even worse, there's no blinds in the front windows. So the foot guy, he's not only deaf, he's blind."

"Or is that supposed to confuse us as well?"

"I honestly haven't given it much thought. But one problem, for you as well as for us, is, uh, all his records are ruined. Paper, computer disks, they're all smeared with horse crap, you can't read anything. And I don't have the time now to call his suppliers, I just do not. But obviously that's gonna have to be done, if we want the serial numbers. But, in addition, the man, Bemiss, he was not very forthcoming about who his suppliers were."

"So you figure, what? A contract boost for the Berettas? Two guys? With crap for vengeance, or another red herring, right?"

"Yeah, that pretty much is what I'm thinkin'."

"So then, uh, what? Check this, uh, Bulldog Security employees, right? Have you done that?"

"No, I haven't even had time to get to their office. But I did ask the woman who answered their phone if they'd fired anybody in the last couple of months. And yes they have. And no, I have not interviewed him. His name is uh, Cozzolino, Cozzolini, Cozzolitti. Lives in Rocksburg, in the Terrace, Delano Drive, but I can't recall the number — or his exact name. It's in my notes. He's who I was gonna start with — whenever I got around to it."

"You happen to ask if they'd been burgled themselves? Had a uniform stolen maybe?"

"I asked. I think she said — wait, I'm not sure. She didn't know or wouldn't say, I don't wanna say which without my notes — I really have been thinkin' about this little girl that's missing. And this woman . . . God, I've never seen anybody beaten as bad as she is. They've sorta taken over my mind, if you know what I mean."

"Yeah. I do. Well, that oughta do it, Trooper. If I think of anything else, I'll give you a call, if that's alright. Appreciate your help. Especially, uh, you know, drivin' me up here."

"Don't mention it. Carlucci, uh, when I talked to him, man, he talks about you with a whole lotta respect. Awe might be a better word. So, uh, anything I can do, be my pleasure."

An extremely broad-shouldered, curly-haired young man wearing surgical clothes hurried into the room, giving the door a knock as he came. "Mister Balzic? Ouu. Police stuff. I can come back —"

"Just leavin'," Milliron said, standing and sliding the chair against the wall opposite Balzic's bed, and leaving with a wave.

"You in trouble? Or you a cop?" the young man said.

"Used to be a cop," Balzic said. "I don't know how much trouble I'm in. You a doctor?"

"Yes. And still making my mother extremely proud. Uh, Mister Balzic, I'm Doctor Fine," he said, extending his very large hand. "We need to talk."

"Yessir, indeed we do," Balzic said, giving the young man very little of his own hand and hoping the doctor wasn't a crusher. He wasn't, though he looked strong enough to lift the whole bed, with Balzic in it.

"Well, to put it the way my Uncle Shelly puts it, you've been dancin' the blood mud polka, and now it's time to pay the band."

"Your uncle a comedian, huh?"

"No, actually he's pretty much a grump, but that one thing he said one time, I don't know, I guess I try to use it for an ice-breaker. Hope you don't mind, but, uh, you look like you mind."

"No, I don't mind — unless it really applies to me, then, of course, I'm gonna mind like hell."

"Well, actually it does apply to you. Uh, I see your wife's not around. I left some pictures with her earlier. It would make it easier to explain, well, here, let me just draw it for you and you can maybe get some idea of what we're looking at here."

"Did somebody say something about pictures?" Ruth said, peeking around the corner.

"Oh good, you're here. Good, good, c'mon." Balzic shrugged up on his elbows and lifted himself toward her.

"Don't move that leg, Mister Balzic —"

"Why not? God I'm in agony here. I don't get to move it pretty soon, I'm gonna have to have an operation on my back. It's killin' me."

"Just listen to him, Mar, okay? Don't

argue with him —"

"Yeah yeah, okay, alright. So, uh, help me out here, tell me why I can't move it."

"It's very simple, Mister Balzic. I made an incision in that artery. It's the second largest artery in your body, after your aorta, and it'll close itself given sufficient pressure, but that pressure has to be constant, and moving around makes it less constant, in which case, if it opens, you're gonna have to lie there at least as long again as you've already been there. That prospect appeal to you?"

"No."

"Just lie back," Ruth said. "I'll hug you, you listen to the, uh, the young man."

"I know, I know," Doctor Fine said, "you've got children older than me, how could I possibly be old enough to be a licensed, board-certified, uh, to use the correct technical term here, heart guy."

"Yeah? So how could you?"

"Well I could, believe me, 'cause I passed all the tests. You have those pictures, Missus Balzic?"

"Yes, here," she said, getting them out of her purse and handing them over.

Fine took them, came around to Balzic's right, turned on the light above the bed, and held up a couple of five-by-seven photos of a grayish-whitish blur with dark lines squiggling around the mass occupying the center of the photos. "That's your heart, Mister Balzic. And I cannot emphasize too much that it is a strong, healthy heart. But what is not healthy are these two lines, right here. Right under the tip of my pen — you can see them, right? You do know what I'm pointing to, right?"

"Yeah," Balzic said, profoundly involved in trying to make sense of what he was being directed to.

"Those are arteries. They supply blood to the heart. One of them closes, gets clogged with the blood mud, the blood sludge, the coronary grease, the capillary goo, the atherosclerotic plaque, whatever you want to call it, the moment it closes, you have what you apparently had earlier today, which for want of a better phrase, we call a coronary event. Some people, that happens, they don't feel a thing. Other people, you for instance, you passed out apparently. Fortunately, you got here in time, the people in the ER, they gave you something to dissolve enough of this goo so that blood flow was restored very soon, then they, uh, sent you up to me to find out what's causing the blockage. And here we have the photographic proof that two of your arteries are fulla blood mud. With me so far?"

"Yeah. I guess."

"Well stay with me, it gets better. This one, in front here? As I told your wife earlier, I think that one's been closed a long time. You see all these little squigglies coming out from the sides? Huh?"

"Yes."

"Those little squigglies — and that's the correct technical term by the way — if this one hadn't been closed for a long time, they wouldn't be there. See, blood wants to flow. It'll make paths for itself, it'll find a way to get to where it wants to go, if you give it half a chance, so now, either you've been exercising a lot or else —"

"Shit I don't exercise —"

"You do too, Mar, you walk —"

"Hell, that ain't exercise —"

"Oh but it is, Mister Balzic. Best exercise there is, if you can do it. Not everybody can do it, some people, you know, bad feet, bad knees, bad hips, bad back, whatever, hey, if you're lucky enough to be able to walk, believe me, you're exercising. Don't stop — well, you're gonna have to stop for a couple of days here, 'cause I wanna do something — with your permission of course."

"What? Whatta you wanna do?" Balzic said, instantly suspicious, instantly apprehensive, instantly frightened.

"I explained it to your wife. See this other one here? See where it's pinched there? Right on that bend? Looks like a bird's beak?"

"Yeah, I see that."

"Well, where it is, where it's closed, on that bend, only way I can open that is with a drill."

"A drill? You're shittin' me. You wanna drill in my heart?"

"No, not in your heart, uh-uh — in your artery here, right where the tip of my pen is. But yeah, drill. It's a small drill. Tiny. Really. It's not a Black and Decker, I won't be kneelin' on your chest and drivin' a hole through your sternum, no, I'll go in the same way I went in today, through your groin, up through your aorta, into this artery —"

"With a drill?"

"Yeah. Same principle as a dentist's drill. You'll be awake the whole time, you can watch it — if you want to, not everybody wants to. But I'll be lookin' at the same picture you're lookin' at. That's how I do it. I'm lookin' at the monitor, movin' the drill around, just grindin' that plaque away."

"If it's mud, or goo, or whatever, whattaya need a drill for?"

"Well those are just nicknames. The plaque is actually sometimes very hard. Sometimes it isn't. Sometimes we can just push it back with a balloon, but not on this bend. I have to drill that. Balloon's not gonna work on a bend like this."

"I have to have it done?"

"Well, if you're feelin' adventuresome, you could take your chances I suppose. I don't recommend it, but you could."

"I could do nothin', is that what you're sayin'?"

"Yes, that's what I'm sayin'."

"And I could have the same thing happen tomorrow?"

"Yes. While you were driving. Or walking up stairs. In which case, obviously there would be other consequences."

"You tryin' to scare me? I mean more than I am already?"

"No no, no, I'm not trying to scare you, I'm just telling you some of the probabilities."

"Does he have time to get another opinion?" Ruth said.

"Oh sure. Of course."

"From somebody who isn't one of your partners?"

"He can go anywhere he wants, Allegheny General, Pitt, St. Francis, Shadyside, wherever. I'll give you the film we took today, you can carry it with you, give it to whoever you want, get it reevaluated, I think you're gonna hear the same thing no matter who you talk to, but please, feel free. You're entitled. And I encourage you."

"But that means I have to get outta here, go there, sweat it out, maybe have them do the same thing —"

"Oh no, they won't — you mean do another cath?"

"Yeah."

"No, they'll just look at the pictures, that's all, they won't do another cath, nah, nobody'd do that   unless his girlfriend wouldn't settle for the Mercedes, she has to have the Porsche."

"Oh you're funny as hell, you are."

"Well, it was either comedy or cardiology. Tough call there when I heard how much Seinfeld was makin' per episode, but . . ." Doctor Fine tried his best to look cute.

"Yeah yeah, okay, so what's the, uh, what's the bad news?"

"Well, I can't lie, as I told your wife earlier, I'm not allowed. Heart attack, stroke, death, they're all possibilities. Not very probable, but if you're gonna have any of them happen, there's no better place to be than right on that table. I mean, the place is just crawlin' with, uh, you'll be surrounded by, as we like to say, health-care-delivery-system professionals. And if you want music, we do three-part harmony on 'Your Cheatin' Heart.' Remember? That old Hank Williams song?"

"I know it," Balzic said.

"You used to play it," Ruth said. "I haven't heard you play it for a while, but you used to."

"Play it? On what?"

"He plays the harmonica."

"Oh don't tell him that, he doesn't need to hear that —"

"He's shy."

"Oh yeah? Bring it in. We'll work up a routine, little patter, little music, hey, who knows, next year this time we could be on *Letterman* — oops, that's my pager. I'll be back. Think it over."

"Think what over?"

"Whether you want it done. Might as well, you're here. Take me forty-five minutes, an hour tops. Bad news, it's not goin' away. Good news, it can be fixed."

"Oh Jesus," Balzic groaned, "all those things you said . . . heart attack . . . stroke . . . death . . . you didn't say anything about . . . holy shit . . . Jeeezzzus . . ."

"Still feeling the pain, Mister Balzic?"

"Like there's an elephant . . . oh shit . . ."

"Tell me, Mister Balzic. What?"

"Steppin' . . . on my chest . . . this is hurtin', I mean really startin' to hurt . . . holy shit . . ."

"Morphine."

That was the only word Balzic heard before the crushing pressure eased, the elephant lifted its foot. "God . . . mouth is . . . mouth so dry. Can I have some . . . so dry . . . water? Please?"

"Go 'head, give him a wipe."

Somebody was wiping his mouth with a cold wet cloth, squeezing drops of icy water on his lips. "Jesus, whatever you want . . . thank you . . . you want somebody killed . . . I'll do it . . . thank you . . ."

"Here we go again, Mister Balzic, ready?"

"Oh shit . . . no . . . yeah . . . like last time? . . . oh Christ . . ."

A high-pitched whir, a female voice counting in numbers that didn't make sense, no sequence to them, the elephant stepping down, harder, the elephant trumpeting, Balzic's chest collapsing, arms swelling, hands swelling, fingers swelling, thumbs swelling, every one puffing up, expanding, stretching, balloons at the ends of his arms, expanding, stretching, Jesus, Mary, and Joseph, they're gonna explode, my fucking fingers are gonna explode . . . holeeee fuck . . . oh shit . . .

"Oh man, this is really startin' . . . to hurt again, this is really — hey, I'm not kiddin' around here . . . oh fuck . . ."

"Morphine."

Whirring stops, voice reciting numbers stops, hallucinatory balloons at the ends of his arms lose their air, thumbs recede, fingers recede, hands recede, nothing's going to explode, the elephant steps off, steps back, stops trumpeting, Balzic exhales, his head sags to the right, his mouth so dry, he's never been this dry, he's in a desert, a white-beige-blue-gray desert, voices everywhere, calm, controlled, calling numbers back and forth, back and forth, no water, no pressure, no pain, never been this tired in his life and still awake. . . .

"You didn't . . . say pain, Doctor . . .

prick . . . bastard . . . you said death . . .
you said heart attack . . . you said stroke
. . . you didn't say pain, you prick you . . ."

"We topped out on the morphine yet?"

"Yes."

"Next time dopamine. Okay, Mister
Balzic. Just a little bit more. Almost got it.
Real close now. One more time I think's
gonna do it, okay? You ready?"

"Wait wait, water . . . please, water."

"Give him another wipe."

More drops of cold water on the cloth
patted and squeezed slowly, wonderfully,
deliciously, across his lips. He tries to swallow it, bite it, suck it, it keeps moving away,
then back, then gone.

"I love you . . . I'll kill for you . . . I'll
bake bread for you . . . I'll come to your
house, I'll cook . . . good cook . . . the
whole meal, bread, wine . . . whatever you
want . . ."

"Oh, how nice, aren't you sweet? But
I know your kind, promise me everything today, won't remember a thing tomorrow."

"Here we go again, Mister Balzic, everybody ready? You ready, Mister Balzic?"

"No . . . fuck no . . . oh shit . . ."

Whirring, counting, stepping, trumpeting, crushing, swelling, expanding, explod-

ing . . . hooooo-leeee fuuuuuuck . . .

"That's got it, Mister Balzic. Look at that! Damn river there, white-water rapids, look at that sucker flow. Can you see that, Mister Balzic? Turn your head to the left. Look up at the monitor. Remember where that pinch was? Huh? Remember that thing that looked like a bird's beak? Look? Can you see it? Course you can't, 'cause it's gone, that's why you can't see it, not there anymore. Regular white-water river there, man, look at that, that's great. Wow, pretty damn wonderful if I have to say so myself — how you feelin', Mister Balzic? That elephant back in the jungle yet?"

Balzic was too tired to talk. He kept trying to see what Doctor Fine was talking about, on the monitor. "Glasses," he croaked. "Need my glasses . . . can I have some water? Please? I'll kill your mother-in-law for water . . ."

"Just a couple more minutes here, Mister Balzic. Don't move anything but your head. Let me get this outta here, get a couple stitches in here . . . get him a drink, go 'head. Did great, Mister Balzic, you did just great."

"What'd I do . . . just laid here . . . tried to get away . . . from that fuckin' elephant . . . man . . . oh God, thank you . . . water . . ."

"Don't lift your head, this straw bends, I'll move it for you."

"What's your name?"

"Renee."

"Renee . . . anything you want . . . really . . . name it . . . if I can do it, I'll do it . . . why am I so thirsty, so dry?"

"Oh we have to dry you out, Mister Balzic, can't have all that liquid sloshin' around inside you, makes it too tough to see what he has to see."

Balzic closed his eyes, blew out a breath, felt the straw in his mouth. He drank and drank until he heard bubbling. The last thing he heard in the cath lab was, "Remember, Mister Balzic, don't move your right leg, no matter what you do, keep it still, okay?"

"Okay, okay," he said, but he was already half asleep. By the time he was wheeled back into his room in the cardiac intermediate care unit, he was hallucinating that itty-bitty guys in satin bowling shirts and women with stiff hair were dancing the "She's Too Fat" polka up and down his arteries, and the band was four elephants, the kind with big ears, and they were playing drums, upright bass, accordion, and clarinet, and the drums were made out of wheels of Parmesan cheese, and the clarinet was made out of pepperoni and the upright bass was made of a huge wedge of fontina cheese and the accordion was made of lasagna noodles that expanded and contracted over meatballs made of greasy beef and pork sausage and eighteen percent butterfat ricotta, and Balzic was in a tuxedo that was so tight every button was popping from the strain against his weight and he was telling everybody in a loud pompous voice like some TV sportscaster how wonderful the band was and how lovely the women were and how handsome the men and wasn't the polka the greatest dance ever invented to make people happy, that was the whole reason it existed, the blood mud polka was what you danced to on your way to the funeral home, and at your wake the elephants played and sang, "She's too fat, she's too fat, she's too fat for me . . ."

"Mario? Mario, what're you saying? Too what? What do you want? More water? Nurse, would you get us more water, please, he's drinkin' it like crazy here."

"They all do when they first come back. Sure, hon, I'll get it, just keep remindin' him, okay? Even if you think he can't hear you, don't move that leg, okay?"

"Elephants . . . every time they quit playin', you know, they have to sit someplace . . . they need a break too . . . everybody needs a break . . . they sit on my leg . . . all four of 'em . . . they play their pepperonis, they play their fontina, their lasagna, makes 'em tired, can't keep playin' all night . . . gotta take a break, you know . . . so, hey, let 'em sit on my leg . . . it's okay . . . I don't care . . . she's too fat, she's too fat, she's too fat for me . . ."

"Boy they must've given him a lotta drugs up there."

"Well, some of them, hon — here's your water, okay? — some of them, they have a real bad time. Not everybody, they don't know why, some people don't feel a thing. Some people, I guess he's one of those, they hurt a lot. Oh but they give 'em morphine, they don't let 'em suffer — but I wanna warn you, hon, when he comes around? He's gonna have an attitude for a while."

"What kind of attitude?"

"It's from the morphine. They get real surly, real paranoid."

"Oh God, he's paranoid enough as it is . . ."

"Don't take it personal, hon, it'll be gone in a coupla hours."

Doctor Fine was holding the most recent photograph and Ruth was holding the one taken yesterday, and Fine was pointing with his felt-tipped pen. "See that," Fine said, "see where it was all pinched yesterday? Look at this. Wide open, see that? It's wide open."

"Yeah, looks great. Can you see that, Mar?"

"Whatta ya lookin' at me for? I can see it, you don't have to look at me."

"I'm just askin' if you can see it, that's all, if there's no glare from the lights, that's all."

"Well just look at the pictures, don't look at me, you don't have to look at me, I'll tell you if I can't see it or not. What I wanna know from you, Doc, is why didn't you tell me about the pain? Huh? You coulda said somethin', coulda warned me, you know? That woulda been nice, be able to get myself a little prepared for that, you know?"

"Well, see, Mister Balzic, not everybody has the pain and if you're not gonna have it, it's not a good idea to put the suggestion in somebody's mind. Maybe the suggestion'll cause 'em to have something they wouldn't've had otherwise, you see what I'm saying?"

"Hey, I'm me, I'm not everybody. Shoulda told me, coulda prepared myself a little, you know? Got my mind right?"

"Mar, it's over, look at the results you got, it's wide open, here, look at the pictures —"

"I've seen the pictures. Show the fuckin' elephant, maybe he'll like 'em. Elephant was stompin' on my chest, man, thought my goddamn fingers were gonna explode. You shoulda told me."

Doctor Fine smiled, patted Balzic's leg, and said, "You're gonna be fine, Mister Balzic. Twenty more minutes you can move this leg, get up in an hour or so, go to the bathroom, have something to eat. It's wide open now, I'll be surprised if all those things you were feeling in your neck, you know, if they come back."

"When can he leave?"

"Couple hours. Just gonna keep him long enough to make sure the artery stays closed, that's all. You'll be sleepin' in your own bed tonight, Mister Balzic."

"Yeah, yeah. Shoulda told me."

Fine smiled hugely, genuinely, chuckled

even, but warmly, without the slightest suggestion of condescension. "Next time, Mister Balzic — if there is a next time? I'll tell you about the elephant. Promise."

"Wait wait, what do I do? I mean, don't you wanna see me again?"

"Oh when you leave, somebody'll give you instructions, before you sign out, sure, about what you can do, can't do, should do, shouldn't do, when to see me. See you in about three months."

"But otherwise, what?"

"Otherwise, take it easy for a couple days, that's all, then, hey, resume your normal life. Do what you feel like doing, you get tired, take a break, that's all."

"Just like that?"

"Just like that. Gotta go. Bein' paged. Nice to meet you Mister Balzic, Missus Balzic."

"Yeah yeah, sure."

"Oh Mario, stop that, he's sweet. He's a kid. He's not as old as Marie — she called by the way. Maybe if you feel like it you can call her when we get home. Emily too."

"Emily called?"

"Of course. Only you would think they wouldn't call. They wanted to know if they should come. I told them I didn't think it was necessary, nobody was giving you last rites — although if you don't change your attitude pretty soon, somebody may have to. They told me you were gonna have an attitude, but boy, I hope you lose it soon."

"Ah, maybe, you know, soon as I get this goddamn bag off my leg. Jesus, my back's killin' me. How long have I been down here now?"

"Well, it's four now, they brought you back around five after eleven. They said you'd have it on four to five hours, you heard him yourself say twenty minutes or so."

"He shoulda told me   "

"Oh Mario, quit it."

"No I'm serious, he shoulda told me. Man, at least now I know what a heart attack feels like. Talk about a crushing sensation in the chest, man, they're not kiddin'. Thought my fingers were gonna explode. You know how you push one part of a balloon, all the rest of it swells up? Man, that's the way my hands and fingers felt like, like this goddamn elephant was stompin' on my chest, pushin' all the air outta my lungs into my arms and hands. And my fingers were all swellin' up, man, thought one time there, they were just gonna go boom! And I was gonna be scattered all over the walls . . . God, that hurt."

"Well it's over now and you're fine —"

"Hey I'll tell ya when I'm fine, okay?"

"Okay, okay, Jesus, Mar, you don't have to snap at me like that —"

"Who's snappin'? I'm not snappin', what're you talkin' about? Ain't twenty minutes up yet? When they gonna take this goddamn bag off, Jesus Christ . . ."

Balzic, on hold with Bulldog Security's personal assistant to CEO David Beckmaier, grumbled aloud as Ruth went by and shut the gas off under water he'd put on for green tea. He'd read a magazine article that green tea was good for the heart. "I woulda got that," he said.

"After you stopped taking your pulse?"

"Why's it bother you that I'm takin' my pulse? I don't get that."

"The cardiologist said you were fine, Mar. You have the pictures to prove it. You never used to take your pulse — not that I saw anyway — and now every time I look at you, you have your finger on your wrist or your neck — why're you doing that? What do you think you're gonna find?"

"I'm just checkin', okay? That's all I'm

doin', checkin' — hello? Missus White-head? Sorry, Miss. Sorry. Yes, I'm still holding — aw crap, not again. This woman's put me on hold three times now, which I wouldn't care about except they have to play this goddamn music. Why do they have to play this music, can you tell me that? Bad enough we gotta listen to this drippy music everywhere we go, now you can't make a phone call, you either get one of these goddamn menus, if you want this, press one, if you want that, press two, and then no matter what you want — which is to talk to some human being — you gotta listen to whatever stupid music they think is gonna make you forget what you called about, that's what this whole music thing is. Elevator music, department store music, telephone music, everywhere you go, you're gettin' some kinda lullaby, they want everybody to go to sleep, so you won't notice everything that's wrong . . . Jeeeeesus, pick up the fucking phone, lady, come on, come on, got-damn . . . yes! Still holding — aw shit . . ."

"Mario, I don't think gettin' all upset, you know? I don't think that's good for you, not anything I've read —"

"Who's upset?"

"Who's upset? Well obviously not you,

excuse me. Oh God, I'm goin' to the Y, there's a yoga class starting, you want me to sign you up? Yoga for relaxation, I'm gonna sign up, I think it might be good for you. Remember that tape Emily sent you? That yoga relaxation tape? You played it a couple times, you got real enthusiastic, and then, I don't know, what? You just forgot about it?"

"Emily sent me a tape? About what, yoga? Oh I remember that, yeah, what happened to that? I thought I lost it — hello, Miss Whitehead, yes, I'm who's been holding."

"Mister Beckmaier is in a meeting right now, is there something maybe I can help you with?"

"Yes, I told you before, I'd be happy to talk to you, I don't have to talk to him just now."

"I'm going, Mar. See you later."

"Huh? Oh yeah. Yeah, sign me up, sure."

"Excuse me? Sign you up? For what?"

"Nothing, no, I was talkin' to my wife. Sorry."

"Oh. Well, alright, what can I do for you? Who did you say you were again?"

"Balzic. Mario Balzic. I'm calling for Attorney Valcanas. He's interested in the security arrangements you had, contracts and so forth, with Freedom Firearms? In the Rocksburg Mall? They were burgled recently — you familiar with any of this?"

"Yes I am, but I don't know how we can help you, we're cooperating with the police and we're conducting our own investigation —"

"Oh I'm sure you are, yes. Uh, I just have a couple questions, that's all, I won't take up much of your time, I promise. Uh, you had an employee named Cozzolino? Ronald Cozzolino? Can you tell me when and why he was fired?"

"Oh I think you should be talking to Mister Beckmaier —"

"No no no, don't put me on hold again, please? Please, Miss Whitehead? Just tell me first, he did work there, correct? Cozzolino? Will you confirm that he was employed there?"

"I think he was, yes, but I still think you should be talking to Mister Beckmaier."

"You think he was? Could you confirm that, please? Could you check your records? You do have access to employee records, right? I mean you are Mister Beckmaier's personal assistant, right? And as such you would have access to all employee records, correct? I mean, if you wouldn't, who would, right?"

"Yes, of course I have access to those records, but they're confidential —"

"Uh, Miss Whitehead, please. I was chief of police in Rocksburg for twenty-some years, okay? And I know that the state police are gettin' ready to subpoena your records, so it's only a matter of time until they become public information, alright?" He was lying. He didn't know any such thing. "So why don't you save us both a lotta time and just confirm some things for me, okay? Such as when Mister Cozzolino was terminated and why, alright?"

"Just a moment," she said. And then he was on hold again, listening to violins playing the Beatles' "Yellow Submarine."

"Oh for chrissake . . ."

Thirty seconds went by. Forty-five. Balzic watched the second hand on the clock above the refrigerator. A minute. A minute fifteen.

"Mister Balzac? Are you there?"

"Yes. Balzic. Not zac, zic. And I'm still here, yes."

"Yes, well, you're correct, Mister Cozzolino did work for us, yes."

"And?"

"And he was, uh, terminated December fifteenth."

"That's this past December, right?"

"Yes."

"When was he hired?"

"Uh, he was hired, let me see here, December first, 1995."

"Uh-ha. Does it say on his records there, anyplace that you can see, that at the time of his hiring he was on probation?"

"Umm, no. No it does not."

"Who does your backgrounding for you? You do that in-house? Or you, uh, outsource that? Isn't that the word now? Outsource?"

"I beg your pardon?"

"Never mind. The fact is — and you can check this the same way I did, Miss Whitehead — you or anybody in your agency there. Mister Cozzolino was on probation for receiving stolen property, which had been kicked down from burglary, that's how come he was only doin' a year's pro instead of one to three which he shoulda been doin'. Would you like to tell me now why he was terminated? Or would you like me to start talkin' to the people in the other stores in the mall about how you background your employees? How you violate state law on hiring people with criminal records to work as private police?"

Click. Another two minutes of stringed

instruments, these playing a melody so incongruously syrupy, Balzic was instantly fascinated. What the hell is that, he thought, I know that song. God, that's awful, what geek thought violins should play that? Oh God what the hell is that — oh Jeeesus, that's "I Can't Get No Satisfaction!" Oh God, Jagger and Richards would need a hundred Valiums. Well at least here it fits.

"Hello? This is David Beckmaier. How may I help you, Mister, uh, Ballick is it?"

"No. Balzic."

"Oh Balzic! Yeah, my girl here, she said, Ballick, I said who the hell is Ballick. Yeah, sure, chief of Rocksburg PD. I remember you, yeah, we met a couple times."

"We did? I don't remember."

"Oh sure, this was a while ago, but yeah, we met, you just had a little lapse of memory, that's all."

"Whatever you say, I really don't recall, but, uh, listen, what I was trying to determine, sir, with your assistant's help, is the reason for Ronald Cozzolino's termination? I know when he was hired, I know when he was fired, what I'm tryin' to find out is why, that's all. And also whether you lost any uniforms to theft recently, employee pilferage maybe?"

"This is in reference to what now?"

"The burglary at the Rocksburg Mall? Freedom Firearms? Owned by Soloman Jacob Bemiss, who has filed a claim with —"

"Oh yes — see, Chief, we're doing our own investigation on that."

"Oh I'm sure you are, but see, I'm doin' one for the insurance agent and his attorney — and I'm not the chief anymore."

"Well yes, okay, but until we complete our investigation, and we're cooperating fully with the police on this —"

"Which police?"

"Uh, until we complete our own work, we're not at liberty to release any information which might jeopardize in any substantive way our own efforts in this regard —"

"Which police? The state police you talkin' about?"

"Sorry, Chief, I'd like to help you out, but, you understand, I can't release any information at this time, I suggest you call —"

"You can't?! Excuse me, Mister Beckmaier, there's no reason for you to not cooperate with me, I don't understand that at all —"

"Uh-huh. Well, as I was saying, call the state police is my suggestion. I'm sure they'll be able to help you, but I'm directly involved with this investigation personally and it's our policy here, I mean, I do not feel at all comfortable releasing any information at this time. Not without a subpoena. But thank you for calling Bulldog Security. Good-bye." Click.

" 'Thank you for calling Bulldog Security good-bye'?" Balzic hung up and laughed out loud, he couldn't help it. "Oh God," he snorted. They get better and better, these guys. What department did that chooch work for? I know I know that name. Beckmaier. Bet he was one of those pricks had a phenomenal clearance record. Hundred percent clearance, two percent prosecutions. Now he's in the see-cure-i-tee business, oh yeah. See-cur-ing his own present and his own future, that's all this jaboney's see-cur-ing. See the opportunity to fleece the suckers, hang 'em up like so many hams, cure them with your own smoke, yowser. Time to try Cozzolino again.

Six rings on the Cozzolino number. Seven. Eight. Nine. "Hello?"

"Hello, Missus Cozzolino? It's me again. Mario Balzic."

"Who? I can't hear you."

"I called before, remember? Mario

200

Balzic? Called a little while ago, you said Ronnie was out. Is he back yet?"

"No. No, he's not back yet. He's at the store. He's gettin' me some stuff. Milk an'at. He shoulda been back already, I don't know what's wrong, probably talkin' to somebody, he's always talkin' to people, he's real friendly, my Ronnie."

"Missus Cozzolino, let me talk to Ronnie, c'mon, put him on, I know he's there. C'mon, this is about a job, you know? He's not workin', right? He could use a job, couldn't he? You wouldn't mind that, would ya, huh, Ronnie went to work?"

"I remember you now, you used to be a cop. You ain't callin' about no job, you ain't foolin' me."

"Oh but that's exactly what I'm callin' about. Yes ma'am, it's true I used to be a cop, but I'm not anymore, no ma'am. I'm callin' about Ronnie's job with Bulldog Security, I'm doin' a little background on this, absolutely, I would not lie to you about this."

"You arrested Ronnie once I think. Yes you did, I remember now, you arrested him once, in high school."

"Not me, ma'am. You're thinkin' of somebody else, I never arrested Ronnie —

in connection with what, ma'am? Refresh my memory here. What did he do?"

"Youns guys, you and that other one, I remember youns now. Youns said he busted into the principal's office, busted all those typewriters or addin' machines, whatever they were, I forget."

"Oh, yeah, that's right, I remember," Balzic said. And he did. It was coming back to him now. He thought Cozzolino's name was familiar, but he'd forgotten the specifics.

"So how old's Ronnie now? What is he, like what, twenty-three?"

"He's gonna be twenty-five next birth-day. Or twenty-six, I forget. He knows how old he is. Ask him, why don'tcha?"

"I will — if you'd let me talk to him. Put him on, okay?"

"I told you, he ain't here —"

"Aw gimme the phone, Jesus Christ — hello! Whatta you botherin' us for, huh? You got nothin' better to do, you motherfucker —"

"Ronnie! Watch your mouth I told you, what's wrong with you, honest to God, you talk like some nigger —"

"Aw go sit down! Who is this? Why you hasslin' me?"

"I just wanna ask you about your job,

Ronnie, that's all."

"About my what? Hey, I got your job swingin' right here — who is this?"

"Mario Balzic, Ronnie. Remember me? Used to be chief of Rocksburg PD?"

"Oh yeah, I remember you, you motherfucker — hey, you're not a cop anymore, you can't hassle me like this — hassle my mother, hassle me, how stupid you think I am, I know somethin' about the law —"

"Oh I know you do, Ronnie —"

"Yeah I do, okay?"

"Hey, Ronnie, shut up a second and listen, okay?"

"Okay what? What? What okay?"

"Bulldog Security, Ronnie, huh? Ring a bell? What'd you get fired for? You got fired December fifteenth last year, right before Christmas, what'd you do so bad they fired you right before Christmas, man, huh? That was very prickish if I have to say so myself, fire a guy right before the holidays? Man, that was cold."

"I didn't do nothin'."

"What're you tellin' me, Ronnie, you got fired for no reason, or you got fired 'cause you weren't doin' what you were supposed to be doin'? Which?"

"I wasn't doin' anything, awright? Fuck

you hasslin' me for, I didn't do anything. So they fired me, so what? Stupid job anyway, all you do is roust kids all night."

"You? Roust kids? That's what they paid you for? C'mon —"

"Yeah, that's right, that's what you do, roust kids. Felt like I was in fucking hell, gonna spend the rest of my life in fucking Rocksburg Mall, hasslin' kids just like you used to hassle me, so I stopped doin' it, okay? So they fired me. And that's all there is to it, okay? Satisfied now?"

"No I'm not — don't hang up! You ever turn in your uniform?"

"What? Somebody sayin' I stole a uniform now? Hey, you wanna come up here, look around? Feel free, motherfucker, I don't have —"

"You're not answerin' my question. Did you ever turn it back in, yes or no?"

"I'm tellin' you I don't have anybody's uniform."

"And I'm tellin' you that's not what I'm askin' you. Listen to the question. Did you ever turn it back in? And if you didn't, which I know you didn't now — what'd you do with it? You sell it? Or you just rentin' it out?"

"Hey, fuck you, huh?" Click.

Balzic pressed the redial button and

waited. And waited. And waited. On the twenty-something ring, Mrs. Cozzolino picked up. "Hello?"

"Hi, Missus Cozzolino, it's me again, Balzic. We got cut off or somethin', can you get Ronnie for me again, please?"

"Ronnie's not here now. He's at the store. He's gettin' some things for me. Milk an'at. He should be back in a little while. Maybe you could call back later, okay?" Click.

"Yeah, sure. Right." Balzic hung up, got up, went to the stove, and turned on the gas under the pot of water he'd put on for tea before Ruth came in and turned it off. Who the hell's Cozzolino related to? He's related to somebody who's a made guy, Jesus, my brain's turnin' to sauerkraut, can't remember anything anymore. I know this kid is related to a made guy, I know he is. Who? Crap, I could stew here for a month, I wouldn't remember. Sit around bitchin' about your memory, call somebody, call Muscotti — oh right, his memory's worse than mine. My brain's fulla sauerkraut, his is fulla Canadian Club.

Balzic went back to the phone, pressed the numbers for Muscotti's.

Vinnie the bartender answered on the third ring.

"Hey, Vinnie, it's me, Balzic, let me talk to Dom."

"Mario? No shit, is that you? I heard you had a fuckin' heart attack — what, you're not dead?"

"Somebody say I was?"

"Said you had a fuckin' heart attack — what, you didn't have a heart attack? Some fuckin' people lie about anything, you know that?"

"Aw will you stop — where's Dom?"

"Nobody here but me and Iron City Steve. And he's unconscious, somethin' new — whatta you want Dom for?"

"I wanna ask him somethin'."

"Don't ask him, what the fuck, ask me, he don't know nothin', he can't remember where the fuck he lives, for crissake. Cop picked him up yesterday, he was walkin' down by that new Arby's, you know? Down South Rocksburg?"

"Get out."

"No. Serious. Cop says, hey Dom, whatta you doin' down here, where you goin'? He says he's goin' home. Cop says you don't live down here, you live the other way. Fifteen, sixteen blocks, he's walkin' the wrong way. Meantime you know how cold it was yesterday? He got a suit on. Thinks he's goin' home, yeah. No

shit. I'm tellin' ya, you fuckin' guys —
whatta you wanna know anyway? Ask me,
I know everything you wanna know, huh?
Every time you wanted to know somethin',
who'd you wind up askin', huh? Me. Go
'head, ask me somethin'."

"Okay, answer man, alright, listen, you
know Ronnie Cozzolino?"

"Huh? Yeah, sure, Ronnie, yeah, I know
him. He's stupid. He's a jagoff. What's up
with him?"

"You got the right guy now? For sure?
About twenty-five, twenty-six?"

"I told ya, yeah, Ronnie Cozzolino, yeah
I know him. So?"

"Who's he related to?"

"Who's he what? His mother and father,
who the fuck you think?"

"You know what I mean, some made
guy, he's related to some —"

"Oh, he's second fuckin' cousins, get
outta here. What, he sayin' he is? He's fulla
shit. In his dreams. He ain't no-fuckin'-
body —"

"No no, I didn't say he said he was. I'm
sayin' is he — you know, is he related
to somebody? And if so, who, that's what
I'm askin'. I know he's not a made guy,
Christ —"

"Oh oh, I see what you're sayin', nah,

he's maybe a nephew or somethin'. Yeah, that's what he is. Yeah, his mother's brother, I know what you're thinkin'. Yeah, he's over in, uh, Knox there. You know, doin' his little thing. That's all, that's the only way he's got anything goin' for him, Cozzolino. And they don't wanna have nothin' to do with him anyway, he's too stupid, you kiddin'? You gotta watch him crossin' the street for crissake."

"So it's the guy in Knox then?"

"Yeah yeah, there's some blood there, but, man, that's stretchin' it. He ain't doin' nothin', that jagoff. I know you were talkin' to Mo the other day, I don't know what you're doin', but this jagoff, uh-uh, he ain't got nothin' to do with nothin'. So you have a heart attack or what? Three different guys told me you had a heart attack, you're tellin' me that never happened now? Why all these people lyin'?"

"It wasn't a heart attack, okay? An event. Coronary event, that's what they're callin' it, you know —"

"A what did you say? Event? The fuck's that?"

"Yeah yeah, event. That's what they called it. Coronary event. Nobody called it a heart attack, I'm tellin' ya."

"Coronary event? What, they sell tickets

to this event, huh?"

"Aw, cute."

"I never heard about no goddamn coronary event —"

"Lotta things you never heard about, what're you, a doctor now?"

"Listen, I know some things, don't kid yourself. Know what I think? I think with that pension you got, that good insurance? You got in there, those fuckin' doctors, they find out you got that good insurance, they tell you, hey, you had an event. Right. That's it. Saw your fuckin' insurance card, that's the only event goin' on. Saw a chance to upgrade the go-mo-bile. Fuck that, c'mon, what happened?"

"I'm tellin' ya, that's what happened — hey, there's somebody at the door, I gotta go. Bye."

Right, that's all I have to do, sit around explainin' that shit to you. Be there an hour. So, what do we have here, Cozzolino's a nephew to that made guy in Knox? Knox, man, that's where that goofy asshole chief is, always talkin' about the war on drugs, he's in the trenches against the drug dealers, always makin' speeches, always got his face in the paper, yeah. Right. They do more drug business on one Saturday afternoon in Braddock than they do all year in

Knox, but not if you listen to him. Fuckin' guy's always out there advertisin', campaignin' for somethin'. What the hell's that guy's name in Knox, the made guy, with the numbers thing, the sports book, that's all he does, he doesn't do anything else. Had Vinnie on the phone, why didn't I ask him — boy, am I spacey. What the hell's his name? I can see him, lower lip sticks out past his nose, all hunched over with a widow's hump, fat as a fuckin' hog, sits around in front of that deli all day, his belly hangin' out, what the fuck's his name . . . God, I can't remember anything anymore. Tuzzoli? No, not Tuzzoli, Christ, he's dead. Oh wait — Cimoli, that's it. Cimoli?! C'mon, Christ, he was an outfielder with the Pirates, holy hell, where'd that come from, Gino Cimoli?! God. Yeah, he played right field against the Yankees when Mazeroski hit that home run, holy Christ, my brain really is sauerkraut. . . .

Balzic thought for another long moment, drawing a blank on a name to go with the face of the made guy in Knox. He pushed the buttons for the Rocksburg PD, hoping to find Carlucci in.

"Rocksburg Police, Patrolman Fischetti speakin'."

"Hey, Fish, it's me, Balzic."

"Mario? Hey, man, how you doin'? Heard you had a heart attack, is that true?"

"No no, uh-uh. No, no heart attack, some kinda coronary thing, you know. Event or somethin' they're callin' it. It was definitely no attack. Maybe a little ambush, you know, but no attack, believe me —"

"So you feelin' okay then? You home?"

"Yeah, fine, yeah, I'm home, sure. Listen, Rugs around? Huh? Lemme talk to him — if he's there."

"He's here, wait a second, he's goin' nuts transferrin' records to the computer. Somebody doesn't do somethin' bad soon, he's about four inches away from total geekhood he doesn't get outta here. Hey, Rugs? Pick up on three — good talkin' to you, Mario — hey, stop around once in a while, you know? You haven't been back since you retired, man, what's goin' on with that? Stop in, for crissake, you act like there's warrants out on you or somethin'. Here's Rugs. See ya, Mario."

"Yeah, Fish, thanks, maybe I will," Balzic said. "Yo, Rugs, it's me, Mario."

"Mario, how're you feelin'? Haven't talked to Ruth since you got home, I guess. You doin' okay?"

"Yeah, fine, I'm alright. Just a little shaky

every once in a while, you know. Feel a little ba-boom-batta-boom in my chest there, you know, start reachin' for my pocket, feelin' around, seein' if I still got the nitro. It's stupid —"

"Aw hey, you know, Mario, gotta expect to feel a little antsy, right? Somethin' like that? Afterwards, you know, who wouldn't?"

"Oh, sure sure, yeah, no big deal. Just, uh, you know, just every once in a while, I, uh, aw never mind — listen, I'm tryin' to think of a name for five minutes here and I'm shootin' blanks, can't think of it, I know you know it —"

"Yeah, sure. Who?"

"Who's the book in Knox? The made guy over there, you know, sits around in front of that deli in the summer, his belly hangin' out, his mouth's always open, looks like he got an IQ about twelve?"

"Oh yeah. Chianese —"

"Right right," Balzic said, giving himself a smack in the forehead. "The Chink, how the hell could I forget that? Chink Chianese — what's his real name again?"

"Arturo, Arthur, Fat Artie, Fat Buddha, those last two, that's what people call him behind his back."

"Right, yes, God, my memory's like cheesecloth anymore, Rugs."

"What's up with him? Somethin' up with him? I haven't heard anything —"

"Chianese? No no, no, I'm doin' this for, uh, Valcanas. That gunshop, you know? In the mall?"

"Freedom Firearms? That one? Tell you right now, Mario, that guy's fulla shit, that's a scam."

"Oh yeah? You know somethin'?"

"No no, just what I read. 'Cause if the numbers were right in the paper — which I'm not sayin' they were — but if they were, those were bullshit numbers. C'mon, I don't have to tell you this, right?"

"Yeah, but do you know something? You got any history with this guy? This Bemiss?"

"Nah, never heard the name before. But no way anybody in this county has that kinda inventory on Berettas, get out. Thirty-eight Berettas? There ain't that many in the National Guard Armory for crissake. Talk to him yet?"

"Not yet. I was tryin' to talk to the guy owns the security agency —"

"Toby Steele?"

"No no, Vanguard's gone."

"They're gone at the mall? Since when? What happened with them?"

"Bankrupt apparently, I don't really

know, that's just what I heard, I don't even know who told me."

"So who's got it now?"

"Uh, some Bulldog Security or somethin' —"

"Aw no, not that fuckin' guy. That's Beckmaier — is that who that is? Beckmaier?"

"Yeah, that's the name, but I don't remember him, he says we met a couple times, but I don't recall him — do I? I mean I just talked to him, but what — you sayin' I should know him?"

"Sure you do. Think a minute. He was a detective in Knox, remember now? Aw he's another one, he's fulla shit three times over. You know him, I know you do 'cause I had problems with him —"

"Oh God, yeah, that's right! I forgot that, holy hell —"

"Oh yeah, for years he was there. Laziest son of a bitch that ever was. But listen to him talk? Man, the greatest clearance record in the county. I know you remember me tellin' you about him."

"Yeah, sure, it's comin' back now."

"Oh yeah, I got stuck workin' a couple cases with him, he was terrible. Wouldn't do shit. Interview somebody in the morning, talk to him maybe ten minutes, he'd spend the rest of the day writin' it up. Next day I'd call him up, he's still writin'. But, man, listen to him? World's greatest investigator — what, he's got the security at the mall? No shit, I don't believe it, I'm tellin' ya —"

"Yes he does."

"Bulldog Security is his? For sure?"

"That's what his personal assistant says. I didn't check corporate records yet, I don't know that I'm goin' to, but —"

"What happened with Vanguard again? Bankrupt?"

"Apparently."

"Man, I thought they were solid, thought they had their shit together. But they're out and he's in — for sure?"

"They're definitely out, he's definitely in."

"Honest to God, those poor fuckers, they don't have a clue what they're payin' for."

"Wanna know who he had workin' for him — for more than a year? Ronnie Cozzolino."

"Aw, see there? That's exactly what I'm talkin' about. And what's he sayin' — he didn't know?"

"He's not sayin' anything, he doesn't wanna talk about it."

"Well naturally, why would he — you said had, right? So when'd he stop workin' for him?"

"They fired him December fifteenth, but they won't say why."

"Aw man, I don't know how heavy you wanna get with this, Mario, but lean on those fuckers. Cozzolino got fired before, right? Is that what you're sayin'? Before the B and E?"

"Yes, before. Right."

"Aw lean on him hard, that weasel. Lean on Beckmaier, too. Get in his face — wait a second, who's workin' this? For the state?"

"Trooper, uh, Milliron —"

"Claude? I know him. Pinky. He's good people — what, he's not leanin' on 'em?"

"He told me he's got a little girl missin' in one of the townships, I forget which one —"

"Oh yeah, that's right, he had the fire department dogs out, I think three days now. Yeah, so he wouldn't be havin' time to mess with those two — but you need to, Mario. I'm tellin' ya, you need to get in their faces, both those creeps. Especially that Beckmaier —"

"Well, see, I'm pretty much doin' this over the phone, Rugs, you know? Kinda

216

soon for me to be travelin' around —"

"Oh oh, yeah, I understand. I sorta got carried away there, I mean I forgot about your, uh, you know, your situation. But wait a minute. Listen. I know this is gonna sound nuts."

"What?"

"What I'm gonna say."

"Oh, go 'head. Didn't mean to interrupt."

"That's okay. But I mean, I know this is gonna sound wacky, but you know what? If I were you? I'd be callin' some people in Knox."

"Whattaya mean? Callin' who?"

"Anybody you know over there."

"Why?"

" 'Cause that chief? You know? That Butterbaugh? Guy's always runnin' his mouth about drugs?"

"Yeah, I know him. What're you sayin'?"

"I'm sayin', hey, if this was mine? And I knew all these people were involved?"

"You mean Beckmaier and Cozzolino?"

"Exactly. If I knew they were involved, I'd start checkin' connections between them and the guy that owns the gunshop and that asshole Butterbaugh. I know, I mean, I know you can't do it right now, you know, with your situation there, but I'd sure be makin' some calls. And I'd sure tell Milliron what I was thinkin', get him to, uh, you know — aw listen to me, I shouldn't be tellin' you how to do this, this is not my business. Sorry, Mario."

"No no, that's okay, go 'head, say what you were gonna say."

"You sure this is alright now?"

"Yeah, hell yeah, go 'head."

"Well, see, first thing I'd do, I'd tell Milliron to talk to one of those cops in that department, ask him if they got new weapons recently, or if they were expectin' to get new ones."

"In the department? You serious?"

"Damn right, yeah. If they heard rumors they were gonna get new ones, you know? Don't you know anybody over there? Somebody with the council? Borough manager maybe, anybody?"

"I used to, not anymore. Used to know the city administrator."

"Well give him a call, ask him."

"Aw hell, he retired years ago, way before I did."

"Give him a call anyway, what could it hurt? Might be surprised what he knows."

"Wait a second, let me get this straight. You're thinkin' these guns're gonna wind up in the Knox PD, is that what you're sayin'?"

"Listen, I wouldn't be sayin' anything if this Beckmaier wasn't involved. But Cozzolino too? And he was workin' for Beckmaier? And he fires him before?"

"Why would he fire him? Wouldn't that make it look too obvious?"

"I don't think so. Because — just my opinion now — but I think that's exactly what Beckmaier would say. Like what, was somebody sayin' he was tryin' to make it look like there was no connection between 'em? Right away, Beckmaier'd say how dumb you think I am? But what better way to have a prime chump? I mean, what the fuck, he'd have it both ways. Cozzolino's the one with the yellow sheet. What's Beckmaier? He's the pretty-boy detective. Plus it's his business, right? Hey, Mario, you know I don't know which way this went, from who to who to who, but, uh, just 'cause of who's involved, just the names? I mean, my antenna go straight up — hey, Mario, I got another call, okay? Lemme know how it goes, I'd really be interested. Gotta go, bye."

Balzic hung up and started thumbing through his Rolodex, trying to remember the name of the man who used to be city administrator for Knox. He gave up after about five minutes; he couldn't connect a single name on his cards with that job. He narrowed his search down to all the names with the Knox telephone prefix, but for some reason he hadn't listed that particular occupation under anybody's name. What the hell was I thinkin'? Boy, there's arrogance for you, thinkin' you're never gonna slip, you're always gonna be sharp. Other people're gonna get old and slip, but not you. No, fuck no, not you.

He started to dial the Knox city administrator's office but something Carlucci said bothered him. He put the phone down and thought about it some more. Rugs couldn't be right. In order for Beckmaier to say he had a prime chump, he'd have to be able to explain why he didn't background Cozzolino, which, if he said that, anybody with half a brain would know he was either lying or in a coma, otherwise he would've known about Cozzolino's record, 'cause the only way he could've hired him was to say he didn't know Cozzolino was on pro. Nah, you can't get away with somethin' that stupid, not if you're in the security business, Jesus. Nah, that doesn't make sense. On the other hand, what the fuck, stupider things have happened. And what's stupider than thinkin' nobody's gonna check — or that somebody else is? Happens all the time. Everybody expects somebody else to check — "No, I didn't check. Hey, that's what I was payin' him for." Heard it a thousand times. Could Beckmaier be that shrewd? Or that stupid, which?

Balzic picked up the phone again, pushed the buttons for Knox City Hall. He tried to find the city administrator he'd been looking for from the woman who answered the phone, but she was only nineteen and the only administrator she'd ever heard of was the one who was her boss. Balzic asked her to transfer his call to the Knox PD, which she did.

Balzic got a civilian dispatcher who very officiously refused to answer any questions about the department, saying repeatedly that if Balzic was indeed a legitimate investigator then he should know better than to ask a dispatcher questions about department policy, personnel, or equipment over the phone. "I'd put you through to the chief, sir, but he's not in right now."

"What's your name?" Balzic said.

"Hapchuk. Melvin."

"Hey, Hapchuk, Melvin, didn't you used to be a cop?"

"Yes sir. Thirty years in this department, yessirree."

"Hey, Hapchuk. I used to be chief of the Rocksburg PD."

"Oh oh oh, you're that Balzic, Jeez, see, I thought that name was familiar, yeah, now I got ya. What can I do for you?"

"Just tell me when you expect the chief back, that's all."

"I don't know, Chief. Last time I seen him he was with one of the councilmen on the safety committee, Charlie Ambrozic, that's all I can tell you."

"What time's he leave for the day, usually?"

"Depends. Can't set your watch by him, that's all I can tell you."

"Uh-huh. You wouldn't happen to know the name of the former city administrator, would you? Would've retired, like, oh, I don't know, five years ago?"

"You mean Ed Lister — is that who you mean?"

"Yeah yeah, that's him. Ed Lister, right?"

"Oh man, whattaya want him for, he's dead."

"He is? Why'd you say it that way? Hell, he wasn't that old. What happened?"

"I don't know how old he was, but believe me, Chief, he's dead, I know. I was there. Had a heart attack. Right in church. Yeah, keeled over two pews ahead of me. Oh man, that was one of the screwiest things I was ever involved with."

"Oh. Man. Died in church?"

"Yeah he did — and I got stuck right in the middle of it, and believe me I didn't wanna be. Oh man, I'll never forget that. He'd just taken communion, went back to his pew, started to genuflect, you know, and then boom, straight down on his face."

"Ouu, man."

"Broke his nose, his bowels cut loose, yeah, I was two pews behind him. It was awful — but believe me it got way worse."

"Oh. Wow." Balzic's right hand went to the right side of his throat, his middle finger prodding, rubbing, probing, pretending to scratch an itch he didn't have, as though hand and finger had a mind separate from the one that's supposed to be between his ears. He knew he was feeling for his pulse, he didn't want to take his pulse, but he couldn't help himself. He had to take his pulse.

"Listen, that was just the beginning," Hapchuk said. "There was a coupla doctors there, so they're doin' CPR, you know, tryin' to get him back, and finally they have to give up, they pronounce him, you know, he's gone, the ambulance comes, they take him away, so naturally everybody starts feelin' sorry for his wife, you know, everybody's tryin' to console her, the priest, everybody. Only thing was — the woman who was with him? Wasn't his wife. Yeah. But nobody knew it. 'Cause she looked just like his wife. Yeah. Imagine that, huh? Brings his girlfriend to church, takes communion, I mean, I'll never forget it, his girlfriend looked just like his wife. Everybody thought it was his wife, it wasn't just me. I knew his wife, I woulda swore this woman was his wife.

"Only the next day, listen to this, I'm workin' the radio and the phones just like I'm doin' now, I get this call, this woman says she's Missus Edward Lister, she wants to report her husband missing. I said Missus Lister, this is Mel Hapchuk, remember me? She says oh yeah Mel, hello, sure I remember you, sorry to bother you, it's probably nothin', but I'm starting to get worried. I says no no, don't you remember me from church yesterday? She says I don't know what you're talking about, I wasn't in church yesterday. She goes, listen I'm worried about Ed, he went out Saturday morning, he was gonna pick up some clothes at the cleaners, he never came back. So I said he's been gone since Saturday morning, it's Monday, you're just now startin' to get worried? She said he does this sort of thing all the time, but usually he never stays gone more than one day. I said one day? She said well, one day and one night. He's always fishin' or huntin' or takin' pictures, she says, he loves to take pictures of deer and raccoons and possums, all those animals that come out at night. She can't stand it, she's got all these allergies, she wished she could go do it with him, but she can't, her nose'd swell all up.

"Honest to God, I'm listenin' to this woman, I knew her husband for years, I never heard him say one word about cameras or fishin' or huntin' or nothin'. But I'm startin' to get the picture, except what threw me was this woman, I'm thinking the woman I'm talkin' to on the phone is the woman I saw in church but she's tellin' me she was never in church, you know what I'm sayin'? But I didn't know what to do. I'm thinkin', what the hell's goin' on here? This woman says she wasn't in church, I'm thinkin' she was too in church, but she keeps insistin' she wasn't, now she's tryin' to find her old man, what the hell am I supposed to tell her?"

Balzic was mesmerized by both this bizarre story and his carotid artery. The more bizarre the details of Ed Lister's death, the more quickly Balzic's heart began to beat, the drier his lips got, the tighter his throat felt. He wanted to break off the conversation, but he didn't know how because he also wanted to know what happened.

"So I had to figure somethin' out, you know?" Hapchuk went on. "I mean what could I say? I told this woman, who I'm thinkin' is Missus Lister, I say I'd have it checked out. So the first thing I do, I call all the funeral homes. The man's already laid out in Zabriskie's, right here in town. Turns out the girlfriend made all the arrangements, that's why nobody called the wife, 'cause everybody's thinkin' the girlfriend's the wife. Can you imagine? Two women, absolutely no relation, they look enough alike to be twins, nobody pays enough attention to know they're not. And this guy's livin' with the both of them. Now that's the thing I could never figure out. If you had to have a girlfriend, if you were gonna do this kinda thing, why would you want your girlfriend to look just like your wife, that's the part that always got me, you know? Still gets me, I mean, I just can't figure that out."

"Yeah, yeah, so?" Balzic said, growing more agitated by the second. "So what happened?" As near as he could calculate, his pulse was up to ninety.

"Oh, hey, I didn't know what to do, I called the priest. I said, hey Father, we got a problem here, somebody has to tell this woman what's goin' on, and, man, I don't know how to do it and I don't wanna do it, this is your line, you know? I don't have the words for this, I'd be too embarrassed for this woman."

"So did he tell her?"

"Oh yeah, course he told her. Yeah."

"Well? What happened?"

"I don't know."

"What?"

"I don't know what happened. I never found out."

"Wait a second," Balzic said, catching the phone as it slipped from his left ear while he was still trying to keep his right middle finger on his carotid artery. "You're tellin' me, after all this, everything you just told me? This is all you know?"

"Yeah. I mean I tried to find out, but the priest never said anything. Not to me he didn't."

"Wait a second. You were a cop for thirty

years before you got this job?"

"Yeah, right."

"And you didn't say anything about this to anybody — besides the priest?"

"Oh no, I didn't say that. I mean I told Chief Butterbaugh, and I know he told Detective Beckmaier, 'cause Beckmaier interviewed me."

"And so what? That's the end of it far as you're concerned? You never heard any more about it, is that what you're tellin' me?"

"Well, the chief, you know, Butterbaugh, he told me to stay out of it, stop talkin' to people about it, it was none of my business."

"Oh for crissake," Balzic said. He was frustrated, disappointed, irritated, agitated for any number of reasons, the principal ones being that a man had died of a heart attack in church after taking communion while publicly violating the sacraments by blatantly violating one of the commandments. "I'm sure it wasn't any of your business, Mel, but now you made it mine and my heart's racin' over here. Thank you very much."

"Huh?"

"Thanks for nothin'," Balzic said, slamming down the receiver.

Balzic tried to clear his throat, felt like he couldn't swallow. What was that? That boom-boom? Yeah, that — what was that? That was nothin'. Where's it at? Where's what? You know what, where's my what? What? Your nitro, you dumb-ass, where's your nitro? It's right there, in your pocket, where you always put it, in your left pants pocket. No it isn't, where'd you put it? I didn't put it anywhere. Well it might've been right there a minute ago but it isn't there now — where'd you put it? I didn't put it anywhere, it's right where it always is. Well if it's right where it always is how come you can't find it — whatta you need it for anyway? You know why, jagoff, what're you askin' for? You mean 'cause you can't swallow? I can swallow, what're you sayin' I can't swallow for? Well if you can swallow what're you all outta joint about? I'm not outta joint — wait wait, there it goes again — you feel that? Don't tell me you didn't feel that. Feel what? That! You felt that, don't say you didn't feel that. Aw bullshit, that wasn't anything. Oh yeah? So how come you're reachin' for your nitro? I'm just checkin', that's all, shut up! Nothin' wrong with checkin'. Lemme just take my pulse here — holy fuck I can't find it! The fuck's my pulse,

229

it's supposed to be right there. In your neck, asshole, quit fumblin' around with your wrist. It's not there! At ease, for crissake, your pulse is still there, calm the fuck down, the fuck you think happened to it, you're still standin', still walkin', still talkin' to yourself, listen to you, you're startin' to hyperventilate for crissake! I can't get my breath, the fuck's wrong here? Aw Jesus you can so get your breath, what's the matter with you? You hear about some guy croakin' out with a heart attack, you gonna give yourself one? You him? No I'm not him, I'm not givin' myself anything, shut up! The fuck's my nitro? Will you quit tryin' to take your pulse, huh? Well why's it beatin' like that? It's skippin', how come it's skippin'? It is not skippin'! I can't swallow. You can so swallow, quit tryin' to take your pulse, slow down, slow your breathin' down, asshole, deeeeep breaths, that's it, slow, all the way out, make your stomach touch your spine, okay, now inhale, that's it, slow . . . slow . . . SLOW! Asshole, you don't know what slow means? Alright I know what slow means, don't shout, that don't accomplish anything, okay, alright, shut up now, I'm not takin' my pulse, I found my nitro, it's right where it always was, right there in my left pocket, alright, I'm slowin' my breathin' down now, exhalin' slow, pushin' all the air out, that's it, touchin' my spine with my belly button, okay, I'm inhalin' now, that's it — wait a minute. Wait a fuckin' minute. I'm gettin' dizzy here, how come I'm gettin' dizzy? You're gettin' dizzy, asshole, 'cause you're forcin' everything, stop forcin' it, don't force your breathin', just breathe, that's all, deep, slow, everything out, then a new one in, that's all, quit forcin' it —

"Mario?"

"Huh?!" Balzic spun around, sucking in air. His heart was hammering, a bass drum in his chest beating so loud and so fast he thought that if he didn't get it slowed down it would explode.

"Jesus you scared me," he blurted. He was on the verge of tears.

"I'm sorry, I didn't mean to scare you, I started calling you as soon as I got inside but you didn't answer me, are you alright?"

"Yeah yeah, I'm fine, sure. What, I don't look okay?"

"You sure?"

"What? Why? Don't I look okay? Whatta you doin' back here anyway, I thought you were goin' to the Y."

"I forgot the checkbook, I got there and I started signing up for the class and I didn't have the checkbook, so I had to come back — you sure you're alright? You want me to call somebody?"

"Why? Call who? What for? Call who?"

"I'm just askin', Mar, that's all. You don't look, uh, you sure you're okay?"

"I don't look what? What — my lips blue or somethin'?"

"No," she said, coming close, and putting her hands on his arms.

He shrugged away from her, took two steps back. "Just tell me how I don't look, okay? Don't tell me I don't look like somethin' and then stand there and not tell me how I don't look, okay?"

"Mar, c'mon, you're fine. He opened the artery that was causing your problem. The other one that's closed, he said — and I believe him, I don't doubt for a second he knows what he's talking about — he said that one's been closed for a long time so you shouldn't feel any different now than you did before —"

"What the hell's he know what I felt like before? I don't even know what I felt like before, how's he supposed to know?"

"All I'm saying is what he said, Mar."

"Look, I'm gonna take a nitro, okay?"

"Huh? Why? You havin' some kinda pain?"

"No. Not exactly."

"Are you having trouble breathing?"

"I'm not sure."

"How can you not be sure — I mean you're either having trouble or you're not, I don't see —"

"Aw what the hell do you know?"

"Mario! Jesus, come on!"

"Ah I'm sorry. Hey, wait." He tried to clear his throat again. It felt like it was closing. Again.

"Hey, Mar, no, uh-uh, I don't wanna hear sorry. If you're having trouble, if you're having chest pain — that's what Doctor Fine said — if you're having trouble breathing or you're having chest pain, or pain in your arms, or in your neck, or in your jaw, then you should take one of those. And if it didn't go away, you should take another —"

"I know what he said, I was there, I was listenin'."

"Of course you were there — that's not what I'm — I'm just repeating what he said, that's all, just reminding you. So if you're having any of those things, you know, sure, go 'head, take one. Then take another. And another. And if what you're feeling hasn't gone away after you've taken the third one, then you're supposed to —"

"Go to the emergency room, I know! I heard him, okay?"

"Well then take it, go 'head. Stick it under your tongue like he said, what're you waiting for?"

"I'm . . ." Balzic hung his head, felt himself sob, felt the tears spill over his cheeks. He turned away from her, coughed, tried to clear his throat again. Now his nose was filling up, the way it always did when he tried to stop crying.

"You're what? Say it, Mar, please? What are you?"

"I'm scared! There, goddammit, I said it, you happy now?"

"Mario, turn around. Look at me. Why would I be happy that you said that? What's goin' on here? You scared of what's happening? Or you scared to take the pill? Turn around, please, I can't see your face, I don't know what's goin' on, c'mon, Mar, please?"

"I'm scared of what's goin' on, I'm scared of takin' the goddamn pill, I never took one, I don't know what's gonna happen."

"Oh, Mario," she said, stepping forward, hugging him from behind, pressing her cheek into his back. "Don't do this to yourself. Take the pill, the worst thing that could happen — he said, don't you remember? The worst thing was you might get a headache. You have to trust him, everybody says he's a really bright guy, very well trained, really knows his stuff, c'mon, Mar, turn around, let me see your face."

"Why? So you can tell me to quit complainin'?"

"What?" Her head jerked back, her arms flew away from around his chest as though she'd been shocked by static electricity. "Why're you saying that, Mar?"

"Because that's what you did. Every time I started talkin' about this, you kept tellin' me, hey, everybody gets old, everybody has problems, that's what gettin' old means, you wake up every day, somethin' new's hurtin', you gotta stop bitchin' about it —"

"Mario, God, I was just talking in general, you know? That's all I was saying, I didn't want us to turn into those people, you know, all they talk about is what kind of medicine they're takin', and why they're takin' it. God, next thing they're talkin' about is their bowels, how many times they go to the bathroom, how many times they used to go, how many times they don't go now, I didn't want us to start turnin' into those people, Mar, that's all —"

"Yeah but you didn't talk about you turnin' into that, you just talked about me complainin', me bitchin', me turnin' into some old fart. Every time I said somethin' about the, uh, you know, this thing in my throat, whatever the hell it is, you'd say, hey, knock it off, gettin' old ain't for sissies —"

"I didn't know you were having specific problems with your artery. How could I know that, I was just talkin' in general, that's all —"

"Yeah? Well now I'm scared to tell you anything about it, okay?"

"Mario, there is no reason for you to feel that way, I didn't mean to make you feel like you can't tell me things —"

"So now I'm not only tryin' to figure out what I'm feelin', I also have to figure out whether I'm allowed to tell you what I'm feelin', 'cause if I'm not feelin' it the way you think I'm supposed to be feelin' it, you're gonna think I'm just some old fart bitcher, that's all —"

"Mario, turn around and look at me, please? I want you to look at me, this is me back here. I am not calling you an old fart, I never called you that, I would never use that kinda language with you, I would never call you a name — you tell me when

236

I did, I wanna know when you think I ever said anything like that to you, called you a name!"

"You never told me to stop bitchin'? Stop complainin'? Huh? You never did that?" He turned around and faced her. Her eyes were burning with bright hurt. He had to look away.

"What I told you, Mario, was stop bitchin'. That's what I said. Stop complainin'. I didn't call you a name. I didn't say you were nothin' but a bitcher or anything like that. Old fart, Jesus — I said stop doing something, I didn't put a name on you! We have never done that to each other, Mario, not in all the time we've been married, we have never called each other names, don't you dare say I did! 'Cause I didn't. I've told you this before — so many times I'm tired of sayin' it — I don't want us to turn into those people who just sit around and talk about their visits to the doctor, what drug they're takin' and how they forget to take it and how nobody takes them seriously and then they start talkin' about how many times they — oh what am I sayin' this for again? I've said it so many times — you know what I'm talkin' about, Mario. You know I have never called you any names, you know I have listened to everything you have ever said, and I never made fun of you or teased you about it or blew it off!

"Mario! Look at me! You can't look at me and say I ever did any of those things. Look at me, Mar! What happened? Something happened while I was gone. What? Tell me what, I wanna know, what?!"

Balzic threw up his hands feebly, rolled his head from side to side, felt the muscles in his neck tightening, tried to look at her, but couldn't hold her gaze because he knew she was right. She'd done what she'd just said, told him to stop bitching, stop complaining, she'd never called him names. He couldn't look at her for that reason and also because he couldn't see through his tears.

He told her about the phone call, about Ed Lister keeling over in church after taking communion.

"Oh God, Mar, you're not him, he's not you. You can't do this."

"Do what?"

"Mar, listen to me." She came close again, put her hands on his arms and gave him one small shake, out of frustration. "You can't do this to you, you can't do this to me —"

"Oh right, I'm doin' this to you now,

right?" He tried to pull away, but she hung on, wouldn't let him back away, came along with him.

"Mario, goddammit, listen to me. There's nobody else here, just you and me. There's never gonna be anybody else here, just you and me, you hear? You and me, that's it! And now you've found out you've got this new problem, you think it's just your problem, and there's nobody else involved. But that's bullshit! 'Cause every time we have a problem, the other one's got it too, understand? It's automatic, whether we want it that way or not, that's the way it is, if I have it, you have it and if you have it, I have it —"

"You don't have this, what're you talkin' about, there's nothin' wrong with your arteries, not in your heart!"

"Mario, the only reason anybody knows there's anything wrong with the arteries in your heart — two! Two arteries, Mar! Will you try to remember that? And they opened the one that just closed, okay? And you've got pictures to prove it — I don't! Nobody's been takin' pictures of my heart! Have they? Huh? So nobody knows what my arteries look like, okay? Not me, not you, not Doctor Fine — nobody, okay?"

"Okay then."

"Okay what? 'Cause we don't have pictures, so mine are alright?"

"No no, that's not what I'm sayin' — all I'm sayin' is, ah, Jesus, you know what I'm sayin' — I have this, you don't —"

"Mario, stop it, okay? Just stop it. You don't have it, okay? You don't have a closed artery anymore, it was opened, it's wide open, you have pictures — before and after pictures, remember? And you don't have to be a cardiologist to see the difference — I mean do you?"

"Do I what?"

"You do know, Mar, don't tell me you couldn't see the difference, you saw the difference, right? Do I have to go get 'em? The pictures?"

"No you don't have to go get 'em, that ain't the point."

"Well what is the point then? You don't want me to tell you to stop complaining? Fine. I won't. But if you think this is only your problem and I'm not involved — directly involved with my whole being here, you're not seein' things right, Mar. There's no other way to say that. Because I am! I'm as involved as anybody can be who doesn't have the problem, okay? Does that make more sense? When I say it that way, huh? Tell me — does it make more sense, can you understand it better, what I'm saying? Or do you still think you're in this all alone, and I'm not here, and I'm not helpin' you, or I don't wanna help you, Jesus, Mary, and Joseph, Mario, look at me! Tell me you don't believe that."

Balzic hung his head, covered his eyes with his right hand, and began to sob. He tried to pull away from her again, but she held on tighter. "It's okay," she said, "Go ahead, it's alright, just let it go, it's okay."

"I'm a fucking coward," he blubbered.

"You are not. Stop that."

"Yes I am, goddammit. Scared outta my mind . . ."

"Of what? What are you scared of? Dying?"

"Hell yeah! Fuck yeah!"

"Why? What exactly are you afraid of? The pain? What?"

"No! No! Fuck the pain . . . it ain't the pain."

"What then? Say it. Can you say it?"

"I don't know. Scared I'm . . . scared I'm gonna be judged . . ."

"Oh Mar. Why? God? You think God's gonna judge you? For what?"

"Everything I did wrong . . . all the people I hurt . . . all the ones I didn't help I shoulda helped . . ."

"Mar, you helped way more than you hurt —"

"Stop it! Don't pump sunshine up my ass, I hate that."

"I'm not doin' that, Mar. I'm not! I'm tellin' you the truth, you helped way more people than you ever hurt."

"How 'bout all the times women came to me, said help me, help me, help me with my kid, help me with my old man, I couldn't do shit for 'em. Blew 'em off. Sent 'em to somebody else. Missus Wrobelewski, remember her? Huh?"

"Missus Wrobelewski? My God, Mar, that was before we were married."

"Yeah, right. Begged me to help her kid, I didn't know what to do with him, told her he'd grow out of it, told her it was some goddamn phase, just teenage stuff, that's all, don't worry about it, that's what I said. Fuckin' kid hung himself — with her clothesline — in their cellar. Don't worry about it, I said, yeah. That's what I told her, he'll be okay. Fuckin' kid wasn't even fourteen . . . tried to go to the funeral home, couldn't get my feet through the fuckin' door . . . woman see me on the street, see me comin', she'd cross the street, wouldn't even look at me." Balzic's shoulders were shaking. He sank to his knees and covered his face with his hands.

"Oh Mar," Ruth said, going down on her knees to rub his back and shoulders and stroke his head. "Why are you remembering that, good God, Mar, you couldn't have stopped that, that boy, he needed to see somebody who knew a lot more than you did —"

"I coulda found somebody for him to see. I didn't go outta my way, that's what I'm sayin', you know? And I should have, goddammit, the woman came to me, she didn't know anybody, didn't have anybody here. After her husband got killed, she was all alone, she could barely talk English, she came to me, I just didn't do enough, just . . . didn't. Could've . . . and I didn't . . ."

"Mar, Mar, my God, we've all done things wrong or things we could've done or should've done that we didn't —"

"You don't understand!" he sobbed. "All my life . . . every day, one way or another . . . I was takin' people to judges . . . that's what I did. When I was on that table, Jesus . . . that elephant that was steppin' on my chest? He was talkin' to me — I didn't tell you that part. He was talkin' to me . . ."

"Alright. He was talkin' to you. What did he say?"

"He said . . . Jesus. He said, How's it

feel, big boy? How's it feel to know you're gonna see the judge?"

"Oh Mar. Oh Mar."

"I'm layin' on that fuckin' table in that fuckin' lab . . . and a fuckin' elephant is talkin' to me . . . all the times I ever thought I was losin' my mind, Ruth, swear to God, I never felt more clear about anything in my life. That fuckin' elephant was askin' me how did it feel to know, huh, big boy? How'd it feel to know I was gonna see the judge . . ."

Balzic opened his eyes warily. He was in bed, but he didn't know how he'd got there. Had he been asleep? Or had he passed out? The last thing he remembered was talking about the Wrobelewski boy: he was kneeling on the floor, Ruth was patting his head and telling him it was all right, and now he was waking up and couldn't remember anything about going to sleep. The thought that he'd passed out bolted jaggedly through his mind, and he heaved himself up onto his left elbow. Just as quickly he realized that Ruth couldn't have put him in bed without help. Maybe he'd begun to get wobbly and light-headed and had told her that's what was happening and she'd helped him — oh this was nuts, this goddamn speculating.

He called out to her. No response. He rolled over onto his right side, swung his feet off the bed, and pushed himself up, reflexively fumbling to find a pulse in his neck. It was a bit fast perhaps — the mere act of sitting up would cause it to speed up — but otherwise steady and strong. He stood up. And took it again. Again, steady, strong. He looked down at himself and saw that he was dressed the way he'd been dressed, except for his shoes, which were on the floor near the foot of the bed.

He put his shoes on, stood up, and tried to saunter into the kitchen, feeling for pulses without touching them in an obvious way, almost like sniffing for them using the tips of his fingers as a nose. He'd found that he could do that best with the pulses at the top of his jaw in front of his ears. He'd thought he'd figured out a way to place his hand on his cheek and rub so that it might look like he was feeling if he needed a shave, and after a couple seconds of rubbing he could assume this reflective pose and nobody would know what he was up to. Nobody. Get that. Ruth. That's who he was trying to fool, and no matter how coolly he tried to front, he knew she'd see through him in a second.

She was standing by the sink washing romaine and smiled at him when he came in. "Feeling better?"

He shrugged automatically. "I don't know. I guess. How'd I get in bed?"

"What do you mean?"

"Well, I was just, you know . . . I was in bed. I mean how'd I get there? Somethin' happen?"

"Something happen? Like what?"

"You know . . . pass out or somethin'. Did I?"

"No," she said, starting to frown but catching herself. "You had a couple glasses of wine, you said you were feeling it, said it was hittin' you pretty hard for some reason, I told you to take a nap, and you did, that's all."

"That's it? Couple glasses of wine and I crashed out?"

"That's it. Maybe you need to go easy on the wine till you find out how it's going to act with the Lopressor. That's the first wine you've had since, uh, you know — oh you know what I mean."

"Really? I haven't drunk any before today?"

"Not that I've seen," Ruth said, shaking

water off the romaine. "Feel like making the salad?"

"Huh? Oh yeah, sure," he said, grateful for something to do. He hunted up a lemon, anchovy paste, garlic, salt, extra-virgin olive oil, Dijon mustard, a hunk of Parmesan cheese, and went to work preparing his version of Caesar dressing, without the coddled egg.

"Uh, why was I drinkin' wine — I mean, I don't remember drinkin' wine."

She shrugged and sighed. "You were havin' such a bad time, I just thought you needed some."

"You mean about Missus Wrobelewski?"

"Yes. God, Mar, I don't think you should be — I mean I had no idea you were still draggin' that around. You should've got rid —"

"Hey, you don't just get rid of 'em, it ain't that simple. And she ain't the only one, believe me."

"It is so simple. It's just not easy and I know it isn't — I mean, obviously not. But nobody's gonna judge you for that, my God."

"How do you know?" he snapped. "No no, wait. I didn't mean that the way it sounded. I don't mean you. I mean how's anybody know? Nobody knows. You get the drill drummed into ya when you're a kid, you think, you know, maybe you can shake it, when you've seen enough shit, how complicated everything gets, you think, hey, maybe the drill doesn't apply — ah, shit, I don't know what I'm talkin' about."

"This is the Catholic drill you're talking about, right?"

"Yeah. Course. What else?"

"Despite everything you've tried to shake it —"

"Not everything I *tried*. I didn't *try* anything. I mean, I didn't purposely set out to shake it — hell, I don't know, maybe I did. The shit that was . . . not anything I did, uh-uh, the shit that was tried on me. You know. Life. That's what shook it."

"Oh. That shit."

"Yeah, that shit. All the things that don't work the way the priests and the nuns say they're supposed to work."

"Oh God, Mar, did you ever really think they knew something the rest of us didn't know?"

"I'm talkin' about when I was a kid."

"I don't believe you were ever *that* young."

"Sometimes I think I don't know anything."

"You know you're scared," she said, dicing dried tomatoes and scraping them into a bowl on top of diced kalamata olives.

"Yeah. Right. *That* I know," he said. "And I also know it never gets easier."

"Some priest tell you it would? Was that part of the drill?"

"Hey, easy, okay? These are my onions you're crushin' now."

"No I'm not. I'm serious. Did you ever really talk to a priest? I'm serious now, about bein' afraid, think about it, in your whole life, all the different times you were afraid, did you ever talk to one? Father Marrazzo, ever talk to him?"

"Nah, uh-uh."

"So then you're doin' what you're always tellin' me to stop doin', you're presuming. And speculating. On really flimsy information too, I could add. You have no idea what a priest is gonna say."

"You tryin' to get me to go back to church?"

"Mario, when was the last time you saw me goin' to church — when it wasn't for somebody's funeral or wedding? I haven't talked to a priest about this any more than you have. You want onions in your pasta?"

"What else you gonna put in there — besides the olives and the tomatoes?"

"Just the onion, if we have a decent one. But just rosemary, garlic, salt, pepper, cheese — if you grate it. Parmesan jar's empty."

"I'll grate it. Have to grate it for the salad anyway." He thought for a second. "Gonna caramelize 'em? The onions?"

"If you want. You want?"

"Yeah. Love them. But nothin' else — I mean don't put anything else in, just what you said — we got any red wine open?"

She shot him a look despite herself, then quickly reached for a Teflon-coated wok, put it on the stove, turned on the gas under it, and opened a cupboard. She frowned at a nearly empty bottle of olive oil. Then, with her back to him, she said, "Beside the microwave. You know where it is. Thought I bought a new one of this. Guess I didn't."

Balzic looked at the magnum of Gallo Hearty Burgundy next to the microwave oven. "This is what I was drinkin'? Before I crashed out?"

She hesitated, then ignored his question and went back to talking about testing her memory about whether she'd bought olive oil.

"Oh, that's cool," he said. Then he

started talking like some pompous narrator on some PBS documentary. "You're showing me through the example of your own memory lapse about the purchase of olive oil that I have nothing to fear because I can't remember why I found myself in bed and what I was drinking before I fell into bed."

"Is that what I'm doin'? I didn't know I was that smart."

"Aw cut it out, okay? Is this what I was drinkin' or not?"

"Yes. That's what you were drinking. And what are you doing?"

"What am I doin' about what?"

"Well for a minute there you sounded like you were auditioning for Charlie Rose."

"Well I was feelin' a little patronized, you know?"

"So you can't remember what you were drinkin', Mar, so what? You've got a new drug in you, you have to learn how you're gonna react to it. You're the guy zonks out on antihistamines, remember? I don't know what Lopressor does — didn't you talk to Doctor Fine about it?"

"I don't remember what he said."

"Well call the pharmacist."

"Ah I don't wanna do that."

"Mario, you need information. What, you can ask everybody in the world the most personal goddamn questions, but you can't ask a pharmacist about your own prescription?"

Balzic screwed up his face and got more intensely interested in making the Caesar dressing. He cut a clove of garlic in half and rubbed the inside of their largest ceramic bowl with it. Then he sprinkled some salt in the bowl, added what he guessed was a tablespoon of extra-virgin olive oil, the juice of half a lemon, about two inches of anchovy paste, and a heaping coffee spoon's worth of Dijon mustard. He grated what he thought would be a good amount of Parmesan into the bowl and then whisked it seriously for nearly a minute. He stuck his finger in it, sucked the dressing off and imagined what it would taste like on the romaine. He put another finger in, nudged Ruth with his hip, and held the finger under her nose.

She smelled it, then started to lean forward with her mouth open, stopped, and said, "Is that a clean finger?"

"I don't double-dip, what's wrong with you?"

She sucked the dressing off, swallowed, then puckered up and scrunched her eyes.

"Too much lemon? Mustard, what?"

"It's always too much everything — until you toss it, then it tastes great. Don't change anything."

"Well at least I remember how to do this —"

"Oh shit, Mar, you think you're gettin' Alzheimer's too — on top of your artery problem — which is not a problem anymore, remember?"

"My problem now is I can't remember what my problems are —"

"Mar, we're gettin' old, you know? Old people forget things. That's our job. Our main job used to be to screw up our kids. We did that. Now our job is to screw ourselves up — forget things, fall down, break our hips, forget to take our medicine, lose stuff, lock ourselves out of the car, drink too much, forget how much we drank — those are our jobs, okay? We gotta learn to do 'em right, big boy."

"Okay, okay, alright, Jesus —"

"Only we are not gonna talk about our bowels, okay? Even if we start fartin' in the middle of lunch, we are not gonna talk about it, okay? I refuse! I absolutely refuse to talk about how much I went or didn't went —"

"Didn't went?"

"You know what I meant — don't interrupt me. I'll be goddamned if I start talkin' about how I go or how often or — God forbid, just shoot me, honest to God, I'm serious, if I ever start talkin' about what it looks like, I want you to promise me you will get a gun and shoot me."

"I don't have a pistol and I ain't gettin' one and it'd be too much trouble to get my rifle. It's locked in the trunk of the Chevy —"

"I know where it is —"

"I probably wouldn't be able to find the keys —"

"I want you to promise me you'll shoot me if I ever start talkin' like Missus Halupa. Honest to God, if that woman tells me once more what color her stools are and what that means medically speaking, I'm gonna kill her and then you're gonna have to shoot me 'cause I'm not goin' to jail — not for that. I mean if anything's justifiable homicide, that oughta be, honest to God. I'm not jokin', Mar, nobody should have to listen to somebody else try to figure out what shade of brown her stools are! Jesus!"

"Why don't you just walk away from her?"

"If I'm workin' in the yard I can't just

walk away, I'm doin' something!"

"Tell her the phone's ringin'."

"She's not deaf, Mar, there's nothin' wrong with her ears."

"All the more reason to tell her. That way she'll know you don't wanna listen to her."

"Oh God, she was a perfectly decent person for, I don't know, lovely person, for God, long as we've lived here. Then she starts with this, uh, what? This stool color analysis, Jesus, you'd think she was askin' you what color to paint her kitchen."

"Water's boilin'."

"Promise me, Mar, I mean it. You'll shoot me, okay?"

"Alright, alright, I'll shoot ya, okay? Jesus. One minute you can't remember why you wind up in bed, next thing you know you're bein' solicited to commit murder. Swear to God, the whole god-damn thing's comin' unglued."

They were just finishing eating and debating about whether to watch the news when the phone rang. Ruth answered it, chatted for a long moment with her back turned to

Balzic, then turned and held the phone out. "It's Mo," she said.

Oh shit, Balzic thought, heaving himself out of his chair. He hadn't delivered even one tape. Oh man. "Yes, Panagios, what's up?"

"Mario, how you feelin'? How's it goin'?"

"Ah, slow, you know. It's, uh, it's goin' real slow."

"But you're feelin' alright though, right?"

"Yeah, you know. I'm comin' along I guess, sure."

"Well, Mario, listen, I've explained to Bertelli, you know, what's going on with you, and he's sympathetic of course, but, uh, he's thinking, you know, maybe, under the circumstances, he should get somebody else. Told him I'd much rather pay you than anybody else, but, uh, can I tell him something? I have to tell him something, you know?"

"Tell him somethin'? Ha. Tell him what? Tell him the truth. I've talked to three of the principals, got nowhere with two of them."

"Well, if I come by, can I have the tapes?"

"Sure, but the only one worth listenin' to is with the state cop who wrote it up. There's nothin' with the security guy, he's

256

strictly fulla shit, the CEO, and, uh, even less with the guy he fired, except the CEO claims not to know the guy he fired was on pro when he hired him and also won't say why he fired him, which, far as I'm concerned, is enough right there to stink up everything."

"Uh-huh. So, uh, when do you think you can get to the rest?"

"Well, I'm sorta doin' this all over the phone, and, uh —"

"Well that's what Ruth said — what, you're not allowed to drive?"

"No no, I'm allowed to drive, that's not it. Ruth said that?" He turned and gave Ruth a look. "Ruth said I'm not allowed to drive?"

"No no, she didn't say that exactly, she just sort of said you were, uh, you know, having a little trouble gettin' back on the horse so to speak. Listen, I'm not trying to pressure you, but, uh, I have to tell Bertelli something, so, uh . . ."

"Look, I just don't feel real comfortable drivin' right now."

"Well at least you can admit it now," Ruth said, as she was putting dishes in the sink. "That's a start."

"Yeah I don't, okay?"

"You talking to me?" Valcanas said.

"No. Ruth. She was just goin' by here."

"Well explain it to him, why don't you?" Ruth said. "You sure don't wanna talk to me about it."

"I don't wanna talk about it at all right now, okay?"

"Look, forget the tapes," Valcanas said. "I just need something to tell Bertelli, that's all —"

"Wasn't talkin' to you, I was talkin' to Ruth —"

"Well how can you work for him and not leave the house?"

"Interviewin' is interviewin', what difference does it make how I do it?"

"Look, you're the one always told me how lousy interviews on the phone were. Said half the interview was observing their reactions, the words were only half the answers —"

"Think maybe I'll come by tomorrow," Valcanas said.

"You can get 'em right now, I'll be here —"

"You better not be thinkin' what I think you're thinkin', Mar —"

"I think I'll get them tomorrow," Valcanas said.

"Fine. Tomorrow. I'll still be here — 'less my wife kicks me outta the house, the way she's lookin' right now, hey . . ."

"See you tomorrow. I'll call first," Valcanas said.

Ruth was glaring at him when he hung up.

"I know what you're gonna say," he said.

"No you don't."

"Yes I do and before you say it, I'm gonna agree you're right. And I'm gonna agree further, you know, it's what you said before, it's one of those things it's real simple, it's just also extremely difficult, that's all, one of life's little onion crushers, you know?"

"Mario, listen to me. You are not gonna lock yourself in this house, not over one artery that used to be closed but is now open. Because you're not just doin' it to you, you're also doin' it to me, and I will not be locked up — not over that."

"I agree," he said, nodding many times. "Told ya before, you're right, already said it, already agree."

"If you already agree, then what? C'mon, tell me."

"Told ya, it's one of those things it's real simple, it just ain't easy. It's a ball-buster, you know? Understand ball-buster?"

"Yes, but what does *this* ball-buster mean? C'mon. Exactly."

"Exactly?" He began to pace, throwing up his hands, banging them against his thighs. "It's a — I don't know — a different kind of fear, that's all, a kind I never dealt with before —"

"Oh God, don't tell me that. There's nobody I know who's dealt with more kinds of fear than you have —"

"Yeah yeah, right, but most of the ones I've dealt with, I mean, hey, they were comin' at me from outside, understand?"

"Fear comes from here, Mar," Ruth said, tapping her chest with her right hand. "You've been tellin' me that forever. It's the whole fight-or-flight thing, doesn't matter what causes it, it all comes from the same place, you know? Inside? So what's different about this?"

"Yeah, right, okay, but the things from outside, you learn how to deal with 'em, you know? You learn which of those things you can deal with and which you can't and what kinda moves you can make —"

"Fear is fear, Mar, you said so a hundred times —"

"No it isn't, no it isn't —"

"Mar, if it all starts in the brain and sends your blood away from your skin and raises your blood pressure and sends your heart rate up —"

"See? That last one you just said, that's new —"

"It is not new, Mar, it's the same old heart rate goin' up —"

"Oh no, uh-uh, no. May sound the same, maybe feels the same, but now, see, it's not comin' from the outside, it's the thing itself that's doin' it, the heart's doin' it, see? And that changes everything!"

"It can't, Mar! You can't let it!"

"It ain't about me lettin' it or not lettin' it. It's not some asshole with a knife at his wife's throat and he's darin' me to make a move, like if he cuts her, you know, it's my fault 'cause he wouldn't't've done it except I made a move on him — that's not what this is! This is all from inside — everything! I know what to do with the asshole with the knife. I don't know what to do with this," he said, slapping his chest with both hands. "This is all me here. I know this sounds stupid, but I'm the asshole husband, I'm the wife, I'm me at the door, I got the knife, I'm the wife, I'm the cop, I'm all here at once, and I don't have a fuckin' clue what move to make. I'm so scared to make a wrong move, I don't wanna make any. Move."

"Oh Mar," she said, shaking her head and coming at him and putting her arms around him and squeezing him. "You can't give up, Mar. You can't turn this house into a jail. You can't, Mar. Some people, that happens, they don't have a choice. But you have a choice, Mar, don't shake your head, Mar, you do!"

"I know," he said, tears rolling down his cheeks. "I know what you're sayin'. I know you're right. I'm just . . . so scared . . ."

"Of what? What, Mar, tell me."

"Missus Wrobelewski . . . all the Missus Wrobelewskis . . . they're all waitin' for me."

She put her forehead on his chin. Then she tilted her head back and said, "Listen, Mar, I'm gonna tell you something. There's nobody waitin' for us. When it's done, it's done. So if you wanna feel bad because you think you didn't do right for this Missus What's-her-ski, go right ahead. But you're wastin' time — and not just yours. Mine too. Thinkin' some judge is gonna be waitin' with an information signed against you, that's just a waste of time."

Balzic pulled his head back and stared at her. "What're you sayin'? You know what you're sayin'? You went to Catholic school same as me — you're sayin' you don't believe there's anything else?"

"Didn't believe it when I was ten, how

262

could I believe it now?"

"Ten? What happened — oh oh, your sister, Jesus, I forgot."

"My sister, yes."

"But wait, wait. From then on, you never believed?"

She nodded emphatically.

"But Jesus, you went through everything, with Marie, with Emily, you mean the whole time, that was all frontin' — because of your sister?"

"Not because of my sister. What the nun said to my mother."

"Oh yeah okay, I remember about the nun and your mother, I mean somebody shoulda smacked her in the mouth, that nun, but, uh, what're you sayin' now — everything you did with the kids, confirmation, confession, communion, all that, that was all front?"

"Yes."

"For who for crissake? Not for me, I ain't buyin' that."

"No, not for you. Everybody else. Mostly your mother."

"You did that for my mother? Why?"

"Oh God, Mar, why do you think?"

"You didn't wanna hurt her?"

"Of course. I loved her, I thought she loved me —"

"You thought? Giddoutta here. Shit, she loved you, you kiddin'? Sometimes a lot more'n she loved me."

"So what was I supposed to do — have some big argument with her?"

"But you told her what happened with the nun and your mother — I know you did — didn't you?"

"Yes. We talked about it a coupla times."

"So, uh, what — you left out how it affected you? You didn't tell her that part?"

"Of course not! What was I supposed to say, huh?" Ruth said. "Because of some stupid brainless twerp nun — Jesus, that still makes me mad. Was I supposed to tell *your* mother that the worst part *for me* was *my mother* kept goin' back to church? Every Sunday. And every Sunday I used to look at her and ask myself, how could she do that? How could she keep goin' back after what that nun said? A doctor screws up, your daughter dies, an idiot nun tells you a good mother wouldn't've let her die — five minutes after you find out your daughter's dead that idiot makes that crack — and you spend the rest of your life beatin' yourself up? Because of this one stupid nun? And — and this is the part I could never get, I still don't get it — you keep goin' back to church? The same church where the nun goes? How do you do that?"

Balzic was intensely relieved to have somebody else to talk about instead of himself. "So, uh, how do you know your mother wasn't doin' the same thing you just said you were doin' — same thing you did with our daughters? How do you know she wasn't? Ever talk to her?"

"About this? No," Ruth said, shaking her head very rapidly. "No, I should've, always regretted not doin' that. Don't look at me like that, I know it was dumb, I just couldn't do it, that's all."

"That's all? C'mon."

"Okay, I didn't think it was right, okay? I didn't think I had any right to talk to her about that."

"So with all the catechism tests you passed, all those A's you got, you were frontin' the whole time? Lyin'?"

"Yes."

"The whole time you were puttin' our kids through the drill?"

"Yes," Ruth said. "Yes! 'Cause it was easier than havin' a fight with my mother, or worse, really, much worse, 'cause I was a lot closer to your mother — it was a lot worse to front for your mother, 'cause I would never've done anything to hurt her."

"You took my mother to Mass every Sunday —"

"Yes."

"And stood right beside her. And crossed yourself —"

"Yes."

"And knelt, and confessed, and took communion —"

"Yes."

"Incredible. What the hell were you confessin' to?"

"That I was a hypocrite."

Balzic threw back his head and roared. "You confessed to bein' a hypocrite? And you were bein' a hypocrite confessin'? Ahhhh, Ruthie, Jesus, you are too fucking devious for words. Just so you wouldn't hurt my mother? And she never suspected?"

"I don't think she did, no. But maybe she didn't wanna say anything, I don't know."

"You're too fuckin' much, Ruthie, swear to God you are. How long we been married? Forty-three years? Fooled the shit outta me. You oughta be runnin' the CIA."

"So see?"

"See what?"

"Quit worryin' about Missus Whositsski. She's not waitin' for you. Neither's anybody else."

"Wait wait, you don't know this, this is just your opinion —"

"Mario, listen to me, Mo's right."

"Mo? What's he right about? How'd he get into this?"

"He told me one time, somebody's funeral, or the wake, I forget, he said, all these people that believe in eternity? They don't know what to do with themselves on a Sunday afternoon if the electricity goes off, what are they gonna do with themselves for all eternity? He said most of the people he knew couldn't sit still for five minutes with nothin' to do without feelin' like they wanted to kill somebody."

"Yeah I've heard that. Still, what people do with it or don't do with it has nothin' to do with whether there's an eternity or not —"

"Personally, Mar, I don't care what anybody does with it. Eighty, ninety years is gonna be more than enough for me, thank you. Especially if I can't walk. 'Cause if I can't get to the bathroom? Uh-uh, I hate bedpans. I'm not hangin' around to make the insurance companies rich. They already have too much money."

"Ruthie, the longer I know you, the

more you surprise me."

"Yeah? Well, it's even goofier you want the truth. 'Cause sometimes I wanna believe. Sometimes I wanna believe so bad I'm praying it's true."

Balzic laughed and shook his head. "Oh this I gotta hear. When?"

"When? Ha! When else? When I think if there's an eternity I'd have enough time to find that doctor — that klutz? That son of a bitch who said it was just menstrual cramps?"

"Yeah, okay, I remember."

"Cramps. The son of a bitch." Tears welled up in her eyes. "Afterwards, he says it was her appendix ruptured — after, he tells us that, not before, the son of a bitch . . ."

"I know," he said.

"Sometimes, I wish there *was* an eternity just so I could hunt the son of a bitch down and kill him. I know it's stupid . . . but I really liked my sister." She buried her face in his chest and sobbed. "I still miss her . . ."

After a minute, she pulled away from him, got some tissues and blew her nose and wiped her eyes. Then she looked at him with a seriousness, an intensity that made him turn away.

"Mar, look at me. I know how scared you are. But you're not half as scared as I am — oh shit, I hate myself for saying this, you know I do, but I can't help it — you've got to get outta here! You can't keep talkin' to people on the phone, Mar —"

"I'm tryin', Ruthie, Jesus Christ, I'm tryin' —"

"Try harder! I mean it, Mar. For your sake, for both our sakes, don't trap yourself in here. You trap you, you trap me, please, please, make yourself understand that . . . please . . ."

Balzic, his throat tight, his chest tight, his jaw tight, trying with everything that was in him to breathe deeply and fully from his diaphragm, pulled his Chevy into a parking slot at the Rocksburg Mall near the back door of Freedom Firearms. He got out in air so cold his nostrils pinched reflexively. He pulled his knit cap down over his ears and his hood up over his knit cap, and, clutching the collar of his parka with his left hand, tramped through about an inch of crunchy snow to get to the back door of the gunshop.

When he was about five steps away he could plainly see the jimmy marks. Nothing subtle about them. But he had no interest in them; what he was trying to do by acting interested was attract the guard from Bulldog Security. On the other hand, he was hoping for all kinds of things — anything — to take his mind off the tightness in his body from his ears to his hips.

Just when he thought the cold had deepened every spasm in his back and neck that his fear was causing him, he heard a vehicle stop behind him. He turned and saw the mall's security Jeep pulling in behind his Chevy, blocking it, and then in a moment someone in uniform was approaching cautiously, calling out to him.

"Yo, what's up, sir? Somethin' I can help you with?"

During all the conflicting emotions he'd felt while getting out of the house today in preparation for coming here, Balzic had not been able to find the letter Valcanas had written for him to carry the last time he'd worked for Valcanas. All the letter had said was that Balzic had applied for a private investigator's license and that it was being processed, neither of which was true, but it had been intended to mollify everybody Balzic might encounter who was too lazy or indifferent to do more checking. Since nobody had ever checked, the letter had succeeded. But because Balzic hadn't found it today, and because he didn't want to admit to Valcanas that he couldn't find it, he'd stuck his Rocksburg PD credentials in his pocket, even though he knew that by showing his chief's badge and ID he was opening himself to a legitimate charge of impersonating a police officer, since he had not been one for nearly two years now. Out of date was out of date; retired was retired.

He thought he could get away with it by holding the case up in his left hand with his index finger over the valid dates, but that would work only if this security guard didn't ask to examine the case. If he did, it wouldn't be just an embarrassment: impersonating a public official was a second-degree misdemeanor, which, as the shysters liked to say, included but was not limited to his own legal fees, court costs, and the likely prospect that he could wind up in front of a judge who had a hard-on for him, in which case, two years max was the legal possibility. And if that wasn't enough stupidity to mull over, Balzic knew that this guard would have to be comatose not to know that this mall in Westfield Township was on state police turf, out of Rocksburg jurisdiction even if Balzic was not retired.

So Balzic held up his ID case, left index finger covering the last date of service, and told the lie that he was assisting Trooper Milliron from the Troop A Barracks in his investigation. What Milliron had said in the cardiac intermediate care unit was that it wouldn't be any skin off his ego if Balzic cleared the case for him, which was not quite the same as asking for assistance. And even as the words were coming out of his mouth, Balzic knew he was sounding stupider by the minute and being stupider, and all because he hadn't been able to find Mo's letter and didn't want to tell Mo that he couldn't find it.

The black security guard stopped four feet from Balzic, leaned forward and held his hand out and motioned for Balzic to turn over the ID case. Oh shit, Balzic thought, starting to shuffle forward, but the security guard stopped him.

"Just stand where you are, sir. Just lean forward and hand it over, okay?"

When Balzic did, the guard took one quick glance at it and said, "This is two years old, man. And you're not the chief in Rocksburg. Maybe you used to be the chief, but you ain't now. Chief in Rocksburg's named Nowicki. And the reason I know that is 'cause I just interviewed with the man for a job. So now what's up, uh, what's this say — chief what?"

"Balzic." Both his arms flew in against his ribs as he shivered convulsively from head to knees.

"Man, you awright? I know it's cold out here, but you don't look so good."

"I'm just cold, that's all."

"Well get on in the Jeep, no need for either one of us to be freezin'. Go 'head on, I'm right behind you."

Balzic crawled into the front passenger seat, but the security guard got in the backseat behind him. He leaned forward and said, "Put your hands on the dash, sir."

Balzic put his hands on the dash, and nodded once. "Whatever you say, Mister Rayford."

"Who?"

"Rayford. That's your name, right?"

"Who told you that?"

"Trooper Milliron."

"Uh-huh. So, uh, I call Troop A right now and get this trooper? Huh? What's his name again?"

"Milliron. Claude. CID."

"Uh-huh. I call him, he's goin' back you on this? And don't be bullshittin' me now."

"You mean back me on the B and E?"

"Now what do you think I mean, sir, huh? That door you were lookin' at just now, it's not the back door of Victoria's Secret."

"Why're you so nervous, Mister Rayford? You didn't have anything to do with this, we both know that."

"Listen to you," Rayford said, snorting. "First you know my name, now you know I didn't do somethin' — this the first time I ever seen you, man, what's up with you?"

"Why're you so nervous I said —"

"If you don't mind, sir, I'll be askin' the questions here, okay?"

"Fine. Ask 'em."

"So what's up with you with your outta-date ID? And no bullshit, sir, okay?"

"Look. Here it is. No bullshit." Balzic explained how he'd been hired by Mo Valcanas, who'd been hired by Albert Bertelli. Balzic explained about Valcanas's letter and how he couldn't find it and how he knew it was stupid to flash an expired ID and even stupider to tell those lame lies, but he thought he was going to encounter the usual rent-a-cop, he didn't

274

know he was going to run into anybody sharp.

"Uh-huh. And you know I'm sharp because why now?"

"Well, look where you're sittin' and look where I'm sittin'. Most rent-a-cops I know woulda never got outta the vehicle in the first place."

"Not s'pposed to get out the vehicle, sir, I got any doubt. S'pposed to do all my talkin' through the PA, s'pposed to keep one hand on the mike at all times. You who you say you are, you know that. You know all I got's the mike — and my four-cell Mag-Lite."

"Yeah? So who was on the mike the night this went down?"

"Excuse me, sir, I'm still askin' the questions here, not you. What're you doin' here? And don't be bullshittin' me now, okay?"

"What I'm doin' here is I wanted to talk to you without goin' through your boss, that's what I'm doin' here." He didn't want to get into the real reason he was there, which was to test his nerve about getting out of the house and driving.

"Say what? Talk to me without goin' through my boss?"

"That's what I said."

"Get out the car, man."

"What?"

"Get out the vehicle. Now! I ain't goin' tell you again. Out!"

"What's the problem?"

"You're the problem. Get out now! Go sit in your vehicle and don't move till I tell ya — and don't be doin' nothin' stupid, okay?" Rayford got out quickly, jerked open the passenger door, and poked his thumb several times over his shoulder toward Balzic's Chevy.

"I'm not your problem," Balzic said, hunching through the wind toward the Chevy.

"Just get in your car, man, I don't wanna hear nothin', okay?"

"I'm tellin' you, I'm not your problem, I just wanna talk to you."

Gloved hands splayed, Rayford glared at Balzic and waited. Balzic got into his Chevy, started the engine, and turned the heater up as high as it would go. God, it's cold, he thought, shuddering and shivering, feeling the cold deep in his chest. He hoped Ruth was satisfied, now that he was out of the house and all, pretending he wasn't scared silly, while one morbid image after another kept bouncing and banging off the walls of his mind: him collapsing in front of mocking strangers, giggly with contempt for his cowardice, who stepped over his body after they grew bored with watching him squirm with fear; him losing control of his bladder and bowels, vomiting, sweating, everything in him coming out and freezing upon contact with frigid air because hell had never been a hot place in his mind. Hell had always been a silvery slippery place with white-hot fire fueled by chunks of ice that burned like coal.

Well he hoped Ruth was satisfied, goddammit. 'Cause here he was in the middle of February, in the parking lot of a mall, a more lifeless place he could not imagine, with a wind chill of minus double digits outside the metal shell of his Chevy. What the hell was he doing here? Couldn't have called this guard on the phone? Talked to him from someplace warm? I'm freezin' my ass doing what exactly — investigating this inside boost? Or defying Ruth, playin' head games with her? What the hell am I doing? Do I know what I'm doin'? Besides Albert Bertelli, is there anyone on the planet willing to give more than one molecule of sweat off their asses about this burglary?

And then there she was, her head right on the middle of the hood, her face frozen in fury at his lazy indifference, his pious police platitudes about teenage stuff, a phase, that's all it was . . . you have to believe me, Jesus Christ Almighty, Missus Wrobelewski, I'm sorry, honest to God I am, I know I should've sent you to see a priest, a social worker, anybody, maybe the kid would've made it, maybe he wouldn't have, I don't know, but you're right, I know you are, I know I shoulda got somebody else involved in it, shouldn't've just given you that crap about so much teenage melodrama . . . aw fuckit, lady, give me a break, what the fuck did I know, I didn't know shit from shoe polish, I didn't know straight up, my kids weren't even born yet, I didn't know what the hell to do with depressed kids, I didn't even know what the fuck depression was — was I supposed to? Hell, my kids were girls anyway, I don't know what I would've done with a boy . . . no consolation to you . . . but how many ways can you say you're sorry? How many ways — oh yeah, right, now listen to me, I'm bitchin' at a goddamn hallucination, tryin' to cop an out with her, good God Almighty, what the fuck is up with me? . . .

"You alright?" Rayford was knocking on the window, peering in.

"Yeah. What? Don't I look alright?"

"Open the other door, sir."

"Why?" Balzic was still slightly befuddled from the vision of Mrs. Wrobelewski's head on the hood.

"Open the door, man, c'mon, it's cold out here."

Balzic reached across the seat and pulled the lock stem up with a grunt. Then he looked at Rayford as he got in, studied him, anything to try to take his mind off himself.

"Checked you out, sir," Rayford said. "Milliron backs you up. So's your guys in Rocksburg. Which, uh, incidentally, you got any juice there?"

"Any what?"

"Juice, you know, pull, influence, connections, power, man, I don't know what you wanna call it, I need a job, that's all I know. I'm starvin' on what these people're payin' me. Got a kid ready to pop in about two months."

"And what? You tradin' information for a job recommendation — is that what this is now?"

"Hey, look around, man, where we sittin'? Middle of a place not a damn thing else happens 'cept trade. People's middle name is trade, this is America, what's wrong with that? You tellin' me that ain't how you clear most cases? Damn near all of 'em? Better tell somebody else, man, I was Air Force CID for damn near four years, that's how we cleared everything. One man's cooperation is another man's confession."

"So, uh, for this recommendation you want from me, uh, what exactly are you gonna give me back?"

"Names of the people you can't get from Mister Beckmaier, and don't tell me he's been givin' 'em to you, him and his girlfriend, 'cause you wouldn't be out here tryin' to talk to me without goin' through him, now would you? Anyway, his Fruit of the Looms are about to get wet, and don't say you don't know what I'm talkin' about."

"His Fruit of the Looms?"

"Yeah, right, the man's about to piss all over himself."

"Why didn't you say anything to Milliron?"

"Hey, I keep lookin' for the man to come back and talk to me, but he ain't so far. But he doesn't have any more juice with the state police commissioner than I do, and I've been on their list since I got discharged. Which, if I'da had my way I wouldn't've, understand? Wife couldn't stand Alabama. Thinks her goddamn sisters're more important than government insurance, or the PX, or the commissary, or per diem, or re-up bonuses. Damn. You have any idea what I got to make out here to match what I made in there? Huh? So damn right I'm tradin' names for job juice. You want 'em? I'll give 'em to you. But you better tell me you're gonna make some serious phone calls with my name all over 'em, otherwise, forget me. Okay?

"And so you know what you're talkin' about when you start talkin' me up? Here's my particulars. Except for basic, four years CID, ninety hours criminal justice U.S. Armed Forces Institute, recommended for reenlistment, Good Conduct Medal, two citations for investigative excellence, two meritorious promotions — damn, don't you think I wasn't sharp 'cause I was. And now all I'm doin' is drivin' around in this dumb-ass Jeep. So what's it goin' be ex-chief, sir? We tradin' or not?"

"Hey, I can promise anything, doesn't mean I can deliver."

"All you have to tell me is you will talk to Chief Nowicki, that's all you have to do to deliver. Remind him he's got my app, he interviewed me, he told me I was on the short list — if no political shit got into it —

and the last thing we talked about was would I be willin' to move to Rocksburg. I told him, hey, right now, for twenty-eight five a year and benefits, I'd move to hell. I ain't got no problem movin' here. That's all you have to say."

Balzic shrugged. "Okay, I can say that. So, your turn now."

"No shit? I got your righteous word? Don't play with me, hear? You know what thirty-six hours of minimum wage buys you? We're livin' with my sister-in-law and her two kids and my mother-in-law's gettin' ready to move in, man, do you hear me? My mother-in-law! And we been livin' like this for a year, man, and now, Momma's comin'! I got to get my wife away from that woman — you hear what I'm sayin'?"

"I hear you, I hear you, you got my word. I will call Nowicki — if what you tell me is worth callin' about."

"Okay, okay, listen up, then you decide. I can say the man in the Jeep the night the shit went down was named Wilbur McFate, dumb-ass redneck from up on Chestnut Ridge someplace. And the man who went in the back door? That was a dude just got fired, name of Cozzolino."

"Keep talkin', I'm listenin'," Balzic said.

"What'd this McFate tell you?"

"Told me Cozzolino told him this waitress in the Ground Round had a thing for uniforms. Told him maybe he should check her out, see if she liked the way he wore his. This was right after he got fired, understand? McFate said he just sorta bumped into him one day out here, Cozzolino, and he knew what days of the week she worked, and what hours, and so on. Now what you gotta understand is, I was not askin' McFate for any of this. He just volunteered alla this, it just come spillin' outta him, I didn't even know what he was talkin' about. All I asked him was what was up, you know, casual chitchat, that's all, when he was handin' over the keys to the Jeep. I'm sayin' hi y'all doin', he's spillin' his guts. It was obvious, man, the dude was scared, which at the time made absolutely no sense.

"Couple hours later now, when I meet Trooper Milliron, I said to myself, oh, so, *that's* what all that bullshit was about. That was his way, McFate's, you know, of tellin' me he knew Cozzolino was the back-door man, and wasn't givin' a damn about his love life, I mean, hey, figure it out. I got all this in about one minute of conversation when he was turnin' over the keys. If I can get all that outta McFate without knowin' what I was doin'? You oughta be able to break him in about five minutes. That boy's scared to death people think he's stupid. Wantsa be cool so bad, you can almost smell it on him. Plus, now he gotta be thinkin' — 'less he's really stupid — hey, you know, that he's up for what Cozzolino did. But . . ."

"Yeah? I'm still listening, but what?"

"Well, you tell me, man. Your guys — your used-to-be guys, you know? Said you were so sharp?"

"Christ, how many people did you talk to? Couldn't've talked to that many, you weren't gone long enough."

"Just two, man. Fish-somethin' and Carlucci. Those dudes respect the hell outta you. So go 'head, you tell me what's up."

"McFate still workin'?"

"He is," Rayford said, smiling.

"And he can't understand why."

"He surely cannot. And?"

"And you found out Cozzolino's got a sheet."

"And?"

"The chief executive officer of Bulldog Security is either a thief or an asshole."

"So now," Rayford said, smiling large, "I believe you can appreciate me wantin' to move my career toward people who actually enforce the law sometimes, 'stead of gettin' blisters on my ass."

"Uh-huh. So now tell me again why you didn't tell all this to Milliron, why's that again?"

"The trooper? 'Cause he was talkin' to Beckmaier, man. And that Bemiss. All standin' right there by the door. He didn't ask me but two questions, you know, what time did my shift start and did I start on time, that's all. When was I s'pposed to tell him?"

"Coulda called him."

"Why? If the man's doin' his job he should be callin' me."

"He's got other things to do."

"Aw shit, man, don't say that. You sayin' they got so few people a damn week has gone by and he ain't got time to make one follow-up call on this? Man, this is a major crime here. See there? See what I'm talkin'? I been on the state police list for a whole goddamn year now, you gotta talk to Nowicki for me, man."

"I will, I will, I said I would. So, uh, you have anything to do with this Cozzolino?"

"Whatta you mean did I? Did I what? What're you sayin'?"

"I'm not sayin' anything — in your work

285

here I'm talkin' about."

"Oh. No. Nothin'. No, he walked, I rode. Saw him a couple times, that's all. Never even spoke to the dude."

"Hear anything about why he got fired?"

"Attitude problem is what I heard. But they coulda said he wasn't wide enough or his teeth was too short, what difference would ita made? How they goin' explain the man had a sheet, huh? And be in the security business? I mean come on. You can't background your own employees how you gonna background anybody else's? Or what else they goin' say? A year after they hired him they found out he had a sheet? Shit. I need to get away from these people 'fore they give me a case of the screamin' stupids — which they got, and stupidity is contagious, man, don't let nobody tell you it ain't."

"Well, lemme see what I can do," Balzic said. "Meantime, I gotta go, okay?" He held out his hand. "Don't squeeze, okay?"

"S'matter? Arthuritis?"

"Huh? No, it ain't arthuritis. It's arthritis. Three syllables. Don't put that extra syllable in there. Ar-thri-tis. Okay? Somethin', yeah. Pleasure, Mister Rayford."

Rayford stared at Balzic for a long moment, still holding Balzic's hand gently but not shaking it. Then he started to chuckle. "Man, what's up with you? Goin' correct my speech and tell me it's a pleasure to meet me in the same breath? Sound like my Aunt Shasta, man, no shit. Hug me so hard like to break my ribs, tell me my breath was bad."

Balzic shrugged, pulled his hand away, and said, "You're a bright guy, I don't wanna recommend somebody's gonna sound like he can't pronounce certain words. Gives people the wrong impression. You wanna move up, you gotta talk the talk, that's all. Nothin' personal. What'd you do after your aunt let go of you, huh?"

Rayford laughed hard.

"Brushed your teeth, didn't ya? Don't lie. You did, I know you did."

"Aw man, go on, get outta here."

"You did. Say it. She let me go, I scooted off by myself, cupped my hand over my mouth and smelled myself, then I went and brushed my teeth. Say it."

Rayford opened the door with a snort. "Damn. My auntie got a soul brother."

"Say it, you brushed your teeth, I know you did. Say it."

Rayford closed the passenger door, came around the front of the Chevy, and stopped by the driver's side. "Okay. Alright. I went and brushed my teeth. You happy now?"

"Yeah," Balzic said, putting the Chevy in reverse. "Happy to recommend you're a man who takes instruction well. That's always good. Now if you'll just move your Jeep I can get outta here."

Balzic drove home through whirling powdery snow, barely enough to cover the ground, the wind sending the snow across the macadam and concrete in weak tornadoes. It was a perfect reflection of his emotions, low, high, spinning first this way, then that, coming, going, nothing substantial enough to buttress a coherent argument or to solidify a point of view. On a scale of one to ten, ten being the worst, his anxiety level was about a seven. He couldn't wait to get home. The hell with this interviewing people face-to-face. Maybe in a week I'll be ready to do this, maybe in a month. Shit. Maybe never. What the hell's so wrong about interviewing people over the phone? Difference between radio and TV, that's all it is. Just have to develop a different attitude about it, that's all. Oh bullshit, he thought

— watch it! Got-damn! Where the fuck'd he come from, you idiot! Just need half the road, that's all I need, stupid sonofabitch . . . oh man, get home, just let me get home, that's all, don't wanna be out here with these crazies, every time you get in the car anymore's a goddamn adventure, take your fuckin' life in your hands, swear to God, just leavin' the house . . . that's the problem, ain't it, Balzic? Huh? Admit it. Scared to leave the house. Got your little bottle of nitro, got your little ninny, yeah, Marie, Emily, remember them, huh? Walkin' around the house, thumb in their mouths, with Marie it was half a bath towel . . . Emily it was a diaper, yeah, sure. With me it's a bottle of nitro, all I need to do is stick my thumb in my mouth, that's all, run around with my little ninny, look at little Mario there, suckin' his thumb, 'bout to piss his pants . . . fuckin' marine . . . yessirree, survived Iwo fucking Jima, hand-to-hand with Japs, starin' down fuckin' machine guns, thirty-some fuckin' years a cop, mind's so fucking addled can't even remember how many years I was a fuckin' cop, all of a sudden the man's scared to death to leave his house . . . two fucking blocked arteries he's about to piss his pants . . . Jesus, Mary, and Joseph. . . .

"How'd it go?" Ruth said, leaning back around the kitchen door frame when he came in stomping drops of water off his shoes. "Go okay?"

"Yeah, sure. Why? Look like it didn't?"

"Just asking, that's all."

"Hey. Nothin' to it. Met a nice kid. Sharp. Pleasure to talk to, really. Asked me to, uh, give him a recommendation."

"A what?"

"Recommendation."

"For what?"

"Ah, he, uh, apparently he just interviewed with, uh, Nowicki. You know. Down the department? Didn't even know they were interviewin'. Hell, how was I s'pposed to know that? Anyway, he, uh, he wantsa get outta where he is, you know, gettin' blisters on his ass playin' Wyatt Earp in a Jeep, so, you know, he asked me could I do somethin' for him, so I said yeah. Sharp kid. Smart. Make a good detective." Balzic was pulling his clothes off, gloves, cap, scarf, parka, hanging them up in the hall closet, clearing his throat, hoping the front he was showing now had more to it than the snow he'd just driven through. God, he needed a glass of wine. A big one. What time was it? Holy shit, it's not even noon, he thought. Fuckit. I'm chokin' here, my fuckin' throat's closin', I got to get some wine in me, this is fucking nuts. . . .

"You hungry?" Ruth said. "If you can wait about five minutes, I'll have this salmon salad ready. Think it's gonna be decent. Want it on some romaine or you just want it on a plate or you wanna make a sandwich? Didn't you make bread yesterday? Thought you made bread. What happened to it?"

"Naw, I don't know how old that bread is. Might be okay you toast it." He opened the fridge door and bent over from the waist. "We outta wine? Jesus. Didn't we just get some? Yesterday?"

"Day before I think. You want wine? For lunch? Don't usually, I mean, you haven't been, uh . . . never mind."

"Haven't been what?"

"Drinkin' wine for lunch — never mind."

"Who said I wasn't doin' that?"

"You did. You said you thought you were drinkin' too much —"

"You think I'm drinkin' too much?"

"I didn't say you were drinkin' too much, I said you said you thought you were drinkin' too much, said you were gonna try to cut down a little, maybe not start so early in the day, maybe not for lunch — I didn't say that, you said that —"

"When'd I say that, I don't remember sayin' that — did I say that? Well who the hell's drinkin' it if I'm cuttin' down? Huh? Carafe's empty. I drink it, then what — I put an empty carafe back in the fridge? Man, I don't know what I'm doin' anymore."

"Yes you do, you're just a little . . ."

"Little what?"

"Just a little, uh, frazzled, you know? Around the edges, that's all. You'll get over it. There's more wine downstairs, I know we're not out. Not of yours. Now I might be out, but I don't think you are. I'll go look."

"No no, I'll look. I can look, you don't have to do that, you're doin' things here —"

"Mario, it's no big deal —"

"I didn't say it was a big deal, I'm not tryin' to make a big deal, I'm just sayin' I can look myself, you know? That's all I'm sayin', okay?"

"Mario, what's wrong? Something happen? Huh?"

"Huh? Nothin' happened. Why? What?"

"You're looking really frazzled, Mar, why

don't you let me go check the wine —"

"Because I wanna get it myself, okay? What, you don't think I can go downstairs by myself, huh? Or come back up? I can go down there, my legs work, nothin' wrong with my legs —"

Ruth backed away and held up her hands. "Sorry. Go then. Go!"

He started down, looked back at her, scowled, started to say she didn't need to be sorry or feel sorry or say she was sorry about anything, but he didn't. He kept his mouth shut for a change and went down the stairs toward the old fridge where he kept the large jugs of wine. He put his hand on the fridge door and felt the tears rolling down his cheeks, and the next thing he knew he was struggling to keep from sobbing. Oh fuck, what is this, what the fuck is this, is this what I'm gonna do now? Huh? Every fuckin' time I turn around I'm gonna start bawlin'? Jesus fuck, this is ridiculous, this is absurd, this is bullshit . . . oh yeah? If this is bullshit, then I shouldn't be scared. But I am. Oh God, what the fuck, why am I scared? What the fuck am I scared of? Missus Wrobelewski? Do I really think she's waitin' for me? Do I think everybody I ever didn't help is waitin' for me? And what the fuck are they gonna do to me? Huh? Where are they waitin'? In hell? In purgatory? I don't believe in that shit. I haven't believed in that shit since Iwo. That was hell. That was purgatory. Iwo was purgatory. If that wasn't hell, if that wasn't purgatory, there ain't any hell. No purgatory either. So? What? Is that where I'm goin'? Back to Iwo? That's insane. Iwo's not hell anymore. It's a fuckin' island in the Pacific, that's all it is. What is this shit? I'm stuck on Missus Wrobelewski and Iwo Jima, blubberin' my guts out? For what? What do I think's gonna happen to me? I'm gonna die? I'm gonna die and have to face all the people I didn't help I shoulda helped? Jesus Christ, they all gotta have better things to do than sit around waitin' for me to settle up! That's nothin' but ego talkin', that's all that is, fuckin' arrogance. Me me me me! I'm so important, all the people who fucked up their lives because I didn't help them — oh God, *this* is hell! *This* is purgatory. This, right here, right now, me doin' this to me, this is hell! Me thinkin' I'm so fucking important I coulda did this or that or whatever to've saved all these miserable bastards couldn't save themselves . . . boy, Balzic, you ever think for a second you had this kinda face, huh? This kinda arrogance? That you were so fucking important to these people they couldn't straighten out their messes unless you did it for them?

Oh, man. Oh man oh man. Now what? Huh? I'll tell you what, Balzic, you ready? This is the problem here, big boy. Get ready. You're nobody. You're nothin'. You don't influence a fuckin' thing. Nobody needs you. It was nothin' but fuckin' arrogance to ever think you coulda had anything whatsoever to do with whether anybody changed their life one fucking molecule because of anything you did, and you can't stand it. You can't stand it that you don't stand for nothing anymore. You can't stand it, you goddamn three-dollar bill, that if you dropped off the face of this planet tomorrow, five seconds from now, the only person in the world who would miss you is right upstairs, and your fucking ego just can't handle that, can it, huh? Big bad marine. Big bad chief of police. Yeah. Right. Scared you're gonna be nothin'. Scared you're goin' into a big black nothin'. Scared you're goin' into a hole in the ground — fuck that. I'm not goin' into the ground, fuck that. That's too fuckin' — uh-uh, I'm not doin' that. Burn this one. Fuckin' right . . . take fire any day, that fuckin' chokin' shit, I ain't goin' that way

— aw what the fuck difference does it make, you jagoff? Huh? You think you're gonna know where you're goin'? Well if I'm not gonna know what am I scared of?

"Mario? You alright?"

"Huh? Yeah. I'm alright. Just, uh, I don't know, just thinkin' down here, that's all. Be right up." He blew his nose into a paper towel from a roll near the washer, wiped his face, opened the fridge, filled his carafe from the jug, made a mental note to get a couple more jugs, and then headed up-stairs, hoping his face wasn't too obvious.

Ruth looked at him while trying to pre-tend she wasn't looking.

"What?" he said.

"You, uh, you've been, uh . . ."

"What? Bawlin', huh? Is that what you mean?"

"Yes."

"Yeah," he said, nodding hard several times with his jaw tight. "Yeah, once again, the big bad chief of police has been bawlin'. Bawlin' for the little insignificant me that I am — or rather, the me that I am not. The me that wishes I was, but who can't bullshit himself anymore into thinkin' he's anybody but who he is, which is a big nobody, and which he can't stand it that he's a big nobody and never was nearly as

296

important as he thought he was. Turns out, you wanna know, hey, I'm just another stiff like everybody else. Imagine that! I mean I'm not a stiff just yet but when I become one, I mean . . . aw what the fuck, I mean I'm scared outta my mind that when I become a stiff, what I'm gonna find out is . . . is nothin'. Like what you said."

"And that really scares you," she said, coming to him and rubbing his shoulders.

"Turns out it scares me so bad, I'm shaking from the inside out, can you believe it? I can't even believe it, why should you believe it? I mean how the fuck did I do the things I did, huh? I wasn't this scared on Iwo, I'm tellin' ya, Ruthie, swear to God. I'm so scared I don't know what I'm doin' half the time anymore. I'm forgettin' stuff, not payin' attention when I'm drivin', Jesus, it's like I forgot every fuckin' thing I ever learned about how to survive. 'Cause I know I'm not goin' to, I guess." He laughed. "Why the fuck's that so funny? What am I laughin' for? Do you know?"

She put her hands around his neck and looked at him. "Mar, you're not — how do I wanna say this? You're not as bad as you think you are, but, uh, oh my. How do I say this? You're not as good as you hoped you were gonna be, that's all. You're just not. But nobody is. Does that make any sense?"

"Not as good as I hoped I was gonna be? Oh yeah, that makes sense. Fuck yeah. But not as bad as I think? I don't know about that one, Ruthie. I think I coulda been a lot better."

"Why?"

"Huh?"

"Why, why? Why do you think you could've been better? What do you think you could've done —"

"Aw shit, c'mon, lotsa stuff —"

"No no, I'm serious, what? Do you think there's something you could've done that would've been better? By whose way of thinking? Yours? Mine? Emily's? Marie's? Your mother's? The mayor's? All the different mayors you worked for? Or those councils? Seriously, Mar, better how?"

He snorted. Shrugged. Smiled. Sighed. "Beats the hell outta me. I don't know. All I know is, I'm scared of dyin'. Scared of meetin' everybody I think I didn't do right by, I mean, you know, like they don't have their own problems — if there is a place for crissake where everybody would be. I mean, where the hell is that? Huh? Downstairs I was thinkin' there ain't no hell, Iwo Jima was hell, I've already been to hell, but that hell's over. So where's hell now? Where's purgatory? I don't know. It's just — it pisses me off that my mind's so small, you know, too small to comprehend the idea that I'm nothin', that I'm gonna be nothin', that I'm goin' into a big black nothin', and that's when I'm thinkin', you know, downstairs just now I'm thinkin' . . . you know, I don't wanna be buried. I mean that just scares the shit outta me, goin' into a hole in the ground, people throwin' dirt on top of me."

"What do you wanna be?"

"I don't know, what the fuck — I don't wanna go!"

"Oh yes you will, Mar. Not now, but someday you will."

"What're you sayin'?"

"Someday you'll get old, you'll get tired, you'll get sick, you'll hurt so much, one day you'll just say the hell with it. And you'll want to go, believe me."

"You want to go?"

"Not yet, no, not now." She laughed, pulling back from him. "My work here with you is not finished. I have much more to do with you."

"Aw c'mon, huh? Quit breakin' my stones."

"Seriously, Mar. I have to get you ready. But I wanna do it someplace warm, okay? I don't wanna shovel snow anymore. I wanna give away all my woolies, I don't ever wanna put on a wool skirt again in this life. I wanna wear cotton and linen and nylon, okay? And the only thing I wanna shovel is sand. At the beach."

"Wait a minute. Ready for what, get me ready for what?"

"Get you ready to enjoy every moment you have left, so that when you're ready to go you won't be scared anymore, that's what."

"And you think you can do that, huh?"

"I know I can. I could just do it a lot better at the beach, that's all. Really, Mar, what's keepin' us here? We have no family here anymore."

"No family? What the hell, what about Marie? Emily?"

"Oh God, there's airplanes. They wanna see us, we wanna see them, there's airplanes. There's telephones. I can talk to them from a condo on the beach just as easily as I can talk to them from that phone right there."

"Condo on the beach? You kiddin' me?

We can't afford no condo on the beach —"

"Don't be so sure, big boy. I've got contacts, I've been reading ads."

"What ads? Since when? I don't see you readin' anything."

"Oh there's lots you don't see me doing. But I'm scheming, Mar. I'm making plans. We're gonna bust outta this joint, you and me."

"You're nuts." He smiled appreciatively.

"That's right, I am. That's why you love me."

"No shit," he said, his eyes filling up again in spite of himself. "Got that right, lady. Love you more than I know how to say."

"Aw go 'head, try."

"Okay. I love you. I loved you from the first time you ever talked to me. I love you more now than I did then. I don't think I'd be alive if I didn't have you to love."

"Oou," she said, her own eyes brimming over. "Wow. Thank you."

Balzic didn't know what to do; he just knew he couldn't keep stringing Valcanas along about this thing because Valcanas couldn't keep stringing Bertelli along. Should've had this wrapped up days ago. Well, yes, but there was this little matter of a couple of blocked coronary arteries. Yes, but they said, all those theys, remember them? Take a couple days off and then resume your normal life, that's what they said. Well, bullshit. Maybe nothing to them, but they're not the ones with the drill bit in their artery, are they? They're the driller, I was the drillee, nothing to it for the driller to say yeah, sure, take a couple days off, resume your normal life, what the hell, it's only one artery. Wasn't like somebody cracked your chest open, pried your ribs apart, opened up a leg and took a foot or two of vein and grafted it in there, hell, it was just one goddamn artery, man! What are you wimpin' around for? Act like it was some kind of major thoracic surgery. This didn't even take as long as a root canal. Yeah? And?

And what?

My question exactly. And what?

I don't feel right, that's what. I'm tired all the time. I'm weak.

Cut the bullshit. You're not tired. Or weak. You're scared. And how many times you gonna go through this scared bit anyway? Every hour on the hour, are you?

Jesus Christ, man, there's a world out there. How many other people do you think've done this? And worse? Jesus, immeasurably worse. Remember that poor sonofabitch used to come in the Giant Eagle didn't have any nose? Remember him? Cancer just eatin' his face away, nose first, his whole face a goddamn open wound, how would you like to try that for the rest of your life? Huh? For as long as your life's gonna give you? Wait a minute. For as long as my life's gonna give me? What kinda circles am I talkin' here? . . .

"Hello, Elmer?"

"Who's this?"

"Mario Balzic, remember me?"

"Balzic? Get the hell outta here — whatta you want, you're retired. What're you botherin' me for?"

"This is private, Elmer, keep your pants on."

"Oh yeah, right, so if it's private, I don't have to talk —"

"Hey, Elmer, just listen first before you get your ass all puckered up, okay?"

"Yeah? So I'm listenin', hurry up, I got stuff to do."

"Anybody tryin' to sell you any Berettas, Model 92F, 9-millimeters, like a bunch, thirty or forty maybe?"

"Get outta here, huh? I don't do that no more, Balzic, c'mon. I'm strictly antiques, armoires, secretaries, china closets, chairs, tables, farm tables're real big with the yuppies now. I'll bet you got a table down in your cellar we could do some business with —"

"I sound like a farmer to you?"

"Who cares? People buy this kinda stuff, you think they're gonna know? You got a table you don't want, bring it in, I got a guy, he beats it up with chains, you know? Wrapped in a towel? Puts dents all over it, paints it, washes it off, throws dirt all over it while it's still wet, washes it off again, paints it some more, by the time he's done with it, looks like it come outta Ben Franklin's cousin's house on the Delaware River, and nobody knows any better, I'm tellin' ya —"

"And we split fifty-fifty —"

"You already sold it to me, Charlie Brown, I'm the one with the merchandisin' skills here, not you. Seventy-thirty."

"Pass, I'm usin' every table I got. So, uh, no Berettas, huh?"

"What you wanna do is talk to Jack Venis, I'm retired."

"You think Jack's gonna tell me what I wanna know, huh?"

"Not as long as you're talkin' to me, he ain't."

"You hear somethin', Elmer? Huh?"

" 'Bout what?"

" 'Bout Berettas, what're we talkin' about? Or maybe a stainless-steel .44 Mag? Or a stainless .357? Both Rugers?"

"Ain't gonna say it again. Jack Venis. Bye."

Balzic hung up and gave his Rolodex a whirl to the Vs. "Venis, Venis, Jack Venis. What're you up to these days, Jackie boy?"

Balzic pushed the buttons for the number he had for Venis and was told by recorded message that it was no longer in service. He called the Rocksburg PD and asked Detective Rugs Carlucci if the number he had for Venis was different from the one he'd just called. Carlucci's number for Venis was the same. He told Balzic to give him five minutes, he'd get back to him. Six minutes later, he called back with another number for Venis.

"Hey, Mario, I meant to say somethin' before, didn't get the chance. Some rent-a-cop called here askin' about you. Said you were flashin' expired ID. Man, I didn't know what to say. Better watch it, Mario. Some of these kids, they got no respect. They'll turn your ass in in a heartbeat. Just for laughs, I'm tellin' ya."

"Nah, that's alright. I got straight with that kid. Tell Nowicki I'm gonna call him about him. Name's Rayford. Hey, gotta go." Balzic was cringing as he hung up, knowing that Carlucci knew he'd pulled that lame stunt with his expired ID.

Balzic quickly called the number Carlucci had just given him, got a woman's smoky voice on a machine. She didn't identify either herself or the number, just gave the usual about not being able to pick up now.

"This is Mario Balzic. I'm trying to reach Jack Venis. If you're there, Jack, pick up, will ya? If not, call me back at —"

"Balzic! What the hell — thought you re-tired."

"That you, Jack?"

"Who else? So you're not retired? What, you like one of those decrepit boxers, huh? Ring's the only place they can keep beatin' people up and not get busted for it. Is that you, huh? Can't quit?"

"This is private, Jack. I'm tryin' to run down some Berettas, like forty maybe. Model 92Fs? Nines. Know anything about 'em?"

"Somebody say I'm supposed to?"

"Your old partner."

"*Elmer* said? Elmer needs bigger fans in his place. Needs to quit sniffin' all that varnish and shellac, you know? Stuff's makin' him goofy. That's why the kids do it, you know? They like feelin' goofy. When you're old, hey, you don't need goofy, you need ventilation."

"So you don't know anything about any Berettas?"

"Who's supposed to've boosted 'em?"

"Ronnie Cozzolino. I think you know him."

"If it's the one I know, if he was hookin' up cable, he couldn't steal the Weather Channel."

"So you know him."

"Well course I know him, Balzic. I know all the Godfather wannabes. Who did they come to before you came to them, huh? What's with you, you sick or somethin'? Somebody said you had a heart attack, maybe it was a stroke. Course if you had a stroke you might not know nothin', would ya?"

"Very funny. So he didn't come to you, huh? Cozzolino?"

"Come on, Balzic, gimme a little credit, Christ. I don't do business with jagoffs."

"Who are ya doin' business with these days, refresh my —"

"Aw c'mon, what're we doin' here, huh? Who do you think? Somebody's not gonna leave his name and number all over everything. Somebody with a little self-restraint, a little ability to postpone his appetites, you know? Somebody doesn't have to have an audience. And that ain't the Cozzolino I know. Some people, you know, the jagoffs, they think because they got the guts and the urge, that's all they need.

"Like my sister's kid, listen to this, Balzic, this is exactly what I'm talkin' about. I put the little shit through college, understand? So whattaya think, huh? Comes to me the day after he graduates, he says he wantsa be a stand-up comedian. I say a what? He says yeah, that's what he wants to do, you know, like this Seinfeld guy. I says you mean the guy on TV? Exactly, he says. Do I know how much this guy makes? Like a half million every show, every week, see? So he goes like this for about ten minutes, finally I can't stand it no more, I say hey kid, listen to me. You been talkin' for ten minutes now, all you said was how funny this guy on TV was, and how much money he makes, and how you're gonna do what he does, and I'm still waitin' for the first laugh. So besides the urge you got, and the balls, and the envy, what the fuck else you got goin' for you here? I mean, no disrespect I says to the kid, I admire ambition, but not once in the whole time you been talkin' here have I even cracked a smile. Don't you think maybe you should be thinkin' more along the lines of somethin' automotive? You know, tires, batteries, the towin' business, a junkyard, Jesus Christ, anything, 'cause the fact is I don't recall ever hearin' you say anything funny long as I've known ya.

"Know what he says? He says hey Uncle, you don't get my comedy, my comedy's all attitude, and it's obvious you don't get attitude comedy. I guess I don't, I says. All I know is, no matter what kinda comedy you think you were doin', I wasn't laughin', and I don't care how bad you wanna make half a million a week."

"Your nephew's a Cozzolino, is that it?"

"Now you got it. If they come in here wantin' to take bows, wantin' to hear the applause, hey, I ain't buyin', simple as that."

"So he did come to you?"

"I didn't say that."

"It's all over what you just said, Jack, c'mon."

"Uh-uh. You ain't hearin' me. I said that's Cozzolino's story from before. He come to me? Especially with that kinda merchandise? I wouldn't even look at it from him. 'Cause you wait a coupla weeks, that jagoff might as well take out an ad in the paper. If he did it, soon as he gets paid, he'll start tryin' to impress somebody, you know this, what am I tellin' you for? S'matter with you, Balzic, you used to be a little more patient about this stuff. You sound like you got the hurry-ups real bad, your voice got a lotta tension in it."

"I heard somethin' about where these guns might wind up."

Venis laughed hard. "The hell's wrong with you? If they're gonna get grabbed for evidence eventually, the hell you care where they wind up? Ain't gonna be there long, so what?"

"I don't want 'em there for even five minutes."

"Ah you worry too much. World was a mess before you got here, gonna be a mess long after you're gone. You always took it too serious, what'd it get ya, huh?"

"I'm doin' alright. Not as good as you, but I'm gettin' by —"

"Not as good as me? Is that what you said? Don't shit me, not as good as me — listen, I gotta buy my own insurance, gotta buy my own retirement, whattaya, kiddin'

me? No fuckin' taxpayers payin' for my retirement like you, Jesus Christ. I had a city
pension the way you do, I'd be in Florida,
Christ, I'd be in the surf every mornin',
catchin' pompano for breakfast."

"Yeah," Balzic said. "My wife wants us
to move down there. I don't know. Layin'
around on the sand all day, that doesn't do
it for me. Does it for her though. She can
lay there for hours, man, readin', watchin'
the birds, takin' a nap. Not me. Too fuckin'
paranoid. When we were down there, she
trieda get me to take a nap, I couldn't
close my eyes for a minute. I was too busy
listenin' for a coupla mopes to come along,
one a bump, the other one divin' for our
goodies."

"That's what I'm sayin', you take the
whole thing too serious —"

"Oh right, I can see you on the beach,
yeah, you'd have your goddamn eyelids
taped open, don't give me that shit —"

"Get outta here, I'd be fishin', wouldn't
be sleepin'. Fishin', only thieves you gotta
worry about are the goddamn herons and
egrets stealin' your bait, or whatever you
catch. I ain't gonna sit around waitin' for
some mope to boost my bag, life's too
short."

"Oh this is beautiful," Balzic said, laughing. "Me listenin' to you tell me how to avoid stress at the beach. You oughta hook up with some travel agency, Jack, you know, tell the tourists how to relax —"

"Don't knock it. I've done it for more people than you know."

"Oh yeah? So okay, counsel me now. Reduce my stress. The only other guns allegedly taken were two —"

"Allegedly? You mean you don't know?"

"How am I s'pposed to know? All I got is this chooch's claim. Listen to me: two stainless-steel Ruger revolvers, one a .44 Mag, the other a .357 Mag. What's that sound like to you?"

"Same thing it sounds like to you, trophies. You sure you didn't have a stroke? Somethin's affectin' your brain —"

"What, am I insultin' your intelligence?"

"Yeah, as a matter of fact."

"Well why don't you just come right out and say it, Jack? Hey, don't hold back on my account, what the fuck —"

"Well what the fuck yourself? You're askin' me stuff I know you know, c'mon."

"I'm just tryin' to get your opinion, you know? Been in the business all your life, help me out here."

"Oh yeah? For what exactly, huh? Suddenly I enlisted in the war against crime?

I'm a volunteer McGruff now? Hey, if you're private, you can't squeeze me, so you want somethin', come up with somethin'."

Balzic tried to calculate how much he could get away with offering, how much either Valcanas or Bertelli would approve. "Uh, I don't know, how's half a yard sound?"

"You shittin' me? I wouldn't give up my first wife's mother for less than a yard, and if I coulda figured out a way to inject cancer cells into her fat ass without her knowin' it, I woulda done it."

"Well then I guess we can't do any business, Jack —"

"Can't do any business?! I oughta send you a fuckin' bill for the time I been on the phone here."

"Save the stamp, Jack, I wouldn't pay ya. You hear anything —"

Click.

"— gimme a call."

Wonderful, Balzic. Your phone skills are exceeded only by your anxiety level. Now that you have nothing to squeeze people with, maybe it's time you learned how to suck up, ever think about that? Would it hurt you? Huh? Mister Paranoia? Mister Personality? Phhhuck. Who else do I know maybe would be willin' to fence this number of guns? Hell with this, I need to call Rugs.

"Hey, Rugs, it's me again. Sorry to bother you, but who would you be lookin' at to fence all these nines?"

"Ah, lemme think. You call Elmer what's-his-face?"

"Yeah. Jack Venis too."

"Well. Hey. Moises Ackerman's dead. Freddy Baker's nuts. David Quarles is also dead —"

"He is? Since when? I didn't know that. What happened?"

"Oh, 'bout a month ago. Somebody put one through and through the back of his neck, mouth first. Tried to make it look like a suicide, but his old lady was naggin' his insurance guy before she even picked out a casket. Got the state guys interested real fast."

"Get out. They lock her up?"

"Not yet. I think somebody in Philadelphia wants her for somethin' else, I think they're workin' it out. So anyway, lemme think, who else here? Uh, Benji Silerno's in the county home, uh, Jeez. I'd try, uh, Buster Grimes, ah no, he's doin' federal time. Jeez, Mario, I'm gonna have to call you back, 'cause I really can't think of anybody else around here with the money or the balls to take on that kinda numbers — I mean if they're for real. Let me call around, okay? I'm thinkin' it's gonna have to be somebody in Allegheny County, there's nobody in this county I can think of offhand that's gonna handle this kinda volume. Let me call you back, okay?"

"Sure. Fine." Balzic hung up, wondering if he was going at this the right way. Maybe he should be trying the other security guard who was in the Jeep when Cozzolino did his thing. What was his name? McFate?

Balzic knew he wasn't going to get any information about Wilbur McFate by calling Bulldog Security, so he pep-talked himself into driving to Rocksburg Mall, fingering his bottle of Nitrostat in his left front pants pocket every couple of minutes, as though it had moved since the last time he'd touched it, two minutes ago at the last traffic light. He drove twice around the mall's parking lot looking for the white Jeep station wagon with the yellow-light bar. When he hadn't seen it during those two circuits, he swung past the parking lot of the Ground Round restaurant, where he found it nestled among the Dumpsters in the back.

It was 4:45 P.M. when Balzic walked into the bar, ordered a glass of white wine, and looked around for Wilbur McFate. He spotted him sitting at a table near the kitchen doors, looking seriously in lust at a waitress backing out of the kitchen with three plates full of chicken wings and hot sauce.

Balzic paid for his wine, took a long swallow, and headed for McFate.

"Mind if I sit down, Wilbur?"

McFate's mouth seemed to be perpetually open because of his very long upper front teeth. When he said, "Huh?" and looked up at Balzic, his mouth fell even farther open.

"I said mind if I sit down?" Balzic said, sitting down.

"Hey that seat's saved."

"No it ain't, Wilbur. She doesn't have time to sit with you, she's workin'." Balzic unzipped his parka.

"How you know that? And how's come you know my name? I don't know you."

"Well, I'd like to say I'm your conscience, Wilbur, but I'd bust out laughin' and you'd get mad for the wrong reason, so, uh, my name's Balzic. I'm workin' for Attorney Valcanas, who's workin' for Albert Bertelli, who wrote the insurance policy on Freedom Firearms — any of that ring any bells for you? It should. I mean, you were supposed to be patrollin' the night it got B and E'd, remember? When you were in here tryin' to find out whether this waitress really liked guys in uniform? Huh? That's what Cozzolino told you, right?"

McFate tried to put on his toughest face, but it was suddenly the wrong color for that. "Hey whoa, I ain't s'pposed to be talkin' to anybody about that. You wanna talk to anybody about that you're s'pposed to be talkin' to Mister Beckmaier —"

"C'mon, Wilbur, you know why he doesn't want anybody talkin' about that burglary. We both know you know that, right? I mean, I've heard you're a smart guy, you know what's goin' on, right?"

"I, uh, I was told specifically by Mister Beckmaier I wasn't s'pposed to talk to anybody 'cept the state police about that —"

"Well certainly that's what he told you, Wilbur, and can you blame him? Man wants to cover his ass — wouldn't you? Right now he's lookin' like a major fuckup here, right? I mean, let's just look at the sequence of events here, okay?"

"Naw, I don't think so," McFate said, jumping up and putting his cap on.

"Sit down, Wilbur, don't make this hard."

"Hey, I don't have to talk to you, whoever you are. You go to hell, pal, I don't know you. But I know you ain't the law or you would've showed me a shield, some kinda ID —"

"Wilbur, I got you on videotape, a whole week's worth," Balzic lied. "Okay? So sit down and listen. I spent a whole lotta money rentin' a videocam, buyin' tape and all that, but I got ya, Wilbur. Hours and hours of that Jeep parked where it is now, 'stead of where it's supposed to be with you in it, you know? On patrol? And I got you in here makin' goo-goo eyes at that waitress, who hasn't been givin' you the time of day. And you know this is not what you're gettin' paid to do, now is it?"

McFate slumped back down onto his chair, but only on the front half. "Aw man. Man. Jeez-ouu. You gonna show it to him? Huh?"

"Who, Beckmaier? Naw, why would I do that?"

"Well who else?"

"Well now who would you show it to if you were me?"

"Oh man you're not gonna show it to them!"

"Who, Wilbur, say it."

McFate hung his head, shook it, and muttered something about he knew he shouldn't have listened to that son of a bitch.

"Listen, Wilbur, you tell me what I wanna know, I'm not gonna show it to the state cops or anybody else. But you gotta help me out here, you know? Scratch my back and all that stuff? 'Cause there's no reason for me to show it to anybody 'cause I don't wanna mess with your livelihood, Wilbur, I mean, strictly speakin', you didn't do anything wrong — not somethin' a half-decent shyster couldn't talk you out of. You just didn't do what you were supposed to do, right?"

"Well not doin' what I was s'pposed to do, you know, I mean, hey, that's screwin' up. Big-time."

"Yeah, if you get a dumb shyster it is. Or a lazy one. But let's not get hung up on that, okay? Let's get back to the sequence of events, okay? I'll lay it out, you jump in if I get anything wrong."

McFate looked like he was trying to decide whether he was going to bawl or throw up. His eyes darted from side to side and he swallowed several times.

"Okay?"

"Yeah," McFate said, looking like that was the last thing it was.

Balzic took two more long swallows of his wine, emptying the glass, which he held up for the waitress to see as she hurried by with both arms full of dinner plates. "Just when you get a chance, miss. Don't make a special trip."

"She'll bring it right back," McFate said. "She's a real good waitress. You watch, you won't have to ask her twice."

This boy's so deep into fantasyland he may never return, Balzic thought. "So, uh, okay, Wilbur, here we go. Ronnie Cozzolino, let's start with him. You do remember him, right?"

McFate winced and nodded.

"Ronnie told you about this waitress, didn't he? I know he did, you don't have to answer that. You wouldn't be here otherwise, would ya? Don't answer that either. But he was real specific about when you should find out, wasn't he? Whether she might have eyes for your uniform, right? Answer that one, Wilbur — did I tell you I'm gettin' all this on audiotape? If I didn't, I am. I don't wanna mislead you, understand? I've just reached the stage in my life where I have to get everything either on film or on tape, know what I mean? It'll happen to you someday, Wilbur. Believe me, someday your memory'll go all to shit and back."

"Uh, what was the question again?"

"The question was how specific did Cozzolino get about you comin' in here, that was the question. 'Member now?"

"Yeah. Uh-huh. Well. Lemme think —"

"Don't think, Wilbur, just talk. You think too much I'm gonna get the idea you're tryin' to spin me dizzy, okay? And I don't want that. Just tell me what happened as best you can recall it, okay?"

"Yeah, okay. Well. See, he told me, uh, you know, I mean, he said this waitress was all crazy for uniforms. Said her father used to be a cop and he got killed or somethin', and every time she sees a uniform she thinks maybe, uh, you know, if she makes love to it, she's sorta somehow, uh, I don't know, I guess she thinks she's makin' love to the spirit of her father or somethin'. Sounded goofier'n hell to me, but one other time some other guy told me 'bout girls like that, you know, sorta like the same thing almost. Little bit different I guess."

"Cozzolino's a regular little psychologist, huh?"

"Hey, I don't know, I'm just tellin' ya what he said."

"Alright. And did he tell you what time she started?"

"Said she started some days around nine. Other days four."

"And the mall closes around nine, right? Isn't that when the mall closes when it's not Christmas?"

"Yeah. Shops close at nine, except for Christmas, right. Ruby Tuesday's stays open way later'n 'at."

"And so does this place, right? And Denny's? And Long John Silver's, right? They all stay open after nine, and you're s'pposed to patrol around them too, aren't you?"

"S'pposed to," McFate said, hanging his head again.

"Now tell me somethin', Wilbur, you bein' a sharp guy? How long before the B and E did you start comin' in here to find out whether she liked how your uniform fit — a week maybe? Two weeks?"

McFate struggled to remember. It was a physical act. He squirmed, chewed the inside of his cheek, licked his lips, and frowned at the ceiling. "It was at least two weeks. Least that."

"And what — you come in every time you spotted her car?"

"Naw. I just come in, you know, looked to see if she was here."

"Ever talk to her, Wilbur? Ever said anything besides coffee please, huh?"

McFate shook his head glumly. "Uh-uh."

"So now, Cozzolino gets fired, and you know about that, right? You did know he got fired, correct?"

"Yeah."

"So how'd you hear about the B and E? I know you didn't find it yourself, while you weren't makin' your rounds. How could ya, right?"

"Huh? Oh no, uh-uh. No. Uh, Mister Beckmaier, he called me."

"He called you when? Exactly, Wilbur, try to remember."

"Next day."

"C'mon Wilbur, what time next day?"

"I don't know. Right before I come to work."

"He called you at home? Around eleven A.M., would you say?"

"Yeah. Around there."

"And how was he? Upset? Angry? Cool, calm, shoutin', what?"

"Naw he wasn't shoutin'. Didn't sound mad or nothin'."

"Did he ask you whether you made your rounds? Or where you were if you didn't? Or whether you saw anything or anything like that?"

"Naw, uh-uh."

"How 'bout since? Asked you anything since? About where you were or what you were doin' — he told you he was conductin' his own investigation, right? Has he ever asked you anything about this, anything at all? And don't bullshit me, Wilbur, 'cause I'll find out just like I found out how long you been hangin' here 'stead of doin' what you're supposed to do, okay?"

McFate shook his head many times. "Uh-uh, no. I thought sure as hell he was goin' to, but he ain't. Not so far."

"Well why do you think that is, Wilbur? Huh? I mean be honest here. Don't you find it a little strange you still have a job here?"

"Well. To be honest? Yeah. I do."

"I mean if it was your security business, you'd be talkin' to your patrolman, wouldn't ya? If somebody B and E'd one of the shops was payin' you to protect it? And took off with all those guns?"

"Yeah. If it was my business, yeah. Guess I would."

"Guess? Shit, Wilbur, c'mon, you know goddamn well you'd be talkin' to your patrolman the second after you hung up from hearin' about it. That's just common sense, c'mon, you're not stupid."

"Well, yeah, I mean, sure I'd wanna talk to me — or him."

"But he hasn't. Not even once, right?"

"Right."

"And now what? A week's gone by — ten days? And he still hasn't talked to you." Balzic put his elbows on the table, leaned forward, and crooked his index finger at McFate. "Know what I think, Wilbur?"

McFate hesitated, then leaned forward himself, shaking his head no as he drew closer. "No. What?"

"I think this waitress ain't as good as you said. I mean, it's been five minutes at least since I asked her to bring me another glass of wine, and where the hell is she? You seen her?"

"No, uh-uh, but she's probably real busy. I mean, this is suppertime, you know? This is her busiest time, right now. Till nine or so."

"Wilbur, tell the truth, have you ever talked to this woman, huh? Have you ever

325

said one word to her about anything except what you ordered, huh? Or askin' her to fill your Thermos?"

McFate blushed again. "Well no. Not exactly, but —"

"Know what I think, Wilbur? I think Cozzolino played you for a chump. Him and Beckmaier both, that's what I think. Know why I think that? Seriously, Wilbur, look at me."

"I can see you."

"Naw, you're lookin' everywhere except at me. Look at me. Think, man, I mean, here you sit, ten days after the fact, you're still dopin' off in this goddamn restaurant here, where Cozzolino told you to come 'cause maybe you could get laid just 'cause you were wearin' a uniform, and your boss hasn't fired you, and yet here you sit, actin' like a lovesick teenager, and you haven't spoken one word to this woman, have you? I know you haven't. Know what, Wilbur? Maybe you're not as sharp as everybody says you are, whattaya think, huh? Can't figure this out for yourself what's goin' on here?"

"They're not gonna do that, uh-uh."

"Not gonna do what? Who?"

"You know. What you said before. Play me for somethin'. A chump or somethin'.

Why would they do that?"

"Oh you don't see the progression here? You don't know where this is headed? Where *you're* headed?"

"Where? I ain't headed nowhere, I don't know what you're talkin' about."

The waitress came then, hovered a glass of white wine in front of Balzic about four or five inches above the table. "Yours was the chablis, right?"

"Good enough," Balzic said. "Say. How's Ronnie? Haven't seen him in a while, he told me to stop in and say hello, you know?"

"You a friend of Ronnie's? Oh yeah?" She flashed a tight little smile and a furiously quick glance at Wilbur and then focused on Balzic again, her eyes softening considerably. "He knows more people," she said, clearly trying hard to remember if she'd ever seen Balzic before.

"Listen, uh, you see him, you be sure and tell him Mario Balzic said hello and we'll be talkin', okay?"

"Oh. Okay. Sure, I'll tell him. I'll be seein' him later on. I better be. Said he'd pick me up, my car wouldn't start today. Battery died." She forced another quick smile, then scowled despite herself, as though she knew she'd said way too much.

McFate's eyes bulged and his jaw dropped. Then he swallowed hard and shook his head no when she asked if he wanted his coffee refilled.

Once she was gone, Balzic said, "So, uh, Wilbur, whattaya think now, huh? Startin' to make a little more sense? Or a little less?"

"Hey I don't know what's goin' on," McFate said, his face flushing a deeper crimson.

"You don't, huh? Want me to spell it out for ya?"

McFate threw up his hands feebly.

"It's like this, Wilbur. The fact that you're still workin' here ten days after a burglary's been committed — that's a first-degree felony in case you forgot, you know? Burglary? And theft, that's a third-degree felony. Two of them together maxed out is seventeen years. You know who does the time, Wilbur? Huh? Press this into your book of memories, okay? Who does the time is the guy who talks to the DA *last*. Still don't understand? Beckmaier used to be a cop, which I'm sure you know. He was a lousy cop, lazier'n shit, but whatever, he understands the game. Wilbur? You hearin' me? He knows how to bargain a plea inside out, guaranteed. And long as he's got a mouth to talk with, he's not gonna do one hour for this. Guess who is."

"Who?"

"Oh, Wilbur, Jesus Christ, who the fuck do you think?" Balzic finished his wine, stood up, zippered his parka, and said, "You need to have a long talk with yourself, man. And then you need to call Trooper Milliron of Troop A CID. 'Cause right now there's a truck headin' for your ass and you don't even look like you know you're standin' in the middle of the road. Wake up, man. You're up for this."

"How? Why me? I didn't do anything! Jesus Christ, I just came in here and had some coffee, that's all. So I wasn't doin' what I was s'pposed to be doin', I mean, holy hell, that doesn't mean I took anything, c'mon! I didn't even know what happened till the state cop showed up, what the hell?!"

"Couple minutes ago you said you didn't know what happened till Beckmaier called you. Now you're sayin' you found out when the state cop showed up. Wilbur, I've already talked to other people here, and if I have, you know the state cop is goin' to. Trust me. Crime, crime prevention, you don't seem to be cut out for either one. I'd start lookin' for another line of work — after I got my buns in the DA's office. 'Cause you definitely don't wanna be last in this parade."

"I'm not gonna do that, you nuts?"

Balzic shrugged, fished a dollar out of his pocket and put it on the table, and said, "That's not for you, Wilbur, that's for the waitress. Remember her? Huh? Ronnie's girl?"

Balzic started to feel a little light-headed, then remembered the last time he'd been drinking and how fast he'd had to lie down afterwards, so he took a couple of deep breaths to steady himself. When he left, McFate was studying his coffee, his right knee bouncing fast and hard.

When he was leaving the mall, Balzic debated whether to chance going to Muscotti's. He hadn't been there since he'd come home from the hospital, but just thinking about going there sent a cold tremor through his stomach. He tried to tell himself it was stupid to be thinking that, even crazier to be feeling it. Muscotti's was as familiar to him as any place he'd ever been, but now it might as well have been Afghanistan. He tried to tell himself he didn't know what had come over him. He'd felt the terrors of acute anxiety many times before, and had, in fact, had one of his worst episodes of it in Muscotti's john.

So now he was feeling compelled to go there. It was as simple as that, as simple as any platitude ever uttered about such fears. When you had them, you had to face them, and the less sensible or logical they seemed, the more compelled you were to face them. You had to, or you wouldn't be able to live with yourself. He'd been hearing some variation of these commonplace words all his life, all requiring no great depth of thought, and easy to recite, like some cockamamie prayer devised for children, or simpletons. So simple, so easy, so quick to rise into consciousness — he wouldn't dare repeat any of them to anyone but his wife.

So when he arrived in Rocksburg and parked and reached for the handle of Muscotti's back door, he wasn't surprised to see his hand trembling. He had to use both hands to pull the door open. He stepped into the smoky winter gloom of the place, his throat tight and dry, itchy with fear, thinking this is what Ruth's been talking about. This is how we build our own jails.

The bar was jammed with the courthouse crowd, recently released from their daily political, judicial, and bureaucratic wrangling. Standing alone at the far end of the bar near the front door, Iron City Steve was locked in a rant with the jukebox, which for some reason Muscotti had moved from the back wall to just inside the front door, near the steps to the john. Steve looked up expectantly when the door opened and waved urgently at Balzic, motioning him to come quick.

God only knew what this was going to be about, but Balzic was instantly grateful. The last thing he wanted was to talk about his heart, his health, procedures in the cath lab, or any other thing medical, and he knew if he stopped anywhere else along the bar, those were the things he was going to be asked about. But Iron City Steve was rarely if ever interested in the here and now, and because of that he suddenly looked like the most interesting drinking companion in the place. Balzic pushed and shouldered his way to Steve, lying three or four times along the way that he was fine, yes yes, everything was fine. "Would I be here if it wasn't?" Well, he'd told worse than that.

Steve was sawing the air with his hands, occasionally giving the underside of his nose a backhanded swipe. As Balzic approached, Steve said furiously, "Did Jesus have cavities or not?"

"Cavities? Jesus?" This was perfect. "Hell if I know."

"I'm drinkin' muscatel. What're you drinkin'?"

A first. Never in Balzic's memory had Steve asked what anybody else was drinking. "Why? You buyin'?"

"No no, no," Steve said, perplexed suddenly in a different way.

"So you're just tellin' me you're empty, is that it?"

"Been empty for years and years," Steve said, though from the amount of red lightning in the whites of his eyes he hadn't been empty for long today. He turned back to the bar and knocked once on it with his empty glass. "Two intelligent fellas like us, drinkin' and thinkin', we can arrive at conclusions. Without conclusions, where's the consensus?"

Balzic shrugged out of his parka and laid it atop the jukebox, saying, "And the question, as I understand it, is whether Jesus had cavities, correct?"

"Said a mouthful there," Steve said, taking his upper plate out and shaking it at Balzic.

"And we're discussing this because why now?"

Steve put his upper plate back in and said, "If you were God, wouldn't you wait till somebody invented the high-speed drill before you had your only child?" Steve weaved from left to right and back again as he fixed his gaze on Balzic's forehead. "What's the rush?"

"I don't know."

"Well the nuns told me Jesus was a real man — told you too, didn't they?"

"Yeah they did. Real and not real."

"Well the real part had real teeth, right?"

"Supposedly."

"Real teeth get real cavities. I had so many cavities, my whole mouth's a cavity. See?" He produced both plates from his mouth and clicked them together while continuing to stare at Balzic's forehead.

Vinnie came down the bar, wagging his finger at Steve. "I told you, stop bangin' that fuckin' glass at me, didn't I tell you that? How many times I told you that, huh? Okay. I'm here now, whatta you want? C'mon c'mon, I ain't got all fuckin' day."

"Whattaya think he wants?" Balzic said.

"A champagne cocktail? The man's only been drinkin' muscatel like forever, you know?"

"Aw what're you now, his PR guy or somethin'? And whatta you gonna have? C'mon, I got a barful here and Dom's at the dentist and my foot's killin' me, so what's it gonna be?"

"What's wrong with your foot?"

"See?" Steve said. "Told ya. Teeth are in the forefront. Even the goombah has cavities. If the Godfather, why not the Godson? Only stands to reason."

"Will you shut the fuck up about those, huh? Fuck's wrong with you? You got teeth on the fuckin' brain or what? That's all he's talkin' about today, all fuckin' day. Nine o'clock this morning, no shit, I open the door, he's standin' there wavin' his teeth at me. Everybody comes in here today, he takes 'em out and shakes 'em at 'em. Fuck's wrong with him, huh? Do me a favor, okay? Take this fuckin' guy to mental health, no shit, get him the fuck outta here. What're you gonna have?"

"Some of that jug chablis. And give him a muscatel."

"You better be payin' 'cause he's tapped out. And it's three days till check time, fucker, huh? Steve? Hear me? Hey, tooth fairy. You listenin' to me? Don't you come in here tomorrow even thinkin' about moochin' nothin', you hear?"

"You're a cavity," Steve said.

"I got your cavity. You got somebody buyin' for ya now, everything's sweet, oh yeah. You come in here tomorrow, tomorrow when you're reachin' into your pants and comin' up zero, then we'll see who's what. Gimme six bucks."

"Six bucks?! For bar chablis and muscatel? A week ago chablis was two bucks. Muscatel's four bucks now?"

"It's two bucks, same as yours, the rest is for my aggravation, and don't gimme no shit, just gimme the money, that's all, I don't wanna hear nothin'."

"If God put fluoride in the rain," Steve said, "maybe you wouldn't be a cavity."

"Gimme five bucks we're square, Mario, c'mon. But you — hey! Take your teeth out at anybody else, I'm callin' the cops, you hear?"

Steve puckered up, pushed his lips out as far as he could, and kissed the air in front of Vinnie's face.

"See that, Mario? Huh? You think takin' that shit all day ain't worth a buck?"

"Not when you're tryin' to get it from me it ain't."

"That's 'cause you're standin' over there. You stood over here once in a while, you'd see what it's like."

"Why would I do that? I got no urge to pour drinks."

"Hey, Vinnie," somebody shouted, "you gonna talk, you gonna work, what's it gonna be?"

Vinnie rolled his eyes, shook his head, turned his lips downward, and used his left hand to make several gestures, palm up, fingertips together, toward the shouter, toward the ceiling, toward Steve, all as though to say to Balzic, see? For this, which is my curse, you have no sympathy. For what I endure every single day of my life you have no understanding. None. What the fuck good are you?

Balzic had seen the gestures and the looks before and knew all their meanings. He was not moved. Instead, he turned to Steve, lifted his glass, touched Steve's, and said, "To teeth."

"Hear hear," Steve said, then swallowed half the muscatel in two noisy gulps. He set the glass on the bar and, fixing his gaze once again on Balzic's forehead, said, "What kinda God had a kid before high-speed drills?"

"Before low-speed drills," Balzic said.

"Before toothbrushes."

"Before floss."

"Show me in the New Testament where it talks teeth. It don't."

"Whattaya think? Fuckup or cover-up?"

"Grounds for su'picion. Investigation is called for. You're a cop. Proceed!"

"Not a cop. Not anymore."

Steve pulled back, gravely troubled by this news. "Since when?"

"Couple years now."

"Oh. Oh this changes everything. I thought, you know, with your help, I could get to the bottom of this. Plumb the depths."

"And what'd you think you were gonna find?"

"Certainty. That's what we're after. Elimination of all doubt."

"Elimination of all doubt, huh? I don't think I coulda helped you, Steve, not even if I was a cop."

"Oh but you did. Oh yes," Steve said, sawing under his nose, elbows flying.

"About cavities? Musta missed somethin'."

"No no. When, uh, you know . . . when she . . . when she passed . . . I came in . . . you touched my arm, bought me wine. You told me it hurt . . . I'd probably never get

338

over it . . . nobody else told me the truth
. . . everybody else thought, you know, buy
me one drink, I'd go away. That's all they
wanted. Just wanted me to leave. You told
me the truth. 'Cause I still ain't over it . . ."

"Oh yeah, truthful, that's me, uh, but
not very helpful."

"Oh no! No! I was the weak one, see?
Helped a lot. Shoulda been me first, see?
She knew how to live, I don't. Never did.
Not till her. And then . . . everybody lied,
'cept you. See, God's a prick. If he wasn't,
he woulda took me first." He picked up his
glass, emptied it noisily, held out his soft,
moist paw for Balzic to shake, then turned
and shuffled out through the front door
into swirling snow.

Balzic blew out a long sigh, turned back
to the bar, and studied his wine for a
moment. Just as he was about to pick up
the glass and drink, he felt a nudge. He
turned and saw a shabby, bony man with
hair like steel wool, gray eyes darting nervously in every direction. It was Charley
Babyak, crank addict, bungler as husband,
and compulsive thief, with a history of
nonviolent burglaries going back to his
early teens. Balzic had himself arrested
Babyak at least four times for burglary and
then had felt so sorry for him the fourth

339

time that he actually tried to make a case for leniency when he was interviewed by a county detective preparing a presentencing report for the trial judge.

"Charley. Lookin' a little more strung out than usual, man, what's up?"

"Hey, Chief, we talk outside, huh? Your car close? Think we could go there maybe? I been tryin' to see ya for a coupla days now, somebody said you were sick, heart trouble or somethin'. I been hangin' around, you know, hopin' you'd show up. You used to hang here a lot, but, uh, this place always did make me nervouser than usual, you know? Nervouser than I normally am."

"What'd you do now, Charley?"

"That's the ball-buster, see? I didn't do nothin'. Hey, Chief, really, could we go talk in your car? I don't want Vinnie hearin' none of this, you know — I don't want nobody hearin' it, but Vinnie, he's a broadcast network, you know? VBS, especially there's anybody around whose ass he wantsa kiss, so, uh, you don't mind, huh? Your car?"

"That important, huh?" Balzic emptied his glass and grabbed his parka off the jukebox. He put it on and led the way out and around the corner to his Chevy. Inside the car, first thing he said was, "Hey, Charley, I'm not the chief anymore. So if this is your usual, I can't help ya."

"I know you ain't. It ain't that," Babyak said, blowing on his hands. He had on two pairs of flimsy cotton pants, at least two faded flannel shirts, and a quilted jacket that was losing polyester fiber from holes around both wrists.

"What then?"

"Listen. You never fucked me around the way some of these pricks did. You were always a little soft on me, I don't know why, I guess 'cause I'm stupid." He hung his head, sighed, and looked away.

It took Balzic a moment to see that Babyak was crying. "That bad, huh?"

Babyak was too choked up to answer. All he could do was nod.

Whatever it was, Balzic thought, it must be a big deal because while Babyak could come up with some of the goofiest excuses why he couldn't possibly have committed the crime for which he'd been busted, he'd never tried to play the victim or to blame anybody else for his predicament, whatever it might have been.

"Gimme a second here," Babyak said. He cleared his throat several times, then turned and looked hard into Balzic's eyes.

"I don't have to tell you all the stupid shit I ever did, but you also know, I mean, once you busted me, I didn't trade nobody and I never copped out. I said you think I done it, go 'head and prove it, and naturally that's what you done, 'cause, hey, we both know how smart I am. But this shit, I'm tellin' ya, I didn't do it. I never done it in my life, I ain't never been no fuckin' short eyes, I ain't never been, never gonna be, not if I live to be a thousand —"

"Short eyes? You?" Balzic laughed. He couldn't help it. While he certainly didn't know everything there was to know about Babyak, he did know that child molesters usually started early, typically around puberty, some earlier, but the pattern was generally set by that age, and if it happened in older men, it was so rare Balzic had never encountered it. Which didn't mean it didn't happen, but in Babyak's case the idea was so far-fetched it was almost too funny to be true. Babyak's problems with sex were just the opposite of short eyes. His was big women, the bigger the better to bump him around. Both his wives had towered over him, psychologically as well as physically, but this seemed to be what he craved. Never in all the years Balzic had known him had Babyak ever shown the slightest interest in children.

"Somebody's pullin' your chain, Charley, huh? You don't think?"

"No. Fuck no! And it's not just somebody," Babyak said, his jaw tight. "It's my uncle! He's the motherfucker spreadin' this shit, it ain't no mystery who's doin' it, I know who's doin' it, I just don't know why. Fucker won't talk to me. I go to his deli, try to talk to him, sonofabitch turns his back. Next thing I know here comes the fuckin' Dobermans, Jimmy and Angelo, outta the back room, and out I go."

"Your uncle? Do I know him?"

"Fuck yeah you know him. Artie Chianese."

"Get the fuck outta here — he's your uncle? I never knew that."

"That's 'cause he never told anybody. Wouldn't let me tell anybody. Told me I ever told anybody he'd feed my tongue to the rats in his cellar. But my mother and him were sister and brother. But he's been pissed at her forever 'cause she married my father. Who was a Slovak. They didn't talk for years, man. Just started up again coupla years ago 'cause she got cancer and he knew she was gonna die, so all of a sudden he started callin' her up, like he got this fuckin' conscience all of a sudden —

crock of shit, but what do I know? Maybe he did. But, see, she did a bad thing, which if she'da asked me first I'da told her never do it. She went to him, without askin' me, understand? And she made him promise 'fore she died, he hada give me a job so I'd have somethin' steady and wouldn't be gettin' busted all the time.

"Worst fuckin' thing ever happened to me, workin' for him. Ten times worse — a hundert times worse than any joint I was ever in, believe me. Busts my balls all day long, every day, from mornin' till night, I'm tellin' ya. If my mother woulda just asked me first, you know? I mean I know she thought she was doin' a good thing, but God I wished she'da asked me, no shit. Coulda avoided all this bullshit —"

"What bullshit, Charley, huh?"

"I'll tell ya what bullshit. He's spreadin' this shit I'm punkin' kids, givin' 'em dope to get in their pants! Yeah! You're lookin' at me like I'm whacked out, but I'm tellin' ya that's what I'm hearin' all over town over there, in Knox. Short eyes, dope dealer, gunrunner, I'm tellin' ya, I'm a fuckin' one-man crime wave, accordin' to him, and the only part that's true is I started movin' a little crank, that's all —"

"What, you usin' heavy again?"

"Hey, you know," Babyak said, nodding hard, "what the fuck, I'm goin' crazy workin' for this two-bit Mussolini, I gotta do somethin'. And then, you know, you gotta move it to score."

"So strictly speakin', you are dealin' dope."

"Hey, I ain't healthy, Chief, you know? I got a bad stomach, I got arthuritis, them drugs cost more than crank, I'm gonna tell ya. So what the fuck, I put some people together, that's all. Some people want crank, I happen to know some people that make it. It ain't exactly like I took over the Colombian coke cartel, you know?"

"Sounds like you're messin' with bikers, Charley. I never knew you to hang with them."

"Don't wanna insult your intelligence here, Chief, but things get rough enough, you'd be surprised who you do what with. Anyway, the motherfucker, after all this other shit he's puttin' around about me, don't you think he goes and fires me, huh?"

"Chianese?"

"Yeah. Course. Who else?"

"Well tell me now how you started workin' for him? Your mother got you this? Doin' what exactly?"

345

"Numbers, you know. Little sports book. Damn little. She made him promise to give me somethin', so he gave me the hunkies over there, you know, since I was half one and all that shit."

"The hell's that mean? I don't know a whole lot about that town, Knox. What're you talkin' about?"

"You 'member where Knox Iron and Steel used to be? 'Fore it closed? I mean all the buildings're still there."

"Yeah, I remember. I was over there a coupla times."

"Well all behind the main plant there, close to the river, for about, like, I don't know, six, seven square blocks, they used to call that Hunkytown. Some people still do. Not the kids. The old people. I guess when all them hunkies came over back in, whenever they come over, whenever the fuck that was, that's where they mostly got together, you know? Mostly Slovaks. Lotsa Ukrainians, Polaks too, but mostly Slovaks, Czechs, like that. That's where my old man was from, you know? Slovakia? So anyway, when my mother got sick, you know, and he starts comin' around and all that shit, they got to talkin' again, and God bless my mother, you know? But she shoulda kept her mouth shut far as I'm concerned.

'Cause she sure didn't do me no favors. 'Cause after I spend my day chained to the fuckin' telephones, every night I gotta go clean up his fuckin' deli for him, while that fat fuck makes jokes about how funny I looked when Angelo sat on me."

"Angelo? Who's he?"

"He's got these two cousins work for him. Goons, you know. Jimmy and Angelo. Last name's Serra. They're related to him somehow, I don't know how. Angelo's about six-five, he weighs about three hundert pounds. Artie told him sit on me one night. So those two fuckers put me on the floor, and he sat on me. Thought I was gonna die. I pissed and shit blood for two weeks. They all thought that was hilarious. Motherfuckers. Now this shit."

"What shit, exactly?"

"First lemme tell ya, before this, no problems, understand? Wasn't no fuckin' paradise, believe me, but never no problems with the fuzz. I'm sure he was takin' care of that, but still. Then all of a sudden, fucker calls me, says that's it, you're finished, you short-eyes punk bastard you, I don't ever wanna look at you again —"

"When was this?"

"Huh? Three days ago. Maybe four. No, three."

"What'd you say before — short eyes, dope dealer, gunrunner, is that what you said? What's that about, that gunrunner business? I don't recall you ever carryin' a piece."

"Exactly! You ever hear such shit? I'm tellin' ya, swear on my old man's grave, that's what that fat prick's puttin' out, I'm sellin' hot guns, man, can you believe that? Me! Who I ain't never in my whole fuckin' life — I'm like you, Chief, you know that. I ain't no robber, man, you know I ain't! Now you know that's true, you know I'm not lyin' about that. I never carried, man, not once, now why the fuck would I start dealin' guns, man, you tell me, that don't make no sense."

"Don't make sense for you to be messin' with bikers either, but you just said you'd be surprised what you do and who you do it with —"

"Yeah right, I know what I said, I ain't gonna say I didn't say it, but that's different, man. I'm scared a guns. Always have been scared of 'em, somebody pulls one out, man, I'm gone. There's only one thing you can do with a gun, that's hurt somebody, I don't want any part of that shit, I ain't no strong arm, I ain't never run with one. But I'll tell ya how bad this has got me. I'm so scared, I'm almost ready to get me a gun, no shit I am, I'm tellin' ya, that's how scared this shit has got me."

"Why now?"

" 'Cause I'm gettin' ready to get chumped out for somethin'. I know it, I can smell it, I can feel it — listen to this. Two years workin' there, not once did I see the chief of police, that jagoff? That Butterbaugh? You know him?"

"Yeah, I know who he is."

"Well, not one time did he ever lean on me, not in two years. You know what? In the last three days since I got fired? Twice! Two times, man, that fucker come up on me in the street, I'm just walkin' along, tryin' to figure out what's goin' on, here he comes, pulls over, puts me up against a wall, pats me down, says what am I doin' there, where am I goin', don't I think maybe I should be someplace else. I say what is this shit, man, why you hasslin' me? Fucker just smiles, man, just gives me this creepy smile, gets back in his car, says whoa, Charley, watch it, be careful, it's a hard world — hard world my ass. If this ain't a setup comin', I don't know what is. I may not be no genius, but I ain't stupid!"

"Take it easy, Charley, you're gonna give yourself a stroke —"

"Hey listen to me! I'm tellin' ya, them fuckers're tryin' to put me in a jackpot, man! And there's nobody I can talk to about this 'cept you. You gotta do somethin' for me, I'm scared to death, I'm not shittin' ya, I never been this scared in my whole life —"

"I can see that, Charley, but you're gettin' so loud you're makin' my ears ring, okay? Just chill down for a minute here, let's see what we got, okay?"

"Already told ya what we got."

"No, no, no, just listen. This thing about guns, what kinda guns you supposed to be dealin'? Just anything? Or somethin' special, you know, semi-auto rifles jazzed up full auto or somethin' like that?"

"Listen, Chief, you know how many houses I went into I found guns? Huh? Know how easy it woulda been? Never once, man. If I passed on one, I passed on a thousand. I'm tellin' ya, I'm scared of 'em — the way some people're scared a snakes, you know?"

"Don't tell me about you, Charley, I know about you. Tell me what you're hearin' — you gotta be hearin' somethin'. Who's dealin' 'em?"

Babyak swallowed, squirmed, kneaded his palms. Balzic could see he was having what for him was a terrible moral dilemma. He'd never traded anybody before, not in Balzic's dealings with him, but he was clearly looking at something a lot more frightening to him than loss of time or mobility. As many times as he'd been inside, it had to be that he didn't want to go in with a short-eyes tag on him. Balzic had heard it said many times there were two things that didn't last long in this life: dogs that chased cars, and short eyes in prison. So he knew better than to prod Babyak. The man was having a bad enough time all by himself.

Finally, Babyak ran his tongue over his upper teeth, squared his shoulders, took a deep breath, and blurted out, "Cozzolino. That's who's runnin' 'em. And the only thing he ain't got is a bullhorn. Fucker might as well be puttin' ads in the goddamn paper. And you know the capper? He's Artie's nephew. Same as me. Only it's his wife's sister — his third wife's sister is Cozzolino's mother, two of the ugliest, stupidest women you ever saw. They both got a nose like a fuckin' red potato, man, and got it in everybody's business 'cept their own. Binky he calls her. Binky. You ever hear such a stupid name as that for a dago woman? I never did."

"Uh, do I know this guy? This Cozzolino?" Balzic wanted to know how Babyak would respond to that.

"Do you know him? Fuck yeah you know him, I know you know him, he's so stupid, he's dumber'n me, if that's possible. You probably busted him yourself couple times. And if he ever heard you're s'pposed to keep your mouth shut, he don't think it applies to him. Worse than a little kid. Them kids in East Liberty? You hear about them, them crazy little niggers? I got a cousin lives in East Liberty, man, lived there all his life. Says it's scarier'n shit there now. Them kids shoot somebody over five bucks' wortha crack at seven o'clock, run in the house and wait for the 'leven o'clock news, man, see if they made it. No shit. Listen to this, my cousin, he busted into a cop's house just to steal his Kevlar vest. Won't go outside the house without it, man, that's how scared he is of them little spades. Thirteen-year-old kids walkin' around with two guns in their belt, man, see somebody they don't like, just start shootin', don't give a fuck who's on the street, who's watchin' 'em, nothin', you're there, you're square, I'm not makin' this up, you can call him up, man, he'll tell you —"

"Charley Charley, whoa whoa, back to Cozzolino, okay? Did you actually hear this from his own mouth? Who told you he was movin' guns? How do you know it's him?"

Babyak twisted his mouth, scowled, wrinkled his nose sniffing, rolled his head from side to side causing loud cracking sounds. "You're gonna think I'm nuts, what I'm gonna say, but I'm tellin' ya, I swear to God I'm not makin' any of this up, this is why I'm so scared."

"I'm listenin', go 'head."

"Don't laugh, I'm tellin' ya. It ain't funny, no matter how stupid it sounds —"

"Okay already, tell me."

"Okay. Here goes. The way I know this, I know the sister of this woman dances in a booth? She been fuckin' this councilman for I don't know how long, long time now, it ain't no weekend fling that's for sure. This jagoff — he books with me too — he's married, he got two kids in some private school someplace out in the boonies, but this woman he's fuckin', it's her sister now who's tellin' me this, okay? That's where I'm gettin' this from."

"You already said that."

"Okay okay, I'm a little nervous here. So, uh, this jagoff, he's been bullshittin' this woman he's gonna leave his wife an'at, and

353

she don't wanna hear it no more, so, uh, to get her off his case, he tells her he's gonna buy her a brand-new Mustang convertible, okay? Which is fine, except he's so strung out on all his lines a credit, he can't make the price on a new one, so he buys a hot one, see? Restored. A '73. Which he stashes in Fat Artie's truck garage, behind his deli, 'cause he doesn't want his old lady to find out about it, right?

"So he done some deals with Artie over the years, I don't know how long he's been councilman, but I guess he figures he did all this shit for Artie, time for a little payback, only he don't know what a cold motherfucker my uncle is, man. Don't have a heart, man. Has a water pump. So anyway, I guess he thought he's storin' that car in the pope's garage or somethin', you know, like Artie's not gonna try to work a scheme. Imagine. Guy asks a favor from Artie and don't know he's gonna have to give one back? What planet's this guy from, you know? But that's what's scarin' me. Somehow, some way, between the three of them, Artie and this jagoff councilman and that asshole chief of police, I'm tellin' ya, they're schemin' and they need a chump and those fuckers decide I'm it."

"Wait wait wait," Balzic said, rubbing his

itchy nose. "You lost me. What's this councilman have to do with anything? 'Cause he bought his girlfriend a car he can't pay for? So what? What's his name?"

"Not the one he can't pay for. She don't want the one he bought — didn't I say that? Name's Tanyar. Herbie."

"No. But what difference would that make?"

"I forgot, that's all. But he paid for that one. Says he paid fifteen, but that's probably bullshit. But it don't matter what he paid, 'cause Artie's got it now, see? And he's squeezin' him 'cause he's the head guy, chairman, whatever, of the safety committee on city council. He's the guy says what the cops and the firemen can buy, what they can't buy, who they got to buy it from, whether they got to get bids, you know this, what am I tellin' you for?"

"So what's the squeeze?"

"Well where Artie comes in with this is, you know, one of his biggest things is, he's real big in salt and cinders, man. Supplies the city every winter, Knox. Other places too, all over the county."

"So I say again, what's the squeeze? If he's already supplyin' the salt and cinders, what's he want?"

Babyak looked at Balzic and sighed.

355

"C'mon. Whattaya think? More money. If you got the deal locked, what's left? More money."

"Lemme see if I got this straight, Charley. I mean, you gotta admit this is sorta off the wall here."

"I know, I told ya. I don't know all the ins and outs, but I'm tellin' ya, that's what it's about. They need a chump for some fuckin' reason and they picked me — and I'm tellin' ya there's no fuckin' way I'm goin' in the joint with that motherfucker taggin' me a short eyes. I know what happens to them —"

"Charley? Charley!"

"I seen what happens to them, it ain't happenin' to me, no fuckin' way. I'll boost a bottle of Valiums, chase 'em with a six-pack —"

"Charley, shut up a second and run this down for me. I know somethin' about this. I'm workin' an insurance thing over a B and E at a gunshop in the mall right now, understand?"

"Huh?"

"Yeah. And the numbers are all wrong. And Ronnie Cozzolino was workin' for the agency that has the contract on the store — all the stores. And the agency is owned by a guy named Beckmaier, who used —"

"Beckmaier? I know that prick. Used to be a detective over there. Collared me once a long time ago. I knew it! I knew it! For sure they're gettin' ready to chump me out — I knew it!" Babyak pounded his knees and started to belch and bawl.

"Whoa down, Charley, okay? All you got is the paranoids, and nobody can do anything with that. You gotta come up with somethin' more than just how scared you are, you know?"

"Oh yeah? Like what? And what the fuck? Why me? Why do I gotta come up with somethin', huh? What the fuck you cops doin'?"

"I'm not a cop I told ya. But a gun would be nice. A Beretta maybe? Or a Ruger? Stainless .357 Mag, that would be good. Or a .44 Mag? You get Cozzolino to unload one of those, people could help —"

"Oh right! He's gonna sell me one of those, yeah. When they're gettin' ready to chump me out? If you think that, maybe you ain't as smart as I think you are —"

"Not you, Charley, what the fuck — a designated buyer, you know? Somebody you hook up with Cozzolino, I know he's not gonna sell you one, not if they're really gonna do what you think."

"Oh they're gonna do it, bet your ass

they are." Babyak grew silent for a moment. "Oh. I see where you're comin' from. Yeah. Okay. Gonna be tough though."

"Why?"

" 'Cause that Butterbaugh? That goofy chief? I heard him say one time, you know, just filed it away, but last coupla days, I mean, I really been thinkin' about what he said."

"What'd he say?"

"Said one day he'd square up with that councilman. That was, uh, you know, when he was, uh, he was in my mother's coal cellar with a videocam, see. Takin' pictures of everybody come down there to book with me. Got the councilman on film pretty heavy."

"Thought you said he never hassled you?"

"He wasn't hasslin' me. Just wanted to take everybody's picture that booked with me, that's all. I figured Artie sent him."

"And this councilman books with you?"

"Yeah. Football freak. Thinks he knows all about it, you know. Don't know shit. All he knows is what he reads in the paper, same thing every other schmuck knows. Slow pay too. Every week only way I get paid is if I say I'm gonna tell my uncle. So they're all out to screw one another, you know? Artie's got somethin' on the councilman, the chief, he's got somethin' else on the councilman, Artie's got somethin' on the chief, it's all a fuckin' daisy chain. Which I don't care except what they're gettin' ready to do to me. I think what it is, tell ya the truth, I think it's all about that fucker Cozzolino wants my job, that's what I think. That's how I think this whole fuckin' thing got started, plus it was 'cause his mother and Artie's third wife were sisters and his father was a full-blood Siciliano and my old man was Slovak, that's what I think the whole thing is. Fuckin' prejudice, honest to God, I think that's the whole thing right there."

"Well that's an interesting theory, Charley, but it doesn't help me help you."

"Well whatta you want me to do?" Babyak shrieked.

"Can you get to Cozzolino? Does he know you? Do you know him?"

"Well course I know him, course he knows me, you kiddin'?"

"Well so what's so hard about tellin' him you're workin' the middle, huh? Tell him you know somebody wants a .357. A Ruger —"

"Aw he ain't gonna go for that, you kiddin'?"

"Why not? Listen. If he's tryin' to chump you out, wouldn't it be sweet if he got you in the middle for somethin' he was tryin' to make you take the fall for? Think about it. You say you know him. Kinda prick he is, don't you think he'd love that? Huh?"

Babyak thought that over, his brows pinched deeply in a frown. "I don't know, man. I don't know."

"Okay, think about this. If you approach him like I said, don't you think it's at least gonna make him wonder what you know and who you told? Don't you think it would slow him down a little bit? Make him wonder how you found out? And who else you been talkin' to? Wouldn't it make you stop and think?"

"How I found out?! Fucker's tellin' everybody! He don't know how to keep quiet, so I coulda heard it from whoever —"

"Yeah, okay, true, true, but no matter who you heard it from, don't you think that goin' right to him, you know? You? You goin' to him? With a deal? I mean if you're right, if they want you to fall, why wouldn't they get their jollies from you comin' to them? Huh? That kinda shit appeals to pricks like that, don't you think?

C'mon, Charley, you gotta see what I'm sayin' here."

Babyak thought for a long moment, alternately blowing on his hands and pounding his knees. Finally he sighed and said, "Who's the customer?"

"His name's Bertelli. Lemme get his phone number here —"

"Wait a second. You talkin' Albert? The insurance guy?"

"Yeah. You know him?"

"Fuck yeah I know him. Used to buy my car insurance from him. Oh he ain't gonna go for this, c'mon, Albert's a fuckin' civilian —"

"Yes, exactly. Who makes a better customer than a civilian?"

"Aw shit, c'mon, Albert?! He wouldn't know what to do!"

"Hey, Charley, I've been tryin' to tell you, I'm a civilian. I'm not a cop anymore. Albert's the guy I've been workin' for on this."

"Oh yeah? Know what I bet? I bet you haven't told him about this, have ya? Bet he don't know nothin' about you puttin' him in the game like this, huh?"

"Course he doesn't. I just now thought of it."

"The fuck you think he's gonna do when

you tell him, huh? I'll tell you what he's gonna do. He's gonna shit."

"Maybe. Maybe not. Let me worry about him." Balzic got his wallet out of the inside pocket of his parka. "Here. This is his card. His numbers, business and home, they're right there on the front. I'm puttin' mine on the back. You memorize these numbers, Charley, then you pitch this card, okay? Don't let 'em find it on you, understand?"

"Yeah yeah, I understand."

"Soon as you give Cozzolino Bertelli's number, you call me, okay? Soon as you can get to a phone. Don't put it off, okay?"

"What if he says he ain't callin' nobody, huh? What if he wantsa be called, then what?"

"Then get his number and call me, I'll give it to Albert, Albert'll call him, c'mon, you're thinkin' too much, Charley, okay?"

"Oh yeah, right. Don't want me doin' that, uh-uh, noooo. Just my ass, that's all. They're tryin' to fuck me around and you're tellin' me don't think too much, just be mister cool. Meanwhile, my stomach's goin' about a hundert miles an hour right now, you know that? Aw man, Jesus Christ, I don't get it, no shit I don't, I never did nothin' to nobody, I never snitched nobody out, never once in my life, what the fuck, never did nothin' to Cozzolino, or this fucker Butterbaugh or that fuckin' Tanyar, that jagoff. Bust my ass for my uncle, what's it get me, huh? I don't get it. Never felt sorry for myself my whole life, man. I'm tellin' ya, I'm feelin' sorry for myself all the time now, and I fuckin' hate it, I really fuckin' hate feelin' sorry for myself. Never used to feel this shit, feel it all the time now. Motherfuckers, I hate 'em for makin' me feel like this."

"I understand, Charley."

"You do?"

"Yeah. I really do. I know exactly how you feel. It's ugly."

"You ain't shittin', that's exactly what it is. Ugly . . ."

Before he got out of the car Babyak grumbled that he hoped Balzic knew what he was doing. Balzic, of course, didn't know what he was doing because he'd never been involved at this level in anything like this in his entire career. He'd always left the cloak-and-dagger stuff to Carlucci or, better yet, to the county detectives or the state police, people who claimed to be trained for it. Whether they were or not was another issue.

Balzic had never been big on buying contraband or prohibited drugs as a way of obtaining evidence, and he'd gone along only when Carlucci or the state or county guys had said it was the only way to get it. As uncomfortable as Balzic had been in authorizing such procedures when he'd been chief, he'd invariably left the details to Carlucci to set up and operate. And when it came down to the actual sting, Balzic generally found a way to be near a phone or radio or tape recorder.

He went back inside Muscotti's after watching Babyak hurry away like the paranoiac that he was, head moving in a different direction with each second step, into a bitterly cold wind. As Balzic sat once again at the bar, he thought, here I am, legally an amateur, a geezer at that, and I pick now to try to run a game. Using Charley Babyak for crissake. Must be these drugs I'm takin', no shit, never did anything this goofy when I was wearin' a shield.

"Fuck you gettin' all chummy with him for?" Vinnie said, pouring chablis from a four-liter jug into a fresh glass.

"Who?"

"That weasel you run outta here with. You know who I'm talkin' about. What's-his-face, that jagoff Babyak."

"Wanted me to help him out a little bit, that's all. What, you don't like Charley?"

"He's no good. Like him or don't like him don't have nothin' to do with it."

"Yeah? What's no good about him?"

"You shittin' me? How many times you bust him?"

"Let me get this straight," Balzic said, taking a couple of sips of wine and squinting at Vinnie. "You're suddenly concerned with me associatin' with known felons? And this is because why? You fear for my soul, Father Vinnie, is that it?"

"He's no fuckin' good, that's all."

"Oh well that's always been my criteria for dealin' with people, you know, accordin' to Vinnie, the noted character analyst, 'he's no fuckin' good' — especially guys that want to trade information. If they're of questionable character, of course I would never dirty my ears with their, uh, you know, their disreputable words, heaven for-fucking-bid."

"Aw see there, you gotta be a wiseass now —"

"Yeah? Okay. Give me specifics. He's no good — why?"

"Hey, what I hear, he's punkin' kids. Usin' dope to do it."

"And you hear this from who exactly? A name please."

"I ain't givin' you no fuckin' name, c'mon."

"Then don't tell me nothin' 'cause without a name that's what you're tellin' me, nothin'."

"Hey, I got excellent sources, don't you worry about it."

"You got *excellent* sources? *Excellent* ain't in your vocabulary."

"Oh yeah?"

"Yeah. So who's your excellent source? Artie Chianese maybe?"

"How the fuck'd you know that?"

"Ohhhuuuu, ho-ho, yeah, don't mess with the information man here. How do you think I know? That's what Babyak was doin' here, whatta you think? Scared out of his mind. Chianese is his uncle, you know that?"

"His uncle? Get the fuck outta here, he ain't got no nephew named Babyak, you kiddin'? He's Siciliano all the way."

"No doubt he is, but his sister wasn't — least not in her marriage, not according to Babyak. And he oughta know who his mother's brother was — is, I mean. So ask yourself why a guy's uncle would start spreadin' that kinda shit around, huh? About his own sister's kid? Who's also makin' money for him, don't forget."

"He don't make no money — Babyak? Giddoutta here."

"He's bookin' for him. Whatta you call that if it ain't?"

"Who told you that — he's bookin' — he told you that? Don't believe that fucker —"

"Why? You believe Chianese — hey, listen to me. Charley Babyak may be in the fuckup hall of fame, but I've known him since he was thirteen or fourteen, that gotta be like thirty years, and I never once knew him to turn anybody. Not once. So now you can say what the fuck all you want, or what Fat Artie wants you to say —"

"Fat Artie don't want me to say nothin' —"

"Bullshit. You know exactly what you're doin'. But I'm tellin' ya, Babyak never did this — what you're doin' to him — never, not once in his life, not to dodge time for anybody. Show me a cop or a prosecutor anywhere who can say otherwise — and don't bring up Chianese again, 'cause if there was ever anybody who was no fuckin' good, it's him."

"I can't believe you're takin' this fucker's word over mine —"

"Oh now it's not Chianese anymore, it's you. Gimme a fuckin' break. What? You seen it, is that it? With your own eyes, you saw him punkin' a kid? Where? When? And if you have evidence of this crime, why have you been withholding this evidence from the duly elected and appointed authorities, who I'm sure would be interested in this, huh?"

"Aw will you listen to yourself, for crissake? Stop crushin' my onions."

"Stop crushin' mine."

Balzic spent the rest of the afternoon and the next two days trying to make a connection with Soloman Jacob Bemiss, owner of Freedom Firearms Inc. Bemiss used every excuse Balzic had ever heard to avoid meeting with him and one he hadn't heard, when Bemiss said he couldn't meet Balzic at three o'clock of the second afternoon because he had to get his prosthesis adjusted.

"Your what?"

"My prosthesis. I got a plastic leg —

well, not the whole thing, just from the knee down."

"Oh. And you have to get it adjusted today? This afternoon?"

"Yeah. Your body's always changin', you know? Especially you lost a piece of it, it changes shape, you know, as it's healin'. Every time it does that, you have to go back to the guy fitted you up, he's got to make adjustments, can't get away from it."

"And you can't see me today 'cause you have to have these, uh, these adjustments made."

"Yeah. Sometimes it takes hours."

"Uh-ha. Well listen, uh, Mister Bemiss, we gotta get together somctime soon, you know? 'Cause there's some information I have to have from you, okay? Can't get away from it."

"Well that's what you keep tellin' me, but, uh, like I been tellin' you, I don't wanna answer these questions just now 'cause I got these other things I gotta do."

"Like get your prosthesis adjusted."

"Exactly. In fact I don't hang up right now and get on the road I'm gonna be late for my appointment, and these guys, hey, they got a waitin' list like, you know, three months you gotta schedule ahead with them."

"So when can we get together?"

"Call me tomorrow, I should be able to give you an answer tomorrow."

"That's what you told me yesterday."

"Listen, I'm tryin' to be polite here, you know? But really, I don't see why I have to talk to you at all, I mean I filled out that claim form, I mean, what're you gonna ask me that's not on that form?"

"Well since I don't know what's on that form, I might not ask you anything that's on it —"

"Well then it sounds to me like you're just huntin' and fishin' and I sorta resent that, so I guess that's why I don't see all this urgency you apparently see. I mean I'll talk to you, but when I get the time, understand? Which ain't now. Bye."

The next day when Balzic called, the first thing he said after he said hello was, "Mister Bemiss, yesterday when we talked you said somethin', uh, I gotta correct you about, okay?"

"Is this gonna take long, 'cause I got people here, you know? Furniture people? I'm tryin' to get my business back in business if you know what I mean, and like every time I turn around I'm pickin' up the phone and it's you. I mean I really can't spend all my time on the phone with you —"

"Mister Bemiss, excuse me, but if I were you and I was tryin' to get my business back in business, the way you put it? I'd work a little harder cooperatin' with me, okay? 'Cause you're doin' a real good job of forgettin' that I'm the guy who's gonna make the report to the guy you bought the insurance from, you know? I wouldn't be always figurin' out some new reason why you gotta be somewhere else every time I suggest we get together, understand?"

There was no answer for so long Balzic said, "Hello? You still there? Hello?"

"Still here. Just lookin' at some fabric swatches, you know, for the chair I'm gonna buy —"

"Well you wanna say somethin'? 'Cause you keep tryin' not to talk to me, Mister Bemiss, that's what's goin' at the top of my report, you know? Subject Bemiss made no effort to cooperate with the undersigned, and in fact came up with some of the more outlandish excuses why he couldn't meet me to verify the details of his claim. How'd you like Albert Bertelli readin' that in the first paragraph, huh? Whattaya think your chances're gonna be of gettin' the kinda furniture you got your heart set on, huh?"

"Aw for Christ's sake," Bemiss said. "What're you doin' now?"

"What am I doin' now? What's it sound like I'm doin' now, huh? Tryin' to make a appointment with you —"

"No, no, uh-uh, I meant what are you doin' right now, can you come out right now, that's what I meant, Jesus Christ, you're so fuckin' uptight, man, I'm tellin' you, you need to get out in the woods and kill somethin', get rid of that anger you got stored up, man, I mean, you're a candidate for a heart attack if I ever heard one —"

"I'm leavin' soon as I hang up," Balzic said, his anger turning up several notches. "And I'm hangin' up right now." He did. Then he said, "And you better be there when I get there, you sonofabitch."

Balzic drew the phone back as though he was going to slam it into the wall, but out of the corner of his eye he caught sight of Ruth watching him. He cleared his throat sheepishly and set the phone in its cradle gently.

"Nice save," Ruth said. "Who was that?"

"Ah some jagoff owns a gunshop. The guy who bought his insurance from Al Bertelli? Who hired Mo who hired me? You know? Jerk thinks he's really helpin' himself by playin' coy with me. Only called him about six times now, and finally he says come on out, he'll talk to me."

"You going? Not gonna do it on the phone?"

"Nah, this one I have to see his face. Uh, who's cookin' tonight?"

"You."

"Me? You sure?"

"It's right there on the calendar. Last night I made beans and greens, remember? We had your bread with olive oil and Parmesan —"

"Yeah, yeah, okay, I remember now. Okay, so I'll figure somethin' out — that won't be pasta primavera, I know."

"It can be pasta, Mar, just see if you can find some different veggies, that's all."

"I was thinkin' of roasted potatoes, you know? Woke up thinkin' about 'em. You know, with rosemary? With oil and rosemary, roast 'em for like forty-five minutes, 'member when you used to do that? Why'd you quit doin' that?"

"Well you got such a thing for them, we must've had them twice a week there for about two months —"

"And what, you got sick of 'em or what?"

"Yeah. More or less."

"Well I wanna have 'em."

"Well if you're cookin', you can have whatever you want. What I'm asking is are we gonna have anything else? Or is that gonna be it, just potatoes?"

"No, I'll think of somethin'. Caesar salad maybe. I just found out you could use Eggbeaters raw —"

"Oh you cannot —"

"Yeah you can, they're pasteurized, says right on the box. You don't believe the box, call 'em up, they got an eight hundred number on there somewhere, I saw it —"

"Well I will call them, 'cause I don't believe that —"

"Well if you're gonna call somebody if you don't believe it, call somebody else, whatta you think they're gonna tell you — what's on the carton is wrong? You can't use 'em raw? We just put that on the carton to play with your mind?"

"I'll call whoever I want," Ruth said. "Go see that gunshop guy, and think of something else, 'cause I don't want just potatoes —"

"Caesar salad I said —"

"Something else —"

"Bread and olive oil, Romano — we still got some?"

"You're standing two steps from the

freezer — look, why don't you?"

"I don't have to look, I know we have some, just grated some couple days ago. I think."

"Just go, I'll look."

"What, you wanna dance or somethin'?"

"Yes, if you wanna know, I do want to dance, I'm feelin' real antsy. Got a lot of crazy energy I want to get rid of. So go."

"Okay okay, I'm goin'. This is me, goin' right now. Have a good time dancin'. Bye."

"Bye."

While he was putting on his parka near the front door, he said, "Oh, listen. If Al Bertelli calls or Mo? Can you hear me?"

"I'm standing right here, Mar."

"Oh. Well if either one of them calls, tell 'em —"

Before he could finish the sentence the phone rang.

"Probably one of them now," Ruth said, going back into the kitchen to pick up the phone. She listened for a moment, then covered the mouthpiece. "It's Emily. Would you like to talk to her?"

"No, not now. Tell her I'll call her tonight, okay?"

"That's what you said the last time."

"C'mon, Ruth, I gotta go. Tell her tonight, for sure."

"Okay," Ruth said, sighing. "I'm not gonna let you forget."

Before she could say anything, Balzic was out the door and heading for his car.

"How you spellin' that?" Bemiss said, sliding around, trying to read Balzic's writing from the side.

"How'm I spellin' what?" Balzic said.

"My first name. Don't spell it like them Hebes spell it. It ain't S-o-l-o-m-o-n. It's S-o-l-o-m-a-n. It ain't Solo-mon. It's Solo-man, as in one who travels alone."

"Okay. Solo-man."

"Yeah, now you got it right. My people are from Germany. My grandfather fought for the kaiser in Big One. And my father was one of the real desert rats, you know? With Rommel? In the Afrika Korps. You look like you're the right age to know who Rommel was, huh?"

"Yes, I know who Rommel was."

"That was a real leader, you know? Real warrior. Not like those clowns we had in Nam. Fuckers shoulda been wearin' skirts."

"Uh, I'm sure some other time, Mister

Bemiss, we might have a, uh, how do I wanna say this? A strenuous discussion about leadership. But right now what I'm interested in is the burglary here, you know?"

Bemiss shrugged. He was large, especially from the waist up, with only a slight paunch. He was very muscular through the shoulders and arms. His graying hair hung four inches or more below the collar of his blue denim shirt, and his hands, wrists, and forearms were tufted with wiry hair that was also graying, as were his full beard and moustache. He was smoking a long, thin cigar like it was a cigarette, inhaling deeply and exhaling the smoke in narrow streams or else blowing rings toward the ceiling, which seemed to mesmerize him as they rose.

The place still reeked of horse manure, even though Bemiss had lit many candles around the floor which burned the odor of vanilla.

Horseshit and vanilla, Balzic thought as soon as he walked through the door, as unlikely a combination of odors as he'd ever thought possible.

"Got somethin' I can write on, Mister Bemiss? Never could take notes just writin' on my other hand, you know?" Balzic said, looking for a flat surface on which to rest his notebook.

"Got a piece a plywood on one of the showcases back there," Bemiss said, nodding toward the rear of his shop.

Balzic let Bemiss go first and then hung back a bit so he could observe Bemiss walking. Bemiss's limp was just a slight hesitation.

"Get your, uh, prosthesis adjusted, did ya?"

"Yeah. Just needed to have a couple spots sanded off. Didn't take him twenty minutes, but it makes all the difference in the world." Bemiss pulled up his right pant leg to show off his prosthesis. "You want me to take it off? Show you where he was workin', huh? I know you don't believe me, most people don't even know I got this thing, then when I tell 'em they all jump to the conclusion I got it in Nam."

"Where did you, uh, I don't know what I wanna say here — lose it or get it or what?"

"Left the original in Southside Hospital. Got this one from some guys in Oakland, work outta the University of Pittsburgh."

"What happened?"

"Ah, I was deliverin' acid to this outfit in the Southside, was puttin' one of the

378

drums on a dolly and the goddamn thing just split open, one of those goofy fuckin' accidents you hear about other people havin'. Shit splashed all over my ankle and foot. I just laid there and watched it take everything down to the bones in like nothin' flat. Woke up about fourteen hours later, looked down at all those bandages, and I thought, hallelujah, my days as a truck-drivin' man are over. Found the right lawyer, and he got a coupla months on some island in the Mediterranean and I got this gunshop. Plus a house and sixty acres and a new pickup, and every gun I ever wanted to kill somethin' with. Then this sonofabitch just comes in here and throws shit everywhere, ruins everything."

"Well, it all looks replaceable to me."

"Yeah sure it's replaceable, it's just you get everything set up pretty much the way you want it, you work your ass off gettin' it just right, you know, then some dickhead comes in and ruins it in one night. Just pisses me off, that's all."

Balzic got out his copy of Bemiss's claim and started asking about the furniture, but Bemiss dismissed him with a wave.

"Most of that was in the Dumpster the day after the state cop took pictures of it. I wasn't gonna keep it around, bad as it was smellin', c'mon, you didn't expect to find any of that stuff here, did ya?"

Balzic pointed to the showcases on the other side of the room. "Well, these showcases, uh, they're still original items, right? Still on the insured list, right?"

Bemiss nodded.

"And, uh, they've still got, uh, well look there, in the front right there on the bottom shelf there, what's that? Looks like horse crap to me, not that I'm any expert, but it sure ain't fly crap, is it?"

"Oh you're a real comedian, you are."

"I'm not tryin' to be wise, I'm just sayin' —"

"Yeah right, tell me what you're just sayin'."

"I'm just sayin', you seem to have the same problem with these showcases, the ones on this side of the room here, but —"

"Seem to have? I don't *seem* to have the same kinda problem, I *had* the same kinda problem, it was just a whole hell of a lot worse in the cases where I had the handguns, that's all. The ones I threw out. The dickhead, you know? He's the one with the problem, not me. I'm just tryin' to live with it — but I sure as shit didn't create this problem, you know? He did, the sonofabitch, he's the one broke all the damn glass, scattered all —"

"Yeah yeah, I know who had the problem, all I'm tryin' to do, Mister Bemiss, is get a clear idea of what you say was destroyed so I can make an accurate report to the man who hired me, that's all —"

"Well get the pictures from the state cop, why don't you? You want a clear idea, take a look at them, they'll show you everything you wanna see, he musta took three goddamn rollsa film."

"I know he did, Mister Bemiss, but I'm talkin' to you right now, I'm not talkin' to him —"

"Yeah and I'll bet you're never gonna get around to talkin' to him, are ya? Wanna bet?"

"Well you'd lose, 'cause I already talked to him."

"You did? Oh."

"Yeah I did. Why's that surprise you?"

Bemiss shrugged. "Didn't know you insurance guys were all that, uh, dedicated."

"If you mean by insurance guy, am I gettin' paid by the insurance company, uh-uh. My pay's comin' from the attorney who's been retained by the insurance agent who sold you the policy, so, yeah, in that sense I'm an insurance guy, but from my point of view I couldn't be any further re-moved."

"Meaning what — you're more dedi-cated than the average bear?"

"Uh, listen, let's change the subject here, okay? For my purposes, it's fine with me, you wanna say that the showcases you had on this side of the room — this is the west side, right?"

"Hell I don't know."

"You sell compasses, don't ya?"

"Course I sell compasses —"

"Well get one out and see which way north is."

Bemiss got a compass off the bottom shelf of a showcase on the opposite side of the room, held it up, and said the wall behind Balzic was the west side of the shop.

"Okay, so the cases on the west side of the shop you've declared to be a total loss, right? And this is also true of your com-puter, all the disks, or floppy disks or what-ever you call 'em, and your file cabinets and all your paper files, that's also true?"

"Yes, right, true. And I have replacement value —"

"I know. But the thing I wanna ask you about, Mister Bemiss, and I'm hopin' you can tell me somethin' about it, is, uh, with your file cabinets destroyed, right? You've declared your file cabinets a total loss, correct?"

"Correct. Clown just jammed shit everywhere, into the locks, everywhere —"

"And also your, uh, computer disks or floppies — can't understand why they call 'em that, they look rigid to me, course I don't know very much about computers —"

"That's 'cause the first ones they made, that's what they were, just got all wobbly and floppy every time you picked it up — you didn't know that?"

"No I didn't. Anyway, they were also destroyed? Whatever you call 'em, the disks?"

"Yeah. Just threw 'em into a garbage bag fulla shit and stomped all over 'em."

"How'd you know they were in there?"

"Huh? In where?"

"In the garbage bag? With the crap?"

"Whattaya mean?"

Balzic shrugged and sighed. "I mean, how'd you know that's where they were? How'd you find them? Were there other bags layin' around?"

"Nooo. All the other ones, uh, they were pretty much empty."

"Just that one, huh? What made you look in there?"

"Hell I don't remember why I looked in that one — what're you gettin' at anyway, what're you tryin' to say? I don't like the look you're givin' me —"

"I'm not givin' you any look, Mister Bemiss, I'm just lookin' at you, and I'm just askin' you a simple question. What made you look in that bag, that's all. Where was it? You remember?"

"Yeah I remember, it was right beside the computer."

"And the computer was also covered with crap, right?"

"Right. Jammed it into every little opening, just smeared the whole keyboard, jammed it into the disk drives —"

"The what?"

"The disk drives. Where you put the floppy disks."

"Oh. Uh, does that mean your computer records are gone? As in destroyed, lost, what?"

"That's exactly what it means."

"Uh-huh," Balzic said, writing yet another note into his book, this one about asking Rugs Carlucci if what Bemiss was saying was true. Carlucci had been backed into learning about computers because apparently no one else in the Rocksburg PD had the time or inclination to do so. Balzic read the note twice to remind himself to not forget to call Carlucci. Then he said, "So, uh, Mister Bemiss, what you're tellin' me, I mean correct me if I'm wrong, but, uh, you have no way to authenticate your loss, am I right in sayin' that?"

"No you're not right — you mean I don't have any proof how many guns were stolen?"

Balzic shrugged and nodded. "Well, what other way is there to look at it — I mean, hey, you tell me how we can authenticate your loss and I'll be glad to do it. I mean, you show me —"

"What're you tryin' to say exactly, huh?" Bemiss took a step toward Balzic.

"Mister Bemiss, you, yourself, just now said in so many words, you have no way to authenticate your loss, is that what I said or not?"

"Yeah that's what you said, but I don't like the way you said. What the hell's that mean anyway?"

"It means exactly what it sounds like — you claim you had thirty-eight Model 92F Beretta, 9mm semi-automatic handguns stolen from this place of business, and, uh, thirty thousand rounds of 9mm ammo, 115-grain full-metal jacket, that's what you claimed, it's right here," Balzic said, holding up the claim form.

"Yeah? And so what?"

"The so what is, all I'm sayin' is you can't authenticate this, not without records you can't, that's all I said, I don't care what you think I said. And if you can authenticate your claim, I'll be happier than hell to listen to it, whatever way you tell me. I mean, for example, give me the names and numbers of the people you bought the merchandise from, can you do that?"

"No I can't."

"Why not?"

" 'Cause their names and numbers were on the records that were either in the file cabinets or on the computer disks."

"This was what, your original inventory purchase, is that what you're sayin'?"

"Yeah. That's what I'm sayin'."

"And you can't remember their names? Not one of 'em?"

"Hey, that was more'n a year ago —"

"Well how many different distributors did you order from?"

"Hell I don't know."

"More than one?"

"Course more than one."

"How many more than one? Two? Six? Twenty?"

"I don't know. Don't remember."

"Well, Mister Bemiss, I mean, hey, if we have to, you know, we'll just go through one of your *Shooting Industry* magazines — you have one, don't ya?"

"Got a bunch of 'em, yeah."

"So, okay, we go through the directory, we eliminate all the dealers west of the Mississippi, you take half and I take half, I think whoever sold you all those Berettas, I think they'd recall that order, don't you? That was a hell of an order, you ask me."

Bemiss thought about that for a long moment. "You keep givin' me this funny look, and it's really startin' to bother me."

"Mister Bemiss, what you gotta understand is I believe you. I do. Unfortunately, the man who hired me, hey, he doesn't care what I believe. All he cares is whether I can prove what I believe, simple as that. And if you can't prove you had these Berettas before you got burgled, how do you expect me to prove it? 'Cause if I had to write the report right now? All I could truthfully say is, you know, owner asserts that X number of firearms and ammo were stolen but he has no proof of purchase, no bills of lading, no inventory sheets, no tax statements — right? You do not have any of those, correct?"

"Right," Bemiss said.

"So in other words, you have nothin' to show that these items were ever in your possession, so, uh, period, end of report. So, uh, if you really wanna cover your loss here, Mister Bemiss, I'd start lookin' up some phone numbers. Whattaya think? Wanna drag out a couple copies of *Shooting Industry*? Huh? You take A to M, I'll take N to Z, nobody west of the Mississippi, and, uh, I'll see you here tomorrow morning, we'll see what we have, right? Unless you have two phone lines — do ya?"

"No," Bemiss said glumly.

"Well, then I'll have to go use somebody else's phone. So, uh, see you tomorrow, then we'll see where we are maybe — oh. Almost forgot. Name Cozzolino mean anything to you?"

"Who?"

"Cozzolino. Know anybody by that name?"

"No. Why?"

"Ever have any problem with the security agency here? Bulldog Security?"

"No. Oh wait. Yeah, now that you mention it. Yeah, one of their guards turned into a real pain in the ass, yeah, kept comin' around, always tryin' to talk me into givin' him some kinda discount, professional courtesy he said, one professional to another. Finally had to tell him to get lost, I was tryin' to make money, I wasn't tryin' to make friends. Professional courtesy my ass, he didn't know what the fuck he was talkin' about."

"What kinda guns was he expectin' you to give him a discount for, you remember?"

"Aw crap he saw on TV, or in the movies, that nigger on *Spenser*, Hawk or whatever, he was always talkin' about this .44 Mag he had. Nickel-plated, with an eight-inch barrel, you know, just made this goofus all gaga. The kinda personal defense weapon some movie asshole'd think you need to look dangerous. Like a .22 can't kill you just as dead. Shit. I do damn near all my shootin' with a .22. Old Colt Woodsman, must be forty-five years old at least."

"Remember his name?"

"Who?"

"The security guard," Balzic said.

"Oh. No. Wait. Ron somethin' — no . . . can't think of it. Ron sounds right, but I don't know. One of those mouthy fucks gets on your nerves just to see him comin', I didn't wanna remember his name. Always talkin' about what kinda gun he'd use to blow all the niggers away, had this Dirty Harry fantasy. Remember those Clint Eastwood movies?"

"I try not to."

"He was the kinda asshole talks about how he'd like to take out a coupla spades just to hear 'em holler, still doin' that nursery rhyme, you know, grab a nigger by the toe, see if you can make him holler? Only he's so dumb he don't know what he's sayin'. Besides, you drop him off in Homewood or Brushton or Wilkinsburg, he'd have a fuckin' heart attack tryin' to get outta there before the sun went down."

"And you wouldn't, of course," Balzic said, wondering what it was going to take to work this conversation to his advantage.

"I grew up in Wilkinsburg, man. I can go back there any time of day or night, go anywhere I want. Wanna know why?"

"I'm sure you're gonna tell me."

"Everybody there calls me Lurp, that's why. Know what Lurp means?"

Balzic shrugged and shook his head no.

"It ain't spelled the way it sounds. It's L-R-R-P. That's Long-Range Reconnaissance Patrol. Know anything about that?"

"No."

"Two of us'd go out for thirty days at a time, man. Dead into Indian Country."

"Dead into where?" Balzic almost laughed.

"In Nam. Indian Country. Right in the middle of the hostiles, s'matter, don't you own a TV or somethin'? Our first TV war and you didn't see it? You don't remember Vietnam?"

"Oh I remember it alright. Just didn't know what you were talkin' about, Indian Country."

Bemiss drifted off dreamily, a tight smile barely showing itself. "Huey'd put us down, me and my spotter. He was s'pposed to find 'em and keep score. But I was the one dustin' 'em. Lemme show you somethin'." Bemiss reached into his back pocket and brought out a long flat wallet which was chained to his belt. He drew out a fading photograph and held it up for Balzic's inspection. There was a tall, muscular soldier, shirtless, mugging wildly for the camera. In his right hand, at shoulder height, he was holding the hair of the severed head of a Vietnamese.

"That was cadre there. VeeCee cadre. Dusted him practically point-blank. Stupid fuck wandered off from his village — course it wouldn'ta made no difference, I'da still dusted his ass if he stayed home. Lucky for me, he came wanderin' out, I just set there and let him come, 'cause he hadn't come out I woulda never got this picture. Ain't too many family albums got one of these in 'em, I can tell ya that."

"I'm sure they don't," Balzic said. "And I can see how proud you are."

"You can get sly all you want, mister," Bemiss said, "but I'm here to tell ya there ain't nothin' in this world'll lift your spirits like killin' somebody that needs killin', and the tougher the shot, the better it makes you feel. Nothin' else in this world'll give you that kinda satisfaction."

"Well. I can see the satisfaction in your eyes. And I believe you."

"You better believe it, it's fuckin'-A well and truly told."

"I'm sure it is."

"Thirty-one confirmed kills, man. That's the record I left for those other boys to shoot at. And that's only the approved targets, understand? Fuckin' spotter wouldn't count the other ones. But I never left 'em with just one to bury, you can believe that."

"I'm sure you didn't."

"Yeah," Bemiss said disgustedly. "Now I have to stay sharp on rats at a landfill."

"Well, you know," Balzic said, holding up his copy of *Shooting Industry* magazine, "we'll be doin' a little long-range reconnaissance right in here — at least I hope you will — you're goin' to, right? Not gonna make me do it all myself?"

Bemiss snorted. "Yeah, whatever."

"See you tomorrow then," Balzic said, giving Bemiss a salute with the rolled-up magazine as he left the shop and headed out into the main mall, shuddering involuntarily twice before he got outside.

Shooting rats to stay sharp, Balzic thought. Thank God for rats.

The next day, Balzic woke at 6 A.M. with muscle spasms in his neck and left shoulder. It wasn't till he was in the kitchen pouring boiling water into a cup of instant coffee that he remembered having called all those gun dealers with the phone in the crook of his neck. Didn't matter that he'd called the gun dealers. All he could do was compare these pains to the intense, crushing pain he'd felt in the cath lab when Doctor Fine was drilling the plaque out of his coronary artery.

Though there was no question intellectually that the pain he felt when he awoke was not at all similar to the pain he'd felt on the table in the lab, it was pain on the left side of his body nonetheless, and he'd heard too many times in his life about the symptoms of a heart attack, every recitation of which included pains on the left side of the body. Ergo, he was caught on the carousel once again: is it or isn't it a heart attack? Multiplying the pain was the fact that he still had to call half a dozen or so dealers whose lines had been busy last night.

When Ruth came into the kitchen and they exchanged their morning hug, he was pulling away almost as soon as his hands touched her back.

"You all right?" she said, studying his face while trying not to look as though she was.

"Yeah. What, I don't look alright?"

"As a matter of fact, no, you don't."

"What? My lips blue or somethin'? Huh?" He was starting to reach for the pulse in his neck when she grabbed his hand.

"Stop that, okay? You look scared, you don't look sick. Are you scared? What about?"

He looked away and sighed. "Shows that much, huh?"

"Well, you know, Mar, mostly that's what I've been looking at lately — you lookin' scared, so it's hard not to see it — I mean when it happens, when you get really scared, I mean it's not something I'm purposely looking for, okay?"

"Okay, okay, I get ya — it's just, ah shit, you know, I made all those phone calls last night "

"So you have cramps in your neck, right?"

"Yeah. Real bad. God, everything just disappeared from my head — what were we talkin' about? Exactly. I can't remember —"

"Huh? That's what we were talking about. Why you were scared."

"Huh? Oh. Well not were. Am. Are. Whatever. Still."

"Are you having some other symptoms? What kind?"

"No I'm not havin' symptoms, I made all those goddamn phone calls, I was holdin' the phone with my shoulder, and my back, my shoulder, Christ —"

"And what? Mar, you look fine, I'm telling you, your color's good, you're not sweating — are you nauseous? You having trouble breathing?"

"No. I'm breathin' alright — ain't I?"

"God, Mar, you have to know whether you're having trouble breathing or not, I can't decide that for you!"

"Okay okay, I'm not havin' trouble breathin', alright?"

"Well if you're not having trouble breathing, and you're not sweating, and you're not nauseous, and you don't feel this pain — I mean the pain might be in your neck and left side, right? But you know it's from holding the phone with your shoulder, right? Why do you do that, I don't understand, you know this happens every time you do it —"

"Yeah yeah, right."

"So quit doin' it then! And can't you tell yourself that's what it's coming from?"

He sighed and shook his head, eyes closed. "Yes, right, I should be able to, I know I should be able to, I know in my head why I should be able to distinguish one kind of pain from another, but . . ."

"But what, Mar? C'mon, say it, what?"

He took off his glasses and rubbed his face hard with both palms. "It's just hard, that's all. I don't know what, it's just . . . just hard to tell yourself what you're feelin' isn't what . . . what you're hopin' it ain't — I know that doesn't make any sense, I'm talkin' in circles — listen, I'm goin'. I gotta get outta here, I'm goin' to the mall, gonna talk to that asshole again."

"Who? The gun dealer?"

"Yes. I been screwin' around with this thing, Christ, a week now, longer, I don't even know how long. Can't remember when I started —"

"Well you can't go now, Mar. It doesn't open till ten — they let the walkers in around nine or so, but stores aren't open —"

"Oh Christ I forgot. I gotta call these other guys anyway, I can't talk to him till I do that — don't know what the hell I'm doin' —"

"Well just slow down, Mar. Do it the best way you can, that's all. Do what you can, and if you have to stop, stop, that's all, you don't have to explain anything to anybody. Just me. You can't not explain to me."

"I tell you everything, Christ —"

"You think you tell me everything, Mar, I know that's what you think, but a lot of those things you think you've told me? Hey, they haven't made it out of your mouth. They might get to your mouth, but they don't get past your lips, okay? You just think they do."

"Oh God, Ruth, too much analyzin'

goin' on, babes, I mean it —"

"No, uh-uh, you just think there's too much, Mar, that's just you thinkin' that 'cause you only wanna think about what you wanna think about, 'cause if I'm thinkin' about it, it's too much analyzing, but if you're thinking about it, it's what? Huh? What is it when you think about it, Mar, c'mon, tell me, I wanna hear this."

He dropped his chin, gave her a half-grin, half-glare, shook his head, cleared his throat with almost a growl, and said, "You're too fucking much, swear to God you are."

"Too much? Or too much for you?" She canted her head, narrowed her eyes, just touched the inside of her lower lip with her tongue. She wasn't quite glaring, not quite grinning, but she was wary, worried, suspicious, more than a hair angry.

Emotionally it was a draw, the kind that comes only after so many decades, so many disagreements, arguments, quarrels, screamings, ragings that they both knew it was time to move on. So, Balzic thought, after you've earned all that history, what you've won is the sense to recognize a draw when you see one, and that recognition meant you knew that even if this thing was worth fighting about, it wasn't worth winning, because nothing would make you feel worse than trying to beat someone who wasn't trying to beat you.

He suddenly wished he could have said all that, but he knew he didn't have one chance in ten of saying it the way he was thinking it, and he thought the best thing to do was just do what he had to do. And hadn't she already said that?

"You're right though," he said. "I can't say the stuff I'm thinkin' — I wish to hell I could, and I don't know why I can't, but I can't and that's all there is to it. But I love you. I know that, and I can say that."

She gave him a playful poke in the shoulder. "You're just sayin' that 'cause you're scared, that's all."

"Now don't go messin' around with me, okay? I just tell ya I love ya, and you got to go messin' around with my mind, no shit, I'm gettin' outta here, don't say another word to me, I mean it."

He started to walk around her, but she stepped in front of him and pulled him to her and kissed him on the lips and looked at him and said, "God, you're hard on yourself. Why are you so hard on yourself? You won't let yourself feel pain but when you feel it you think it's the end of the world and worst of all you think you deserve it except you're just shakin' in your shoes what's waitin' for you. God, Mar, give yourself a break! I mean it. Take a break!"

"Wish the fuck I knew how."

"Oh poor baby," she said, mocking him, shaking him, hugging him. "Poor poor baby. You work so hard to stay so tough, and you're almost as scared to let people see you're scared as you are to let yourself feel scared. Honest to God, Mar, you got to lighten up on yourself, you're not that bad, I mean it. Why do you think you are?"

"Missus Wrobelewski would probably have a different —"

"Oh piss on Missus Whojeewhatski! Mario, goddammit, you've gotta stop this —"

"Look, I wish I could, I wish I could shut my mind off — or my brain or what-ever's in there runnin' my thought motor," he said tapping his temple hard three times.

"Don't do that! My God, you're gonna break the skin — look at that, you scraped yourself with your nail — cut it out, Mar!"

"Okay okay, that's it, c'mon, lemme go, I gotta call these guys." He tried to pull away from her.

"Look, I don't know how you stop your thoughts or your mind or your brain or whatever you think you ought to do to give yourself a break. Maybe you need to talk to somebody, I don't know, there has to be somebody around who can tell you how to give yourself a break — there has to be, Mar —"

"Yeah, okay. Where? Who? Tell me, I'll go talk to him."

Ruth nodded, licked her lips, let go of him, and backed away. "Let me think about it. I know somebody I can ask. Let me see what I can come up with, okay? Would you let me do that for you?"

"I'd let you do damn near anything for me —"

"Damn near?" she howled. "You better start callin' people, buster. Damn near my foot."

"That was a joke."

"Oh what, now you gonna tell me I don't have any sense of humor?"

"No no, hell no, I wouldn't say that, believe me, that's the last thing I'd ever say to you. I swear on my mother's grave I'd never say anything that dumb to you, never." He was moving toward the dining room where he'd left his briefcase. He was trying to collect the things he needed to start making calls again.

"Mar?"

"What?"

"Promise me. If you need to take a break, do it, okay? Don't make yourself crazy, okay? Promise?"

"Okay okay, I promise."

"Whether you're makin' calls here or out, whatever, okay?"

"Okay. I promise. I'll take it easy."

Then he was trying to playfully shove her out of the way so he could get to his briefcase.

"I don't know who you think you're gonna call, Mar," she said, pointing at the clock above the fridge. It was 7:29.

"Oh Christ," he said, blowing out a long sigh and shaking his head. "Well, what do I do now?"

"Go back to bed for a couple hours, why don't you?"

And that's what he did, before calling the dealers who hadn't answered his calls last night. To the last, their response was the same: they had no record of selling any firearm or ammunition to Freedom Firearms Inc.

It was five to noon before Balzic finally got through to the last distributor on his part of the list in *Shooting Industry*. During lunch of black bean chili and bread dipped in olive oil, he grudgingly promised Ruth that if it didn't get warmer they'd go to one of the malls tomorrow morning to walk.

Ruth had always been more careful about what she ate, and she'd always been more active, doing the housework, gardening, mowing the grass, going up and down the cellar stairs to do the laundry, walking in the neighborhood, exercising along with shows on TV, and, in the last year or so, dancing in the house. After he'd retired, it seemed natural to her that walking was a thing they could do together, and she took every opportunity the weather gave them to get out and moving.

His "cardiac event" further strengthened her resolve; now she had medical opinion behind her, and she showed him every newspaper and magazine article she found about the benefits of walking. She kept insisting that nothing would be worse for him than to sit around "looking for pings in his engine." What he needed to do was walk, she said: Doctor Fine had said so, Doctor James had been saying so for years, the American Heart Association was saying so, every exercise guru on TV and in print was touting its benefits.

Balzic tried to tell himself that walking was medicine, no different from one aspirin a day or 50 milligrams of Lopressor, but when he did get out and walk, he had a hard time dealing with the fact that the person who was most persistent about getting him moving was also in much better shape than he was. Balzic just couldn't keep up with Ruth, and so he urged her to not hold back to his pace and deny herself the exercise she wanted and needed. Of course when he was left behind, it gave him more time to listen for new pings in his engine.

And when he watched her pulling slowly away from him as they made their circuit around the mall or around town or around the quarter-mile track at the high school, Balzic halfheartedly consoled himself that he was four years older and many pounds heavier and that was the difference. But that was baloney and he knew it; he just hated the idea of walking for exercise, because to him it was just walking in circles, and nothing gave him more time to think about everything that he had or had not done in his life than walking in circles. Walking in circles in the malls was much worse: the hard floors pained his feet, ankles, and knees; and the short circuit amidst all that twinkly commerce bored him, giving him all the more reason to think about himself.

Temperamentally, Ruth couldn't sit still for more than an hour at a time, and it had to be an exceptional TV show or rental movie to keep her on the couch for that long. Even the best of books or magazines couldn't hold her on her chaise lounge in their bedroom. He joked that they'd had to have the chaise recovered because she wore it out getting up and down to do other things while she was supposedly reading. . . .

Balzic locked his Chevy and hurried through biting cold wind into the mall, where he found Soloman Bemiss standing aloof outside his shop. Bemiss gave a dismissive wave in the general direction of people going past his shop and said, "Look at these people. In here every day."

"What?" Balzic said. "Who's in here every day?"

"Every day," Bemiss said disgustedly.

"Never buy a damn thing, just use up oxygen, take up space. Hell they tryin' to prove?"

"Who you talkin' about?"

"These people that come in here every day and all they do is walk, around and around and around, Kee-rist. They open up the damn place for 'em early every day, why don't they come then? Why they gotta come when people're tryin' to do business, clog everything up?"

Balzic shrugged. "If these stores were alongside streets in town, Mister Bemiss, you'd laugh at yourself for sayin' that."

"Huh? I'd laugh at what now?"

"Some people would call that window shoppin'. In the big department stores in Pittsburgh? When they still had a few? Used to be a job called window decorator. 'Cause some people just like to look. And some people don't have enough money to do anything else, ever think about that?"

"Oh bullshit —"

"Well maybe not everybody wants to be doin' business all the time, Mister Bemiss. Some people're just tryin' to stay alive. And some of 'em are probably tryin' to prove they're still alive. You know, long as you're still movin', pretty hard for somebody else to put you in a hole and throw dirt on top of ya."

"That'd drive me nuts, goin' around and around and around, every day same old, same old," Bemiss said. "What they need to do is go hunt somethin'. Track it and kill it. Or if they're so goddamn squeamish, they could at least go outside and grow somethin'."

"In this weather?"

"Hell you can grow stuff in this weather. Just gotta think a little, that's all, do a little plannin', build you some low-level greenhouses, it ain't like it's never been done, lotsa people do it, New England, Canada, hell, all over the world. But, Christ, get outside, do somethin', anything. If you really wanna get your heart pumpin', if that's what they're tryin' to do, go hunt something. Get your heart pumpin' real fast."

"Yeah, so I've heard you say before." Balzic stepped across the threshold of Bemiss's shop and went toward one of the showcases in the back. He set his briefcase atop it and said, "Well, Mister Bemiss, you find the dealer that sold you those Berettas?"

"No. I was hopin' you did."

Balzic stared at Bemiss for a long moment. "You were hopin' I did? What're you, shittin' me?"

"Excuse me?"

"Hey, I was on the phone till nine o'clock last night. Only time I stopped was to eat. And this mornin', I started dialin' at nine sharp, all the ones I missed last night. Got through to the last one at five to noon, and now you're gonna stand there and tell me you're hopin' I found him? Hey Mister Bemiss, I mean, uh, either you bought those guns from somebody west of the Mississippi, which I strongly doubt, or else you're lyin'."

"What? Hey I don't like people talkin' to me like that."

"Yeah? Well, the distributors I called, nobody heard of you, so that leaves the people you were supposed to call, and now you're tellin' me you hope I found him? Either you didn't make the calls, or you bought the guns from somebody else, or you never bought the guns from anybody. You can call that anything you wanna call it, but lyin' is the least of it.

"And before you say another word, Mister Bemiss, I'm gonna tell ya a couple things. You don't start cooperatin', I'm gonna tell the lawyer who hired me your claim should be denied in total. And then I'm gonna call the DA's office and talk to them, and if they're not interested, then I'm gonna call Alcohol, Tobacco and Firearms and tell them a whole lotta pistols are on the loose, and I'm sure somebody from that outfit's gonna wanna take a look at your license. So you wanna huff and puff about how you don't like bein' talked to, hey, fine. Then come up with a better story, or I'm gonna do what I just said."

Bemiss said nothing for a long moment, just pushing out his lower lip, breathing heavily through his nose, and looking everywhere except at Balzic. When he finally brought his gaze around to meet Balzic's, he said, "I don't think I need to talk to you anymore. I think I need to talk to the man who sold me the policy and, uh, I think probably that'll happen in my lawyer's office, so, uh, the only thing I got to say to you is, uh, good-bye, motherfucker."

"Hey. Fine with me, Mister Bemiss. Hope you got a sharp lawyer, 'cause you just said good-bye to your money." Balzic closed his briefcase and gave Bemiss a sarcastic little salute as he left.

He drove over slickening roads and streets to Panagios Valcanas's office and did exactly as he'd promised, but not to Valcanas, who was out of the office deposing somebody for a traffic accident case.

That's what the woman he'd never seen before had said when he asked her where Mo was. She said she was a temp substituting for Valcanas's personal assistant, who was sick with the flu, and she wouldn't let Balzic into Mo's office because she didn't know him and wasn't going to have that on her head if he was some kind of crazy, so Balzic had to sit in the waiting room and talk to his tape recorder, which he did for forty-five minutes, saying in great detail that Bemiss's claim should be denied.

Then he tried to give the tape to the temp but she said she didn't know what to do with it so he asked her for a large envelope, which she found after going through every closet in the suite before finally landing on the one with the stationery supplies. Balzic wrote across the outside, "Bertelli, Freedom Firearms claim, M.B." and then sealed the tape inside and handed it to the temp, asking her to please be sure that Valcanas got it.

He then walked to the courthouse and took the elevator to the third floor and the DA's office after the temp looked at him funny when he asked if it was alright if he used Mo's phone to make a couple of calls.

410

Balzic ran into another temp working as a gatekeeper to the DA's office. She was young, loud, brash, and officious, altogether very impressed with herself. She didn't know who Balzic was, didn't care, all she knew was she had her orders, which were to admit no one until further notice. She didn't know why. She thought it was probably because they were having a meeting.

"They're always having meetings," Balzic said. "That's what they do in the DA's office. Just call somebody, okay? Tell 'em I'm out here? Mario Balzic? And I want to file an information? Please?"

"Have a seat, sir. They told me no calls and nobody goes in until further notice," she said.

Balzic took a seat and tried to read the *Rocksburg Gazette*, holding out for almost fifteen minutes before he felt a wave of anxiety getting ready to wash over him. He stood abruptly, dropped the paper on the chair he'd been sitting in, told the gatekeeper once again who he was and asked her once again to make sure DA Failan called him at his first opportunity. Then he headed for the elevator, and when it seemed to be stuck on the second floor — no doubt somebody having a meeting while holding the doors open — he scurried for the steps, trotted down them, and hurried back to his car parked behind Valcanas's office and then home.

There, without taking his parka off, he hunted up his most recent copy of the Pittsburgh directory and looked up the number for the Bureau of Alcohol, Tobacco and Firearms. He dialed it and spent many minutes being passed from one agent to another's personal assistant to another's until he finally was connected to one who had time to listen to him. That agent listened politely to Balzic but concluded the call by saying he was sorry but that further investigation would depend upon several factors, primarily case backlog and personnel workload.

"And since I'm not privy to that information, sir, all I can say is I'm not gonna promise any investigation will be conducted by this office, but we certainly appreciate your call and we certainly appreciate the work you've done, the effort you've made to collect the information you've collected. But if my supervisors do decide to proceed, I'm certain someone will be in touch with you. Thank you very much, sir, and, uh, you have a good day now. Good-bye."

So there, Mister Bemiss, take that, Balzic thought as he dropped the phone into the cradle. Nothin' like makin' threats other people are not real sure they're gonna have the time or the inclination or the manpower to carry out.

By the time Balzic hung up from that call, it was 3:35. He found a note from Ruth saying she was at the Y doing the yoga class and for him to get some balsamic vinegar if he was going out again and might be passing near a market. He was nearly hoarse, his throat was dry and itchy, and he was thirsty, so, for the second time in two days, he headed for Muscotti's.

"Rugs Carlucci called lookin' for you," Vinnie said while Balzic was draping his parka over the back of a chair at one of the tables. As Balzic was sitting on a barstool near the kitchen, Vinnie said, "Hear what happened to your buddy?"

"When'd he call? He want me to call him back? What buddy?"

"What're you gonna have?"

"A big glass of water —"

"Hey, you want water, go to the Y, fuck I look like, huh?"

"You don't want me to answer that."

"Then tell me what you want and don't say water."

"I'm sayin' water 'cause that's what I want — first. Second, I want a glass of whatever you're callin' dry white wine, and put some ice in it since I know you ain't keepin' it in a cooler where it oughta be, but first I want the water, but don't hurt yourself, okay? Now what buddy you talkin' about? What'd Rugs want?"

Vinnie filled a tumbler full of water and ice and then filled a draft beer glass nearly full of ice which he then filled with wine from a green jug whose label read Taylor California Cellars Chablis.

"Your buddy, you know, that Charley what's-his-face you went outta here with coupla days ago. Wine's two-fifty. Water's free. How should I know what he wants? He ain't callin' me, he's callin' you."

"Your prices go up and down faster than the stock market. Couple days ago it was what — seven bucks for a chablis and a muscatel?"

"Wasn't seven. But whatever, that was for aggravation. He ain't been around today, Steve, and so far you only got on

414

my nerves once."

"Uh-huh. So, uh, Rugs want me to call him?"

Vinnie shrugged. "Whatta you think? First thing outta your mouth is water, so whatta you want me to say?"

"How about sayin' what you started to say, how about that?"

"About what?"

"This Charley you're talkin' about, that's what. You said did I hear about my buddy, now I'm waitin', you haven't said anything else —"

"Charley Babyak."

"Yeah? So? What's up with him?"

"Got himself in a jackpot. Got grabbed with a buncha dope, buncha pictures a naked kids, buncha guns."

"Get outta here."

"I'm tellin' ya! Heard it on the radio when I was drivin' in. Got busted in Knox, musta been late last night, early this morning."

Balzic pursed his lips and tapped them with his fingers. "You sure you got the name right, wasn't somebody else sounded like him?"

"Hey. How many Charles Babyaks you think there are, huh? One's too fuckin' many."

"And you heard this when again?"

"Drivin' in here this mornin'. Eight fifty-five, local news, WRKB."

"Say where he was bein' held? Say anything about bail?"

"No. Bail?! What're you, shittin' me? This is WRKB — five minutes of news before the hour, whatta you want for crissake."

Balzic shrugged and shook his head.

"What're you shakin' your head for?"

"Nothin'. Gimme some quarters," Balzic said, pushing a dollar at Vinnie and thinking what to do. If everything Charley Babyak had said the last time they'd talked was true, and if Arturo Chianese was behind it as Babyak had said, then the next step was as logical and as inevitable as day following night.

"Look at you," Vinnie said, snorting. "Gettin' ready to do somethin' for that jagoff, he ain't worth one of my yesterdays —"

"Just gimme the quarters, okay?" Balzic said, draining the glass of water. "And fill that up again, will you please?"

"Fuck you so thirsty for? It's the middle of winter, somebody look at you they'd think it was July."

"Quarters, huh? I gotta go to a bank or somethin'?"

"Wastin' your time on that jagoff," Vinnie said, making change in a register behind him. He slapped the quarters on the bar and continued to harangue Balzic as he went to the pay phone near the back door.

"I'm callin' Rugs, is that okay with you?"

"What're you tellin' me for? I look like I care?"

Balzic called the Rocksburg station, asked for Detective Carlucci, and had to wait only moments before Carlucci picked up.

"Yo, Rugs, it's me, Balzic, what's up?"

"Mario, hi ya doin'? Listen, uh, I got a call from Eddie Plasjac little while ago. Remember him?"

"Vaguely. Oh oh, yeah, goofy-lookin' guy, real skinny, head like a football?"

"That's him. Told me somethin' while he was tellin' me somethin' else. Said he heard Knox PD collared Charley Babyak — remember him?"

"Yeah, course I do. Just talked to him couple days ago."

"Yeah, well, seems they got him with a whole buncha kiddie porn, you know, videos and magazines —"

"Aw bullshit."

"What, you know about this already?"

417

"No no. Just somethin' he said to me, that's all."

"For a second there, it sounded like you knew already —"

"Nah, nothin' like that. So go 'head — there's more, right?"

"Yeah. The thing I thought would interest you was, uh, now this is from Plasjac, who's generally reliable, uh, they apparently got him, Babyak, uh, in addition to all the porn? They got him with a buncha handguns, Berettas, and I was thinkin' that's what you were lookin' for, about this, uh, Freedom Firearms? Right? Berettas?"

"Yeah. Berettas, absolutely right."

"But what? This doesn't make you happy?"

"Tell ya the truth, no. 'Cause see, Babyak came to me three days ago, two days maybe, I forget — I was in here, Muscotti's, and he said his uncle was gettin' ready to chump him out, he was all frantic. I mean, he's never been what you call a calm guy, but he was really wired that day. I know he's usually never very far away from some crank, but, uh, see, now I don't know what to think. Uh, you remember when we first talked about this, you remember what you told me, huh? About where these guns might wind up?"

"Yeah."

"You also remember that Babyak was harmless?"

"Yeah. Compulsive thief but harmless, yeah."

"He told me he thought his uncle, you know? Fat Artie? Chianese?"

"He's Babyak's uncle? I didn't know that, no shit."

"Neither did I. Now I knew Cozzolino was his nephew — Artie's — maybe it was you told me that, but, uh, so is Babyak it turns out. So whattaya think Babyak told me, huh? Said he was scared his uncle was gonna chump him out because he thought Cozzolino wanted his job. You know, bookin'? Now your guy tells you this, and Babyak told me Cozzolino's who boosted the guns, he's runnin' his mouth all over the place over there, which was what I figured soon as I heard he got fired from Bulldog Security —"

"Oh yeah, sure," Rugs said. "I told ya, didn't I? Didn't I say, hey, given the people involved? Didn't I say it wouldn't surprise me where those guns wound up? Look where they are."

"Yeah, right, but as evidence —"

"Yeah — so far! But who knows how many are evidence, huh? Anybody sayin' that? Who knows how many didn't get inventoried, logged into the property room, huh?"

"I haven't talked to anybody over there yet — have you?"

"No, just, uh, Plasjac, that's all."

"So then it's just you speculatin' and surmisin', right?"

"Yeah, but it's a solid surmise, Mario, I'm tellin' ya. So did you ever talk to anybody over there? You said you were goin' to —"

"Nah, I mean everybody I know there's either dead or retired. I don't know anybody in that department except that chief, Butterbaugh, that flake. Guy's got drugs on the brain."

"Yeah, he's nuts, I know. But, listen, Mario, what I said before still goes, I still think those Berettas're gonna wind up in that department, I mean it. Just because of who's involved. You talk to the guy owns the shop yet? Last time I talked to you you hadn't —"

"Yeah. This afternoon. Finally agrees to see me — I mean you can't believe this guy. Puts in this claim, then every time I tried to get him to sit still for it, he blows me off. Instead of tryin' to offer me ten percent, he didn't wanna give me ten minutes — hey, I just thought of somethin'. You know a lot about computers, right?"

Carlucci sputtered a long laugh. "Mario, I don't know shit about computers, trust me. I know a guy who knows about computers, and thank God I do, 'cause if it wasn't for him I'd be crazy, believe me."

"Yeah, well what I mean is, I think you might know the answer to this, I wouldn't know who else to ask — and if you don't know maybe you can put me in touch with this guy you know."

"Oh, okay. Go ahead. I probably won't know, but, uh, what?"

"Well this guy, Bemiss, owns the gunshop. He just really jerked me around about who his distributors were and he's been claimin' all along he's got no records, everything's got horse crap smeared over it or on it or in it. But somehow, I seem to remember hearin' somethin' one time about somebody thought he'd destroyed all his records on his computer but it turned out he didn't. Turned out somebody got his computer and found all this stuff he thought he'd destroyed —"

"Oh yeah, absolutely. That was that, uh, that Oliver North guy, ran all those covert operations out of the cellar in the White House, yeah, I remember that."

"So it's true?"

"Well it depends what you mean is true. You mean can somebody knows what they're doin' recover those records?"

"Yeah, yeah, I guess that's what I mean."

"Well, see, what it depends on is if his hard drive's intact —"

"His what?"

"Hard drive. Think of it as his main file cabinet."

"Oh okay, I got ya now."

"Yeah, if that's intact, if that hasn't been corrupted by anything physical or chemical, yeah, whatever's on it, sure, there are programs to recover that, oh yeah — if you have the programs and you know how to use 'em? Nothin' to it — not me now, I can't do it, but sure, yeah, that's how they got North. Yeah, he, uh, smashed all his floppies, and he killed all his files manually, but he didn't know there were programs on there that meant you couldn't kill 'em off his hard drive, that's how they got him. Course, didn't make much of a difference, he's a big star now anyway, so what? But if your guy's sayin' all his records are gone 'cause his floppies are ruined — is that what he's sayin'?"

"Yeah, exactly."

"Well, if he's still got the tower — you know, the box where all the guts are stored?"

"I don't know what you're talkin' about, Rugs, I'm just takin' notes here, that's all."

"Well if he says he's still got the original box with the original hard drive in it, all you gotta do is have, uh, somebody, Milliron, somebody from the DA's office, serve a search warrant on him, grab the tower, I'll give you the name of my guy, he'll tell ya exactly what you wanna know. Depends how busy he is, but, actual work, I don't know how long it would take him. Certainly no more than a couple hours, I don't even know, I'm just givin' him lotsa room, you know? Hey, Mario, I gotta go, my pager's goin' off —"

"Yeah okay, Rugs, thanks. I'll see ya."

Balzic hung up and got the number for the Knox PD in the tattered phone book chained to the bottom of the phone platform. Once connected, he asked to speak to the duty sergeant or the watch commander, whoever was handier. The watch commander, a Lieutenant Leffert, came on. Balzic remembered him vaguely, probably from an FOP picnic or some such, but it had been years ago and Balzic couldn't put a face with the name.

Balzic explained his interest in Charley Babyak by focusing on the kinds of guns supposedly found in Babyak's house.

"And your interest would be what again?" Leffert said.

"I'm workin' an insurance claim for a guy owns a gunshop in the Rocksburg Mall, said he lost a buncha handguns. I'm wonderin' if these are maybe his, that's all. I heard about your collar from a guy heard it on the radio, this morning." Balzic wasn't going to say he'd heard anything from Carlucci.

"So what do you wanna know again?"

"The guns, you know, the make, model, caliber, how many, how many magazines, how much ammo if any, okay?"

"I don't think I can release that information — who'd you say you were again?"

"Mario Balzic. I was chief of Rocksburg PD for twenty-some years, okay? Hey, Lieutenant, what's the reluctance here? I'm workin' a burglary claim for an insurance agency, I heard your department collared a guy with a buncha guns. All I'm doin' is lookin' to see if they're from my case, so what's the problem?"

There was a short pause, then a cough, then Leffert said, "Think maybe you'd better talk to the chief, okay? Maybe he remembers you, I'm havin' a hard time placin' you right now. Hold on."

"Yeah, right, I'm holdin'." Balzic started watching the second hand on one of the many clocks advertising beers around the walls and backbar. Five minutes later, after he'd used the last of his quarters and was calling for Vinnie to bring him another dollar's worth, a voice came on the line.

"Chief Balzic? Earl Butterbaugh here. What's up, ol' buddy? Long time no see, no hear, no nothin', whatcha up to these days?"

"Ah, you know how it goes, Chief, right now I'm workin' for an insurance agent. He has a claim for a B and E on a gunshop —"

"Gunshop? Is that right? Which one?"

"The one in Rocksburg Mall? Freedom Firearms?"

"Is that so? So what's he claimin' he lost?"

"What'd your guys confiscate?"

"Asked you first."

"Semi-auto Berettas. Nine-millimeter."

"Um, I'd have to take a look at the property log, Mario. Got a minute? Wanna hang on, or you want me to call ya back?"

"I'm at a pay phone, Chief, but otherwise I got all the time in the world." Balzic put his hand over the speaker and yelled to Vinnie, "You comin' with those quarters anytime soon or what?"

"Aw keep your skirt down, will ya, Jesus Christ." Vinnie stopped at the end of the bar to argue with two customers about which numbers had hit yesterday and the day before, stopping again after starting toward Balzic to go back and lament how for three days in a row last week he'd missed by only one digit.

Balzic rolled his eyes and let out a long breath through his nose. Just as Butterbaugh came back on the line, an automated operator said time was up and to deposit another quarter to continue the call.

"Yo! Vinnie? Quarters?"

"Hey. This was my place?" Vinnie said, handing over the quarters. "First fuckin' thing to go's this phone. Wish I had a penny for every dollar's wortha change I ever made for this fuckin' thing. Wish I had another penny for every time I said, no he ain't here. Coulda fuckin' moved to Lauderdale ten years ago."

"Yeah? A month after you got there, you'd be tendin' bar," Balzic said, taking the quarters and dropping one in the slot and redialing the Knox PD number.

"What's that mean now — I don't know what to do with myself? Like I'm fuckin' stupid?"

Balzic had to go through the dispatcher again before reconnecting with Butterbaugh. "You said it, I didn't — yeah, Chief? Balzic again. Yeah — got the property log?"

"Yes I do. Let me see here. We confiscated Berettas, that's correct."

"Model 92F?"

"Correct again, Model 92F 9mm semi-automatic handguns —"

"Thirty-eight?"

"Thirty-eight? Jesus. Why'd you pick that number?"

"Well how many?"

"Is that what the gunshop's sayin'?"

What the fuck, Balzic thought. Why's this guy so coy? "Thirty-eight, yes, that's the claim."

"Damn, that's a lotta pistols, you know? That's a lotta inventory for a shop in this part of the woods."

"I know, Chief, I know, that's been one of the problems from the start. That and how much ammo he's claimin'. How much did your guys get? Ammo I mean."

"Ummm, I don't think my people've finished countin' it yet, tell ya the truth. See,

427

we've had to log a damn ton of porno magazines and videos. Just disgusting crap.
Kids, animals . . . makes ya sick."

Balzic let that pass for the time being.
"Uh, any other guns, Chief? Revolvers,
rifles, shotguns?"

"No," Butterbaugh said. "Nothin' else
listed here, uh, no, that's it, just the
Berettas. So does that sound like your
claim?"

"Well that's one of the makes he's
claimin', one of the models and bore sizes,
but he's claimin' other guns are missin'
too. So, uh, listen, any chance I could talk
to your collar?"

"Huh? Wanna talk to him? Well, I don't
know, see, we've been interrogating him all
day, and I think it's gonna be a while
before we're done with him, and, uh, some
councilmen, see they wanna talk to him,
they're all upset about the kid porn, you
know, which I don't blame them for bein'
concerned, I mean this is really disgusting
stuff."

"So you've still got him."

"Well course we do."

"Well I was just sayin', you know, maybe
you had him in the county lockup and you
were goin' back and forth —"

"What? No, we don't do that. No, he's

here. And he's gonna stay here till we get everything inventoried and logged into evidence, and finish our interrogation, then we're gonna see where we are, probably won't call the DA till maybe tomorrow afternoon, day after even, I don't know yet, I wanna talk to this guy myself. See, I'm really disturbed about these magazines we found, really disgusting crap, Mario, wait'll you see it."

"Aw that's alright, Earl, I don't need to see that stuff, uh, I'm just interested in the guns, that's all. But I'd really like to talk to him about those, you know? But I got no standing, so, uh, it's all on your good graces. I really would appreciate you lettin' me have him, you know, soon as you can, for, oh, say a half hour, forty-five minutes, that's all I'd need. And I'd really appreciate it."

"Well normally, Mario, see, there wouldn't be any problem, but it's not just the guns that, uh, that's the issue here. I mean, in addition to the porn, there was drugs confiscated, and I don't mind telling you, a rather large amount, and, uh, so that's another area we're gonna have to be looking at, and, uh, you wanna give me a call in a day or so, I'll probably know a lot better where we stand, see? I mean, I can appreciate your interest, but, uh, hell, you know, put yourself in my place. What would you be sayin' if our situation was reversed? Would you just let me walk right in — in the middle of your investigation, you know, come and interview this guy? I don't think so. I don't think you'd do that —"

"Well that's what I'm sayin', Chief Butterbaugh, that's why I'm askin'. It's up to you. Whenever you say, you know, it's your call."

"Well I'm glad you appreciate that — oh, listen. Just thought of something. You have history with this guy, don't you? Collared him a couple times yourself, didn't you?"

"Yeah. But that was a long time ago, it's been a while. Why?"

"I don't know, let me think on it. Maybe we can scratch each other's back here."

"Well, tell ya the truth, Chief, really, I've got some problems with this, uh, you know, this guy and child porn, that just doesn't sound right to me. That was never his thing, kids. I mean, he had problems with sex, but it was always with big women, it was never with kids — least not in my experience with him. He always liked big women, you know, to bully him around, make him crawl around on his hands and knees, that kinda stuff, but I don't ever recall him messin' with kids, I really don't."

"People change, Mario, people change. Just like with the drugs, they start with the marijuana, and the next thing you know they're spikin' it with PCP and LSD, and then the next thing they're onto heroin, morphine, and amphetamines and cocaine, it's an old —"

"Yeah, well, with some people that's true, no doubt, I'm not gonna argue that, but with a lotta people it isn't true — and that's another thing, I don't recall Babyak bein' a volume dealer. He was a user, that's for sure, most hyper guy in the world, and then he'd get so he'd have to sell some just to buy some for himself, and then he was tryin' to stay awake longer than everybody else, and that's why he was partial to crank — course you didn't say what kinda dope you found —"

"Whole buncha crank, that's exactly what it was, crystal methamphetamine. Can't tell you the exact amount 'cause I haven't heard back from the lab on either quantity or purity yet, and I don't know when we're gonna hear, backed up as the state boys are, but I'm callin' this a significant operation, a major arrest, you know, a major interruption of a major dealer's operation —"

"Ah c'mon, Chief, Babyak's never been a major anything. In fact, you want the truth, I'm real real surprised about the guns."

"Well hell, Mario, that's three for three. So far you've been surprised about the porn and the, uh, dope, and now it's the guns," Butterbaugh said, snorting and laughing.

"Well yeah, to be honest with ya, Earl, yeah, I don't see him with guns. Never have before. Never knew him to carry 'em, never knew him to boost 'em. I remember one house he went in, guy had at least a dozen centerfire rifles, buncha shotguns, plus a couple rimfires and a couple air rifles. Babyak never touched 'em. Now he took the old lady's collection of Elvis dishes and a portrait of Elvis on black velvet which she was really pissed about losin', but he never touched the gun case. Six grand easy wortha rifles, scopes, and shotguns, and he didn't put a finger on the case. In fact that's how we knew to look for him. I know you find that hard to believe, Earl, given what you have there now, but it's true."

Butterbaugh chuckled. "Well maybe

when you get over here, Mario, eventually, you know, whenever that is, maybe we'll have a long talk with him, maybe he'll be nice enough to tell us both how come all those illegal things just happened to be in his house when we got the tip."

"Oh this was from a tip, huh?"

"Sure was. Best intelligence we've gotten in a long while, I mean, what with the result we got, hey, you know, in the major interruption in this guy's life who you say is no dope dealer, and is no gun thief, and who, uh, likes his jollies with the big girls —"

"Women, not girls."

"Whatever."

"Uh-huh. Okay, Earl. So I'll be waitin' for your call, okay? When it's okay for me to come and talk to him? And I really do wanna talk to him, I really wanna know whether he's involved with the guns —"

"Oh he's involved alright," Butterbaugh said, chuckling. "But, uh, yeah, I'll give you a call. Sure. Then we'll both give a listen to what Mister Babyak has to say. I think it should be interesting."

Balzic spent the next day and a half rereading all the pamphlets about coronary artery disease he'd been given when he was discharged from the cardiology department of Conemaugh General Hospital. It was the only way he could take his mind off Charley Babyak and what was going on in the Knox Police Department.

He read about his medication and its side effects, about what he should and should not eat, and about what exercise he should do and how, and about what he should or shouldn't do if certain symptoms appeared. He loved that phrase: ". . . if certain symptoms appeared." Yeah, right. Like you were walking from the bedroom to the kitchen and all of a sudden who should appear but Mister Shortness of Breath? Who was running from Mister Buzzing in the Throat, who was accompanied by his pistoleros, Mister Burning in the Esophagus, Mister Tingling and Numbness in the Extremities, and the goombah, Mister Crushing Sensation in the Chesteroonie. Oh yeah, certain symptoms do appear, and when they do, what you should do is sit down, calm down, breathe deeply, stick a nitro under your tongue, and never, ever panic, oh yes, absolutemento, unless, of course, the nitro doesn't help, in which case you are probably having a heart attack and should have someone drive you to the nearest emergency room, or you should call an ambulance, but under no circumstances should you attempt to drive yourself there, oh my no, because you might pass out and drive up onto a sidewalk and take out a pedestrian or two as well as a very important and expensive utility pole! Duh. Oh that's right, mock it, sure, easy to mock it — when you're not feelin' any of it. . . .

They're getting ready to chump Charley Babyak out and there's not a damn thing I can do about it because they're not gonna let me near him. And they're certainly not gonna let him call me, which means he's as good as boxed, wrapped, and in the bus on his way to Southern Regional Correctional Facility, period, end of story.

Just before dinner on the first day, he was going over for the fourth or fifth time how important exercise and a low-fat, high-fiber diet was, when the phone rang. He heard Ruth answer it, and then she poked her head into the dining room where he'd been reading, and said, "It's Marie. You didn't call her — or Emily either, did you?"

"Forgot," he mumbled and got up and took the phone. "Marie, hey, kiddo, what's up, hi you doin'? I was just gonna call you —"

"Yeah, right. God, Daddy, you're getting as bad as some of the marketing creeps I have to deal with."

"Okay okay, so I forgot. You put me in the same league with marketing creeps now? 'Cause I forget to make one call?"

"Okay, so you're not that bad — yet. Listen, did Momma tell you what I called about, huh?"

"Yeah, she told me, but you should probably tell me yourself —"

"Oh Daddy, you're not as bad as the guys I work with, you're worse!"

"Okay, okay, take it easy, she told me, she said, uh, you found some books you think maybe I should be readin', right?"

"Yes. Well. You actually remembered what I called about — course I guess it was on your talk list that you had all prepared for me —"

"You know, Marie, if someday, God forbid, you should ever, you know, decide to get married?"

"The bozos I've been meeting, that's not very likely," she said.

"Uh-huh, okay, but in the remote possibility that should ever happen? I'm warnin' you right now I'm gonna tell whoever it is you have this tendency, uh, toward negative aggressive guidance? N-A-G?"

"Negative aggressive guidance — God, where'd you get that?"

"Well when certain people keep bustin' my chops about somethin', that's what immediately comes to mind, mentionin' no names of course."

"Oh, right. Daddy, could we move on? Like, did you ever hear of a doctor named Dean Ornish?"

"Yeah, somewhere, but I don't know where. He in Pittsburgh?"

"No no, he's a cardiologist in California? And he's written a whole lotta books about reversing heart disease? I've been reading a couple of them, and I'm gonna send them to you, okay? Promise you'll read them?"

"You send 'em, I'll read 'em, okay, but why do I have to promise?"

" 'Cause I know you, Daddy. You start out with the best intentions in the world, like that yoga tape I sent you? Last year. Momma said you were all excited about it, you watched it a couple times, then that was it. She can't remember the last time she saw you watchin' it —"

"Hey, I do that stuff, she doesn't have to be lookin' at me for me to do it —"

"You do?"

"Every morning, absolutely, faithfully — well I haven't done it since, uh, you know, the hospital, but I'll get back to it. What, you think I have to watch the tape every day? Huh? In order not to forget? I'm not that old —"

"I didn't say you were —"

"Yeah, but that's what I was hearin', cutey pie."

"Well that's on you, 'cause that's not what I was sayin'."

"Okay, alright, so what's so great about this Orfish guy?"

"Ornish, Daddy, not Orfish, God, you're terrible."

"Orfish, Ornish, okay, so what's his agenda?"

"Agenda?! He's a doctor, he doesn't have an agenda —"

"Oh right, yes — listen, I'm not sayin' everybody has an agenda, just most people, huh? Most people're tryin' to sell you somethin' —"

"Most people?"

"Yes, definitely yes, not just the marketing creeps you work with. Yes, absolutely, most people have an agenda, Marie, and the smoother they are, the bigger they get, the bigger the agenda gets, and the worst ones are the ones who pretend they don't know what anybody's talkin' about when the word agenda comes up. Trust me on this one, kiddo, I've spent a lotta time with people dealin' in confidence —"

"Daddy, this man has had patients who reversed their artery disease and he didn't do it trying to sell them something. He put them on a real low-fat diet and got them walking and taught them meditation and he didn't use drugs, he wasn't trying to sell them something — I know what you're thinking, you're thinking he had to have a deal with some pharmaceutical company, or some hospital where he did surgery, but that's just it, he's saying you *don't* have to take expensive drugs or have surgery —"

"Oh yeah? What, some chooch goes down in the street, this guy comes up on him, the chooch is turnin' blue, he's sweatin', he's grabbin' his chest, and what? This Orfish bends over him and says, 'Excuse me, pal, but what you need to do is come to my place, I'll put ya on a diet, teach ya how to meditate, and tomorrow you can start walkin',' huh?"

"Daddy, that is *not* what the man's saying at all — at all!"

"Oh yeah, right, excuse me, but at that point, if I'm the chooch on the sidewalk? I would like to think if the guy didn't have any first aid in his bag of tricks, the least he would do is call nine-one-one, save all the talk about the diet and the meditation till next week — you know? If the chooch survives —"

"Well that's exactly what he'd do, Daddy, he's not an idiot! If you're grabbing your chest of course he'd give you first aid and call an ambulance — he says that, in plain English. But what he's also saying is that afterwards, you know, if you change your diet, I mean really cut down on the fats, and start walking and meditating? You've got a real good chance of not just stopping what's clogging up your arteries, but of reversing it, you know? I mean actually reducing the amount of the goop in your arteries, and he's done studies that prove it —"

"Whoa, wait, wait. Marie, do you know they used a drill on me? Did you know that? Huh? A drill with a carbide tip? You know what carbide is, huh? It's real hard stuff, close to diamonds, you know?"

"I know what carbide is, Daddy, and I

440

know they used a drill on you, yes —"

"Yeah, and right, right, exactly, that's what they did, so now this guy's proposing what again? That by changin' what you eat and walkin' and meditatin' — like I know how to do that —"

"He explains that, Daddy, he gives very specific instructions, and I've been doing it for a couple of years now — at least I think I'm doin' it — and his instructions are as good as anybody else's I've ever read "

"Yeah but what I'm sayin', Marie, you know? If this stuff was so hard they hada use a drill to get it outta my artery? How's this stuff just gonna vanish — is that what he's sayin'? By doin' these things, whatever, this stuff's just gonna dissolve? Go away by itself?"

"Yes, Daddy, that's exactly what he's saying! But no, not by itself, and you can't just wish it away, you do it by changing what you eat and with the walking and the meditating — you really need to read these books yourself, you'll see, I mean, you owe it to yourself, Daddy, honest, promise me, okay? If I send them you'll read them, okay?"

"Okay, you send 'em, I'll read 'em, I already said I would, I promise, and I'll keep an open mind, even though the only thing this guy's tryin' to sell is books, okay?"

"Daddy! Jeez —"

"Well he is chargin' for the books, right? He's not givin' 'em away, is he?"

"Oh God, Daddy, you're — what'd you used to say all the time about some people? They were incorrigible? Well that's you —"

"Hey, Marie. Listen. We just got a copy of the bill, okay? For when I had this done? Listen to me, okay?"

"I'm listening. What?"

"I was in there, wasn't even in there two whole days, okay? Went in the one day, they do the thing the next morning, I'm outta there that afternoon, okay? You know what the bill was? Huh? Ready for this? Twenty-one thousand plus. You hear what I just said? Twenty-one thousand dollars —"

"Well that's what I'm telling you — read these books, that's what he's saying, you know? The price of conventional therapy, it's just ridiculous, it's outrageous. And he's saying his treatment is way way cheaper and you can save yourself a lot of money —"

"Not me, Marie, the insurance company. Thank God we got insurance, they're gonna cover everything except the deductible, which is five hundred bucks —"

"Yes, but what if you didn't have insurance?"

"But I did, I do, so that's not the issue here —"

"Yes, but what if you didn't? And think of all the people who don't. I mean, imagine if you didn't have insurance, Daddy, God, what would you do? What would you've done?"

"I don't know, paid 'em a hundred a month till I croaked and then let 'em fight it out with the executor of my will —"

"Yes, but do you think they would've done that if you didn't have insurance? What would've happened if you didn't have insurance?"

"Now who's the cynic here, huh? Little while ago, you're cappin' on me 'cause I'm sayin' most people got an agenda, now listen to you — what woulda happened if I didn't have insurance — like what? They woulda let me croak out in the ER?"

"Oh Daddy, God forbid hospitals ever let anybody go untreated because they didn't have insurance —"

"God forbid, Marie, you *are* worse'n me, way worse, Jesus, you're bad as Vinnie, that's what he said. Only reason they even bothered is 'cause they found out I had good insurance —"

"Oh that's not what I'm saying at all, Daddy, and you know it —"

"Hey, listen, you're gonna run up your phone bill here —"

"It's a toll call, Daddy, I call you guys all the time, you're just tired of talking to me, admit it, 'cause every time you don't wanna talk any more, all of a sudden my phone bill becomes an issue —"

"Hey, somebody gotta worry about it —"

"Daddy, I'm making twenty-nine five a year for nine months' work and I get five more for managing the swimming program in the summer, I think I can afford to pay my phone bill —"

"You only get five for the summer? As many hours as you put in? You need to talk to somebody about that, that ain't right, Jesus, I didn't know that's all those cheap pricks were payin' you —"

"Daddy, quit trying to change the subject, I want you to learn how to meditate, it'll be really good for you —"

"Okay, I'll make you a deal, alright? You learn how to negotiate, okay? I'll learn how to meditate. You talk to those cheap bastards, you learn how to negotiate yourself a raise, I'll learn how to meditate —

for what purpose I don't know, but I'll do it —"

"You learn how to meditate to learn how to focus, Daddy, to give your mind a rest, to try to reduce the stress your mind puts on your body by thinking all these useless thoughts —"

"How do you know they're useless?"

"Oh they are, the Buddhists know they are. Buddhists think we're addicted to thought, we can't get enough of it, everything we do we tell ourselves it gives us time to think, no matter what we're doing, washing dishes, cleaning the toilet, we never just try to do one thing at a time and focus on it —"

"You wanna focus on cleanin' the toilet?"

"Yes! If that's what you're doing, yes! The Buddhists think you should focus on whatever you're doing, you should never just go through the motions and tell yourself you don't have to think about it, whatever it is, it gives you time to think about something else. The Buddhists say that's just wasting your life, you're never here now, you're always only partly here, or only vaguely here when you're doing one thing and thinking about something else. Buddhists believe you should apprehend reality without thinking about it, just focus on it without analyzing it to death the way we do, or thinking about something else —"

"How come you know so much about what the Buddhists think?"

"How come? It's all your fault, Daddy, if you wanna know —"

"My fault? How's it my fault? What the hell'd I do now?"

"Remember that book *Zen in the Art of Archery*? You were always reading it, remember?"

"Not always, whatta you mean always?"

"Well, every once in a while you'd be reading it, I saw you, and one day, you know, I got curious, I picked it up, I read it, and then, you know, I read it again, and I was really having a bad time that year with swimming, I just got sick of it, you know? Bored sick? And I didn't know how I was ever gonna get through that summer, and, uh, I don't know, somehow, you know, I just — I can't explain it very well now, but I just know that book got me through that summer. I couldn't've done it, I would've quit. 'Cause I really hated swimming that summer. That book got me through it. I learned how to focus — well, not great, but good enough to make practice bearable, you know?"

"Really? I didn't know that, you never said anything to me."

"Well, you know, I was getting ready to quit and you know how you are about quitters —"

"Aw come on —"

"Yeah, well, Jeez, I wasn't about to make you mad at me, so I got, like at one point, I remember one day, I had this strangest feeling, I was focusing so hard on breathing and moving my hands through the water in a certain way that it felt — this is gonna sound really strange, but it was like I wasn't even in the water, I forgot completely I was in the pool — I really don't know how to explain it, but that was what changed it for me, swimming, you know, that book made it so I could stand it I guess. I really didn't understand most of it, just that part about breathing and doing each thing in time with my breathing, that was what got me through that summer. Anyway I didn't quit."

"Uh-huh. And that got you interested in the Buddhists?"

"Yes. It did. Ever since, whenever I'm in a bookstore or a library, I find myself just sort of gravitating toward the religion section and I pick up something that a Buddhist monk or teacher wrote —"

"Why didn't you ever tell me about this before?"

"Oh Daddy! I did! I've told you a buncha times, sometimes you don't listen very well, really, sometimes you make me so mad —"

"Hey, listen, there's somebody at the door, I gotta go. Love ya. Bye." He hung up without giving her a chance to respond.

"Mario!" Ruth said, poking her head in from the kitchen. "You have to stop doing that to your kids! I mean it, that's not right —"

"Doin' what? I wasn't doin' anything, what're you talkin' about?"

"Oh God, don't say you don't know what I'm talking about! How can you say that?"

"What, 'cause I said there's somebody at the door?"

"Of course! You can't do that to your own daughters, that's rude!"

"Hey, I'll tell ya how I can say it, okay? There's three women in my life, you and my two daughters, and there's nothin' pisses me off faster or keeps me pissed off longer than hearin' one of them say I don't listen, okay? And I don't wanna talk about it now either, okay? Just let's me get back to what I was doin', and you go back to

448

what you were doin', and Marie can go back to what she was doin', and we'll all be fine, alright?"

"No. It's not alright. We will not be fine — *you'll* be fine, or you *think* you will, but it's not gonna be fine for Marie —"

"Well it's gonna have to be 'cause I'm not talkin' about it now, okay? She said she's gonna send me some books, I promised her I'd read 'em, that's the end of it. Period. Some other time, you ladies want to discuss my listening powers, hey, fine, lemme know when you're done, then I'll file my, uh, my minority opinion, okay?"

"Mario, you have to stop doing this," Ruth said. "I mean it. You keep doin' that, you're gonna lose Marie, she won't stand for it. She's not Emily. Emily's easier, she puts up with more, she doesn't take it so serious, but Marie, I'm telling you, you can't just keep blowin' her off like that. You wouldn't do that to anybody else, you certainly wouldn't do it to Mo, and you know you wouldn't —"

"How many times does Mo call here — aw wait a second, I'm not doin' this now. I don't wanna do this now, I'm not gonna do this now —"

"Okay, fine, have it your way, big boy," Ruth said, rolling her eyes and retreating into the kitchen. "But sooner or later, you're gonna have to have it out with Marie about that. She doesn't deserve to be treated like that. She loves you too much. And neither do I."

Balzic slumped back onto the chair in the dining room where he'd been reading before the phone rang and rubbed his nose and cheeks with his thumb and index finger for a long moment, thinking about that phrase Marie had used about the Buddhists when they said we were "addicted to thought." So here I sit, trying not to think about everything that passed between Ruth and me about Marie and how lousy a listener I am and what do I do but think about being addicted to thinking. Aw it's too fuckin' confusing, sometimes, no shit, I mean, hey, it just is. . . .

Before calling Knox PD Chief Butterbaugh about talking to Charley Babyak, Balzic waited badly through the next day and a half, fidgeting and fussing around the house. He made two kinds of dark bread, working from complicated recipes involving molasses, baker's chocolate, instant coffee, cider vinegar, and whole-wheat and rye flours which led to stiff, heavy doughs that were hard to knead. Between risings he tried playing his harmonicas, but one of them sounded flat and he tried to repair it by reading instructions out of a book that said to file the reeds with an emery board. Since he'd never done it before, he didn't know when enough was enough and wound up with three draw reeds playing almost identical sounds. He threw the reed plate into the kitchen garbage and asked himself what the hell he thought he was doing. But he knew what he was doing and knowing it pissed him off. He knew he was making bread and playing the harp because he didn't want to talk to Ruth about what was going on, and what was going on was him avoiding Ruth and also looking like he wasn't trying to squirm away from fear of his own body while trying to make it look like he wasn't doing either.

He tried relaxing with yoga, but was so anxious about overexerting himself that every posture of relaxation quickly degenerated into one of strain and pain. He wound up sweating and panting, ratcheting his anxiety up, scaring himself even more.

Then he tried again to meditate, which was worse in a different way than doing the yoga postures. As far as he could figure out from the pamphlet given him at the hospital, he was supposed to sit or lie quietly, inhale through his nose while focusing on the air going through his nostrils and filling his diaphragm, and then exhaling and focusing on the air leaving his diaphragm and coming out his nose while saying the word "one." According to the pamphlet, this was the method explained in the book *The Relaxation Response*, written by a doctor named Benson, who used the principles of Western scientific inquiry to validate Eastern methods of meditation, thus establishing their therapeutic value. In other words, Balzic thought, if American doctors and hospitals wanted to pass out this particular information to discharged patients, American health insurance companies, thanks to Doctor Benson, could now tell their stockholders they were justified in paying for it.

Balzic found that he could do only one or two breaths as described in the pamphlet before his attention skidded away to Ruth or Marie or Emily or his mother or Charley Babyak or Chief Butterbaugh and the drug menace — his breath and breathing seemed to lose their attractive power almost immediately. Then he cussed himself out for not being able to concentrate, and then he thought about what Marie had said about the Buddhists saying that we were addicted to thought. He'd forgot to ask her which *we* that was: Americans? Caucasians? Or just me and her?

Naturally, he was immediately fascinated by the idea that a person could be addicted to thinking, which seemed to be the very opposite of addiction. Addiction implied compulsion, whether physical or emotional made no difference, and compulsion meant doing something repeatedly in spite of thoughts to the contrary. Not only that, thinking was something he'd been told all his life was ideal behavior, by his mother, his teachers, priests, nuns, superior officers, supervising politicians; all in one way or another had told him to think before he acted or spoke, to not let any person or situation provoke him to do or say something he'd regret — and up to now he'd had no reason to doubt them. Not that he'd ever been able to live up to that ideal behavior. His quick lip had gotten him into more trouble than he wanted to think about. But whether he could do it or not, he'd always believed, or been led to believe, that a civilized, reasonable, obedient man thought first and then spoke or acted, to say or do the right thing the right way for the right reason. All of which implied thinking, thinking, thinking.

But now? At this stage of his life to be told that a part of what was wrong with him physically might be a direct result of his being unable to stop thinking? Something he believed without question — until now — to be a good thing? To hear now that this good thing was an addiction? And that his inability to overcome this addiction, to give his mind a rest, had put a direct strain on his coronary arteries? How the hell could that be?

This was the goofiest kind of merry-go-round to be on, and one so obvious it was almost comic because the more he tried to focus on his breathing, the more his attempts were interrupted by — what else? Thinking. About every damn thing except his breathing. And he couldn't stop himself. It was infuriating! The more he tried to focus on his breathing, in, out, through the nose, down into the belly, back up and out, then say "one" — the harder he tried, the more his mind wandered. His breathing was a greasy rope he couldn't hang on to for more than twenty seconds, sometimes less.

During another attempt at not thinking,

he thought of a conversation years ago with Father Marrazzo, who'd told him about some Frenchman who'd said that all man's troubles came from the fact that he didn't know how to sit alone in a room. Was that what meditation was? Learning to sit alone in a room? And then he remembered another conversation, one he'd had with Mo Valcanas, who was talking about some poet named Dickey who'd said something about a man alone being in bad company. What the hell?! I *am* in bad company when I'm alone, Balzic thought angrily. Always have been. Is this why? 'Cause I don't know how to be alone? 'Cause I'm addicted to all the silly shitballs that bounce around the inside of my skull? That I think are so wonderful I can't get enough of them? What is this crap? . . .

After he took the temperature of the second loaf of black bread and decided it was done, he set it on a cooling rack, took a deep breath, picked up the phone, and dialed the Knox PD.

"Hello, Chief Butterbaugh? Mario Balzic. How're things lookin' over there? Any chance you can slip me in, give me a half hour with Charley Babyak?"

"No, can't do it," Butterbaugh said with a heavy sigh.

"Aw c'mon, Chief, hell, you've had the man thirty-six hours now, at least. Babyak was never that tough, not when he knew you had the physical evidence —"

"That's not what I mean —"

"What — you can't get rid of the god-damn pols, huh? Tryin' to show their phony concern about the kid porn?"

"No no, that's not it, the man's dead."

"What? You're shittin' me. How? When?"

"Don't know yet. John Leffert, he was watch commander, he went in to wake him up this morning, the man was hanging by his belt to the bars. Leffert called me —"

"By his belt?!"

"That's what I said, so then he called the coroner, so a deputy coroner showed up, I mean what was he gonna say? Couldn't very well say anything else, so we shipped the body to Conemaugh General."

"I don't believe this," Balzic said.

"What's not to believe, the man hung himself —"

"With his belt?! You didn't take his belt away, his shoelaces? Fuck kinda lockup you run?"

"Hey, I resent that —"

"Resent whatever you want, you don't take a prisoner's belt and shoelaces, you don't know what the fuck you're doin' —"

"Hey, Balzic, you're outta line here, I don't need you to tell me how to do my job —"

"Oh no, right, yeah, you got a prisoner dead with a belt in a cell! And you put him there! You don't like me tellin' you how to do your job, whatta you think the coroner's gonna say? Whattaya think Grimes is gonna say, huh? And the DA after him?"

"I don't care what anybody says —"

"You will!"

"Oh bullshit, this conversation's over." Click.

"I'll be damned," Balzic said, hanging up. For a long moment, that was all he could say, all he could think. His mind, which only minutes ago had been so overactive he was cursing it, was now utterly blank. Then slowly, it started working again.

They hadn't just wanted to chump Babyak out, they — whoever they were — wanted him dead. Nah, nooooo, that didn't happen. That would require more cooperation and coordination of motives and methods than that collection of jagoffs had ever thought about having. Over a bunch of pistols? Over a bookie's job? Nah, Butterbaugh's a fucking idiot. He had drug fever the way some Republicans used to have commie fever; everywhere they looked they saw a communist or a communist wannabe. Everywhere Butterbaugh looks he sees a dealer or an addict.

With a belt?! Bullshit. Incompetence doesn't explain that. There can't be a turnkey alive who hasn't heard he's supposed to remove belts and shoelaces. They may not all issue jumpsuits, but there can't be one around anywhere who can say with a straight face he didn't know he was supposed to remove belts and shoelaces.

Balzic took off his glasses and rubbed his face. He remembered what Babyak had said about going inside again with a short-eyes tag hanging on him. What did he say? Something about he'd take a hundred Valiums and wash them down with a six-pack before he'd ever go inside as a short eyes. He knew what happened to them inside and it wasn't gonna happen to him. Son of a bitch, Balzic thought. I gotta go see Grimes. Anything weird here, he'll find it.

Balzic, with other things than his own heart or mind on his mind, had a somewhat easier time emotionally going to Conemaugh General Hospital. Still, he had to keep reminding himself of what Doctor Fine had said when he was enumerating all the hazards of the Rotoblator procedure: "If something's going to go wrong with your heart, couldn't happen in a better place than in the cardiac unit."

So even though he was going to the pathology department, it was only a short elevator ride away from the cardiac unit. He kept repeating what Fine had said over and over, first silently and then out loud, stopping only after he became aware that a woman in a minivan was gawking at him while they were waiting out a red light.

Once inside the hospital, he hurried to the basement to get to Coroner Wallace Grimes's office, out of the ridiculous belief that the faster he moved the harder it would be for others to put him in a box and cover him with dirt.

Grimes wasn't in, but the door to his office being unlocked as it usually was, Balzic went in and sat in a straight-backed chair beside Grimes's desk. There he toyed morosely with the idea that if quick movement would save him then logically he ought to be sprinting everywhere. Which would've been fine, except that he hadn't sprinted anywhere in thirty or thirty-five years, not since he'd had a walking beat. He then tried to come up with a plausible story about why Grimes should allow him, now just another civilian, to observe the postmortem. And while he knew there wasn't any plausible reason for Grimes to let him observe, he also began to consider the possibility that maybe he'd gone round the bend because he'd let himself tumble so easily for the nonsense that speed of movement would deter his death.

While Balzic was spinning deeper into his own confusion, Grimes walked in, calm, comported, businesslike as usual.

"Mario. What brings you here?" Grimes said, putting manila folders into separate baskets on his desk before hanging up his topcoat in a locker.

"Uh, guy named Babyak? Get a chance to look at him yet?"

"Just did a quick walk-around, that's all. Why?"

"When you get to it, uh, mind if I watch?"

"Watch? You're retired, aren't you? From the city police?"

"Uh, yeah. But I have a real special interest in this guy."

"You working for the state AG? I heard you were doing some work for them, contract work, some sort of thing like that, uh, no?"

"Uh, no, not on this. Not this one, no, uh-uh, but, uh —"

"So, uh, you're not with any legitimate authority?"

"Well, no, but I'm workin' for an attorney who's workin' for an insurance guy, there's a phony claim I'm investigatin', least I'm about ninety-nine percent sure it's phony, and this guy was involved —"

"Mario, I know you know my rules, which I'm guessing are no different from any other coroner's rules. No legitimate reason to observe, no observation, period."

"The man died in a lockup —"

"I know where he died."

"Yeah, okay, but listen. Just gimme a minute here, okay? Can't hurt, okay? The guy was collared for theft involving a whole lotta guns, same kinda guns this dealer is tryin' to make this claim for, the one which I'm thinkin' is phony —"

"Mario, if you stop now we won't have any problems, alright?"

"C'mon, Doc, there's somethin' I want you to look for —"

"Mario," Grimes said quietly, patiently, "I know where the man died, I know how to do my job. We've enjoyed years of good

461

professional relations, and I don't want to spoil that now and I don't think you do either, so please, let me get on with it, and, uh, if no judge says there's any reason to close the file on the case you can read my report like anybody else, but, uh, right now, I'm going to have to ask you to please stop asking me anything, alright?"

"Yeah yeah, okay. Just one thing, okay? Measure the belt, okay? Put it around his waist, not his neck, okay? See where the crease is, you know? On which hole, okay?"

"Mario, please."

"I'm thinkin' it's not gonna be his belt, okay?"

"Mario, stop it, will you?"

"Okay, okay. Uh, you call anybody over in Knox yet?"

"I'm waiting on them now. Also called Troop A CID and the DA's office. Told them they might want to send a couple detectives over."

Balzic shrugged and said, "Oh. Okay. Okay if I wait here?"

"Fine," Grimes said with a faint smile. "Make yourself some coffee if you want. Just, uh, you know, when you're eavesdropping at the doors? Try to not look too obvious, alright? I don't know how you do

462

that exactly, but at least make some pretense at it, okay?"

Balzic nodded and shrugged, mumbling something about trying, and then made a pot of coffee while Grimes changed into his greens. Minutes later, when the coffee was finished dripping, the people Grimes had called started straggling in. Chief Butterbaugh and Watch Commander John Leffert from the Knox PD arrived first, then Trooper Claude Milliron from Troop A CID, and finally two county detectives Balzic knew on sight but had never worked with. They introduced themselves to Grimes as George Sporcik and Lou DeSantis. Sporcik, who was the older, larger, and quieter of the two, nodded to Balzic and gave him a quizzical look, but said nothing. Both of them looked irritated about something, maybe just having to be there, though DeSantis kept trying to joke about how they'd gone months without a murder and now it was raining bodies. Balzic found himself wondering what the others were laughing at.

Balzic quickly forgot about the rest of them because as soon as he caught Trooper Milliron's eye, he approached Milliron with his hand out, telling him how good it was to see him again. Just as quickly he noticed the others noticing him with Milliron. Without a word, they turned their backs to the rest, and inquired about each other's health in the hushed, slightly awkward tones of one who'd been aided in a time of physical crisis and as the other who'd given that aid. After about two minutes, Balzic found himself with nothing else to say and nodding stupidly at Milliron for no particular reason. He was actually relieved when Milliron had to leave because Grimes said he was ready to begin.

Balzic watched them all go into the lab before he took up what he hoped was an explainable posture and position near the lab's double doors. He decided that if he stood with his back to the doors, it might look as though he'd been hired to keep everybody else out. That also got his ears near the opening between the doors. Still, he could hear only snatches of what Grimes was saying, but what he heard first was Grimes perfunctorily ruling out natural causes and an accident as cause of death. Which left either suicide or homicide. When the PM was over, those two were still left. Grimes hadn't ruled out either one.

Balzic ducked away into Grimes's office

when he heard them starting for the doors. There he once again took the same seat he'd been sitting in when he'd been begging Grimes to let him observe, and almost as soon as his rump hit the chair it occurred to him that in the whole time he'd been standing at the doors eavesdropping, he'd never once thought of himself, his pulses, his arteries, his mind, his thinking, his not thinking. During all that time, nothing except what was being said on the other side of the doors had mattered. It was wonderful. Paying attention to somebody else was also a way to give your mind a rest, a way to stop focusing on all the pings in your engine. It was wonderful but also terrible. Because he couldn't very well spend the rest of his life eavesdropping on other people's business, and unlike Charley Babyak, he had the rest of his life to live, as stupid as that sounded.

Grimes was in the room before Balzic could let go of that last thought.

"Mario? Still here, eh? Heard anything interesting lately?"

"Huh? Oh. Yeah, well, uh, what I didn't hear was anything about a belt. I mean I heard about the V-bruise goin' the right direction and all that, but I couldn't hear what you said about the belt."

"Well if you want to know about the belt, you're going to have to talk to the state police. It's headed to their lab."

"Oh. Okay, I'll do that. Uh, you hear anything about any detectives bein' on that scene? All I heard about was the watch commander and the chief and the EMTs, and the, uh, the deputy coroner, I didn't hear anything about any detectives. And nobody from Troop A CID either. Course I couldn't hear everything, lotta times I heard somebody talkin', I couldn't make out one word."

Grimes shrugged. "Mario, further conversation between us about this would be, uh, very difficult for me to justify, okay?"

"Yeah, okay, just one thing? You rule? I couldn't hear —"

"No, not until the tox work's done. Two weeks at least."

"Yeah, sure. Okay, Doc. Thanks, uh, you know. Thanks."

"Mario? I know they all saw you, but, uh, still, I don't want it coming back to me, okay?"

"Huh? Oh no, Doc, no, I wouldn't do that to you."

"Thank you. Now I really do have to get to work."

"It was murder, wasn't it? He didn't

hang himself, huh?"

Grimes said nothing for a moment. Then he sighed and said, "I have work to do, Mario. I really do have to get to it."

"Well you're not tellin' me it wasn't, are ya?"

"I'm not telling you anything."

"Yes you are. You're just not talkin'."

District Attorney Howard Failan was not his usual politically congenial self; the cherubic smile for which he was justly famous was barely visible, which for him meant he was practically on the verge of a scowl.

"Mario, detectives are working the case, talk to them. Until they come to me with something, I'm as ignorant as you are —"

"They're not workin' the case, they're workin' two other cases, and who said I was ignorant?"

"Excuse my presumption," Failan said, picking up the pace of his stride, merely waving and nodding at people in the hall on the way to his office instead of stopping every couple of steps to shake hands and inquire about somebody's mother, father, spouse, or children. The man couldn't help himself; he tried to let on that what he was doing was campaigning but Balzic had long suspected that the man simply had too much blarney in him to pass up even mundane conversation. Could it be that Failan was addicted to chatting?

Ever since Marie had told him about thinking as an addiction, Balzic was starting to see all kinds of behaviors as addictions. The DA could pretend he was campaigning if that's what he wanted people to believe, even though the next election was years away, but Balzic now suspected the man was hooked on yakety-yak. Couldn't help himself. And now neither could Balzic. He was starting to see addicts everywhere, just like that idiot Butterbaugh when it came to druggies. Well, maybe he wasn't as bad as Butterbaugh. Yet.

He had to hurry to keep up with Failan. "Hey, c'mon, Failan, gimme a coupla minutes here."

Failan said nothing until he was in his office and sitting behind his desk. "Mario, seems to me you've been in this office more in the last week than you were in the last two years you were chief in Rocksburg. Have I missed something? This guy cure cancer? My understanding is he was a small-time burglar, bookie, crank addict —"

"Hey, the guy came to me couple days before he was killed, he told me they were gettin' ready to chump him out for things he did not do —"

"Which you have told me at least three times now, and I keep reminding you, I direct the prosecutions, I don't work the investigations, though why I have to tell you this is beyond me. Talk to the detectives and please quit bothering me —"

"Ah the detectives, c'mon, it's a week now, what're they doin'?"

"Mario, you know very well what they're doing, I'm not gonna explain again that we've got two cases with a little higher priority than the one you want us to have. They know what they're doing —"

"They do? Then why ain't they doin' it? A week? There are principals they haven't interviewed yet, c'mon."

Failan bit down on his lower lip and looked up at Balzic over his reading glasses. "Mario, you've got way too much free time —"

"Well hell yeah I got too much free time, I'm retired. Time's what you get when you retire, you know? They bring it to ya in trucks, dump it on your front porch. Here, wha-whoomp, it's yours. Fuck's that have to do with anything?"

"I say again two things. I have much work to do, one, and two, I don't know why you're so worked up about this guy, God knows he didn't bring peace to the Middle East —"

"Oh right, so he deserved to have somebody slip a belt around his neck — not his belt either, huh? Belt was a size 42, Babyak was a 35 waist —"

"I'm sure it's being looked at —"

"And no prints either, huh? Troop A lab says no prints on that belt. What, he stayed awake long enough to wipe his own prints off?"

"You've been talking to people in the lab? Who? Who told you that?"

"Nobody. I was eavesdroppin' —"

"Mario, who do you think you are, Miss Marple? You're real close to the line here," Failan said, standing.

"Oh what — you gonna charge me with interfering with the police in the performance of their duty — that would be good if they were performin' their duty I guess — hey, I'm doin' their duty here —"

"Mario, I understand your situation, but understanding it or not, you're pushing it. Leave now, no problem. Keep talkin' at me, there's gonna be a problem, and just to put it in perspective for you, we had ten homicides in the county last year. We've had three in one week, and I've had to make some decisions about priority. I don't care whether you like my decisions or not, but a murdered child and a murdered wife are more important to me than the murder of your career thief. Neither of those innocents deserved what happened to them —"

"I understand, Failan, I do, honest to God I do, but there's somethin' else involved here, remember? Guns? A buncha nines. Right now, they're in the property room in the Knox PD — or they say that's where they are, and even if that's true, even if that's where they are right now, they're not gonna be there long, I'm tellin' ya, 'cause real soon they're gonna be in the holsters of every cop in that department, I'm tellin' ya, that's what's gonna happen, that's what this murder was all about, that's what makes this one different, and that's not all, hold it, just lemme say this one other thing and then I'm gone, okay? The security outfit that has the contract on the mall? The guy that runs it, I got a witness puts him in the mall, in uniform, gettin' ready to punch clocks the night the B and

471

E went down and he used to be a detective in the Knox PD —"

"That's it, Mario, out. Out! Talk to the detectives. Good-bye."

Balzic started backing out of the office, hands up, still trying to sell his opinions, but Failan suddenly pushed his chair back and came toward him so fast that Balzic instinctively retreated. Failan started to slam the door, but caught himself, and just shut it firmly in Balzic's face.

Balzic didn't hesitate. He turned around and set off toward the detective bureau office where he asked the female gate-keeper if he could speak to either Detective Sporcik or DeSantis. She made a call, hung up and told him with a smile to take a seat, both detectives were busy and one would be out as soon as he was free.

Balzic found a seat, a rumpled *Rocksburg Gazette*, and was halfway through the first section of it when it occurred to him that he'd been in the courthouse for nearly an hour without once checking his pulse or listening for pings in his engine. Wasn't even thinkin' about any of that stuff. And right now, I'm not thinkin' about it, I'm thinkin' about how I'm not thinkin' about it, how I wasn't thinkin' about it, so all I'm doin' here, if I got any kind of a handle on this, is I'm feedin' my addiction to thinkin', yeah, by congratulatin' myself on thinkin' about what I wasn't thinkin' about. Which may be the trick. Jesus, wait'll I tell Ruth — oh man, what's she gonna think? No no, it'll be alright, she'll be okay with this, yeah, 'specially if she talks to Marie about it, yeah. If I try to explain it, I'll fuck it up, but Marie, she could explain it . . . I'll bet. I hope. Oh that would be real good if she could do that. . . .

"Okay, who wantsa see a detective — oh man. Balzic, you ever think about movin' to Florida?"

"Oh that's cute, DeSantis, real cute. You wanna hear what I know or you just wanna crush my onions, huh?"

"Alright, Christ, c'mon back — unless all you're gonna do is tell me how I shoulda done somethin' already — 'cause if you're gonna do that, I'm tellin' ya right now, I'm not puttin' up with that, I'm too tired."

"Well, as a matter of fact, you wanna tell me why you guys haven't charged that fucker with destroyin' records, tampering with records?"

"See, that's just what I mean," DeSantis said, stopping short in front of Balzic.

"Didn't you hear what I just said, huh? I'm too fuckin' tired, okay? And which fucker you talkin' about? Bemiss?"

"Yeah, Bemiss, of course Bemiss, who else?"

DeSantis splayed his hands wearily. "Every fuckin' time I turn around for a week now, you're bustin' my balls about this Babyak, and now you wanna talk about tamperin' with records? What the fuck, huh?"

"Hey, you guys get anybody talkin' yet? About anything? This guy's a start, and the records are a good way to scare him —"

"A start? What start? Start how, fuck you talkin' about now?"

"Have you interviewed Bemiss, yes or no, just tell me that —"

"Oh please, look around, what do you see, huh?"

Balzic looked around the office, saw five other detectives, each on a phone talking to somebody, each looking raw-eyed and dog tired. "Yeah? So?"

"Where do you think everybody else is, huh? They're out on two crime scenes. I'm so fuckin' tired, I had to stand up or I was gonna fall asleep, that's why I come out to see who wanted to see a detective, okay? That temp didn't recognize you, 'cause if

I'da known it was you, you'd still be sittin' out there, and here you are and the first fuckin' thing you say is some shit about tamperin' with records. Why can't you remember you're a civilian, I don't get that. Is this what's gonna happen to me when I retire, huh?"

"Listen, I've talked to some people can really help you out, okay? I talked to a guy places the owner of Bulldog Security, remember him? David Beckmaier? Used to be a detective in Knox, now he owns —"

"I know who he is, Balzic, Jesus, gimme a fuckin' break —"

"You want the witness's name or not?"

"Yeah, okay, go ahead, go ahead, Jesus Christ," DeSantis said, taking a notebook out of the middle drawer of his desk.

"Roger Johnson. He works for the mall, walks around with a broom and a pan, sweepin' up butts."

"Oh."

"Oh? Hey, besides the foot patrol from Bulldog Security, the only people ever talk to this guy are some of the clerks, you know? Everybody else don't even wanna look at him. Worked for Westinghouse for thirty-some years, now he's sweepin' up butts, believe me he knows who talks to him and who treats him like he ain't visible. He knows all the foot patrol, he went out of his way to introduce himself to them, you know, so he could have somebody to talk to? And that night there was a new guy. So he introduced himself, okay? 'Cause he didn't want this new guy feelin' left out, you know? Guy introduced himself, you ready? Huh? David Beckmaier."

"Yeah? So?"

"Whatta you mean yeah so? The guy owns the agency is walkin' foot patrol? That night, huh? Of all nights?"

"Maybe he's shorthanded, I don't know, shortfooted, what the fuck? You ask him?" DeSantis slumped onto his chair and put his chin in his left hand.

"You really tired, or you usin' that as an excuse to be a wiseass or what, huh? You know Beckmaier doesn't have to talk to civilians and you know I know you know it, so what's goin' on here, huh?"

"Is that all?" DeSantis said, closing his notebook.

"No that's not all, so don't be closin' your notebook there."

"Alright, what? What else, c'mon, let's hear it, c'mon."

"Am I borin' you?"

"Hey, man, look around, whatta you see,

476

huh? Everybody's bustin' their asses in here —"

"So you said."

"Huh? Hey, I ain't speakin' for anybody but I for one haven't been in my own bed since Tuesday, huh? Ever since the girl was found, you know anything about that? Or the woman? Huh?"

"Hey, DeSantis, what I'm talkin' about involves guns —"

"Tell my boss, don't tell me, I don't get to pick which case I work, so just give me the information, okay, and lemme get back to what I'm supposed to be doin', alright?"

"Okay, okay, listen. First, Detective Carlucci, Rocksburg PD —"

"I know who he is, Jesus —"

"Yeah? Well he told me Bemiss's computer, uh . . . gimme a second here," Balzic said, unable to recall Carlucci's words.

"Yeah, what? All of a sudden you can't talk now?"

"I'm not sure how to explain this."

"Oh man —"

"No, it's a little bit complicated when you don't know that much about computers, and I don't, so gimme a second here."

DeSantis yawned and his chin slipped off his hand with a jerk. "Anytime now'll be fine with me."

"Okay, here. What I think Rugs said was, uh, this guy's hard drive? If nothin' corrupted it, you know, the horse crap? There are guys know how to get whatever's on there, there are programs that can get it off, uh, off that thing. The hard drive."

"And assumin' we get the okay to hire one of these geeks, assumin' we got the money to hire one, and assumin' he knows what he's doin', this is gonna tell us what now?"

"Aw man, c'mon, he said he didn't have any records of where he bought the guns, from which distributor, you know? So he was supposed to call half of the distributors, he didn't do it, I did it —"

"Which you already told me at least three times now —"

"And I found the distributor, and he's mailin' me copies of the bills, okay? With serial numbers, okay? So all you gotta do now is match them against the guns in the Knox PD, and then you get Bemiss's records off his hard drive and you got an absolute lock — aw, man, look at you, fuckin' fallin' asleep while I'm talkin'."

DeSantis's eyes were fluttering shut. The pen dropped out of his fingers, rolled off the desk, and fell to the floor. Balzic picked it up and tapped DeSantis on the hand with it. "Hey. Yo. DeSantis? C'mon, man, wake up, Jesus Christ."

DeSantis's eyes closed and his head bobbed forward.

Balzic sighed, looked around at the five other detectives involved in their calls, and thought, what the fuck, he's gonna get around to it sooner or later, might as well leave him a plan. He turned DeSantis's notebook around and wrote out a to-do, to-call, to-interview list.

1, interview Roger Johnson, custodian Rocksburg Mall, places D. Beckmaier in uniform punching clocks night of Freedom Firearms B&E.

2, get copy of bills from North Carolina gun distributor from M. Balzic in re Freedom Firearms B&E.

3, search Knox PD's property room for Beretta 92Fs, compare serial numbers w/bill from N.C. distributor. Also include officers' persons, lockers, B&Ws, personal cars in warrant, case pistols gone.

4, search S. Bemiss's computer hard drive, compare records, serial numbers with bill obtained from N.C. distributor.

5, iv Jackie Slaney, address unknown,

waitress Ground Round restaurant, Rocksburg Mall, prob unwilling accomp to burglar R. Cozzolino, fired foot patrol Bulldog Sec, owned by D. Beckmaier. Pressure from mother to separate self from Cozzolino, Slaney ready to talk, esp if arrest threatened.

6, iv Knox city Cclmn Herbert Tanyar, chrmn safety comm, prob prepared fraudulent requisitions and bids for B. 92Fs, look for backdating, etc., with identical serial nos on Bemiss's order from N.C. dist. Also, prob can squeeze in re '73 Mustang, check Pa, Ohio, FBI hotsheets.

7, iv Regina Hitalsky, aka Gina Hite, dancer in Leo Buckles's shop on Rt. 30 south of Knox. GF of Cclmn Tanyar, could be squeezed generally, specifically in re '73 Mustang.

8, iv cousins Angelo & James Serra, address unknown, employees of Art Chianese, Knox. One or both should be considered suspects in Babyak's death.

9, iv Lt. John Leffert, Knox PD, watch commander time of Babyak's death. Should be considered accomplice, aiding abetting entry/exit from lockup.

10, iv Chief Earl Butterbaugh, Knox

PD, principal accomplice and co-conspirator, with Tanyar, Leffert, Chianese, Beckmaier, Cozzolino in FF B&E, subsequent Babyak homicide.

11, iv Ronald Cozzolino, address Delano Drive, Rocksburg Terrace, primary suspect perp B&E FF, co-conspirator with Beckmaier in B&E.

12, iv Wilbur McFate, Bulldog Security motor patrol Rocksburg Mall time of FF BE, unwitting accomplice Cozzolino/Beckmaier FF B&E. Will talk if arrest threatened. Maybe best to start with him.

Balzic felt someone hovering by his side. It was Detective Sporcik, DeSantis's partner. "Hey, Balzic, what're you doin'? Huh? What're you doin'? Hey, Lou, don't sleep like that, go lay down on the cot, you're gonna hurt your neck, c'mon, Lou, wake up. What're you doin' with his notebook, huh? He takes a snooze, you grab his notebook, what the fuck —"

"I wasn't readin' it."

"Lemme see that." Sporcik snatched it away from Balzic. "What's this? You writin' him a *to-do* list? You think we don't have enough to do, you gotta write us a list? Hey, Lou, wake up, man, guy's fuckin' with your notebook here, c'mon, Lou, go back on the cot, lay down for a half hour, you're gonna get a crick in your neck you stay there — and you? Balzic, huh? Go home! Stop bustin' our balls over this —"

"Hey save your breath, I already got my ass chewed by Failan, I'm goin'. But I can see what's gonna happen here, plain as fuckin' day. You're gonna bust a boyfriend for the little girl, you're gonna bust the husband for the woman, you're gonna waste all this time on two no-brainers and meanwhile you got a homicide while in custody which oughta be top of your list, and while everybody in this whole fuckin' office is on these no-brainers, those ass-holes in Knox, they're gonna think of every way they can to cover their asses and you're gonna wind up with nothin' over there, that's what's gonna happen."

Sporcik closed his partner's notebook, held it up, and talked into it like it was a microphone. "Thank you, Nostradamus, for sharing your cogent predictions with us miserable dickheads. Live from the Cone- maugh County Courthouse, this is George Sporcik, now back to you, Sally."

"Aw that's real cute. I don't understand, why don't you guys get this, huh? This I really don't understand. You're s'pposed to be a sharp guy, Sporcik, everything I been hearin' about you, you're supposed to be a real good detective, why don't you get this?"

Sporcik took a quick look around, then, lowering his voice, he said, "Meet me at Wendy's out on 30, by the east entrance to the mall. Five o'clock."

"Huh?"

"You heard me. Now get outta here."

Balzic didn't protest. He turned on his heel and left, moving quickly, shaking his head, but not making another sound.

Balzic was fifteen minutes early to Wendy's. Sporcik was five minutes late. Balzic was nursing a cup of decaf when Sporcik walked in, brushing snow off his shoulders and stomping slush off his shoes. He spotted Balzic back in a corner booth, started to come back, then veered toward the counter and ordered chili and coffee. When his order came, he motioned for Balzic to follow him outside, and he led the way to a blue Ford, a county car. Balzic waited before getting in while Sporcik arranged the seat so he could eat in relative comfort and then made small talk as he opened his container of chili and sipped his coffee.

"You eat?"

Balzic shook his head. "I don't eat in these joints."

"Chili's decent. Not great, but speed's the attraction, huh?"

"Uh-huh. So, uh, what's this about?"

"Somethin' you said. I just wanted to clarify somethin'."

"Yeah? What'd I say?"

"You said we don't get it. That pissed me off."

"Oh yeah? Why?"

" 'Cause we get it. Maybe some of the other ones don't, I'm not speakin' for them. But DeSantis and me, we get it. You're the one's not gettin' it."

"Huh?"

"Hey, you turned in your report, your job's done, right? So why don't you take the money, and move on, and quit worryin' about it? It ain't worth worryin' about, believe me. It's the new world order."

"Excuse me?"

"The new world order, man. Remember? Georgie Bush? That thing he was always yakkin' about but he never explained? You haven't figured that out yet?"

"Apparently not."

"Hey, can't get what you want one way,

you get it another, that's all it is. Georgie Bush trieda tell ya, but he was practically tongue-tied. But the guy in there now, he ain't tongue-tied. Never shuts up. And he's sure tryin' to tell ya, ol' Billy boy is. You owe it to yourself — and to us — to start payin' attention, man, I'm serious."

"Hey, Sporcik, this would be interesting if I knew what you were talkin' about, but I don't, 'cause I thought this was gonna be about what I wrote in your partner's notebook —"

Sporcik smiled and ate more chili. Then he started talking to his plastic spoon. "Here we are live in Wendy's parking lot, talkin' once again with Nostradamus. Say, Nosty, how 'bout a couple more predictions for the folks at home, whattaya say? Alright, don't mind if I do. How's this for starters? I predict that a certain retailer will, through the magic of modern technology, recover his records. I further predict that this retailer will revise his original insurance claim to say, oh, half what it was. And the half that he will now claim he lost, I further predict that his records will show that the serial numbers in his inventory will match the serial numbers on the guns in the property room of a certain police department —"

"Aw bullshit, nobody's gonna make the bill from the distributor go away, that's bullshit —"

"Please don't interrupt Nosty when he's on a roll. I predict the pistols this retailer will now claim he lost, they will suddenly be found, and not only that, they will be returned to him by the aforesaid police department, and he will quit his insurance claim on all the pistols whose serial numbers don't match. I further predict that nobody nowhere, except for one geezer ex-cop, is gonna give two shits for this guy who got his ticket punched in a certain lockup. And I predict that because everybody got what they wanted, nobody's gonna pay any attention to anybody who claims that what they wanted wasn't right. That's my final prediction. Back to you in the studio, Sally."

"You sonofabitch."

"Hey, don't sonofabitch me, I'm tellin' ya I got it as soon as I heard what went down and you didn't, and lookin' at your face now, I think you still don't get it. So I'm sayin' it again, it's the new world order. People with juice take from those who don't have the juice and give it to the people who gave them the juice, that's the deal, it's that simple. What makes it new,

Balzic — everything else is the same old, see? The new part is, now they do it with computers."

"This is what you got me out here to tell me, huh? That this is gonna slide because there's juice here? Who? That fuckin' idiot Butterbaugh? And that councilman can't keep his dick in his pants?"

"Yeah, exactly," Sporcik said between spoons of chili. "And don't forget the Fat Buddha."

"*This* is the new world order? *This?* Those two clowns and that fat fuck?"

Sporcik nodded emphatically. "Plus computers. Yessir, that's exactly what I'm tellin' ya. That's the it we get, and you don't."

"Aw bullshit. New world order my ass, you're talkin' bought pols and cops and a fat prick can't get enough of whatever he wants, this is as old as dirt —"

"See, that's what I mean, you don't understand the computer part."

"So explain it, if that's what you got me out here for, do it!"

"First, I'm from Knox, okay? Born there, raised there, went to public school there, as a matter of fact two years behind Dave Beckmaier. Yeah. We played football together. He was an end, I was a tackle.

487

Played right beside him every game his senior year —"

"Oh so now what? I'm gonna hear how you learned all about this guy from playing football with him? Jesus, the man's a weasel, you think I give a fuck how he got that way?!"

"That ain't what I'm gonna tell ya. Just listen. We lived there, my family, because my old man worked at Knox Iron and Steel. He was in the furnace gang. Every time they hada rebrick the ovens, that's what he did. You know anything about that?"

Balzic shook his head no.

"All I know is what my old man told me, 'cause when he was dyin' he told me that if he found out I ever went near a mill he'd come back and haunt me. I had four brothers, all older, he wouldn't let any of us even think about workin' there. 'Cause he had the hardest, dirtiest, stinkin'est job in the mill, takin' the worn-out fire bricks outta the ovens, puttin' new ones in. He was doin' that shit before they gave 'em masks, you know? With filters? Before they even knew that what those guys were blastin' away with their jackhammers was full of all these carcinogens, which once it got in their lungs, they were history. Took decades to get 'em, thirty-two years for my father, but all the guys that were around the same age as my father? The ones that were workin' before masks, huh? They all died of lung cancer. Just like my old man. Most of 'em were niggers. Niggers and hunkies that couldn't speak English, that's who worked in the furnace gangs. His last year, man, I wouldn't do that to a rabid skunk what that . . . that shit did to him. I was twelve."

"Sorry," Balzic said halfheartedly. He was burning from Sporcik's tone and attitude.

Sporcik shrugged and ran his tongue all around the inside of his mouth. "It was a lot tougher on my mother and my oldest brother than it was on the rest of us, but, yeah, it was no picnic. So, uh, anyway, couple years later, I'm playin' alongside Beckmaier. Whose old man also worked for Knox I and S. 'Cept he was white-collar. Accountant, bookkeeper, I'm not sure exactly. All I know is he lived long enough to collect his pension. He's still alive. Down in one of those, uh, islands off the coast of South Carolina, Kiawah or somethin' like that."

Sporcik finished the chili, put the container, cover, spoon, and napkins carefully into the paper bag and set it on the dash. "One time, after the season was over, Beckmaier and me got to talkin' about our fathers, you know, I guess we thought we were buddies 'cause we went through some football bonding bullshit or somethin', but when I told him about my old man, who'd been dead like three years, he said somethin' I never forgot. He said, 'You know, he didn't have to work there. He didn't have to do that job. He could've worked anywhere he wanted. This is America, you can work anywhere you want. So it's not the mill's fault he got cancer.'

"I can't tell you how many times I've run into that attitude in my life, like there's this special information somewhere that mill hunkies were just too stupid to know they could even look for it, or understand it if they found it, like they were incapable of knowin' what guys like Beckmaier and his old man knew, or know. I ran into that so much, it got so bad, it started to affect me so much, there was a time I actually thought about changin' my name. Yeah, no shit. I thought about changin' it to somethin' like Beck or Meyer, yeah, you're smilin', you think that's so pathetic it's comic, but no shit, I actually thought about doin' that once. I mean, 'cause I said to myself, if all I'm ever gonna run into is assholes with attitudes like that, if I'm ever gonna get anywhere, you know, someplace that wasn't that fuckin' mill, which my old man didn't want me near, then hey, I was gonna do whatever it took."

"So why didn't ya?"

"C'mon. That woulda been like spittin' on my father's grave, you kiddin' me? He wasn't the sharpest guy in the world, that's for sure, he never did learn how to read or write English, but he worked, man. If he missed work, it was before I was born, 'cause I never saw him stay home. And he kept the weather off us, roof and clothes, he kept our bellies full, he never smacked any of us around, not that he didn't like to shout every once in a while, he did. And when he did, hey, that's all he needed to do, that got my attention real fast.

"But the point I'm makin' here, Balzic, it's this. Everything else is the same old, same old, you're right. Cops on the pad, pols on the pad, stinkballs like Chianese greasin' 'em, shakin' 'em down for the salt and cinder contract, that shit hasn't changed. And the guys that owned Knox Iron and Steel? Still there, man — the ones that ain't in caskets or nursin' homes. They're still in the big houses out on Country Club Road, all around Knox Country Club, Country Club Estates, they're all still there. They built the country club, they still own it. And they also still own Knox I and S — except now it ain't in Knox anymore. Now it's in Brazil. And that's where the computers come in.

" 'Cause they still live here, those guys, five, six months a year, you know, good weather. Then every winter they're off to wherever, Boca Raton, Palm Beach, the Virgin Islands, who knows? Meanwhile, all the dirty faces? They're squeakin' by on Social Security. 'Cause when those fucks moved their operation to Brazil, their shysters busted the union contract, man, fucked those guys outta their pensions, half of which had been skimmed off anyway before it even got to court. Yeah. They skimmed half of it, and then their shysters went to court and took the other half, all nice and clean, all the i's dotted, all the t's crossed, fuck you very much.

"But right now, here's what I want you to know, Balzic, okay? This is the part I want you to listen to, understand? I want you to hear me, I want you to listen, I want you to understand. You're makin' me sick harpin' about this shit."

"Excuse me?"

"No, no fuckin' excuse you. Listen up. If you think there's anybody on this planet wants to hang a murder rap on Dave Beckmaier more than me, you're not gonna find him. That guy doesn't exist. But Knox Country Club does. And Howard Failan, my boss's boss? He's a member there. And has been since a month after his election, what, twelve years ago? Huh? So you put it together. Where do you think he got most of the money to run on, huh?"

"Hey, Failan's straight, Sporcik, you're not gonna tell me he's bent, I'm not buyin' that."

"Course he's straight. That's what he gets paid for. To be straight as he needs to be. And I'll give him that, he's the best DA we've had in my memory. I'm not that old, but I know he's straight. I never saw him bend a case. But you know what? I've heard about some, some DUIs, some pot busts, acid busts, coke busts, some sixty-through-a-twenty-five zone with blood alcohol twice the legal, roaches in the ashtray, coke under the seat, hey, that stuff suddenly isn't enough to make a case if it comes attached to the right address. You hear what I said? *If it comes attached to the right address —"*

"Yeah, yeah, I hear ya, what's that have to do with the fuckin' idiots in the PD over there?"

"Just listen, I'm comin' to that. That dinky shit I just told you about, that doesn't bother me. I'm a big boy. And we don't need to waste our time fuckin' around with those stupid rich kids anyway. But your boy Babyak, hey, that's a different thing. That bothers the shit outta me. 'Cause I can't do anything about it — and don't you fuckin' dare say won't, 'cause you're gettin' ready to. You like to ride the high horse, man."

Balzic shook his head. "Can't, won't, what's the difference?"

"Huge difference, goddammit, whattaya think I been talkin' here? There's no way we're goin' anywhere with that. So you see these notes, huh? You wrote for my partner? Insultin' both our intelligence, huh?" Sporcik took folded papers out of his inside coat pocket, the two pages Balzic had written on in DeSantis's notebook. "See these? Watch?" Sporcik rolled them into a ball and shoved them into his mouth and started to chew.

"Aw what the fuck," Balzic said.

"Yeah, right," Sporcik said after he'd

swallowed the paper. "Not real tasty, but edible, you know. Not as good as the chili, but, hey, I really wasn't expectin' much."

"You got a real problem here, Sporcik —"

"Yes, right, I do have a problem, goddammit, which is exactly why I don't need you comin' around with these fuckin' to-do lists, okay? Three times you were in there this week, but today was a first with this, uh, this list shit. You can't do that to me, man. No more, you hear? I feel shitty enough about this *all by myself* without you comin' around, 'cause if the guys in Country Club Estates — you get this? If those guys wanted somebody else in City Hall in Knox, huh? They'd be there. Wouldn't be Tanyar, wouldn't be Butterbaugh, and that fat fuck Chianese, where do you think he'd be if he stopped deliverin' what those sweet pieces wanted, huh? It's what they call a symbiotic relationship, man. You know symbiotic? If you don't, look it up. But just do me and Louie a favor, huh, and stop buggin' us about this shit we can't do anything about and let us do the thing we can do somethin' about, you know? We find the creep killed this little girl, we're heroes. Everybody loves us. We get to hold our heads up for a while, you know? Don't tell me you don't know what that feels like, I know you do."

"Cops aided and abetted with Babyak —"

"Oh please, what the fuck?! What, you knew this Babyak, is that it? I mean besides him comin' to you beforehand and tellin' you what was gonna happen — I mean do you have other reasons for this super superior conscience of yours, huh?"

"Hey. Watch it, Sporcik, I'm not that old —"

"Oh what? What're you tryin' to do, huh? Shit me you never bent a case? Sell that one to your wife and kids, don't try to sell me that bullshit —"

"That's not what I'm talkin' about —"

"Then say what you're talkin' about. 'Cause I know you know what's goin' on in Knox. Ain't any different there than it is in Rocksburg. I watched you go out, man, you think we weren't watchin', huh? We were watchin', don't think we weren't. So I know you know what I'm talkin' about. Besides which, I had a couple long conversations with Rugs Carlucci about that, when Rugs got his blindfold off about who he was really protectin' when he took the oath? To serve and protect, huh? I know you understand all that, then why the fuck

don't you understand how you're pissin'
me off comin' around throwin' it in our
faces — 'cause you know we can't do anything about it? What the fuck's the mental
block here? You do anything about your
fire chief, huh? Still fire chief or not?"

Balzic hung his head, took his glasses
off, and rubbed his eyes.

"Yeah, that's it, rub your eyes, that's
good, that'll help —"

"Why're you such a wiseass?"

"Because you can't get it through your
fuckin' head that comin' around all the
time bustin' our balls about Babyak is
doin' nothing' but throwin' it in our faces
there's nothin' we can do about this! Why's
the fire chief still around, huh? And the
guy owns the paper? Huh? Both papers?
Case you didn't know it, he's owned the
paper in Knox for about two years now.
He's bought every newspaper in the county
in the last two years, you keepin' up with
that, huh? And how about the guy owns
the dirt under both the malls, huh? The
guy who built 'em, still owns the dirt under
'em, how come they're all still around and
you ain't —"

"It was time for me to get out —"

"That's not what I'm talkin' about!
What're you, gettin' senile? I'm talkin'

about they're the guys who decided it was time for you to leave, not you. Don't fuckin' sit there and tell me you don't know that, I'll punch you in the mouth you try to tell me that lie —"

"That's it, that's enough, I'm gone," Balzic said opening the door and starting to get out.

Sporcik grabbed Balzic by the arm and said, "Go read the papers, man. Won't take you long to read the Knox paper, it only comes out once a week. But read the *Gazette*. And read the one from Pittsburgh. See the way they play these three murders, the girl, the wife, and your guy. And what, you don't watch TV news, huh? How those fuckers been playin' 'em, huh?"

"I don't watch TV news, no —"

"Then ask somebody who does! And you'll know what I'm sayin' when I'm tellin' ya I don't need you comin' around throwin' it in my face, okay? I know there's nothin' I can do. I already know that, understand? Every time I read the fuckin' paper or watch TV, I know *they're* throwin' it in my face — and they don't even know they're doin' it. I know they don't know any better, 'cause if they did they wouldn't be workin' there, 'cause soon as they tried to say what was really goin' on, they'd be out the door. Bad enough I'm gettin' it from them, who don't know, why the fuck do I also have to get it from you, who should know better, but is actin' like he don't, huh? Why do I have to have *you* throwin' it in my face — *you,* that's the part I don't get?"

"Let go of my arm."

"Yeah, right. That tells me you really get it. Go on, go, go read the papers, see what I'm sayin'. But I'm warnin' ya, don't come in the office anymore. I have to take this shit from newsies that don't know their ass from a sewer pipe, but I'm not gonna take it from you anymore, you hear me?"

Balzic got out of the Ford without saying anything. He walked to his Chevy without looking back. He was seething.

Balzic drove to the *Rocksburg Gazette* building, identified himself to the female gatekeeper as an investigator for Attorney Valcanas, who needed to have some facts checked about an insurance problem, and asked to read through the last two weeks' worth of papers. The gatekeeper made a couple of internal calls, and momentarily a security guard appeared to escort Balzic to a narrow room on the first floor near the pressroom, where the previous thirty-five days' papers were stacked in wooden bins from floor to ceiling along one wall. There were no chairs and the floor was littered with cigarette butts and candy wrappers.

Balzic took the oldest edition he could find, spread it in a corner, took off his parka, and folded it carefully on top of the papers. Then he went looking for the first stories about all three deaths, none of which had been officially ruled on yet as to manner of death because Coroner Grimes was still waiting on the toxicology reports. What Grimes had said about the deaths of the girl and the woman so far was that they were not the results of suicide, accidents, or natural causes, and on that basis homicide investigations were being pursued. But when it came to Charles Babyak, Grimes had ruled out only accidental and natural causes, leaving homicide and suicide both as possibilities. What was frustrating Balzic was that all the investigators involved, state, county, and local, seemed to have been assigned to the deaths of the girl and the woman and were doing next to nothing about Babyak.

So Balzic went thumb-licking through

the papers even though he knew that what Sporcik had said about how the three deaths were being played in the paper was going to be true. Plodding on as much to test his memory as to confirm Sporcik's prediction, Balzic took note of which page and in which of the four sections of the paper the stories first appeared and what happened to them subsequently.

The paper's first section was dedicated more or less to international, national, state, county, and city news, editorials, and the weather. The second section was dedicated to sports and the comics; the third to business, obituaries, and classified ads; and the fourth to local news, lifestyle, entertainment, and food, though it soon became apparent to Balzic that these categories and sections tended not to be very rigid. Sometimes, for instance, the classified ads and comics appeared at the end of the sports section. Two days a week the food section was greatly expanded; the rest of the time it got no more space than the so-called lifestyle section, which could be about anything from reports of charity dances to octogenarian bridge clubs, church and fraternal dinners, engagements, weddings, births, and retirements.

Balzic was looking for where the stories

first appeared as well as their size and general content; how many, what color, and what size photos accompanied the stories; and finally for the progression through the paper as the story aged. He also paid attention to the content and attitude of the editorials, considering that there had been three violent deaths in one week in the county as opposed to ten in the whole previous year. He read the editorials because where most other people tended to see coincidences, editorial writers tended self-importantly to see trends, but these three violent deaths seemed to have left the *Gazette*'s editorial writer with nothing to say. There was only one pro forma call for the community to support the families of the victims and to assist the police wherever possible.

It took Balzic about ten minutes to find the page-one story when Emmylou Drosser, aged six, was first reported missing. Her story remained on the bottom of page one of the local news section until two days before Charles Babyak's murder, when her body was discovered by Rocksburg Fire Department bloodhounds buried in a shallow grave less than a mile from the house where she lived with her mother, Maryann Tomko Drosser, and her mother's boyfriend, Eric John Anderburg. That story dominated the top of page one and was wrapped around color photos, one of the girl's body being placed in a Mutual Aid ambulance and the other of a volunteer fireman petting his bloodhound.

Because investigators were naturally saying as little as possible, there was the usual journalistic speculation about where, when, and how the girl had been killed, whether she had been attacked sexually, whether she knew her killer, and why it had taken her mother nearly two hours to report her missing, as the girl had been in first grade all day and had been seen coming home on the school bus by every one of her classmates who rode that bus. The mother's call to 911 had been received at 4:31, two full hours after the bus reached the stop where the girl got off every day. The mother was cooperating fully with the authorities, "though she was so distraught that investigators frequently had trouble understanding her responses to their questions." The boyfriend was identified by name, age, and current employment, but little else was said about him.

The next day that story was pushed to the bottom of page one by the death in

Conemaugh General Hospital of Florence Marie Tucker Wohlmuth, who had been beaten allegedly by her husband, Frederick James Wohlmuth. The husband had been missing since the day his wife had accused him of the beating as she was being admitted to the emergency room, last seen in his Ford Ranger pickup truck by his brother Irvin at a gas station near the Donegal entrance to the Pennsylvania Turnpike. Irvin Wohlmuth claimed to have no idea where his brother was going, but didn't believe his brother had beaten his wife. "They always got along okay far as I could tell," Irvin said. "I never seen him hit her or nothing."

The next day, when Charley Babyak's body was found in the Knox PD lockup, the Drosser girl's story started on page one and broke over to an inside page, while Mrs. Wohlmuth's story had been moved to the front page of the local news section, as investigators were releasing no new information. Most of the space about both those stories was taken up by color photos of the residences where both victims had lived, which, as far as Balzic could see, did nothing but illustrate how little real information the paper had about either case.

Meanwhile, the story of Babyak's apparent suicide was told on the bottom of page one in about twelve inches of type wrapped around a color photo of Chief Earl Butterbaugh conferring with county detectives George Sporcik and Louis DeSantis outside Knox City Hall's front door.

Babyak's death was reported from the first day strictly as a suicide. There was a summation of the charges on which he had been locked up, the emphasis on drugs, porn, and guns in descending order, but otherwise there was no speculation, no analysis, no interviews with either the coroner or state, county, or Knox police about the death itself. There was also no editorial questioning either custody procedures in general or the Knox PD's custody procedures specifically. Nor, in the days since, was there ever a letter to the editor suggesting that perhaps the Knox PD warranted an investigation because a prisoner in their custody had allegedly committed suicide by hanging himself with a belt, a fact which, if true, flew in the face of all custodial theory and practice.

In three days, Babyak's death had been moved from page one of the first section to the second page of the local news section to the very last news page of that section where it had been reduced to a three-inch story that said the investigation was continuing, pending a final ruling by the coroner on the manner of death, which was mistakenly called the "cause" of death.

While the beating of Florence Wohlmuth continued to be reported in progressively smaller stories on the front page of the local news section, the disappearance and murder of Emmylou Drosser continued to be reported prominently on page one. Every day there was at least one story and sometimes two about the girl, or her mother, or her mother's boyfriend, or the neighbors, or her classmates, or her teachers, and, finally, after a week, an interview with her natural father, who'd been located in Clearwater Beach, Florida, working as a bartender on a gambling boat. There was also a long interview, dealing mostly in hypotheticals, with a Pittsburgh police detective, a woman, whose special interest and expertise was violence against children.

When Florence Wohlmuth died, her story went back to page one of the first section, where it too followed a progression nearly identical to the story about Emmylou Drosser: interviews with relatives, neighbors, co-workers, and a family counselor often used by Family Court, who spoke hypothetically about domestic violence, especially against women.

Balzic sensed through all the stories about Emmylou Drosser and Florence Wohlmuth that there seemed to be implicit a considerable interest in whether sex had been a motive in either death. Without a direct quote from either the coroner, state police, or county detectives, the *Gazette*'s reporters typically found some way to imply that the girl's murder had occurred to cover up sex with her, leaving little doubt that they were convinced it was the boyfriend who had murdered her. Balzic, of course, had believed that from the beginning, just as he'd had no doubt that Florence Wohlmuth's husband had beaten her, even before he knew she'd accused him to at least five witnesses in the ER before she lost consciousness.

Balzic then went back through the papers to find the story about Babyak's arrest by Knox police. He wanted to see how that had been reported, especially in light of Earl Butterbaugh's boast that Babyak's arrest had been a "major interruption of a major illegal drug operation."

Balzic found the arrest story on the bottom of page one of the local news section. It was wrapped around one color photo of Knox Chief Butterbaugh pointing at some bags of white powder and several stacks of magazines and videotapes on a table. The handle of one pistol was all that was visible, the rest apparently obscured by Butterbaugh's torso, while Butterbaugh himself looked appropriately somber as he considered the importance of his department's stellar skirmish in its war against drugs and pornography. The story was a straight-ahead who, what, where, when, and how, and Butterbaugh was the only person quoted, so his version of what went down preceding and during Babyak's arrest thus became the news.

The *Gazette*'s reporter, somebody named Will Butler, focused entirely on the drugs and the porn, barely mentioning the pistols until the last two paragraphs. What a coincidence, Balzic thought. Butterbaugh is the only person quoted. This Butler should've been a butler if this crap is any indication of his investigative curiosity.

Balzic searched for follow-ups on this "major interruption of a major illegal drug operation" but found none, not another word about Butterbaugh or Babyak until the latter was found dead in his cell. And that story had moved to the back of the paper as fast as anything Balzic had ever seen.

He replaced the papers in their respective bins, collected his parka, and went back to the front desk where he asked the female gatekeeper if reporter Butler was available. She said Butler usually worked nights but it so happened she'd just seen him leave with a photographer to wait for a jury to come in. Said he was probably in the paper's office in the courthouse or else would be catching a bite to eat, maybe at Muscotti's.

Balzic called the paper's courthouse office from a pay phone inside the front door and learned that Butler was in Muscotti's. Balzic drove there and, once inside, asked Vinnie if he knew a reporter from the *Gazette* named Butler and to point him out if he was there. Vinnie pointed at a table near the far wall where a pair of twenty-somethings was drinking coffee.

"One of you guys Butler?" Balzic said, approaching the table.

"That's me," one said, standing and holding up his coffee cup in Vinnie's direction. He was short, broad-shouldered, with the build and gait of a wrestler. His left ear was well cauliflowered. When he returned with fresh coffee in his cup, he said,

"What's up? Uh, do I know you?" He shifted his mug to his left hand and, wiping his right on the back of his pants, studied Balzic to see if he knew him.

"No," Balzic said, introducing himself as Valcanas's investigator. "Don't squeeze," he said as he extended his hand. Butler looked like a squeezer.

"Okay," Butler said, offering Balzic his fingers and letting Balzic shake them. "What's up?"

Before Balzic could reply the other fellow put on his parka and said he had to go to the courthouse and warned Butler not to linger. "Vinnie don't always give good messages, okay?"

"Yeah I know," Butler said, still looking as though he should recognize Balzic.

Balzic took a chair, stated his interest as quickly and as generally as he could, and then said, "Uh, you mind tellin' me why you didn't do any follow-ups on the drug bust?"

Butler shrugged. "Mind? Why should I mind, I don't mind, probably had other stuff to do. I mean, uh, that's my beat, Knox. I have the school board, City Hall, council, the cops, the firemen, uh, everything over there, pretty much."

"So you were workin' on, uh, routine

stuff, is that what you're sayin'?"

"Yeah. Probably. Why?"

"Well, you know, it seems to me there was a lotta stuff included in that one bust, you know? The drugs, the crank, the porn, all those magazines, videos, uh, you almost didn't even mention the guns."

Butler squinted and shook his head. "Uh, so what — there's a problem with that or somethin'? I mean, you're lookin' at me like, uh, like I don't know what — what's the issue here, I don't know what you're sayin'."

"What I'm sayin', Mister Butler, is, uh, why you seemed to think there was nothin' worth followin' up there, I mean, given that, uh, within a couple days, the man was found dead, you know?"

"Oh. Well. He hung himself, that's all there was to that. Cons off themselves all the time, I mean —"

"He wasn't a con — not for that. For other things, yeah, but not for that bust. They hadn't even filed an information with the DA's office yet."

"Oh no? I didn't know that. But, uh, so what?"

"Uh, Mister Butler, you know anything about custodial procedures, huh? What police are required by law to do when they arrest a citizen, huh? Detain him? I mean besides Mirandizin' him, you know?"

Butler's shoulders went up, the corners of the mouth went down, then his left thumb came up. Then he shook his head slowly. "I don't know what you mean."

"Okay, forget that for a second. You remember seein' the pistols? That day you covered that, the first day, you remember, uh, on the table there when you did the first story, huh? The picture that ran? I mean, I saw the butt of one pistol in that picture, you know? Who took that picture by the way?"

"Me. I took it. But, yeah, I remember the guns."

"You happen to count 'em?"

"What, the guns?"

"Yes the pistols. You wrote thirty-eight. Did you count 'em?"

"No. That's the number they gave me, why would I count 'em?"

"To check on 'em maybe?"

"To check on 'em? Who, the cops? Wait wait wait, you think I should be checkin' on the cops over there? Whoa. You know what happens I start checkin' on what they tell me, huh? Hey — oh man, they don't tell me anything ever again. Bango, closeo, that's it, I'm shut out. It took me like, whoa, two years to get to where they'd even let me ride with 'em once in a while, you kiddin'? They think I'm checkin' what they tell me? Man, they're on the phone to my boss, and I get a new beat, which means I gotta start all over again — or else I'm lookin' for a new job. Believe me, Mister, uh, Mister Balzer, there aren't a whole lotta newspapers hirin' these days, you know?"

Balzic peered at Butler, trying to make up his mind whether Butler had any idea what he was saying. "Uh, just to clarify somethin' here, you know? You tellin' me you think it is not your job to check what a cop tells you? Is that what you're sayin'?"

"Oh not just cops. Anybody. What, you think I'm supposed to check out everything somebody on the school board tells me? What, I'm supposed to check all the bids, huh? For construction or remodeling, or, uh, uh, school supplies, tablets, pencils, band uniforms, computers, whatever? What price they got, what price they coulda got from somebody else, like that you mean? When, uh, when am I supposed to get the time to do that? I mean, I got City Hall and the school board over there, okay? City Hall means all the departments in the city, street, electrical, building inspectors, the cops, Christ, you kiddin'? And during football season I gotta cover high school football games every Friday and Saturday night for the sports department. This is in addition, you know, to the rest of my beat, which also includes writin' ad copy for any business over there that has a minimum three-month ad contract in the zoned edition."

"Well, I'm sure you have a lot to do, no doubt, but, uh, Mister Butler, listen to me. I was a cop my whole life, I never did anything else. And for the last twenty years I was chief right here —"

"Oh oh, you're Balzic, I thought I recognized you, wasn't sure —"

"Okay, so you know me now, alright, here's my point. You don't think it's your job to check out what public officials tell you?"

Butler snorted and laughed. "Hey, whoa, whoa, wait a second here, okay? Lemme tell you somethin', okay? Strictly between us? Okay?"

"Yeah. Okay, I'm listenin'."

"Okay, for your ears only now, don't screw me around on this, alright?"

Balzic nodded. "Won't go anyplace."

"Okay, alright. Uh, my boss? The managing editor? He doesn't want me checkin' stuff. On anybody. I wrote a piece one time right after I got assigned over there, in Knox, you know? About how a coupla contractors doin' city work weren't buyin' workmen's comp insurance? So I wrote it, worked my ass off on it, and I turned it in to the guy workin' the desk that night — hey, never saw it again. I asked him about it couple days later, man, he tells me don't bother him about that stuff, I wanna know what happened to my story, go talk to the managing editor. So when I did, the managing editor tells me the law department has it, my story, they're checkin' it out, makin' sure I got all my facts right, 'cause in case I didn't know, our libel deductible had just got kicked up to a hundred thousand.

"So that story, hey, it never got outta the law department, which I don't even know who or where it is, okay? It's sure as hell not in the *Gazette* building. 'Cause if it is, it's behind some secret panel or somethin' 'cause I haven't found it. And that was three years ago. And every time I tried writin' anything like that again? Same thing happened. Exactly. The law department was checkin' on me, checkin' my facts, checkin' my attribution, that was always the answer whenever I asked. Oh yeah. So, uh, hey, I don't pretend to be the smartest guy in the world, Mister Balzic, but, uh, you know, I don't have to get hit with a brick either, man. I mean, later if not sooner, you know, I get the message. Now I'm not gonna sit here and try to tell you what newspapers used to do, or are supposed to do, or anything like that. All I know is what this particular paper does and what it does not do, because that's how I keep gettin' paid every two weeks, okay? And what this paper does not do, is investigate anything or anybody."

"You shittin' me?"

"Nope, that I am not. Ask any reporter there, don't take my word for this, you know, get 'em off the record somewhere like we're talkin' here, hey, they'll all tell you the same thing. After somebody else investigates it now, yeah, okay, then it's news, then we report it. But if the cops, if old Chief Butterballs, if he tells me he confiscated thirty-eight guns, then that's what he confiscated, man, thirty-eight. You think I'm gonna stand there right in front of him and count 'em? He'd throw me outta the building, man. Physically. And I'd have to really kiss his ass to get back in — but I would've been shifted to a new beat before I got a chance to pucker up —

or I'd be fired — 'cause he would've made the call to my boss right after he threw me out. I mean we get our beats rotated, you know, routinely about every three years, but if you can't get along with the people on your beat? Hey, you get two chances, that's it. Second time the boss has to listen to complaints about you from anybody that you have to rely on as a source, you're gone, bye-bye, don't even think about gettin' a third chance. I've only been here five years and I've seen two guys go. Same scenario. Exactly."

"What happened to all the president's men?"

"Huh? Oh you mean Woodward and Bernstein, huh? Those guys?"

"Nobody does that anymore? Huh?"

"Oh yeah, I'm sure in the big metros there are still investigative reporters around. But, uh, not here, man, c'mon — at the *Rocksburg Gazette*? You kiddin'? That's fantasy."

"So you never check anything any public official tells you, elected or appointed?"

"Not just public, man, hell no. For every business over there with an ad contract for the zoned edition? Part of my job is to write advertisin' copy once a week, on a rotating basis, for, uh, like, I think, well, it varies, but probably right now it's between twelve and sixteen businesses. So basically what I'm doin' there is fakin' an interview with somebody from the company, usually the owner, sayin', you know, what a great product or service they have and how terrific they are 'cause they been in business there since, uh, you know, 1972, and, uh, they're your neighbors so buy their stuff. That's advertisin', man. You think I check what they tell me?" Butler laughed and shook his head. "Look, essentially, what I do is, uh, I retype press releases, man, that's all I do, from everybody, man, school board, city council, the school bus company, the food service that runs all the school cafeterias —"

"Don't you go to council meetings?"

"Sure, yeah, of course, but what — you think I'm gonna hear somethin' there that wasn't prearranged? Hey, the only thing that's not prearranged is if some citizen gets up and starts bitchin' about somethin' that's pissin' him off in particular, c'mon. I mean, I walk in, the secretary hands me a copy of the agenda, I just put it in my own words for the paper, that's all. If two members of the board are arguin' about somethin', I report that, you know, that's my big exposé for the week. But, what —

you think I'm gonna check to see what's behind their beef? No way, man, never happen. First place, like I said, I don't have time, and even if I did, it wouldn't get printed."

Butler fiddled with his spoon, running it around the rim of his mug. "Listen, man, I'm no crusader, okay? I read about them, those, uh, old muckrakers, Ida Tarbell, Mother Jones, and I read *Mother Jones* magazine, you know? I'm a subscriber, man, I know what real investigative journalism looks like. But I'm gettin' ready to get married, and my girlfriend is between jobs now, and her car's fallin' apart and mine, hey, my Tercel's got like a hundred and thirty thousand miles on it. But that, you know, I mean, that's not even the worst part, shit." He sighed and shook his head.

"Mister Balzic, you ever tell anybody I told you this stuff, I'm gone, you know? I don't know whether you know this or not, but in this state, man, you don't have to have a reason to fire people, okay?"

"I know," Balzic said.

"Yeah, well it's not just that the employers got everything stacked their way, it's like . . . oh man. It's like it's worse than Alice in wonderland, I'm tellin' you. Do you know that in the last three years, the publisher has bought up every newspaper except one in this county — did you know that?"

"I'd heard something like that, yeah."

"Well, listen to this. And then you explain it to me, okay, 'cause I'm still tryin' to figure this one out, okay?"

"I'm listenin'."

"Okay. Here it is. If the publisher owns all the newspapers except for one in the county, how could anybody talk about competition between papers he owns, huh? But that's what I got one day. I mean, I turned in a routine story about the school board over in Knox, you know, just like I always did, the day after. And the managing editor calls me up, he says, no shit now, you gotta believe what I'm sayin', I'm not makin' this up. He says we got beat on that story, direct quote. I said excuse me? Beat? How? By who? He says *Knox Weekly Review*. I said I thought the publisher bought that paper two years ago, he says yeah he did. So I said, well if the publisher owns both that paper and this paper, you know, maybe I'm not seein' the big picture here, but how are we competitors with them? Aren't you the executive managing editor for all his papers? He said yeah he was, right, but that didn't make any difference, the *Knox Weekly Review* had almost everything I'd written, a day ahead of my story. So I said well, hell, all they did was get a copy of the school board agenda a day before I did, that's all. 'Cause they're a weekly, right? And I'm not gonna repeat the rest of that conversation, because that's the way the rest of it went, but I thought, hey, I'm in wonderland, man. I mean, here's this guy who won't let me write anything ever about anybody that isn't comin' off a press handout, and he's talkin' to me about a competition that doesn't exist because the publisher owns both papers, only I can't make him understand, I mean, where's the competition? I mean if he woulda said, you know, that what I did or didn't do somehow made him personally look bad for whatever reason, though I can't think of what that would be, I mighta been able to understand that, but otherwise, him just talkin' about *how we got beat?* I mean, that missed my head by about three feet.

"So I asked him again, weren't we all workin' for the same guy? I said, really, you know, without tryin' to be wise, I was really watchin' how I said it, I said, you know, the concept of gettin' beat by a competitor just seems real illogical to me if the same publisher owns both papers, you know? And he just gave me this look, like, watch it, you're real close, you know? So I said yeah, right, I knew and I booked, man. But I don't know. I really don't. Must be too subtle for me. Do you? Can you explain that?"

Balzic shrugged. "No, not logically, I mean. I think the guy was just layin' a power trip on ya, that's all, tellin' ya where you both stood on the ladder and he was up and you were down. 'Cause otherwise, it doesn't make sense."

"Well, so then, with that kinda stuff lookin' at me, I think maybe now you can understand why I don't count guns when Butterballs tells me he confiscated thirty-eight. He says thirty-eight, then thirty-eight is what I write."

Balzic nodded and splayed his hands. "Okay, Mister Butler. You've, uh, you've given me what I really didn't wanna hear, I guess. Okay. Sometimes what you don't wanna hear is exactly what you need to hear. Thanks. See ya around."

Eight days after talking to Will Butler, Balzic was sitting in Muscotti's trying to read one of the books Marie had sent him, *Stress, Diet, and Your Heart* by Dean Ornish, M.D., while listening to Iron City Steve railing about the permanence of impermanence to a clock shaped like a football above the cash register. "Fast as you think the second hand's on the second, it's on the next one. Around and around and around . . . impermanence . . . permanently. Every day . . . 'at's all you got left."

"Wish t'fuck you'da left twenty minutes ago," Vinnie said. "Twenty minutes? Shit, listen to me — twenty years, how 'bout that?"

"See," Steve said, shuffling back three steps, then lurching forward one. "Even you. I go home, you're not there. I come back, here ya are. You're worse than a second hand . . . impermanence is a trap. Permanently . . . you're trapped in impermance —"

"Aw shut up, now you can't even say it for crissake," Vinnie said. "Im-per-ma-nence, not im-per-mance."

"I'm impaired," Steve said, weaving slowly. "That's why I can't say impermance. I'm impaired. Impairmence is impermance when you can't say impermance. It's how you know you're impered. Paired. Huh?"

"Aw sit the fuck down, go to sleep, don't bother me, fuckin' impairmence, impermance — now you got me doin' it. You hear that, Mario? Huh? Everybody's worried about bartenders gettin' cancer from secondhand smoke, you hear 'bout that? California, they're gettin' ready to pass a law out there about no smokin' in bars, all the bartenders and waiters, they're worried they're gonna get cancer from secondhand smoke. When's somebody gonna get worried about secondhand bullshit, huh? All the secondhand bullshit I gotta put up with in here, you think that don't affect me? Ten times worse on my brain than smoke on my lungs, I guarantee ya. Every day of my life in here I'm fightin' off tumors on my mind."

Balzic splayed his hands indifferently, shrugged, and returned to reading a section on visualization. His concentration was so poor he was rereading what he'd read at least twice before.

"Anger is not always inappropriate,"

Ornish wrote. "Sometimes it can be quite healthy to be angry, and it is usually better to express anger than to repress it and turn it inward. Meditation and visualization can help to make you more aware, both of your feelings and of those of others. But they also help to put things in perspective. After a few weeks of regular meditation, you may find that you are not as distressed by trivial events that used to be so upsetting. And when you become angry, you can feel it clearly, express it constructively — and let it go. It is when you hold on to anger long after it has served its purpose that it may become destructive.

"When you forgive people, it does not absolve them from responsibility for what they have done. It does not excuse them — it simply frees you from being affected in a harmful way.

"Likewise, forgiving yourself does not absolve you from your responsibilities, but it will help to free you from the pain, stress, and guilt that you may impose on yourself. You will then be able to see more clearly and accomplish whatever needs to be done in a more constructive way."

Balzic closed the book and tried again to sit calmly and focus on his breathing while trying, as Ornish had instructed in another part of the book, to visualize a healthy heart with all arteries open and blood flowing unimpeded, feeding oxygen to every organ, sustaining healthy life. But this time, like every previous effort, Balzic's visualization was interrupted by the memory of him in his cellar a couple of weeks ago. He'd been filling his wine carafe when it had struck him with blindingly painful clarity that he had not been nearly as important as he'd thought and that his ego couldn't handle this sudden recognition of his unimportance. Recognizing it was one thing; admitting it had been almost more terrifying than his fear of death and dying.

Then, as abruptly as memories of that moment blocked his focus on his breathing, here came memories of Mrs. Wrobelewski's face appearing on the hood of the Chevy in the mall parking lot, of her crossing the street years ago to avoid him after her son had committed suicide by hanging himself. All his guilt, pain, and remorse buzzed by him like bullets. As hard as he tried to focus on a healthy heart with clean arteries pumping oxygen-rich blood, the images of Mrs. Wrobelewski and her son kept tripping and trapping him.

Still, he persisted. He sighed and once again tried to focus on his breathing. Then for some reason he recalled the preceding page in Ornish's book about visualizing a person "with whom you are angry."

"Imagine someone who has done something to you that you have never quite been able to forgive." That's easy, Balzic thought. Butterbaugh. "Try to see this person's face in as much detail as you can." Balzic failed. All he could see when he thought of Butterbaugh was judgments, not details: self-importance, vanity, pompous self-righteousness. But slowly details began to creep into Balzic's consciousness. Butterbaugh had a roundish face, double chin, narrow nose, blotchy complexion, brownish-grayish eyes. His left ear was longer than his right, and it stuck out farther from his head than his right. He had brownish hair, graying, starting to bald in the middle of the back of his head. . . .

"Now, imagine that you are reliving the incident. Remember as many details as you can and include these in your visualization." I wasn't there for the incident, Balzic thought. Can't relive it. Have to make it up. How that bastard, or one of his subordinates, probably Leffert, how they let somebody in, probably a couple of Artie Chianese's goons, opened the cell door for them, and then just fucking turned around and left them there with Babyak screaming — is that what happened? Fuck yeah that's what happened. What else?

"Notice how you feel — including the changes in your breathing, heart rate, muscular tension." Hey, no doubt about it, I'm gettin' mad all over again just sittin' here tryin' to visualize it. "Since the incident occurred, physical and emotional stress has often resulted whenever you have thought of this person." Bet your ass it has. Not only him, all the fuckers who won't do anything *about* him. "In this context, you have given to this person the power to produce these unpleasant and potentially harmful changes in you." No shit. "Your anger is not affecting the other person, but it may be hurting you." Not as much as I'd like to hurt him.

"You are not able to change the other person — but you don't need to." I don't wanna change him, I wanna lock the bastard up — well not me, 'cause I can't, I'm not in any position to do that, but somebody needs to do it, the afterbirth of a bastard rat. Calls himself a cop. "Simply by changing the way you view him you will change the way you react and the way you feel." I don't wanna change the way I view this piece of shit, I don't wanna change the way I react to him — oh fuck me, man, listen to me, Marie's right, this is my problem right here. This is exactly my problem. Ornish is right, Marie's right, Ruth's right, I can't change Butterbaugh, I can't change the situation, all I can do is keep pokin' people to do somethin' about him. Aw fuck him. No, not fuck him. Fuck me, I'm the one has to change the way I react to him.

"To accomplish this" — accomplish what? What am I tryin' to accomplish? Oh. Change the way I react and how I feel. Oh yeah, fat fuckin' chance — hey. Stop this fat-fuckin'-chance stuff. Why're you so fuckin' high and mighty scornful here? Anybody has to read everything two, three, four times should not be so contemptuous. Okay, okay, so where was I? Okay, here. "To accomplish this, transform the way that you are visualizing this person. Instead of seeing him as being malicious, evil, or heartless" — what the fuck, that's what he is! Okay, shut up now and try to do this now. ". . . see him as a small child" oh bullshit ". . . or as an ignorant adult, one who should know better but does not." Yeah, okay, that's fuckin' stretchin' it, but that I can buy maybe, alright, that's what he is, ignorant — willfully ignorant but ignorant, yeah — who damn sure oughta know better, but yeah, okay, ignorant, I can go with that. "If you prefer, choose another image — whatever works to transform your feelings of anger or hatred" — how about him bein' strapped on a gurney for a little lethal drip juice, huh? How's that for a different image? Aw shit, lost my place again, Christ, man, focus, c'mon! Oh. Here. "Isn't it sad that he's that way, but I don't have to let it affect me." Fuck, you kiddin' me? That's what everybody says, don't let it affect you, yeah, right, this fucker keeps on doin' what he's doin', who's stoppin' him? "I can forgive him for what he did" — I don't wanna forgive him, let God forgive him, I ain't God — "it doesn't matter anymore" — no, not to anybody else apparently, sure as fuck doesn't. "It's all in the past — it is only in the present because I'm keeping it here." All in the past for Charley Babyak, right, fuckin'-A, he's history. Where else am I supposed to keep it if not in the present? Sure as shit, nobody else is keepin' it in the present. "Once I forgive him, then I'm freer." No, I ain't — what?! I'm freer? 'Cause I forgive that rat bastard?

"Continue this process for a few minutes (or as long as you feel comfortable)." I don't feel comfortable at all. "If at any time you feel too uncomfortable, simply redirect your awareness to observing your breathing." Okay, breathing, right, alright, that's what I'm doin' now, redirectin' my awareness to observin' my breathin' 'cause I'm too fuckin' uncomfortable thinkin' about forgivin' those bastards.

C'mon, man, get back to this. Focus! Concentrate! Marie's gonna ask you about this, what're you gonna tell her, huh? That you're arguin' with every fuckin' sentence? Can't get through one fuckin' paragraph without pitchin' a fit? Yeah right, that's exactly what I'm doin', how do I tell her, huh? Okay, okay, where was I, c'mon, Christ, Balzic, what're you doin', man, huh? Okay, here we go. "After you feel comfortable," okay forget that, okay, "keeping your eyes closed" — how the fuck can I read with my eyes closed? Aw stop arguin' with the guy and just read it, okay? Why do you have to be such an asshole? Jesus. Okay. "Keeping your eyes closed, bring to mind an image of yourself. In particular, imagine an episode in your life that you regret" — yeah, right, only got a couple hundred of those — "something that you did or did not do, for which you never have quite forgiven yourself. (You

531

don't have to tell anyone what it is, of course, just visualize it.)" Well that's easy. Missus Wrobelewski's kid.

"As before, imagine that you are reliving that episode." No, thanks, I don't wanna relive that episode, thank you very much, Doc, I'll just pass on that. I've seen that kid's purple face enough in my dreams. "Remember as many details as you can, and include these in your visualization." No fuckin' way I'm doin' that again, uh-uh.

"Again, notice how you feel" — like two poundsa shit in a one-pound bag — "the changes in your breathing, heart rate, muscular tension, and so on." Okay, right, yeah, I'm gettin' the message, everything's up that shouldn't be up, heart rate, breathing, tension, fuckin' right.

"Now, transform the way in which you are visualizing yourself. Feel the same compassion for yourself that you extended to the person in the previous visualization." Yeah, right, me on a gurney in line behind Butterbaugh, strapped in, gettin' ready for the bye-bye buzz. "In your mind, hear yourself saying, 'I made a mistake and learned from it.' " I wish. " 'I was ignorant — perhaps I should have known better.' " I *was* ignorant. But I should've known better. " 'The past has passed — I have suffered enough. I forgive myself what happened.' If you are sincere you probably will notice that you feel more relaxed." If I'm sincere? Ha! Yeah. Once I learn how to fake that, yeah, all the rest is gravy, I'll be able to tell myself anything . . . aw fuck, what am I doin' here? Look at me, I'm sittin' in Muscotti's, reading a book, talkin' to myself. Least I ain't talkin' out loud. Forgive myself? How? The way I forgive Butterbaugh? No way I forgive that prick, I forgive him I may as well lay down and die myself — oh listen to yourself, man, Christ, you're readin' a book your daughter gives you to get you out from under stress. The man writin' the book says stress is as hard on your arteries as eatin' animal fat, and you're sittin' here tellin' the inside of your skull you're not gonna forgive anybody, which means, asshole, how you ever s'pposed to forgive yourself for Missus Wrobelewski's kid? Wait wait — is this 'cause he hung himself, huh? And Charley Babyak got hung? You tryin' to glue these two together? No wait, no don't confuse the issue here, you were seein' Missus Wrobelewski's head on the hood before they even busted Charley Babyak, before he even came to you with that story about his uncle, which was long before he got hung, so don't be confusin' things here.

C'mon, man focus, concentrate! Aw look there, you're right back to where you were five minutes ago. "Anger is not always inappropriate . . . da-da, da-da, da-da. . . . It is when you hold on to anger long after it has served its purpose that it may become destructive.

"When you forgive people, it does not absolve them. . . . It does not excuse them — it simply frees *you* from being affected in a harmful way.

"Likewise, forgiving yourself does not absolve you from your responsibilities, but it will help to free you from the pain, stress, and guilt that you may impose on yourself."

How many times am I gonna have to read this before any of it starts to stick, huh?

He read it all again, starting with the part about bringing "to mind the image of a person with whom you are angry." He tried to make himself understand how he and Butterbaugh were both forgivable not because what either had done was forgivable but because not forgiving either Butterbaugh or himself was hurting only himself. In its own goofy way that made sense. Forgive the person, but not the act? Whether it was an act of commission like Butterbaugh's with Babyak or omission like mine with Missus Wrobelewski's kid? No, wait, there's something wrong with that. It's doing the right thing for the wrong reason. It's forgiving somebody not for the sake of forgiveness but to save your own ass. Or soul. Or whatever.

Well what the fuck's wrong with that? Don't know. Can't say. Is it something I heard from a priest? If it's done for the wrong reason, it's wrong? But maybe what this Ornish is sayin', maybe you have to stop thinkin' everything has to be done with the purest motives. Maybe he's sayin' it's one of those things where if you do it often enough, if you really work at it, practice it, maybe sooner or later it doesn't matter why you're doing it, the results are what counts. If you forgive somebody, anybody, even yourself, you help your arteries by the act of forgiving. Is that what he's gettin' at? So okay, so say he's right, this Ornish. So what hurts you is draggin' the old emotions around, the anger, the guilt, the regret, the pain — that's the stress, haulin' all that crap around. Fuck whether you're fakin' the forgiveness, you gotta start somewhere. Somehow, you have to find it in yourself to forgive yourself. "Forgive us our trespasses as we forgive those who trespass against us." No, wait, that's askin' God to do it. I'm not gonna dump this off on God, uh-uh, this I gotta do myself. Yeah. Forgive me for trepassin' against Missus Wrobelewski's kid as I forgive those who trespassed against Charley Babyak — at the same time I bug the shit outta Sporcik and DeSantis and Howard Failan to bust those bastards. I can forgive 'em all — long as somebody arrests 'em, locks 'em up, and sticks a fuckin' needle in their veins, yeah, I can forgive 'em that way, shit, that ain't no problem. . . .

"Hey, Balzic, just the man I'm lookin' for." It was Detective George Sporcik, and he was beaming, flushed with an edgy kind of excitement, an aggressive glow of self-satisfaction. "I'm gonna let you buy me a drink, Balzic. Gonna let you help me celebrate."

"Oh yeah? And why would I wanna do that?"

"Just cracked that son of a bitch. Eric John Anderburg."

"And for that I'm s'pposed to congratulate you?"

"Absolutely."

536

Balzic snorted. "How long'd it take you — eight days? Christ, you oughta be able to crack the devil himself in eight fuckin' days."

"Yeah? Well the devil in this instance had a girlfriend, you know? Who was fulla such guilt she just couldn't bring herself to stop denyin' it. She's who took eight days, not him. Once we got her to tumble, hey, Anderburg, he went in about five minutes. So, uh, listen, you ain't gonna rain on my parade, Balzic, no matter how hard you try. Fact, I'll tell you what, you don't have to buy me one, I'll buy you one, how's that? What're you drinkin', what is that, coffee?"

"I'm ready for wine," Balzic said, closing his book, slipping it into the pocket of his parka, and following Sporcik to the bar.

"Hey, Vinnie? Yo, Vinnie?" Sporcik called out. "Double VO, water back for me, and give Balzic here whatever. I'm not gonna do this too often, Balzic, so, uh, don't hold back."

"Okay, I won't. I want you to get your ass over to Knox and start doin' what you're supposed to do, what we pay you to do, you know?"

"Told ya, man, that ain't gonna happen. Not in this life." Sporcik looked directly and intently into Balzic's eyes. For a man

537

who was claiming to have just had a major success, Sporcik was looking very hostile. "Just tell the man what you want to drink, okay? You wanna talk other stuff, I'll talk, but don't keep the man waitin', we all know how super valuable Vinnie's time is, right, Vinnie?"

"Fuck you all grinnin' about?" Vinnie said, pouring the VO.

"Just cracked a perv, that's what I'm all grinnin' about. Fact, I'm so pumped, Vincent, I'll even buy you one."

"You got it," Vinnie said, hurrying away to the beer cooler to get himself a long-neck bottle of Miller. He set that down, then, without asking, he put a wineglass in front of Balzic and filled it with white wine from a jug. "I ain't even gonna ask you what you want no more."

"Well fuck me very much."

"Just hoist it and drink it, huh?" Sporcik said.

"What're we drinkin' to now?" Vinnie said.

"Crackin' that short eyes. Full confession."

"You mean that little girl? What was her name?"

"Emmylou Drosser," Sporcik said, tossing back his double. "Single this time.

C'mon, Balzic, lemme hear it, congratulations, Detective Sporcik, the way in was through the mother, excellent police work. C'mon, man, say it, I wanna hear you say it." Sporcik turned to face Balzic squarely.

"Okay," Balzic said, turning to face Sporcik. "Okay. Congratulations. For a no-brainer. Ya got the boyfriend goin' through the mother. Took you long enough, but what the fuck's time matter, huh? When evidence is not bein' collected, when interviews are not bein' done in another case, huh? Involving fucking police, huh? Yeah. I congratulate you. Drink up. I'll buy you one. Pour him another."

"What, younz two gonna do somethin' here?" Vinnie said, reaching slowly for the bottle of Scagram VO. "Hey, younz gonna do somethin', take it outside now, don't start no shit in here —"

"There ain't nothin' gonna happen here," Sporcik said. "I'm just pissed I gotta beg for congratulations, that's all." He glared at Balzic and chewed his teeth, his jaw muscles rippling. "You're gonna love this, Balzic. Remember that belt you kept buggin' me about, huh? It's missin'. Whattaya think of that?"

"Excuse me?" Vinnie said. "What's missin'?"

"He knows what I'm talkin' about," Sporcik said, turning back to the bar and putting both hands on it. Then he picked up the single shot, tossed it down, and glared at Balzic again. "What, ain't got nothin' to say, huh?"

"Where'd you hear that?"

"Right after I finished doin' the paper on Anderburg, I thought, you know, I might actually make an attempt at, uh, somethin', you know? An actual investigation maybe, huh?"

"I don't know what younz fuckin' guys're talkin about," Vinnie said digustedly.

"Don't worry about it," Sporcik said. "Just pour me the one Balzic's payin' for, okay? He knows what I'm talkin' about. Besides, I still got a lotta celebratin' to do."

"So what're you sayin', Troop A lab told you it was gone?"

"No, uh-uh, never made it to Troop A lab. Never got logged in, no belt, not size 34, not size 42 —"

"Bullshit!"

"No bullshit. No belt. Gone. Poof. I'm tellin' ya —"

"And I'm tellin' you, bullshit, Trooper Claude Milliron signed it outta the coroner's office —"

"You're not listenin', that's not what I'm

sayin', I'm sayin' it wasn't logged into Troop A lab —"

"Bullshit! I talked to a tech up there, he told me there were no prints on it —"

"So you've said. A coupla times. And I keep askin' you, which tech, huh? Gimme a name."

"Uh, uh, ah fuck, I can't remember his name, lemme think —"

"Which is what you say every time we do this little cha-cha-cha. You talked to a tech, he told you there were no prints on the belt, you called me twice, you came into the office at least twice, every fuckin' time you talked to me about this sooner or later you got around to this belt, and every fuckin' time you told me, you never mentioned the name of the tech who told you there were no prints on it —"

"No, I'm havin', uh, havin' some problems that way —"

"And of course even though you know you're havin' problems like this, you didn't bother to write his name down anywhere, did ya? Huh?"

"Yes. No. I don't know." Balzic was very flustered. He could feel his face flushing. "My notebook's, uh, all my notes, tapes, they're, uh, they're all in Mo's office. Valcanas's —"

"But you're the one bitchin' me out for bein' lazy, right?"

"Well it's your case, it ain't mine, I got no weight here —"

"So every time you called me and every time you came into the office and told me what you were tellin' me about this belt, you never had a name to go with that information, did ya? Yes or no?"

"Did you ask me for a name?"

"Oh that's fuckin' gorgeous. You can't remember the name but you're gonna stand here right in my face and ask *me* if I asked *you* for a name, right? You're handin' out toys like you're Santy Claus but you can't remember where the fuckin' North Pole is, oh man, you're beautiful. What the fuck —"

"Well you were supposed to check, you weren't supposed to take my word for it, what the fuck yourself?!"

"Well it doesn't matter anyway, does it, huh? Who you talked to or whether you can remember anybody's name, 'cause I don't care who you talked to, or who you think you talked to —"

"I didn't *think* I talked to somebody, I talked to somebody!"

"— it ain't there now, this fuckin' size 42 belt with no prints on it, you hear me? It ain't there, it was never logged in, 'cause I just talked to the OIC and he told me it's not on the custody sheet, period, end of story, you hear what I'm sayin'?"

"Well bullshit! Aw this is unbelievable — hey, somebody's name's on that fuckin' custody sheet, Milliron signed for it when it left Grimes's office and somebody else's name is on it when it got logged into the lab and anybody says otherwise, his mother's a whore with AIDS, I ain't buyin' that bullshit in a million years —"

"You better buy it, man, 'cause there's no belt, you listenin' to me? Huh?"

"Well what're you doin' standin' here, huh? You know this? What the fuck you tellin' me for? Get your ass movin'! Start with Grimes. He told me right after the post, the belt was on its way to the lab, and there was only one state cop there, and that was Milliron, and nobody's gonna tell me Milliron lost that belt! That I will not believe!"

"Yo, Vinnie, one more here," Sporcik said, holding up his empty shot glass at Vinnie, who was talking to other customers.

"Hey, you don't need another shot, you needa go to work, do your fuckin' job!"

"Hey, you're not my boss, okay? You're

not anybody's boss."

Balzic squinted at Sporcik. "Why'd you come in here? You come in here and tell me this and you're not gonna do anything about it? What, you just bustin' my balls, is that it?"

"I came in here so you could congratulate me for crackin' that short eyes, that's why. I told ya before, cases like this, I get to hold my head up. I want you to look at me holdin' my head up, okay? This is me, right here, holdin' my head up, see? Look at me, man, don't turn away from me, look at me!"

"You're fulla shit, Sporcik, you're in here lookin' to bust my balls, that's all you're doin' —"

"No that ain't what I'm doin'. You're not listenin' to me, Balzic. And you're not thinkin'. You were in Grimes's office before he did the post on Babyak. I know you were there 'cause I was there, I saw ya. Just like I know that belt was there. I was standin' not two steps away from Grimes when he put it in an evidence bag. 'Cause it came in with Babyak. It was layin' right beside him. I saw it."

"Then what the fuck're you doin'? Fuck's goin' on here?"

"Told ya, I'm celebratin'."

"Aw celebratin' my ass, what is this?"

"Celebratin' that I was right about how it was gonna go, remember? You remember that, huh? Remember me tellin' you how this was gonna go over there in Knox? Or can't you remember that either?"

"Hey. Watch your mouth. You got somethin' to say, say it."

"I already did. I told you how this was gonna go. But I was guessin' then. It was good guessin', but it was still guessin'. But now? Hey. Now this belt's gone, it ain't a guess anymore, man. When was the last time you talked to your insurance guy? Why don't you do that, huh? Go 'head, right now, call him up, ask him if that creep owns the gunshop filed a new claim. C'mon, I wanna see if I'm right — I mean I know I am, but I'm still just guessin', although the guessin's gettin' easier all the time, especially now the belt's gone. Get it? Huh? Go 'head, call him — what? You need a quarter? I got a quarter. Here."

"I have my own quarters, I don't need your quarter. You want me to call him, I'll call him. Why not? Fuck's with you, man, I don't get you, you're comin' at me — I don't know what you're tellin' me here."

"Just call him, huh? I'm anxious to hear how right I am, go 'head, call him."

Balzic went to the pay phone near the rear exit and called Al Bertelli's office. When Bertelli picked up, Balzic said, "This is Balzic. Did that Bemiss? You know? Guy owns Freedom Firearms? He, uh, he file a new claim? Or an amended one?"

"Huh? Oh. Yes he did. Hi ya doin', Mario? Feelin' better?"

"I'm fine, yeah. Listen. Uh, what's he sayin' now, this Bemiss?"

"Is this important, Mario? I didn't think you were still on this. Is this something you have to clear up for Mo or what?"

"No no, it's just, uh, I'm curious, that's all. There's a cop tellin' me some things, he said Bemiss filed an amended claim. You say he did, okay, he did. Which way'd it go, up, down, what?"

"Oh he cut the number of guns way down. Instead of, uh, whatever it was, thirty-eight? Huh? Does that sound right? Thirty-eight? Yeah, that's right. Now he's sayin', uh, two."

"Two?! Fuck. Is he also sayin' why he's sayin' that?"

"Huh? Oh yeah. Said he got some computer geek, some kid, to, uh, recover his, uh, whattaya call that, data, yeah. From off his hard drive? He said he knew the last number was an eight, he just forgot the first number was a one instead of a three."

"Wait a minute, I'm not followin' this. The last number was an eight, what the hell's that mean?"

"Uh, the original claim he said he lost thirty-eight pistols of one kind, and two different ones —"

"Yeah, yeah, okay."

"So it turned out, or he says it turned out, he only lost eighteen, that's what I mean by the last number was eight. Eighteen instead of thirty-eight —"

"Wait, he doesn't have any paper from his distributor?"

"Says the distributor's out of business. Bankrupt. No records."

"You're shittin' me. The distributor's name's not in his records? Get outta here, I don't believe this."

"I'm just tellin' you what the man said."

"So, uh, you're not gonna check?"

"Check what? What for?"

"The distributor?"

"Why should I check? Maybe I didn't explain this right. No, Bemiss, he's sayin', see, he says now he only lost eighteen Berettas and all of those were recovered by the police over there in Knox. So all he's claimin' now is for the furniture, the display cases and so forth — and those other two pistols, that's all. He sent printouts along with the amended claim that show he only received eighteen Berettas. So the only guns that're still missin' are those two, uh, oh what's the word?"

"Magnums?"

"Yeah, those. So what am I gonna do? I don't have any problem with the claim now. Have to pay him."

"So he's sayin' the Knox PD recovered all the Berettas he said he lost? Son of a bitch."

"Huh?"

"Nothin', nothin'. Uh, thanks, Al. Sorry to bother ya."

They exchanged some small talk, then Balzic hung up and went back to the bar where Sporcik was grinning again. Like before, there was nothing happy about his grin.

"So? Sound like anything you heard before? From me maybe?"

"Yeah, okay, so you're psychic —"

"Oh no, not psychic, uh-uh, not me. And I'm not done either," Sporcik said, looking edgier, more aggressively self-confident than before. "Remember that '73 Mustang, huh? The one ol' Councilman Tanyar bought for his girlfriend Gina Hite? 'Member her? Regina Hitalsky? You put her name in Louie's notebook, remember that? Said we should interview her, maybe get to that asshole Tanyar through her, huh? You rememberin' any of this, Balzic, or is this more stuff that's gone bye-bye from your brain?"

"Yeah fuck you. What about her?"

"Not her, Balzic, it. I predict you're really gonna love this."

"Whattaya mean it? What're you talkin' about? Christ —"

"Okay. Get this. You ready? Washington Township firemen just pulled it out of a creek off nine-eighty-one."

"What?"

"Yeah. Upside down in Coleman's Creek. That beautiful restored '73 Mustang."

"Get outta here —"

"Oh no, nooooo, I'm not gettin' outta anywhere. Only get this. Not a body in sight. No work for the coroner, just for the salvage truck. And I feel very confident, even before seein' any of the evidence, understand? Talkin' to any of the traffic cops, huh? Firemen, drivers of the aforementioned salvage trucks? I feel extremely confident that the ruling will — ta-ta! Vehicle homicide. Yeah. Further investigation will reveal that Councilman Tanyar's beautiful restored '73 Mustang was a victim of vehi-cle homicide. Get it?"

"What the fuck you talkin' about?"

"Don't get it? Huh? They killed his car, man. Murdered his beloved Mustang. Took his beautiful restored Mustang out on lonely ol' nine-eighty-one and pushed it off the road there so it would come to a real sudden stop, you know, with the rocky bottom of the creek? You know what I'm sayin'?"

"You're makin' this up."

"Ha! Listen to you, makin' it up. Funny man. I don't make anything up, Balzic. I don't need to. Reality's way fuckin' better at makin' stuff up than I'll ever be. Yeah. Ol' Gina Hite there, she thought she was the councilman's girlfriend. But Fat Artie, he knew who the councilman's real girl-friend was. Bet your ass. It just happened to go over on a stretch of nine-eighty-one where the guardrails had been down from a previous accident, whattaya think of that little coincidence, huh? C'mon, Balzic, your eyes are all buggin' out, man, what's goin' on back there, huh? Any good thoughts? Huh? For me and my partner maybe? Gimme somethin' good to tell my partner Lou. Like maybe there's somebody else you think we should interview, huh?"

"When'd this happen?"

"Nobody knows when exactly, imagine that. No witnesses. Not yet. I'm thinkin' probably never. But some stiff out deliverin' papers, you know? Deliverin' the *Knox Weekly Review* back there, he just happened to glance down, saw that car upside down in the creek, called nine-one-one, and what do you think the top story on the front page of that paper was he was deliverin', huh? C'mon, Balzic, take a guess."

Balzic sighed. "Why don't you just tell me, huh?"

"Hey. Why guess? Here. Read it for yourself." Sporcik pulled a newspaper folded three ways out of his topcoat pocket and spread it on the bar in front of Balzic. "Take a look, huh? Big picture of Police Chief Earl Butterbaugh and Lieutenant John Leffert of the Knox PD, holdin' up one of their brand-new 9-mm Berettas, huh? For City Councilman Herbert Tanyar? Chairman of the safety committee there, huh? How ya like that, Balzic? You like that? I can get ya your own copy of that paper, you want it for your scrapbook, you know? What, you look like you don't want it? No?"

Balzic studied the photo for a long

moment. Butterbaugh was on the left, Leffert on the right, both smiling at the Beretta cradled lovingly by Butterbaugh in both hands, supposedly for Councilman Tanyar's inspection. Tanyar was not only not smiling, he looked utterly stupid. His mouth was open, his eyes half closed.

"You lookin' at Tanyar, huh? See there, Balzic? That's how you tell the world what's goin' on."

"What're you talkin' about?"

"You know what I'm talkin' about. Look at Tanyar there, look at his face. How many pictures you think that photographer took there, huh? Guarantee you he took more than that one. They always catch somebody lookin' stupid like that when they got a group. That's why they always take at least two, make sure everybody's eyes're open. But who decided to print that one, huh? That's a picture designed to make a joke of somebody. That was printed to make an asshole outta him. So every time he thought of it, he'd remember what an asshole he looked like. Don't say you don't know what I'm talkin' about, c'mon."

"Sporcik, where you comin' from on this? What'd I ever do to you you gotta bust my balls like this, huh?"

"If I'm bustin' anybody's balls, man, they ain't yours."

"Aw what the fuck —"

"Hey, didn't I tell you, huh? Didn't I say how it was gonna go? That's who we are, man. We put the pervs away, the Anderburgs, yeah, we hold our heads up, but when there's real shit goin' down, belts come up missin', nobody signs anything, what they're supposed to sign, huh? Look at Tanyar's face there, man. That's a man in over his head, that's a man just heard about his beloved Mustang, and he knows he's in over his head. I guarantee he's doin' all the paperwork for 'em right now, puttin' in the right dates, the right amounts that didn't have to be cleared on bids, guaranteed he's makin' all the numbers come out right. I know that without even lookin'. Me and Louie could go over those papers for a month, we wouldn't find a comma in the wrong place. But I bet you a thousand bucks against a dime he didn't know how far in he really was till they told him what was gonna happen to his car. And how it was gonna happen. And as slimy as he is, I guarantee you that asshole never felt sorrier for anything in his life than his precious little Mustang."

"Hey, how you know all this? This ain't

predictions, this ain't guessin', you ain't guessin' here, you know somethin', you fucker —"

"Bet your ass I know somethin'. Told ya. I'm celebratin'. I been workin', man, that's where I'm comin' from, Balzic, I been workin'. I'm from Knox, remember? That's where I grew up. That's my town they're fuckin' with. And don't tell me you don't know what I'm talkin' about. I watched you do the whole thing with the fire chief here, remember? And his buncha elves got their money stashed with three different brokers, huh? All those bingo games and raffles and street fairs, and they don't even pay to maintain their own buildings, huh? City pays for that, right? The taxpayers. The schmucks. Us. Us, Balzic. You and me. We're the schmucks. I watched you and that councilwoman, man, I watched you two suck wind behind that. Jesus. Just like I'm suckin' wind now.

"Yo, Vinnie, another one." When Vinnie came back down the bar and swept up the bottle of VO to refill Sporcik's glass, Sporcik said, "I think it's appropriate you should be pourin' 'em for me, Vincent, my man, seein' how your boss used to be the goombah, huh? Where is ol' Muscotti these days, huh? Haven't seen him around in a while. Think he could tell us how things're gonna go over there in Knox, huh, Balzic? Bet he could tell us plenty he wanted to."

"Hey, Sporcik," Balzic said, "you're forgettin' somethin' real big. Grimes hasn't ruled on it yet. But he's gonna rule homicide on Babyak, he knows that wasn't suicide, and they're not gonna be able to make that go away, I don't give a fuck who they are. And he'll testify he bagged the belt. And signed it out, and nobody's gonna turn Grimes, that'll never happen, Grimes is the straightest arrow ever was."

"Hey, Grimes can rule homicide till he's purple, that's not gonna change anything, 'cause they're gonna say they didn't lose the belt. They're gonna say that belt got disappeared after Grimes signed it into evidence, and at least five people saw that belt in his lab, man — him, me, my partner, Butterbaugh, and Leffert, never mind the EMTs that brought Babyak in, never mind you. But it won't matter, 'cause they'll stonewall us, man. Those motherfuckers over there? All they have to do is keep pointin' at Grimes and Troop A, sayin' hey, we didn't lose the belt, you wanna know who lost the belt? Ask them, don't ask us. One of them lost it, we didn't lose it. And what're we gonna do then, Balzic, huh? Nothin', that's what. Who do you think's gonna talk over there now that the Mustang's dead, huh? Hey, Balzic, you know as well as I do why that car's crashed out. It's junk to make sure Tanyar doesn't say anything except what he's told to say. Which leaves nobody else. And try to remember you heard it from me.

"Hey, Vincent — where the fuck'd he get to now? He was just here. Ho, Vinnie. Fuck is he? Is this a fuckin' saloon? Or a self-serve gas station? Next thing you know, Balzic, listen to this, I'm tellin' ya. Some rich prick's gonna try to cut his overhead, turn these places into self-serve, just like gas stations. And don't think they ain't tryin'. Once they figure out how to computerize these places, huh? Balzic? Once they figure out how to get computers to do it, measure the booze, count the bottles, hey, believe me, they'll do it. People'll be payin' with credit cards just like they do in gas stations. Only a matter of time. 'Cause the rich pricks, hey, they got people that never sleep, always tryin' to cut the overhead, and the simplest way to cut the overhead is to cut the people —"

"You still got one in front of you," Balzic said.

"Huh?" Sporcik looked down at the shot glass filled to the white line. "Well lookee there. No shit. The celebration has officially begun. Startin' to forget shit already. Just like you, Balzic. Just like you. You're forgettin' Rocksburg, I'm forgettin' Knox. We're both forgettin' where we come from. Gets easier every day, don't it?"

"I don't know what you're talkin' about."

"Fuck you don't, man. You can try to bullshit me all you want, you can't bullshit yourself. Not and drink as much as you do."

"You don't know how much I drink, you don't know nothin' about nothin'. You're drunk."

"That's the idea. Yes sir. I bust the Anderburgs, and the Butterbaughs, the Chianeses, the fuckers out on Country Club Road, they laugh at us. We're a fuckin' joke."

"Speak for yourself."

"Who you think I'm speakin' for? Wouldn't presume to speak for you. Respect ya too much. But when I wake up in the middle of the night and I'm sweatin' and I go try to read in my little office at home, you know? I look up on the wall and read my commendations, huh? For crackin' the short eyes and the nigger drug dealers, huh? How come that don't make me stop sweatin', huh? Fuckin'-A I'm speakin' for myself. Think I'm speakin' for you? The great Mario Balzic? Ha. Yeah. This is the great George Sporcik, speakin' only for himself. Yeah. Face it, Balzic. Only ones we put away are the ones have to take a number and get in line in the public defender's office, that's all. Yeah. The great George Sporcik. Riiiiiight . . ."

Winter ended finally. Spring came. Then summer. Then summer started to wind down.

Ruth took care of the yard, cut the grass, grew rosemary, basil, tarragon, chives, and Sweet One Hundred cherry tomatoes in pots on the deck, and Nova plum and Burpee's Big Early tomatoes in the yard. Balzic talked her into growing more globe and lemon basil than sweet or purple because globe was easier to harvest and lemon had become his favorite flavor among the basils. Even when he made basic pesto from sweet basil, he had taken to adding the juice of half a lemon to the blender and subtracting a like amount of olive oil.

With Ruth's help, her insistence really, he changed his diet to restrict animal protein to no more than three meals a week, mostly fish. They ate one big salad every day, experimenting with various fruits, greens, and nuts, and made their own dressing, finding that they could control the amount of oil much better that way than by buying so-called low-fat bottled dressings. Ruth also expanded her menu of stir-fries, after she learned from watching a Chinese cook on PBS that she didn't have to use nearly as much oil as American recipes called for. All she had to do was get a well-made Teflon-coated wok.

It seemed to him that every time he turned around, she was thrusting a piece of fruit at him, saying, "Eat this, it's good for your lower tract."

"My poop factory, what's-his-face used to say."

"Bill. Spiegel. Yeah. I still miss old Bill. Remember what he said the day we asked him if he wanted to go see the air show?"

"Yeah. Piss on the Blue Angels."

They walked four, sometimes five days a week, at the high school track or around town in good weather, in the malls in bad.

It took Balzic months to decondition himself from feeling angina. He had to remind himself every time he walked for the first couple of months that the artery which had been closed was now open and that the sensation he felt in his neck was nothing more than a conditioned memory of what he had originally felt before the Rotoblator procedure. Sometimes he thought the most difficult thing he'd ever tried to do was to wrestle intellectually, physically, and emotionally to separate angina, a fear of angina, and a conditioned memory of angina, which he named the three demons of doubt. Twice, he made Ruth drive him to the emergency room because he couldn't make the distinction among them, and then, of course, he felt like a fool when no evidence of new coronary problems could be found.

He made the most progress in distinguishing among the three demons by simply giving his brain stern pep talks, after he'd read another book sent to him by Marie, this one titled *Healing Back Pain* by a doctor named John Sarno. When Balzic argued with Marie that his back wasn't the problem, she argued back that Sarno was saying most physical pain was a result of the brain telling the body it didn't want to deal with an emotional problem, so the brain would send pain messages to some part of the body because Americans believed in physical pain and especially believed in dealing with it through chemicals or surgery. Marie said Sarno said that, after genuine physical problems had been ruled out, the person feeling the pain simply had to tell the brain, in so many words, to knock it off, there was an emotional problem to be dealt with and these physical symptoms were just a smoke screen.

Balzic read the book just to get Marie to stop calling and asking if he had. But once he had read it, he had no trouble accepting the book's premise because he knew he had an emotional problem he couldn't resolve. He was scared of dying because, as much as he tried to shake the idea, he thought judgment and retribution were waiting for him in the next life for all his failures in this one. What made the problem absurd was that he didn't believe intellectually there was a next life while emotionally, of course, he was convinced of it.

So he walked in emotional circles, so to speak, always coming back to where he started. But whenever he felt some physical symptom, usually one of the three demons of doubt but not always, he lectured himself that he had a problem unresolvable because of the limits of his intellect, but that was no reason to keep feeling pain in places where logically there should be none, no reason to continue to beat himself up. Sometimes the lecture worked. Some days he walked without any pain anywhere, without so much as a hiss, hoot, or howl from one of the three demons. Despite that, he still couldn't keep up with Ruth, though he wasn't falling nearly as far behind as when they'd first started walking for exercise after his trip to the cath lab.

It also helped that he'd learned from another of the books Marie sent him that walking itself could be a meditation; it turned out to be far easier for him to focus on walking than on breathing while sitting or lying on the floor.

He'd also managed to overcome his struggle to relax while doing yoga postures. Ruth helped him with that, showing him how she inhaled when she arched her back and exhaled when she humped her back, which were corroborated in almost identical words in Ornish's book. Ruth convinced him that if he could coordinate his breathing with those two body movements, it didn't matter what position he was trying to get into, eventually he would relax into it. And he did, though it took him months to reach the point where he felt that his body actually understood what his mind had been hearing.

Between the walking and the yoga, Balzic was gradually learning how to come back to the here and now every time his mind skittered away, which it still did, but less and less and for shorter periods. He was also learning how to talk himself down from his anger, how to label the emotion as soon as he felt it rising, how to characterize situations that he knew would provoke him if he let them, that would escalate his anger into rage, thereby raising those numbers cardiologists liked to count: pulse, blood pressure, cholesterol. He didn't understand the science Ornish put in the appendix of *Stress, Diet, and Your Heart,* but overall the premise that anger was as bad as a fatty diet made sense to Balzic, so he believed it.

Besides, he needed every meditative crutch he could carry, because he'd never felt so frustrated in his life. For three weeks after Charley Babyak's death no one did anything about his body, never mind his murder.

During those weeks, Balzic learned that both Babyak's parents were dead; he had no siblings; his first wife had died in a fire she probably started herself by falling asleep while smoking; his second wife insisted that she'd never legally been married to him; and he'd had no children by either woman. Worse, his only living relative was Arturo Chianese, who found it hilarious, for one brief moment at least, that anybody, never mind a former chief of police, "cared what happened to that little hunky's body. Put it out on the curb, why don'tcha?"

Balzic left Chianese's deli only after the cousins Serra appeared out of the back room when Fat Artie said he was "tired of talking about that fuckin' scum. He was okay when he was doin' what I told him. But then he thought he should be able to do somethin' for himself. I didn't need that shit. Besides, Balzic, you ain't nobody no more. Get t'fuck outta here before I tell Angie to sit on ya."

Balzic shrugged, left, and went straight to Coroner Grimes's office and asked him whether anyone had expressed interest in Babyak's body. Grimes shook his head no and said if Balzic had a plan he'd certainly be willing to hear it. Something had to be done; the body couldn't be kept in the lab indefinitely.

Balzic said he'd be in touch. He went home and, after many phone calls, arranged a funeral for the next day in St. Malachy's Cemetery in Westfield Township.

Retired Rocksburg Police Sergeants Bill Rascoli, Joe Royanowicz, and Vic Stramsky bought lumber and built a box; funeral director Sal Bruno drove the hearse; Rascoli, Stramsky, Royanowicz, and three painters hanging out between jobs in Muscotti's carried the box to the plot; Father Marrazzo from St. Malachy's said the words. Afterwards, in Muscotti's, Balzic paid for the drinks and hot sausage sandwiches with peppers and onions on hard rolls, which Vinnie served up while bitching that he couldn't believe anybody had wasted even five minutes worrying about burying Babyak, never mind actually doing it. The ex-cops, meanwhile, ate, drank, and swapped Babyak stories.

Rascoli told about the time he responded "to this call about a B and E on Washington Street in the Flats, so I'm walkin' around the house in the back, I hear somethin', I bend down, shine my light under the back porch steps, there he is. I said, what the hell you doin', Charley? He says, I'm lookin' for Pete. I says Pete? He says yeah, my pet python. I says in your fuckin' dreams, come outta there. Bastard never blinked. He said, you ever seen that movie *Harvey*? Jimmy Stewart has this big rabbit nobody can see it but him. I'm the only one can see Pete but he's here, I'm tellin' ya, I can smell him. I was laughin' so hard I snapped the cuffs on my thumb, gave myself this huge blood blister. 'I can smell him,' Christ."

Stramsky told about the time while he was still driving a patrol car he responded to a complaint from people that lived below Babyak in an apartment building on the east end of town with his first wife. "She was a big woman," Stramsky said.

"All his girlfriends were," Balzic said.

"Yeah, well this one was like six-one maybe, a hundred and eighty pounds easy, and she wasn't fat. I get there, the neighbors are bitchin' 'cause they can't sleep, he gotta get up, go to work, couple times a week upstairs they're screamin', carryin' on, raisin' hell. So I go up, knock, she comes to the door, pulls it open wide. Naked. Woman got no clothes on. But she looks at me like she got all her clothes on, you know, didn't try to cover up nothin', and she says, What? You know, real snotty. What?! I tell her about the neighbors, have a heart, you know, the guy gotta get some sleep, go to work, I hear this ca-lump, ca-lump comin' at me. I step around her, there's Babyak, he's tied to this kitchen chair, he's walkin' it across the floor like some kinda inchworm, ca-lump ca-lump. She got him tied up with clothesline, and got a red hanky gaggin' him. I go over, I untie the gag, I says what the hell's goin' on here, Babyak, the neighbors are complainin'. He says, 'Ouu, you know, we're just doin' it, that's all. She can't help herself, she gets loud.' I look down — don't ask me why I didn't notice till then — he's naked too. Not only that, got this big hard-on. I says for crissake, Babyak, can't you figure out some other way to do this, huh? How about some other time maybe, you know, give the people downstairs a break? He looks at me, shakes his head, with these big gooey eyes, he says, 'You know, Officer, Marge works days, I sorta work baker's hours myself, so gettin' together's a problem for us, you know.' Baker's hours, Jesus Christ, I just looked at him. I said just try to keep it down a little bit, have a little consideration. Baker's hours. You believe that, huh?"

567

"Hey, that was his shift alright, eight P.M. to four A.M."

Balzic got Dom Muscotti to tell about the time he saw Babyak on TV. "Somebody busted in a buncha houses in Penn Hills, and this reporter, he's interviewin' somebody, it's the eleven o'clock news. He's talkin' to one of the stiffs got robbed I guess, and there's this jerk behind him wavin' his arms, goin', you know, hi Mom? I says to myself that looks like that goof Babyak. So right then, honest to God, that exact friggin' instant, the front door opens, Babyak walks in, he sits down, we're both watchin' him on TV makin' an ass of himself like it's somebody else. When it's over, he says to me, 'You know, Dom, it's true. You *do* look fatter on TV.' I just shook my head."

Now that Babyak was in the ground, the far more frustrating problem gnawed at Balzic: no one was doing anything about Babyak's murder, despite Coroner Grimes's ruling that it had been indeed exactly that. Two days after doing Babyak's post, Grimes had reexamined the body and then told Detective Sporcik, who told Balzic, that he'd found an unmistakable bruise on the top of Babyak's left trapezius muscle. The bruise was in the shape of a left hand pushing down and squeezing as the belt was pulled up and behind Babyak's left ear, which created the characteristic V-bruise of a hanging, as opposed to a straight-line bruise of a strangulation. Grimes also found bruises on the outside of Babyak's ankles where someone had tied something, cloth, a sheet or a shirt perhaps, to keep him from kicking.

Balzic interviewed and reinterviewed Trooper Claude Milliron about who at the Troop A lab had logged in the belt he had signed out of Grimes's office. Milliron never wavered. He said that all of Babyak's clothes, including the belt, had been logged in by a tech he'd never seen before and had paid so little attention to that he wouldn't guess at a description. The only things he was sure of were that, one, the tech was a male and, two, that his failure to record the tech's name was a violation of procedure worthy of an official reprimand.

The first time Balzic interviewed Milliron he admitted that he'd been working so hard on the Drosser and Wohlmuth cases that he'd simply failed to make a note of the tech's name because he was bone tired. He knew his failure was inexcusable, but still, he hoped Balzic understood that when you're that tired you tend to make mistakes.

Balzic understood. He did. He sympathized. He told Milliron he remembered plenty of times when he'd been that tired or that stressed-out on particular cases, but he was sorry, his sympathy went only so far. Milliron's failure to identify the tech was an insurmountable gap in anybody's investigation of the chain of custody, not just Balzic's. Balzic, after all, had no business investigating any of this, and nobody knew it better than he did. He was reminded of that every time he tried to interview the techs who'd worked that shift that day. None of them would admit to Balzic that they'd logged in the evidence; none would admit telling him or anybody else at any time that no fingerprints had been found on the belt. Most of them wouldn't even talk to him except to say that they wouldn't unless they were ordered to. And nobody gave that order.

On the contrary. The fourth time Balzic tried to interview them, the lab's duty OIC appeared, one Sergeant Lloyd Cummings. His order to Balzic was brief and to the point.

"You been buggin' people here and I been lettin' you get away with it, but no more. You got ten seconds to get outta this building, mister. You're not gone, I'm gonna bust you for defiant trespass. And if I even see you in the parkin' lot again, I'm gonna bust you for harassment and for obstruction, understand? I know you used to be chief of the Rocksburg PD so I know you know what I'm talkin' about. Nobody here wants to talk to you, nobody here has to talk to you, not without a court order, so leave! Now!"

Take that, you fucking nobody going nowhere, Balzic said to himself when he was getting into his Chevy and heading for home. And he said it, and said it, and said it again, until Ruth said, "Mario, we have to talk."

After their talk, Balzic didn't say it anymore. What he did instead was write letters. Or print them. His typing was almost as bad as his script was illegible. So, while labeling his rage and focusing on his breathing and on being here and now, he laboriously printed his outrage over the handling of Charles Babyak's murder and mailed the letters to Conemaugh County District Attorney Howard Failan, Conemaugh County President Judge Milan Vrbanic, Pennsylvania Deputy Attorney General G. Warren Livingood, and U.S. Attorney J. Howard Moseby of the Western District of Pennsylvania.

For the first two months, he just wrote to Failan and Vrbanic. After that he wrote to them all once a week, and once a week he received replies ranging from the politically polite to the professionally bureaucratic, all saying essentially the same thing: nobody in any position of authority was interested in when, where, how, or why Charley Babyak had been murdered or who had murdered him.

He also wrote once a month to the Bureau of Alcohol, Tobacco and Firearms. Their first reply said their investigation had determined that only two revolvers had been stolen from Freedom Firearms Inc., all others had been accounted for, and a theft of that limited magnitude was a matter for local police. Their second said their case was closed.

The only reply that truly bothered Balzic was the one he kept getting from Warren Livingood, deputy state attorney general. A couple of years ago, Livingood had personally hired Balzic to investigate a post-conviction appeal that led to a complicated and grotesquely ugly case of police corruption in Deer Mountain Borough, Wabash County, which led to further investigations, not involving Balzic, of judicial and prosecutorial misconduct. A judge of the Court of Common Pleas of Wabash County was impeached, and the district attorney was indicted, prosecuted, pleaded out to charges of misfeasance and malfeasance, was sentenced to probation, and eventually disbarred. Livingood made headlines across the state for his work in that case, and the stories invariably noted that his name was being mentioned more and more in Republican circles as an attractive candidate for the U.S. Senate, in the event Arlen Specter should retire.

Balzic thought he could play upon his part in that case to cause Livingood to pay attention to Babyak's murder. But after an initial cordial response rejecting Balzic's personal appeal, Livingood answered Balzic's letters with form letters. And after July 4th, Balzic quit writing to him, concentrating instead on the others for whom he had no personal feelings.

Balzic's days began with a hot shower to loosen his back and neck, followed by a half hour of yoga. Then, after breakfast, he walked to the library and read all the local newspapers and, whenever they came in, the weekly newsmagazines. He also tried to keep track in the *Knox Weekly Review* of the drug wars over there. Charley Babyak's arrest apparently had been the "major interruption of a major illegal drug operation" Chief Earl Butterbaugh had declared it was at the time because, since then, Butterbaugh's drug warriors, armed with their Beretta Model 92Fs, had made only four drug arrests, all for possession of marijuana. All suspects were still awaiting trial.

As the days became weeks and the weeks months, there were times when Balzic had trouble remembering what Charley Babyak had looked like alive. And Balzic had made a point not to look at him in the pathology lab. The last thing he wanted to add to his emotional baggage was another memory of another hanging. Once Balzic even tried meditating on Charley Babyak's face, as though by sheer force of will he could conjure up a likeness of the man. It hadn't worked. All Balzic could remember was that Babyak had hair that looked like a used soap pad.

The Tuesday after Labor Day, Balzic was in Rocksburg Mall, shopping for a pair of walking shoes. He started in Sears, then went to the Foot Locker, then Athlete's

Foot, and finally landed in Famous Footwear. He was on his hands and knees trying to find his size in black Rockports when he heard somebody approaching and asking if he could be helped.

"No thanks, I'll find 'em eventually — if they're here. These bifocals, uh . . . makes it hard when you're tryin' to find somethin' near the floor —"

"Chief? That you, man?"

Balzic squatted back on his heels, shoved his glasses up his nose, and felt his tongue slipping out the corner of his mouth as he focused on the face.

"I know you?" Balzic recognized the face immediately. That wasn't the problem. There just wasn't any name bubbling up beside it.

"Well I know you if you don't know me," the young black man said, smiling broadly. "Rayford, William, you know. You talked to Chief Nowicki for me? Remember? About the job in the Rocksburg department?"

"Oh oh, yeah yeah," Balzic said, heaving himself up onto one knee. "Gimme a hand, will ya? Knees about to come unglued here."

"Oh sure, here, grab on." Rayford extended his forearms so Balzic could catch hold of them and pull himself up.

"Hell you doin' here?"

"Workin', man, whatta you think? Yeah. Least here, I don't have to smell anybody's feet, like I did the last place I worked."

"You not with Bulldog Security anymore?"

"Oh yeah, sure, I'm still there. But I never get more than thirty hours with them. Here I get maybe sixteen, some weeks twenty-four, depends who's sick, who's fed up, you know. Then I'm on call with this funeral home, anytime they need a body picked up, I do that too."

Balzic shook his head. "Sounds like all you do is work."

Rayford shrugged. "Gotta do what you gotta do. Which I wouldn't care if I was makin' some money, you know? Worked forty-six hours last week, man, took home an astounding total of one hundred and eighty-nine nineteen. But my wife just gotta be near her momma, understand, can't live in Alabama, nooooo, man. Can't deal with what the United States Air Force pays, you know, all that money, plus free health care, man, commissary, PX, no, she just has to come home so her momma can move in with us — listen to this, you're not goin' believe this. Last month, this woman

— her momma — I can't call her my mother-in-law, I can't put the word *my* in front of anything has to do with that woman, man. She brings home this voodoo priestess, man, says she from Haiti. Voodoo priestess, hear what I'm sayin'? Gonna take care of everything. I said take care of what? She said, fool, you know, get you a good job, take care the baby, make sure everything come out right —"

"Your wife didn't have it yet?"

"Naw, any day now."

"There some problem?"

"Naw, just my wife's momma — listen to me, I got to tell somebody this, I mean, this stuff is just drivin' me crazy. Brings this voodoo priestess into our apartment, man, I come home, they're chantin', dancin', she's throwin' chicken bones around on the kitchen floor, man. Told my wife, said, I come home and find chicken blood anywhere in this apartment, that chicken better be in a pot, 'cause if it ain't, that voodoo bitch is goin' be on the street and your momma goin' be right behind her — man, I can't believe this shit when I'm sayin' it.

"So I checked her out, right? This voodoo priestess from Haiti? Madame Maiesha Duval? Who my wife's momma is

577

givin' money to? For throwin' chicken bones around on the floor? And lightin' candles all over the kitchen and readin' these bones? Readin' bones, man, what kinda shit is that? And she's gettin' the money from my wife's momma? Who's gettin' it from my wife, who's gettin' it from me? Madame Duval is very well known to the Pittsburgh bunco squad, plus the NAACP, plus the Urban League. Everybody in Pittsburgh 'cept my wife and her momma know this bitch graduated from Westinghouse High School in 1981 and was born in Pittsburgh Hospital 1963, name Charmaine Jones. Been workin' this voodoo hustle for at least ten years now —"

"Hey," Balzic said, "I'll give Nowicki another call, see what the holdup is —"

"Aw you don't have to do that. I'm not tellin' you this for you to do anything, no. Nowicki told me council's just draggin' their ass, he doesn't know what their problem is. Talked to him last Friday. He said I'm still on the short list, but hey, who knows? All I know is, I don't get it, my black behind is goin' be flyin' to the Air Force recruitin' office, man. I am not goin' be workin' fifty-two hours like I did one week last month, took home two hundred and fourteen dollars and fifty-eight cents — and then know part of that money is goin' to that voodoo hustler? Man, I don't care how much my wife loves her momma. She wanna stay here with that nastiness, I'm sorry, I'm goin' be wearin' Air Force blue. She wanna come with me, fine, she don't, that's fine too."

"Well it's been a while since I talked to Nowicki," Balzic said, "but he told me you were either first or second in all the tests —"

"First or second? Oh yeah? Man. He didn't tell me that. I asked him straight out — well, what was he goin' say, you know, I mean, that was stupid, I shouldn't've asked him, but, hey. I got a little carried away when he said I was on the short list, but, uh, you know, still." Rayford shrugged. "Anyway, listen, man, I wanna thank you. Seriously now. You know, whether I get it or don't, I really appreciate you talkin' for me."

"If I didn't think you were worth it, I wouldn't've talked."

"Yeah, I know," Rayford said, smiling again. "That's what Carlucci said too. Said I musta done somethin' right —"

"You talked to Carlucci?"

"Yeah. Couple times. First time, 'mem-

579

ber? When you flashed that outta-date ID on me? Back door of that gunshop? Then, uh, when that shit happened with, uh, you know, Cozzolino and McFate? He interviewed me, oh man, musta been like half hour we talked —"

"Wait wait, what shit with Cozzolino? I don't know what you're talkin' about."

"You didn't hear about that? Cozzolino and McFate? Huh? Wilbur? 'Member him? Dude was supposed to be in the Jeep the night Cozzolino busted into —"

"Oh yeah yeah, I remember 'em. Sure. What about 'em?"

"You didn't hear about this? No joke?"

Balzic shook his head. "I don't know what you're talkin' about."

"Man, I thought much as you were involved with the insurance end, Carlucci'd for sure be tellin' you —"

"I don't know what you're talkin' about. Rugs hasn't called me about anything, hell, for a coupla weeks at least."

"Oh man, you're not goin' believe this. Two nights ago McFate come in the Ground Round? Where that waitress works? Slaney, huh? 'Member her? Jackie Slaney?"

"Yeah, yeah."

"Well, McFate's in there, I guess he's

still tryin' to feed this fantasy about her or somethin', here comes Cozzolino, man, starts bustin' her chops about somethin', gettin' loud, carryin' on, but then he grabs her — this is what I got from the bartender — and from her too. Both of 'em told me this —"

"You were workin' that night?"

"Oh yeah, sure. I punched in five to midnight, Burnett, he gives me the keys to the Jeep, off I go. Twenty minutes later, man, I hear a nine-one-one call from the bartender in the Ground Round, you know, callin' in a fight, so —"

"He called nine-one-one, he didn't call you? Where was McFate? You said Burnett, you didn't say McFate —"

"Oh you don't know? That's right, how would you know? They fired McFate way back, uh, like a month, six weeks, maybe, after that burglary, and, uh, he can't get a job nowhere —"

"So he was just there, huh, moonin' over the waitress?"

"I guess, I don't know what else. All he was drinkin' was Pepsi so he wasn't drunk. Course I haven't talked to him now, so I don't know what he was doin' there."

"But the call wasn't for you? You just happened to hear it?"

"C'mon man, we're the last ones they call —"

"Yeah, okay, so?"

"So I hear it, I was only, like, uh, maybe a hundred, hundred and ten yards from their turnoff when I heard the call, so I just turned right in, you know, and I drive around the side, and there's McFate, man, this little chipmunky-lookin' ridge-runner, I mean, he's doin' a Gregory Hines on Cozzolino. I'm tellin' you, man, between the time I first saw them and when I got out the Jeep? Whoa. McFate musta kicked him five times, man, the last time, the last one puts Cozzolino back in his car — his door'd been open, see? Obviously he was tryin' to get in his car when McFate caught up with him —"

"I'll be damned —"

"Wait wait, that's only half of it, man. 'Cause the next thing I see is a bright orange flash and POW! Yeah, man. Comin' out the car, POW! And McFate, he goes spinnin' around grabbin' his left arm or side, I don't know what he was grabbin' at that time, found out later it was his arm, but not then, he's just screamin', and I just hit a glass wall, I mean I went backsteppin' fast as I could move, got down behind the door of the Jeep, and McFate's hollerin' and I'm thinkin' Cozzolino got a piece and what do I got, huh? I got a four-cell Mag-Lite, what the fuck am I doin' there, you know? And before I could think of anything, here comes Cozzolino, man, just burnin' rubber right on by me. So I look back at McFate, he's all doubled over, moanin', holdin' himself, I can see blood drippin', and I grab the mike and call nine-one-one for an ambulance, you know? And I still got the mike up to my lips, and damn if McFate doesn't go get in his car, man, and burns rubber outta there just like Cozzolino, so I'm thinkin', hey, cancel the ambulance, you know, McFate's takin' himself to the hospital.

"Wasn't five minutes later, I'm talkin' to the bartender and to this Slaney — I mean they're talkin' at me, you know, tryin' to tell me what happened? What got all that shit started? And I'm hunkerin' around, seein' if maybe there's a casing, 'cause I don't know whether it was an auto or revolver, and I hear another nine-one-one call, and this one's comin' from the emergency room up at Conemaugh General."

"They both went to the ER."

"Yeah man, exactly — I can't believe you didn't hear about this —"

"I haven't read the paper last couple

days. All this shit about how the governor wants to give all our taxes to those fuckers own the Pirates and the Steelers, you know, just pisses me off so much, I had to take a break from even lookin' at a paper —"

"Yeah, I know what you mean. Piss me off too. Man act like it's his money. But anyway, you know, when McFate gets inside? Up the ER? Sees Cozzolino, man, starts in on him all over again. Little chipmunky fucker, surprise me I have to say it, man, got some guts, you know? Carlucci told me the dude took a .357 wadcutter in the arm, damn near blew his bicep off, and he's *still* kickin' the shit outta Cozzolino. Carlucci told me took every security they had in the hospital plus two city cops to get him offa Cozzolino and cooled out.

"Cozzolino's in bad shape, man. Maybe not gonna make it. And if he don't I'm goin' feel real sorry for McFate 'cause that motherfucker had it comin'. And you know the DA goin' use that ride from the Ground Round to the ER as time to premeditate —"

"Not necessarily."

"Huh? Why not?"

Balzic shrugged. "Who's to say he knew

where Cozzolino was goin'? All he has to say is he was tryin' to get himself to the ER, that doesn't mean he knew Cozzolino was tryin' to get there too."

"Yeah, but still, Carlucci said both cars were in the lot right outside the dock where the ambulances pull in, Cozzolino's first, McFate's behind, so he knew that was Cozzolino's car soon as he got there, he had to be thinkin' Cozzolino was inside, so maybe it wasn't a premeditation ride, but it could've been a premeditation walk from the parkin' lot inside —"

"Maybe it was, maybe it wasn't. Just because he saw the car of the guy that shot him doesn't mean he went there for any other reason than to get himself taken care of."

"I don't know, man, Cozzolino croaks out, that sounds like a first-degree ride, or walk, or run for sure. Had five minutes to think, you know? Or five seconds from the time he got outta his car. 'Cause I still think it'd be easy to say it was a first-degree walk from the time he saw the car till he got inside and jumped Cozzolino's ass again."

"Anything's easy to say, Rayford. Little tougher to prove."

"Yeah, I know. Still. Dude use me like

Cozzolino used him, I'd wanna kick his ass too. And this ain't funny but I can't help it, man, it's funny but it isn't, you know? Know what that Slaney told me, that waitress? Told me McFate has never said a word to her except what he wants off the menu. Goes in there all the time, don't do nothin' but look at her. So I'm thinkin' the dude's goin' do time for defendin' pussy he ain't never touched. Never seen, man." Rayford closed his eyes, rubbed his eyelids with his thumb and index finger and shook with small, sad laughter.

Balzic didn't have to try not to laugh, though he knew that someday he probably would. For now, he just shook his head. "Uh, Rugs hasn't said a thing to me about this. I'll have to give him a call. Hey, uh, listen, not to change the subject, but, uh, you got any Rockports in eleven wide? Black? All I see down here is ten and a halfs and twelves."

"Oh yeah? If we don't have 'em, I can get 'em. That's just a couple phone calls. Lemme take a look." Rayford squatted down and ran his fingers over the boxes. "Nope. I'll check the back. We don't have 'em back there, I'll call around, I'll get 'em for you, Chief, no problem."

"Uh, don't call me that, okay? I just, uh

. . . I'm not, okay?"

Rayford smiled. "Whatever. 'Mister' okay?"

"Mario's better."

"Nah. Anybody talks for me, it's mister."

Balzic shrugged. But after leaving the mall, after Rayford had said they were out of the Rockports and he'd have to call around, Balzic drove straight to Rocksburg City Hall and beat Chief Nowicki's ear about Rayford for more than five minutes. Nowicki listened patiently, nodding his head all the while Balzic was talking, but saying finally that Balzic was talking to the wrong person. Who he needed to be talking to was Councilman Egidio Figulli. Figulli was the holdup, not him.

Balzic chewed his cheek. "That my chair you're sittin' in?"

Nowicki shook his head no.

"But it was mine, right? Looks like it. Or you order a new one?"

"No, I didn't order a new one, why would I do that? It's a good chair. But it wasn't yours when you were sittin' in it, Mario, and it isn't mine now. Belongs to the city."

"Oh yeah? Huh. Maybe that was my trouble." Balzic stood and headed for the door. "Rugs around?"

"I don't know," Nowicki said. "He was trying to clear that case from the ER the other night, had a buncha statements he was tryin' to put together. And if he's not doin' that, then he's turnin' paper into plastic. Wish I could get somebody to help him with that. Fuckin' council won't move. All those people we were short when you left? We're still short. And that asshole Figulli? He's still — I can't believe that stupid fuck, every goddamn meeting, he's still tryin' to introduce an ordinance to create an all-volunteer department, do you believe that? Says we got volunteer firemen, no reason in the world why we can't have volunteer police. Only thing standin' in the way is the FOP. But they're gonna go, he says, just like the United Steelworkers and the United Mine Workers, everybody's sick a unions, he says. This sonofabitch has belonged to the pressmen's union at the fuckin' *Gazette* his entire fuckin' life and every month he comes into council and makes the same fuckin' stupid speech. Says private prisons are the wave of the future, volunteer fire departments have proved their efficiency all over the nation, no reason in the world not to consider volunteer police. I'd like to strangle the fucker.

"Lemme ask you somethin', and, uh, keep it here, okay?"

Balzic shrugged, but he was immediately on guard. Nowicki liked to take people into his confidence to expose their gullibility. "Yeah? What?"

"I mean it, you gotta keep it here now."

"Yeah, okay okay, what?"

"Sec, the thing is, I'm startin' to have dreams about stranglin' that prick. Figulli. And, uh, the worst part — and this gotta stay in this room, Mario, okay? You can't say anything about this —"

"I already said I wouldn't. So what? What?"

"Uh, I wake up, uh, I mean I have the dream, you know? And then I wake up, and, uh, I got my hands around my dick."

"Aw Jesus —"

"Naw no, c'mon, I'm serious, this is startin' to get to me. You think I needa see a shrink, huh? No shit, Mario, I'm startin' to get a little worried, you know? Whattaya think?"

Balzic threw up his hands. "If the only thing bad you ever wanna do is strangle Figulli, forget about it, okay?"

"No I mean the part about wakin' up with my, uh, you know, my hands, uh, you know . . . where they are — after that particular dream? They connected, huh? You think?"

"You're askin' me if I think you need to see a shrink? I'll tell ya why you need to see one. 'Cause you're askin' *me* whether you need to see one. Christ, Nowicki, c'mon, that's the kinda stuff you tell a shrink, that's not what you tell people to find out whether you oughta be seein' one, Jesus. I'm not your boss — hey, I gotta find Rugs, I'll see ya."

"Yeah but wait, wait. What if you were my boss? What would you tell me, you know, if I come in here and told you that?"

Balzic rolled his eyes and headed for the door. "Let me put it to you this way, okay? What if one of your guys came to you with that story, huh? What would you tell him? And remember, you're the boss now, alright? So you gotta have an answer. So what would you say?"

Nowicki thought for a moment. "I don't know. It's a toughie."

"That's what you'd tell him, huh? You don't know, it's a toughie? Well. Hey. My chair, your chair, the city's chair, whose ever chair it is, it's under your ass now. I'm gone."

"Hey, Mario, wait a second." Nowicki stood and came around the desk until he was a step away. "You know, I haven't seen you since, uh, I got the job. You mostly never come around, which I understand. But there's times things come up around here, you know, I'm throwin' darts at the answers."

"Yeah? So?"

"Well, you know, I think sometimes, maybe — ah, what do I wanna say here? Look, I asked Rugs one day if you thought, if he thought, you know, if you'd mind if I, uh, called ya, you know, asked you for some advice, some counsel —"

"Listen, Nowicki. The reason you and I always had a little bit of a personality clash — I think that's the phrase I wanna use here — is because you like jaggin' people off, you like pullin' their chains, you like stickin' the needle in, you know?"

"I know, I know —"

"Yeah yeah, you know, right. But then you get serious — or you try to make people think you're gettin' serious, but they don't know whether you're serious or not, so that makes it hard to know how to respond. 'Cause nobody likes gettin' jagged off. Nobody, not me, not anybody, I don't care what people say about how thick you gotta grow your hide, that's all bullshit, 'cause nobody likes gettin' their chain pulled, man. Nobody likes bein' made to feel stupid. It hurts. It pisses people off, man. But for some reason, that never got through to you, I don't know why, but I'll tell ya what it does. You tell me that story about dreamin' about stranglin' Figulli and wakin' up with your hands around your dick, and I'm thinkin', this fucker's jaggin' me off again, bigger'n shit, and I don't wanna hear it. 'Cause what I'm waitin' for, is for you to start laughin' and sayin' *gotcha*. 'Cause you did it too many times —"

"I know, I know," Nowicki groaned. "But see, now I could really use some help, you know, no shit. Maybe I do need to see a shrink."

"Okay, maybe you do. But, uh, you didn't ask for this, I'm givin' it to ya for free. You do that, don't tell anybody. And pay for it yourself. Don't put it on your insurance. 'Cause that gets out, you're gone. And don't believe that confidentiality bullshit from the insurance companies, that's just bullshit. You go see a shrink and you pay for it with your insurance card? Fuck, you might as well get a bullhorn and stand in the middle of the intersection by the courthouse and say, Hey, people, ain't you lucky to be livin' and workin' here?

I'm the chief of police and I'm seein' a shrink, I'm havin' my head shrunk on a regular basis.

"Your ass'll be outta that chair so fast you won't know it was ever there. But if you're jaggin' me off right now, Nowicki, I'm gonna tell ya in advance, okay? Fuck you. But if you're not? Yeah, okay. You can call me. If it's somethin' I can help you with, I'll help."

Nowicki extended his hand. "Thanks, Mario. I mean it."

"Yeah, right. You're welcome. I think. And don't forget this Rayford, okay? Do what you can for him. He'll make a good cop. I gotta talk to Rugs, I'll see ya."

Balzic couldn't get away soon enough. He still wasn't sure Nowicki wasn't pulling his chain. Years ago, at an FOP picnic Nowicki had Balzic believing that Nowicki had a tumor in his large intestine and probably had no more than a year to live. Balzic had never forgotten, or forgiven. About some things, Balzic was proud to say he had no sense of humor.

He found Carlucci in the city clerk's office waiting to use the copying machine.

"Yo, Mario. What's up?"

"What's up with you? Heard you had a wild one the other night."

"Yeah. Cozzolino and, uh, McFate. Man, are they in some shit, those two. That McFate, he took a wadcutter in the left arm, .357, tore up the bottom end of his biceps, all kindsa tissue damage, bone damage, nerve damage, and lost a lotta blood too."

"What about Cozzolino?"

"Yeah, then he's up for that too, McFate. Cozzolino has a busted collarbone, at least two busted ribs, his wrist, jaw. His jaw's destroyed, man, just shattered. But the worst thing is his lung's messed up. They had to put him on a ventilator. Doc told me that was the real problem, all those breaks would heal one way or another, but the lung was really bad news. Man, some people, Mario — I know you know this — hey, just don't know when to stop."

"Cozzolino gonna make it?"

"Depends what happens with his lung. Way it was described to me, all I know was I hope it never happens to anybody I like."

"So you didn't get a statement from him."

"Not from either one of 'em. He can't, and McFate won't. So, uh, I'm just puttin' it together from what I got from the ER staff and the people at the mall, you know, security, and Ground Round. One funny thing, though. This morning I went up to see if maybe Cozzolino was awake and could write what happened with his good hand. There was this humongous fucker sittin' between him and the door. Didn't wanna let me in. Turns out he's one of Artie Chianese's goons. They heard about it almost soon as we did, can you believe that?"

Balzic nodded. "That surprises you?"

"I guess. I don't know. I just think, you know, some people, I just wonder how they hear these things, you know, fast as they do?"

"Scanners. How else?"

"Yeah, but you're not gonna pick up names off a scanner. Everybody's switchin' frequencies so much, you know, how do they keep up?"

"I don't know. But they do. Always surprised me how fast people got hold of my phone number, and there were times I was changin' it every three months. You tell me how they do it, I don't know. They get it from somebody. So, uh, what'd Chianese's goon have to say?"

It was Rugs's turn to use the copier and he did that while talking. "The usual, you know, what do you want, you can't come in, who are you — till I showed ID, then of course he's nothin' but a friend lookin' out for a friend. But I told hospital security, if they had anybody, they needed to put him on McFate's door. He's not gonna be there that long, from what I was told, but still, we don't have anybody to put up there. I don't know if they have anybody either. They didn't act like it. So I told McFate, I said you got any relatives or friends, you need to get 'em in here. He just shook his head. I said it's your ass, man, we can't protect you, you need to understand that. He said he did. So I came back here. I need to talk to that waitress. She's the only one I haven't talked to. So hi ya doin', Mario? Lookin' good, lookin' healthy. Takin' care of yourself?"

"Tryin' to. It's a struggle. I keep strugglin' with myself, you know, over what I can eat, what I can't, how much I should exercise, and where, and when, and all that shit. Mostly, my struggles are all between my ears. Like everybody else's I guess."

"Yeah. Christ knows, that's where mine are. Hey, I'll see ya, Mario, I gotta go talk to this waitress. You know, the one thing I did get from her, she has a PFA on this prick Cozzolino, you know? She called the state cops right after this went down, they tell her, they had one body in the whole fuckin' county, can you believe that? What is this, the fourth most populated county in the state? Fuckin' state cops had one body on patrol that night. State got all this money for new cells, man, don't wanna hire no cops. Unbelievable."

"Yeah," Balzic said, heading for the door. "Unbelievable alright. But true. See ya, Rugs."

Balzic came back to the kitchen after getting the charcoal going in the chimney. He knew the charcoal had caught fire when the smoke changed from billows hovering just above the lip of the chimney to a stream turning to billows three to four feet higher. He went back inside to the fridge, reached into the deli drawer, and took out a package of turkey kolbassi. He read the label and shook his head in disgust. To Ruth, who was peeling skin off peppers she'd just roasted, he said, "Why'd you let me buy these? Got way too much fat in 'em."

"Tried to tell you you didn't like them. Last time you bought them you said you'd never buy them again. But, hey, you had them in the cart and you had that look —"

"What look?"

"That one that says no cholesterol gremlin is gonna keep you from eating what you want, so I just said it and moved on, I wasn't gonna argue with you."

"I didn't hear you say that."

"Well I said it."

"And you let me buy 'em anyway?"

"C'mon, Mar, okay? You stood there and you read the label, you looked at me, you said what do I think, I told you you didn't like them and you'd said you wouldn't buy them again — what else you want me to say? Don't use them. You know Marie's not gonna eat them, and Emily's not gonna want too much, and after Marie gets through raggin' her, she probably won't want any, even though she'll try to say she doesn't care how turkeys get raised."

"So what am I s'pposed to do with these — pitch 'em? Cost almost four bucks."

"Take them back, tell them you forgot you're not supposed to eat that stuff anymore."

"Man, all the things I don't eat anymore. Kolbassi, sweet sausage, hot sausage, hot dogs, cheeseburgers, Jesus. Used to be, Labor Day was the day grunts tried to get fat, you know? I remember hearin' people

— did I ever tell ya this? When I was a kid people used to see a fat guy, they'd say, man, he can afford to eat that good, he must be rich. All that food, remember? Huh? People used to say —"

"That food's rich," Ruth interrupted him. "Or it's too rich."

"Yeah, exactly. Meanin' only rich people could afford it. Butter, cream, eggs, sugar, chocolate, yeah, right, rich people's food. Now the only people you see eatin' that stuff are the ones either haven't heard the party line from the American Heart Association or else they don't wanna hear it."

"Oh no, that's not true, uh-uh. When I was waiting for you to wake up the first day you were in the hospital? And I was in the cafeteria? You know who I saw eating a cheeseburger?"

"Who?"

"Your cardiologist, that's who, except at the time I didn't know he was."

"Doctor Fine? He was eatin' cheeseburgers and he's tellin' me don't eat 'em? You saw him?!"

"You don't like them anymore anyway. Every time I make something with beef in it you can't stand the smell — that's what you say."

"I can't. Anyway, all I do anymore is grill veggies."

"And what? You gonna say now you don't love them? You eat them all. Then you start lookin' at my plate, and you always say you should've grilled more."

"I know, I know. I don't know, it's just stupid nostalgia or somethin'. Kinda picnics we used to have, man, all that grease drippin' onto the coals, I used to remember it smellin' sooooo good. I don't know, maybe I'm just sick of bein' so goddamn healthy all the time —"

"What? God, Mar, listen to yourself! Only you, I swear, nobody but you would say that — sick of bein' so goddamn healthy? What's bitin' you, you've been grumpin' around all day today, ever since you got up."

"I don't know," he said, shrugging. "Kids're comin'. I guess."

"*The kids?* Not the kids, uh-uh. Not *the* kids. Marie."

"Alright, okay, okay. Marie."

"God, Mar, scared of your own daughter now? What? Scared she's gonna give you a test, ask you how you're doing?"

"Not scared, no, c'mon. Just, you know, I don't know, she, uh, what the hell I wanna say here — she kinda makes me, you know, feel like I, uh, like I'm not up to it, you know? Like, just lookin' at her, she doesn't have to say a thing. But I know she's thinkin' she sent me all these books, and what am I doin' with 'em, you know? Am I readin' 'em? Am I gettin' better because I'm readin' 'em? Or am I too dense to ever get this stuff, you know, this meditation stuff? Man, another one came yesterday — I didn't even tell you about that one."

"I saw it."

"You did? Yeah, well. Meditation of the month. Remember last month, huh? *Wherever You Go, There You Are*? I'll be wrestlin' with that one when they wheel me into the furnace, Christ. Now she sends this one, get this, you ready? *Being Nobody, Going Nowhere.* Yeah. Christ, I open it up, take one look at the title, I say yeah, right, this is exactly what I need. Some Buddhist monk in Sri Lanka or wherever, he's gonna tell me how I been feelin'. Whatta you mean, you saw it?"

"I saw it, yes, you left it on the dining room table. Besides, she told me."

"Huh? She told you she was gonna send that one?"

Ruth nodded and dragged the garbage can over to the edge of the table where she was peeling the peppers. She scraped all the charred skin into the can, pushed it with her foot back beside the fridge, and then collected the peppers in a bowl and scraped them into the bowl of the food processor.

"Hey, Mar, am I goin' nuts or did we buy a hunk of Parmesan yesterday? I could swear I bought one, I knew we were out, I put it on the list, but I looked in the fridge a little while ago, looked and looked and I can't find it. I need a quarter-cup for this. We buy some or not? If we didn't, I'm really startin' to lose it."

"It's here somewhere," Balzic said, opening the fridge and looking, starting in the deli drawer by putting the turkey kolbassi back. "I know it's here, 'cause I took it outta the plastic wrap and put it in a Baggie —"

"You ate some?"

"I didn't say I ate any —"

"Why'd you take it out of the wrap then? Mar, you ate some, you promised me you wouldn't and every time I buy cheese I think is he gonna eat some, should I buy this? You tell me you won't and then you do it anyway —"

"I just took it out to put it in a Ziploc, that's all, I didn't eat any," Balzic groused.

But he couldn't find it. He went top to bottom twice, moving jars and bottles around. "Sonofabitch, it's in here, I know it is. I grated some to put on my rolled oats, that's what I did, I didn't just slice off a hunk and eat it like that. I shoulda grated enough to fill the jar — what the hell'd I do with it, doesn't make sense."

"Well reach around while you're there and get me a towel, huh? This one's soaked already," Ruth said, standing behind him with her hands over the sink.

"Can't find it," he said, shaking his head. Still squatting by the open fridge, he turned and opened the towel drawer to get a fresh one, and said, "Oh, Jesus."

"What?"

"You're not gonna believe this. Look."

"Huh?" She bent over his shoulder and peered into the drawer and started to howl. "Oh God, Mar."

Balzic straightened up with a grunt. "Oh man. Really startin' to lose it, Ruthie, no shit."

Ruth was laughing so hard she was gasping.

"Oh now wait, wait now, c'mon, I'm gonna tell ya what happened," he said. "Listen, no, I know what happened. You're havin' way too much fun with this, Ruthie, c'mon, listen, I know what I did. I took that plastic wrap off, I grated some onto my rolled oats, and I didn't wanna use a new bag, so I got one outta there, used one, you know, and then, uh, hey, what the hell, I put it in the bag, and, uh, boom, musta just dropped it in there, that's all. Ain't gonna hurt nothin', c'mon, they don't refrigerate this stuff — c'mon, hey, it ain't that funny, okay?"

"Oh God, Mar," she grunted through her laughter.

"Aw c'mon, it's not that funny —"

"No no," she said, trying to catch her breath. "I didn't tell you what I did. Oh God, I have to stop laughin', I'm gonna hurt myself."

"What? You did somethin'? Dumb as this? C'mon, what?"

She nodded, gasping, tilting forward from the waist, hugging herself. "Two days ago, I went to lunch with this woman I met in the yoga class. She asked me, and I didn't know how to say no to her, so anyway we went to that Chinese place, you know where I'm talking about — in front of the bank there?"

"Yeah?"

"So we had soup and egg rolls, I really wasn't very hungry, I just ate the soup, and we were talking, she's not my type, you know, we could never be great buddies or anything, she's just way, way too much into her family and kids and grandchildren, and, so anyway . . ." She had to stop talking because she started laughing again.

"Yeah? C'mon, what?"

"I took one bite of the egg roll," she sputtered, "and I wrapped the rest in a paper napkin. So this morning I was lookin' for the checkbook . . . oh God, there it was. In my purse! Two days, Mar!"

"Oh Christ," Balzic said, shaking his head and sighing. "We're losin' it, Ruthie, bigger'n shit, we're goin' round the bend —"

"Oh it's funny, Mar, c'mon," she said, bursting into laughter again. "God, Mar, you look so serious, c'mon, this is funny! You have to laugh at stuff like this or you're gonna go nuts — listen, Mar, you have to know this is funny, you're not gonna get all bummed out about this, c'mon, you're not gonna do that, I'm not gonna let you, uh-uh."

He shook his head and chewed his lower lip.

"Listen, you," she said. "I was in the parade all the while you were takin' your pulse, every time I turned around you were takin' your pulse, every day some new pain, some new sign your heart was gonna attack you, ambush you, I just shut my mouth, bit my lip twenty times a day, but I was here, Mar —"

"I never said you weren't —"

"Oh yes you did, plenty of times —"

"Oh okay, so we had some problems, yeah, I'm not gonna argue that, but you were here, no argument now, not from me. We had some problems in the beginning, yeah, we worked 'em out —"

"Yes, right, we did, Mar, we worked them out. And I was still here, still marchin', Mar — still marchin', all the way through Missus Wrobelewski and her kid, all the way since February when she first started showin' up on the hood, remember? Huh? And then through all the rest of the winter and spring and summer with Charley Babyak and the cops over there in Knox, right? And you in the DA's office, and with the detectives, and through all the letters you wrote to the attorney general, and the U.S. attorney, every one of them I checked your spelling, didn't I? You asked me to read them, check your spelling, I did that. I was here, Mar, okay? Through all that, I was here! I'm still here!"

"I know, I know —"

"Okay, you know, but what I'm talkin' about is now, Mar. Right here, right now, that's what I'm talkin' about. All this Buddhist stuff you and Marie have been givin' me —"

"I'm givin' it to you 'cause I want you to know what I'm tryin' to do for myself, that's all, I'm not tryin' to sell it to you. And 'cause Marie's givin' it to me, don't forget —"

"I didn't say you were tryin' to sell it to me —"

"Well good. Long as you know that —"

"Mar, that's not what I'm sayin', listen to me. All this stuff about how you have to learn to live in the here and now, you know? With full awareness? Huh? Can't be livin' in the past, can't be livin' in the future, be here, be now, that stuff, huh? I'm still here, Mar, you know? Okay? Still marchin', Mar. Still right here, right now, still marchin' right beside you. But, goddammit, Mar, someplace in all that be-here be-now stuff there has to be room for laughin' at dumb shit, c'mon! And puttin' Parmesan in the towel drawer is dumb shit! And wrappin' an egg roll in a napkin and keepin' it in my purse for two days is dumb shit, but it's funny dumb shit,

Mar! Mar, you can't get all mopey and scared about this, I won't let you. You get all mopey over puttin' cheese in the towel drawer and I swear, Mar, one of these days I'm gonna stop marchin', I'm tellin' you. I don't care — oh shit, Marie's here. God, how long's she been listenin' to this? Go let her in, Mar, okay? I have to finish this pepper thing."

"So she was listenin', so what?"

"Oh c'mon, I'm not gonna march in your parade anymore? Please."

"Hey, you were just talkin', that's all."

"Yeah, you know that and I know that, but Marie doesn't always understand the way we talk to each other — go let her in, please?"

"What were we sayin' that was so bad?"

"I just wanted to finish it, that's all. Just wanted to say what I wanted to say without bein' interrupted — oh shit, please go let her in — quit foolin' around, let go of the towel, c'mon, Mar."

"Hey, what if I don't want to? What if I think holdin' on to the towel while Marie's on the front porch while you didn't get to finish what you wanted to say, what if I think that's funny, huh? What if I think this is funny dumb shit, what — you're not gonna march in my parade anymore?"

"C'mon, Mar, let her in, c'mon, let go of the towel —"

"Aw take the towel, I'll let her in — yo, Marie! You're early. What's up? C'mon in, kiddo, be here be now with us nobodies goin' nowhere, c'mon. What'd ya bring me — no more books I hope. You send me any more books you'll have to stick 'em in my coffin —"

"Oh Daddy, God, you're terrible. What, did I get here at a bad time? You two havin' a fight?"

"Fight? Us? Noouuu, we don't fight. Too old to fight. We were just talkin', about dumb stuff, laughin', you know. But you're right, I am terrible. But at least I'm alive terrible, I ain't dead terrible. Which isn't much to brag about, but, hey, I'm here, I'm now, you know, 'cause wherever I go, there I am. C'mon, gimme a hug."

"You're lying, Daddy," she said into his chest.

"Me? No. Never lie to you, kiddo. C'mon in the kitchen, give your mother a hug. She misses you. Me too. And seriously, thanks for the books, they're really helpin', no kiddin', they are."

"No kidding?"

"Yeah, yeah. I'm tellin' ya, I'm really startin' to understand bein' nobody. I mean it. Goin' nowhere. It's helped me. I don't get nearly as mad as I used to —"

"Except at me," Ruth said, coming out of the kitchen with her arms out for Marie.

"Well you, hey, you're different. You're important. Course I get mad at you. If you weren't important, why would I care?"

"Hear that, Marie? Caring to him means gettin' mad. Only to him would that make sense."

"I know," Marie said, pulling them both together and hugging them hard. "He's terrible. Emily not here yet? Jeez, I'm starvin'. What'd you guys make? Oh-oh, I smell kolbassi. God, Daddy, you tell me these books are helping you? And we're having kolbassi? You said you read Dean Ornish —"

"Kolbassi?! Noooo, you kiddin'? I'm takin' that back, I was just readin' the label. Think I wanna make Dean Ornish mad? Or you? C'mon, grilled veggies, that's what we're havin'. Lots of 'em, too, you're gonna love 'em, healthy as hell."

He winked at Ruth. She rolled her eyes and shook her head.

"You guys," Marie said, groaning. "Gawwwwd, you ever gonna stop treatin' me like I'm a kid? So you're havin' a fight.

What're you fighting about? You can tell me, c'mon, what?"

Balzic sighed and laughed. "Nah, I don't think so. It'd take too long and, hell, you'd probably wind up tellin' us how dumb we are, and we already know that. Don't we, Ruthie?"

"Speak for yourself, big boy. I'm makin' pepper spread."

"Awww you guys . . ."

"I gotta check the charcoal," he said, starting for the door onto the deck. He stopped and said, "Okay, okay, strictly for myself now, you know, little ol' me, bein' here, bein' now, bein' nobody, goin' nowhere. I'm, uh . . ."

"You're what?" Marie said. "What?"

"Uh . . . I don't know," he said. But he couldn't say any more. He couldn't remember what he was going to say because he was stunned. Because suddenly in the fire now showing above the lip of the charcoal chimney he'd lit earlier, as clearly as a photograph, there appeared the top of a head. Just the hair. Hair like a used soap pad.

"What, Daddy? What?"

"Huh? Nothin'. Nothin'."

Marie came and put her arm around his waist and looked up at him. "God, Daddy, you alright? You're all pasty white — you okay?"

"Yeah yeah, I, uh, I just forgot what I was gonna say, that's all. Stuff like that, I, uh, I can't help it, it just, uh, just bothers the hell outta me, uh, when I forget what I'm gonna say, makes me think I'm goin' round the bend, you know, losin' it? You don't know what I'm talkin' about now, someday you will. Ask your mother, I gotta check the fire here."

He shrugged away from her and went out onto the deck, staring at the barely visible flames. As quickly as the top of Charley Babyak's head had appeared it was gone.

Balzic rushed to put on two hot mitts and quickly upended the chimney into the grill and busied himself arranging the glowing coals on the floor of the grill.

Marie followed him out and asked him again if he was okay.

"Yeah, sure, sure, I'm fine. Someday, you know, you'll understand, you live long enough, you get old enough, it'll happen to you, you'll see. Happens to everybody, they live long enough. Anyway, hey, it was probably some smart-ass sarcastic thing I was gonna say, and you know, with all the stuff you're givin' me to read, I'm learnin' how to catch that stuff, that sarcasm before it gets outta my mouth, you know? Just caught myself, that's all, gettin' ready to say somethin' wise, and, uh, you know, if it's a smart-ass thing, I don't wanna remember it, you know? Uh . . . never mind."

He cleared his throat, dropped the hot mitts on the table, and hurried back inside the kitchen. "Hey. How about some vino, huh? Little vino? You ready, kiddo? Marie? Yo, Ruth? Ready for some chardonnay? Oh man, Emily's here. Let her in, Marie, I think I locked the door again. Hey, I'm ready for some cold chardonnay if nobody else is . . . am I ever. Whoa . . ."

"Hi, everybody," Emily called out. "Happy Labor Day."

"Right, exactly," Balzic said, pouring himself a large glass nearly full of California chardonnay. "Time to celebrate, right. Labor Day in America, right. Man, this wine smells great. Can't wait to taste it . . ."